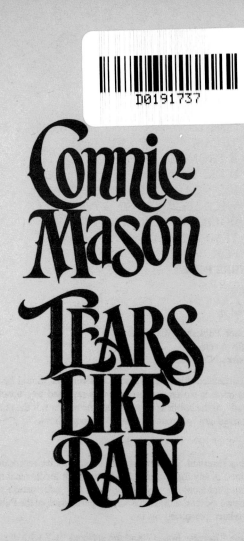

Connie Mason

Tears Like Rain

LEISURE BOOKS NEW YORK CITY

A LEISURE BOOK®

July 1994

Published by

Dorchester Publishing Co., Inc.
276 Fifth Avenue
New York, NY 10001

Printed in the United States of America.

LOVE SLAVE

Zach stood his ground, fists clenched at his sides, his mouth taut with anger. He hated the way Tears Like Rain stared at him as if inspecting her property and finding him lacking. Zach refused to be intimidated by the little savage, despite the disadvantage his nudity gave him.

"Where are my clothes?"

Tears Like Rain gave no hint of understanding. Zach reached out and touched the fringe of her tunic. "My clothes. I want my clothes."

Abruptly Tears Like Rain walked past him, rummaged in a parfleche hanging on a pole and returned with a small bundle. She thrust it into his hands, then withdrew quickly, as if contact with him repelled her.

Puzzled, Zach shook out the brief swatch of material and was stunned to find that she had given him an Indian breechclout. Surely she didn't mean for him to go around in something as indecent as this, did she?

Prologue

Colorado Territory—Summer 1850

Glancing over his shoulder, ten-year-old Ryder Larson noticed that his little sister, six-year-old Abby, was lagging behind and waited for her to catch up.

"Hurry, Abby, you know what Papa said about dawdling. He wants to make Fort Lyon by dark."

Abby's chubby little legs churned vigorously as she tried to keep up with her adored older brother. "Can't I rest for a minute?" Abby asked plaintively as she plopped down on a rock and refused to budge.

Recognizing the stubborn set of Abby's pointed little chin, Ryder heaved an exasperated sigh, grasped her hand, and urged her to her feet.

"C'mon, Abby, you can rest when we reach the wagon. You know Papa has been nervous since we left the Oregon Trail with the Matthews. Before we left the wagon train, the wagon master warned us that Crow and Sioux Indians were on the warpath."

Zeb Larson had left the Oregon Trail near Ogallala, where he was joined by the Matthews. Both families intended to settle near Denver. Now, with Fort Lyon within easy reach, Zeb had advised the two older children not to dawdle as they gathered buffalo chips to feed their fires.

Abby's eyes grew round as she cast a furtive glance over her shoulder. Her brother's warning must have had the desired effect, for she jogged beside him without further protest. Between them they toted a basket filled with dried buffalo chips.

Without warning, the prairie erupted in a frenzy of activity as a war party of Crow Indians burst over the crest of a hill, their bloodcurdling cries echoing over the plains and bouncing off the hills. The children froze, their faces stark with terror as Indian warriors, their bodies painted in hideous designs, swept toward the two defenseless wagons.

"Mama, Papa!" Abby's agonized cry released Ryder from his stupor. Dropping the basket, he grasped Abby's arm and pulled her toward an outcropping of rocks.

"Be quiet!" he hissed, pushing her down and shielding her with his body. He could feel her small frame quaking in fear, and for her sake he tried to control his own mounting terror. But deep in his heart, Ryder Larson knew there was little hope for the survival of their parents. He grieved for them, and for his little sister, Sierra, who was too young to accompany him and Abby on their little foray this morning.

Staccato bursts of gunfire and screams of agony turned the once peaceful prairie into a valley of death and destruction. Crouched behind the rocks, Ryder closed his eyes and ears against the atrocities he knew were taking place, focusing instead on keeping his little sister safe. The eerie sound of silence brought his head up with a jerk, and what he saw turned his blood to ice water. Flames licked at the Matthews wagon, leaving little beyond its metal ribs. Lying on its side, its contents scattered over the ground, the Larson wagon had not yet been set ablaze. Indians danced around the burning wagon, some shaking spears and coup sticks while others brandished weapons high in the air. Bodies lay scattered on the ground.

From a distance, Ryder saw that very few of those bodies belonged to the raiders. Every instinct told him that his mother and father were dead, and so were Sierra and the Matthews. When he saw one of the painted warriors sprint toward the remaining wagon with a flaming brand in his hand, Ryder closed his eyes. He couldn't bear to see all he owned in the world be destroyed. Except for Abby, all he loved and held dear was lost to him forever.

Had Ryder opened his eyes, he would have been stunned to see a hunting party of Cheyenne, mortal enemies of the Crow, cresting a nearby hill. Once the Crow spotted them, they reacted by turning tail and fleeing. Outnumbered two to one, the Crow rounded up the horses, took what loot they could carry with them, and rode away before they had set the Larson wagon ablaze. The ungodly war whoops and resulting battle brought Ryder's eyes open with a jerk. He was shocked to see the raiders fleeing toward the hills, driving the stolen horses before them. Another band of Indians was close on their heels. Ryder didn't know what it all meant, except that it was too late to save his parents and three-year-old sister, Sierra.

Slowly Ryder rose to his feet, bewildered by the course of events that had just made him and Abby orphans. Confused and disoriented, Abby stood beside him, tears flowing copiously from her luminous gray eyes. They realized their mistake too late. One of the Cheyenne braves had spied the children and called out to his companions. Several braves broke from the main group and reined their ponies toward the rock behind which the children were crouched.

"Run, Abby, run!" Ryder cried as he tried desperately to drag Abby along behind him. But Abby, immobilized by shock and fright, merely clung to her brother and wailed.

The Indians drew abreast of the children, and with easy grace, one Indian brave bent low and scooped Abby up before him onto his horse's withers. A second Indian did the same with Ryder, easily subduing the lad's brave resistance. Then the band split up, some riding toward the hills after the Crow and the others returning to camp with the children in tow.

Behind them the wagons lay in ruin, one burned beyond recognition and the other toppled over on its side, its contents scattered to the wind. Two dead Crow lay among the remains of the four slain emigrants. The Larsons had been so close to their goal that a few hours would have taken them within sight of Fort Lyon.

Chapter One

September 1864

Tears Like Rain stared dispassionately at the wounded white soldier lying at her feet. Though she didn't join the other women, who were spitting on and taunting the gravely injured man, she felt as much contempt for him as did her friends.

"He's handsome for a white man, isn't he, Tears Like Rain?"

Tears Like Rain directed her gaze at her companion, Summer Moon, then glanced back down at the soldier who had just been dragged into camp behind the horse of her father, White Feather, chieftain of their small band of Cheyenne. The captive's blue uniform clung to his body in tattered shreds, soaked with bright

14

red blood from numerous wounds, the result of Cheyenne lances and arrows. One of the deadly missiles was still embedded in his thigh.

"All white men are ugly," Tears Like Rain confided in a somewhat uncertain tone. Actually, despite the man's deplorable condition, she thought him passably attractive for one of his race.

His tawny hair reminded her of prairie grass at the end of summer before the frost turned it brown. And his frame was every bit as impressive as that of her brother, Wind Rider. Visually measuring his length where he lay sprawled on the dusty ground, she noted that he was very tall. Beneath his tattered uniform, his muscles bunched and tensed in involuntary response to his pain.

"I heard your father say the soldier is from Fort Lyon. He is the sole survivor of the patrol that was attacked today by warriors of the Shield Society," Summer Moon revealed. "Tonight he will wish he had joined his men in death."

Tears Like Rain flinched. She knew what would happen to the hapless white soldier tonight. She had seen it many times in the twenty years of her life. Tonight there would be a huge celebration, with dancing around the campfire and much boasting about today's exploits by the warriors of the Shield Society. Every member of their small band would attend. The young men would dance and feast, and the women would join the men

15

as they tormented the captive—providing he was still alive by then. The end of the evening would culminate with the soldier's death.

It was the way of things, Tears Like Rain reflected, after the way the white man had lied to the Cheyenne, Sioux, and Arapaho. Until the white-eyes came, making treaties and breaking them, the Cheyenne had been a religious, thoughtful, and fun-loving people. Now they fought for their survival. The Cheyenne nation was on the warpath despite Black Kettle's continued efforts to mend the peace with more meaningless treaties.

Tears Like Rain had seen firsthand what happened to her people when they refused to leave the territory granted to them by treaties. In 1857 the cavalry had charged her people at Solomon Fork in Western Kansas, using sabers to force them to retreat. Innocent women and children had been killed, and she had been wounded when she attempted to help her mother, Gray Dove, who had perished in the attack. She had been only thirteen at the time, and the loss of her mother had been devastating. She thanked the Great Spirit that her father, brother, and grandmother had been spared.

Suddenly, Summer Moon grasped her hand and tugged her forward. "Come, Tears Like Rain, I want to join the other women in tormenting the soldier." She picked up a sharp stick lying nearby.

Tears Like Rain hung back, her distinctive gray eyes troubled. Though she had watched often enough in the past, she did not enjoy torturing a wounded man. Summer Moon noticed her reluctance and jeered, "You are too tender-hearted. Think of the atrocities he and men like him have visited upon our people."

Dragging Tears Like Rain behind her, she jabbed the sharp point of the stick into the fallen man's ribs with unbridled glee. When she had finished, she shoved the stick into Tears Like Rain's hands. "Here, now it is your turn." The man, not as senseless as Tears Like Rain had assumed, opened his eyes and tried to twist away from the new onslaught of pain.

Captain Zach Mercer's body was on fire. The arrow that protruded from his thigh was not the least of his numerous wounds, but it was probably the most serious. He was pierced in so many places that he felt his life's blood slowly seeping away. And now, being ruthlessly prodded by these bloodthirsty squaws was the last straw. Zach had no idea how many miles he had been dragged behind his captor's horse and was surprised he had survived the ordeal.

Consumed by pain, Zach almost wished he had been killed outright like his men. He knew enough about Indians to know that more painful torture was planned for him.

Zach grunted in pain when another sharp jab found his ribs, and his eyes flew open. He had tried to remain stoic, tried to ignore the pain, but when the women of the tribe started tormenting him, it added a new dimension to his suffering. A human body could endure only

17

so much. His eyes sought those of his tormentor as he twisted to avoid further torture, and settled disconcertingly on a young Indian woman with startling gray eyes—eyes that could not possibly belong to an Indian, not by any stretch of the imagination.

Tears Like Rain drew in a startled breath. The captive's eyes were the sharp, clear blue of a summer sky. And they were fixed on her with almost desperate urgency. The stick fell from her hand. With a snort of disgust, Summer Moon retrieved it and thrust it into the captive's ribs. The only indication that Zach felt the resulting pain was the rapid blinking of his eyes.

"He is very brave," Summer Moon allowed. "But not as brave as your brother. Wind Rider belongs to the fierce War Dog Society." She sighed dreamily. "Father would be ecstatic if a brave warrior like Wind Rider were to court me."

Tears Like Rain barely heard her friend, so intent was she on the captive. He hadn't shifted his eyes from her since they had found her, and it appeared that he was trying to convey some kind of message. Couldn't he tell how much she despised him and his kind, who were trying to destroy the only life she had ever known?

"Our father counted coup many times this day." A tall, bronze-skinned warrior strode up beside Tears Like Rain and Summer Moon. He spat with contempt at the wounded soldier.

"Wind Rider!" Tears Like Rain greeted her brother enthusiastically, relieved to find someone other than the captive and his plight on which to concentrate. "Were you with Father today? Did you also count coup on the enemy?"

"I wish I had been with Father," Wind Rider complained. "Instead of counting coup on the enemy, I was hunting with a party of Dog Soldiers. But we did not come home empty-handed, little sister. I have a fine buck to show for my efforts. We will have a grand feast tonight."

"What of the captive?" Tears Like Rain asked. Though she knew better than to inquire, she couldn't help herself, and it made her angry. Something about the captive struck a responsive chord in her. The hatred she felt for those of his race was still there, but beyond that was a strange, compelling compassion that she had never experienced before.

Wind Rider shrugged carelessly. Four years older than his sister, he had been a warrior for many years, shortly after he received the vision that provided him with his name. Since then, he had witnessed many acts of cruelty by both white-eyes and Indians. Personally, he would rather count coup than kill an enemy. Anyone could kill an enemy, but it took a brave man to touch the enemy and count coup.

"The pony soldier will provide the entertainment tonight." He glanced sharply at his sister. He knew she didn't enjoy torturing and killing any more than he did, but their people had been driven to it. "You don't have to attend the celebration," Wind Rider reminded her.

Tears Like Rain's small, pointed chin rose, and her lips firmed. Wind Rider smiled, recognizing it as a sign of her stubborn nature. He recalled when they were children and . . . His thoughts skidded to a halt. Those years were behind him now. Nothing mattered but the beleaguered People and their struggle to retain their rights and their dignity.

"Father would think me a coward if I didn't attend," Tears Like Rain said.

"You have never been a coward," Wind Rider said fondly. He loved his sister dearly. "Painted Horse would be the first to agree with me. When are you going to put him out of his misery and marry him?"

"Negotiations are still in progress," Tears Like Rain informed him. "You know how lengthy they can become. Father is still waiting for Painted Horse's family to offer gifts. If they aren't sufficient, he will consider another."

Just then the captive groaned, diverting their attention. "Perhaps he won't live until tonight," Wind Rider opined.

Tears Like Rain's expression underwent a subtle change. For the first time in her recent memory, she felt a faint, stirring compassion for a white man, and it angered her.

Zach listened in silence to the exchange between the beautiful Indian maiden and the young brave, unable to understand a word.

He had been in the West only a short time, but he knew they were speaking the Cheyenne language. His disappointment had been keen when he was assigned to the Western frontier to join the fight to quell the Indians before the War Between the States was over. True, the war was slowly but surely coming to an end, but he had wanted to be a part of the victory when the South surrendered. Instead he found himself serving at Fort Lyon. Now here he was, wounded and likely to lose his life before he reached thirty.

Zach didn't fear death. If he did, he wouldn't have joined the Union Army. What made him angry was the fact that he wouldn't be allowed to die with dignity. He'd be humiliated, tortured, and mutilated. And the half-breed Indian maiden with compelling silver eyes would witness his humiliation. As Zach continued to stare at the Indian maiden, he thought he recognized a spark of something akin to compassion, and hope flared in his breast.

Obviously the girl had a white mother, probably a captive, and perhaps somewhere in her heart she held a small regard for those of her mother's race. If he could play upon that regard, Zach thought, he might be able to convince her to help him. He waited until the brave she had been speaking with departed and the other women, weary of their games, had turned away before speaking to the maiden.

Tears Like Rain watched her brother and Summer Moon walk away before turning back to stare at the captive. His blue eyes, bright with fever, were still fixed on her. From the corner of her eye, she noted that the other women had become bored with their game and were drifting away. Soon the captive would be dragged to the center of the village and tied to a post, where he would remain until the celebration tonight. Realizing that she had no excuse to linger, she turned away.

"Don't go!" Zach's voice was rough with pain, as if his words were forced through the rawness of his throat.

Tears Like Rain stared at him curiously. The white man's tongue was foreign to her, yet . . . Like some distant memory, it stirred her in strange ways.

"Help me. I know you're half white. Do you understand what I'm saying?"

Tears Like Rain shook her head in vigorous denial. She understood nothing of what the captive was saying.

"Do you speak English?" Zach rasped. The will to survive beat fiercely within him.

Her eyes wide with sudden comprehension, Tears Like Rain felt a shock go through her when a word that was utterly foreign to her came unbidden from her lips. "No."

Zach attempted a smile but failed miserably. "I knew you spoke English. Will you help me?" Silence. "You're part white, for God's sake!"

"No!" Turning on her heel, Tears Like Rain fled as if the devil himself was after her. The shock of realizing she understood the white soldier's words sent fear and denial coursing through her. Since as long as she could remember, she had pretended ignorance of the language.

She wasn't white! She wasn't! Tears Like Rain denied as she took refuge in the tipi she shared with her brother and father. White men were more vicious even than their old enemies, the Crow and the Pawnee, who were treacherous and lazy and repulsive. She was proud to be Cheyenne, proud of her father, White Feather, and her brother, Wind Rider. Though she darkened her white skin and sable hair regularly with dye made from boiled walnut shells, there was nothing she could do about her gray eyes. But inside, where it counted, Tears Like Rain considered herself pure Cheyenne. Nothing would ever change that. Why did this particular white man have to remind her of things that had no place or meaning in her present life?

At dusk the beating drums summoned the People to the celebration. Summer Moon had already stopped by with her friend Morning Sky, but Tears Like Rain had sent them on, insisting that she wasn't ready yet. She sat before the fire now, distractedly running a buffalo-horn comb Wind Rider had carved for her through her waist-length black hair. The comb was one of her most prized possessions. Suddenly the tent flap opened, and Wind Rider stepped through the opening.

"Why aren't you at the celebration, little sister? Is your stomach too weak for such entertainment?"

His gentle teasing set her teeth on edge, and she frowned at him. "I could ask you the same question, brother."

Wind Rider smiled. He was so handsome, Tears Like Rain thought. No wonder all the maidens vied for his attention. But thus far no one had captured Wind Rider's fancy. Tall and sinewy, his firm bronze skin flowed smoothly over rippling muscles.

"I leave for Fort Weld in the morning," Wind Rider said. "I'm to accompany White Feather. We go to engage in peace negotiations forced upon us by white soldiers and their government. Their continued attacks and atrocities must stop if there is to be peace. Black Kettle hopes these latest negotiations will put an end to the war between our nations." His voice turned bitter. "Black Kettle is an old man who dreams of a peace that will never come."

"I don't blame you and your friends for being bitter," Tears Like Rain said vehemently. "The white-eyes will not be satisfied until every Plains Indian has been wiped out or herded onto reservations, where we will die in poverty. I hate them all. I fear for you and Father."

Wind Rider laughed. "We can take care of ourselves, little sister. It's you I worry about. The Shield Society is to remain behind to protect the camp, and since Painted Horse is recovering from a wound, he will also remain behind. I have asked him to look after you."

Tears Like Rain bristled. "I can look after myself. I can shoot and hunt and ride as well as you, big brother."

"Nevertheless, take care, Tears Like Rain. We are true brother and sister." His gray eyes, so like hers, spoke eloquently of his meaning. They didn't need words between them to convey their close bond. "This is the last chance before I leave to bid you good-bye. Tonight's celebration will go on till dawn, and I will sit beside Father at the council. There will be much boasting and storytelling tonight. Coup was counted many times by our brave warriors this day, and their deeds deserve praise."

"None is braver than you, brother. Summer Moon finds you irresistible. When are you going to choose a wife and make one of the young maidens happy?" She flashed him an impish grin.

Wind Rider was not impressed. "When I am ready." He reached for her hand. "Come, it is time to attend the celebration. Father will wonder where we are."

"Does the white man still live?"

He looked at her curiously. "I watched you earlier. You seemed uncommonly interested in the captive."

Tears Like Rain bit her lower lip, as if trying to come to a decision. Suddenly she asked, "Do you ever think about—about our real parents?" She flushed, fearing Wind Rider would ridicule her for harboring such thoughts.

"No!" Wind Rider said explosively. "The Cheyenne are our people; don't ever forget it. You have seen how cruel white-eyes are, how they lie and cheat and covet our lands. Many of my friends have been killed by the soldiers who try to wrest us from our homes. They attack innocent women and children and force the Cheyenne to retaliate in kind. Once we were a peace-loving people. Some, like Black Kettle, still are. But I fear we are all doomed if we don't fight back. Do you think the white-eyes would welcome us into their society? No, little sister. You and I are Cheyenne. We will always be Cheyenne."

Wind Rider's impassioned words were just the medicine Tears Like Rain needed to put her life back into perspective. She had seen the Cheyenne brutally slaughtered by soldiers, and her hatred for them had never wavered. Whatever had caused her momentary lapse, allowing her to feel compassion for the tawny-haired captive, was gone. He was her enemy. His death meant nothing to her. Squeezing her brother's hand, she followed him through the tent flap into the gathering dusk—a dusk that was swiftly turning bloodred against the brilliant backdrop of the campfire.

Hovering at the edge of consciousness, Zach knew his time was limited and tried to disassociate himself from the events that would soon take place. He had heard enough about Indians to realize that the pain he was suffering now was nothing compared to what he would experience during the course of the night.

Unaccountably, his thoughts drifted back a few hours to that terrible moment when he had been dragged into the Cheyenne camp at the end of a rope. He had passed out from pain, and when he had opened his eyes he had seen the half-breed Indian maiden staring down at him with a look of utter contempt. He couldn't help thinking about her despite his desperate straits. She was a nubile young beauty whose delicate features and smoky-gray eyes belied her Indian blood. Slightly taller than the other women, her slim curves could not be disguised beneath her doeskin tunic. If not for her inky hair and dusky skin, he would never have suspected that savage blood flowed through her veins. Compared to the other moon-faced females he had seen today, the gray-eyed beauty's features were finely drawn and pure Caucasian.

And she hated him. Hated him without even knowing him. Unfortunately, white man's greed had made it impossible for their two cultures to live side by side in harmony. Though Zach had not been in the West long enough to have participated in any of the despicable Indian massacres, he was still part of the system that authorized and made those raids possible.

Around the huge campfire, the dancing became more frenzied as both men and women joined in the festivities. Zach knew his torture and death was to be the highlight of the evening, and though he was not a coward, he dreaded the long ordeal ahead of him. Nearly intolerable pain pulsed from the place where the arrowhead was still embedded deep in his thigh, even though the shaft had been broken off and discarded before he had been dragged to the center of the camp and tied to an upright post. His legs no longer supported him and he hung by his arms, confined by rope bindings, clinging desperately to consciousness.

Abruptly the drums grew silent and the dancing stopped. Zach knew his time had come and stiffened his spine. No matter what these heathens did to him, he intended to give a good accounting of himself. His eyes were defiant as he stared at the band of grotesquely painted, nearly nude Indian braves, unconsciously seeking the half-breed maiden he had seen earlier. Somehow it seemed important to him to let her know he wasn't afraid to die, that a white man could be as brave as any Indian.

Tears Like Rain did not feel the same kind of elation over a man's brutal death as did her family and friends. She had never felt comfortable with this kind of thing but tried to conceal her revulsion. Sometimes she chose not to attend these ceremonies, but tonight she couldn't have stayed away even if she had wanted to. Something deep and profound compelled her to be present tonight. But when her gaze met that of the white soldier straining against his bonds, doubts began to assail her.

Despite his grievous wounds, he was not screaming and crying for mercy as she had seen other men do. Somehow he had managed to stiffen his spine and raise his head, staring at her with hollow eyes. Instinctively she knew he was a proud, brave man who wouldn't give in easily. He would die with as much dignity as her people allowed him. When his mouth formed silent words, her thoughts scattered.

Desperate, Tears Like Rain thought. His eyes looked desperate as he searched her face. What was he trying to say to her? Why should she care?

Suddenly the drums began to beat again, even more franticly than before. Tears Like Rain was pulled forward, dragged along by the momentum of the crowd advancing toward the captive. She was close enough now to reach out and touch him. The drums stopped again, and White Feather stepped forward, shaking his coup stick high in the air. His elaborate, feathered ceremonial bonnet trailed the ground as he prepared to give the signal the warriors had been waiting for. Dancing around the captive, the warriors shook their weapons in Zach's face, wanting to prolong his agony before beginning the actual torture.

Tears Like Rain wanted to turn aside, wanted to run back to the seclusion of her tipi, but something compelled her to remain.

"Isn't it exciting?" Summer Moon trilled as she sidled up beside Tears Like Rain. "We are placing bets on how long the captive survives once our fierce warriors begin the torture." The Cheyenne dearly loved games, especially betting games and placing wagers.

Tears Like Rain shook her head, unable to take her eyes off the captive. Flickering flames from the campfire turned his tawny hair the color of a brilliant sunset, and she was standing so close to him that the brilliant blue of his eyes nearly blinded her. If she lived to be one hundred, Tears Like Rain would never know what made her act as she did.

It was foolish.

It was irresponsible.

It was an act of raw emotion.

As if in a dream, Tears Like Rain stepped from the crowd, shielding the captive with her body. Abruptly the drums stopped, and her father whirled to stare at her as if she had lost her mind.

"What is the meaning of this, Tears Like Rain?" White Feather asked gruffly.

"Is it not tribal custom, Father, to spare a captive's life if a member of the tribe comes forward and claims him as their slave?"

White Feather scowled. It was indeed the custom, but one rarely invoked in regard to male captives. Female captives were rarely tortured or put to death, for they were usually claimed by one of the warriors. "You know our customs as well as I, daughter."

White Feather's fierce countenance nearly made Tears Like Rain lose her nerve. But something inside her rebelled at the thought of torturing and killing the handsome, tawny-haired captive. Her people might scorn and ridicule her, and she probably would hate herself later for sparing his life, but she could not let him die.

"I claim the white soldier as my slave," Tears Like Rain said in a loud voice. An angry cry rose up among the Indians. To be thus denied did not sit well with them, and they looked to White Feather for direction.

Zach sagged against the ropes that bound him, unable to understand all that was being said but astute enough to know that the gray-eyed maiden was speaking up in his defense.

Suddenly Wind Rider stepped forward, his compelling gray eyes probing his sister's face. "Why would you do such a thing, little sister?" Brother and sister were so close that Wind Rider could tell by the stubborn angle of her chin that nothing would dissuade her from the course she had set for herself.

"Must I have a reason?" Tears Like Rain asked obstinately. "Death is too easy. Anyone can see the captive has a proud spirit. Doing my bidding as a captive will not be easy for him and will be more of a punishment than death."

"He is very close to death now," White Feather observed. "Why deny us the pleasure of ending his misery?"

"Do you refuse me, Father?" Tears Like Rain knew her father could refuse her nothing. Both he and his wife, Gray Dove, had loved her well and spoiled her outrageously.

White Feather's scowl grew even more ferocious. He loved his daughter and son with fierce pride. Finding them at a time in his life when he had thought never to have any children of his own had been a gift from the Great Spirit. He had taken three wives and had no children from any of them. All but Gray Dove had taken other husbands who could give them children. Tears Like Rain and Wind Rider had filled his lodge with happiness. After Gray Dove's death, he had not taken another wife in order to devote his life to his two adopted children and pursue his dream of freedom for the Cheyenne.

Tears Like Rain stood her ground, waiting for her father's reply. As chieftain of their small band of Cheyenne, he had the power to grant her wish. She glanced at her brother, seeking his approval, but saw that he was as puzzled by her rash act as she was herself. What she was doing was entirely out of character.

"You know I can refuse you nothing, daughter," White Feather said at length. "If you want the captive, he is yours. But heed my warning. All men except the very old and very young leave tomorrow for Fort Weld to begin lengthy peace negotiations. If I didn't know you hated the soldiers as much as I do, I would never grant your wish. I will speak to our shaman, Spirit Singer, and to your grandmother, Cow Woman. They will look after you while I am gone and see that your slave obeys you."

"The captive will do as I say, Father," Tears Like Rain assured him. "I despise him and his kind. I cannot forget that soldiers took Gray Dove's life. He will suffer, Father, never fear."

Raising his coup stick and shield into the air, White Feather spoke to his disgruntled people. Their disappointment was keen, but because they respected White Feather's decision, they returned to the campfire to resume their dancing. Within minutes, Tears Like Rain was alone with the captive. She turned to face him, her eyes dark and stormy.

Zach had no idea what had just taken place, but he knew he owed his life to the slim girl who now faced him with a look of utter contempt on her face. "Thank you," he said simply, wondering why she had saved his life if she hated him as much as her expression indicated.

Something stirred inside Tears Like Rain. She had heard those words before, but their meaning was deliberately suppressed somewhere in her distant memory.

"I understand you not, White-eyes," she said in rapid Cheyenne. She was rewarded with a blank stare. "You are too proud, but soon you will come to look upon me as your mistress. As my slave, you will do as I bid, no matter how repulsive or menial the task. Perhaps the day will come when you will wish I had allowed you a quick death."

"Please," Zach pleaded, nearly at the end of his endurance, "speak English. I understand nothing of what you say. Why did you save me? Or did you save me? Have you only delayed my death to impose a new kind of torture on me?"

"Silence!" Tears Like Rain ordered harshly. She had no wish to give her people the impression that she felt sympathy for the captive. She must remain firmly in control. "I will come for you in the morning." Turning on her heel, she marched away.

"Wait!" Zach cried desperately. "Release me. Whatever your plans for me, they will come to naught if my wounds aren't treated."

His words were lost to the wind and the darkness. Tears Like Rain had already disappeared into the night.

Chapter Two

Dawn hovered on the edge of darkness, but sleep eluded Tears Like Rain. The drums had ceased, and both White Feather and Wind Rider were in the purification lodge, banishing evil spirits from their bodies before departing for the "Great Smoke" with the soldiers at Fort Weld. But no matter how hard Tears Like Rain tried, she could not dispel the disturbing image of the white captive she had left tied to the post in the center of the village. He was her slave now, to do with as she pleased, yet the thought of his suffering and death gave her no joy. The knowledge that he might die from festering wounds was not comforting.

The rain began during the predawn hours. A torrent of cold raindrops pelted the tipi with drenching fury. Surrendering to the stirring within her heart, Tears Like Rain rose from her pallet of hides and furs, pulled her soft deerskin dress over her nude body, strapped her hunting knife to her slender waist, and slipped through the tent flap. The camp was quiet. One of the sleeping dogs awakened and crept from the shelter of a nearby tipi to sniff at her heels, then quickly retreated to escape the soaking downpour.

Tears Like Rain needed no light to guide her as she walked unerringly to the center of the camp, where the captive slumped against the post. Soaked to the skin and looking thoroughly miserable, he appeared oblivious to her presence until she squatted before him in the mud.

At that moment Captain Zach Mercer would have bet his last dollar that his life wasn't worth a hill of beans. His predicament was so desperate, he was convinced that if the Indians didn't kill him, infection would. Since he hadn't been tortured and killed last night, he wondered what the Indians had in store for him, and if the cold-blooded half-breed squaw had devised some particularly cruel method of ending his life.

Zach flexed his hands, finding them numb clear to the wrists. His left leg was so grotesquely swollen that he feared it would take a miracle to save it. His body was no longer flesh and blood but a mass of throbbing, excruciating pain. And the solid sheet of cold, drenching rain added insult to misery.

Why didn't they just kill him?

Immersed in agony, he failed to see her until she crouched before him. She was so close, he could feel her sweet breath fan his cheek. She looked nearly as wet and bedraggled as he felt. His eyes widened when he saw the hunting knife clutched in her hand.

"So this is it," he said, aware that she did not understand him and resigned to his fate. "Go ahead, put me out of my misery. I welcome death." His throat was so parched that his raspy croak was barely recognizable as speech. "If my death is inevitable I may as well die at the hands of a beautiful woman."

"Quiet, slave," Tears Like Rain hissed in Cheyenne as she raised the knife above his head.

Zach braced himself for the slashing blow, hoping it would be quick and clean. Shock shuddered through him when he found his hands suddenly free. He moaned as they fell helplessly to his side.

Tears Like Rain made short work of the rest of his bindings, then sat back on her heels, her expression inscrutable as she regarded him. "Can you walk?" she asked in Cheyenne.

"I—I don't understand," Zach rasped. "Can you speak English?"

Briefly, Tears Like Rain considered summoning her father or brother, both of whom could speak English. Someone needed to tell the captive what his circumstances were to be, since her own command of the language was sadly lacking. Then she discarded the idea, deciding it would be rude of her to interrupt their time in the purifying lodge. Perhaps there would be time before they departed at dawn for them to tell the captive what was expected of him.

Motioning with her hand, Tears Like Rain indicated that Zach should stand up and follow her. Though Zach understood, he didn't think he could stand if his life depended on it. He pointed toward his wounded leg and shook his head.

"Bah," Tears Like Rain spat in harsh disapproval. "The weakest Cheyenne maiden has more stamina than most white men."

Zach realized he was being ridiculed, and his temper flared. During the war he had performed many daring acts, and his courage was never in doubt. How dared this half-breed heathen infer that he was a weakling? Spying a sturdy stick lying nearby, no doubt discarded by one of the women who had tormented him earlier, he reached for it and levered himself off the ground. The stick slipped in the mud once, twice, before he was finally upright.

Tears Like Rain smiled inwardly, secretly pleased at the captive's courage and stamina. The Cheyenne greatly admired courage. Their men were the bravest among all the plains tribes, and their women the most chaste.

Once Zach was on his feet, she indicated that he should follow her. Gritting his teeth against the tearing agony, Zach pulled himself forward with the help of the makeshift crutch, dragging his wounded leg behind him. By the time they reached the tipi, both were soaked and shivering. Zach made it as far as the yawning opening before collapsing. When Tears Like Rain turned to see if he was still following her, she found him sprawled facedown in the mud. His eyes were closed, his breath was shallow, and he was as pale as death.

Tears Like Rain let out a startled cry as she grasped the soldier's arms and dragged him inside the tipi. She could feel the torrid heat of his flesh through the thickness of his uniform and realized that he must be treated soon or die. She didn't want the white slave's death; she wanted his total submission. After she settled him on her pallet, she covered him with a thick fur, then rushed back into the freezing rain to the lodge of Spirit Singer. If anyone could save her slave, it was the shrewd old shaman.

Zach's body was on fire. He was cold. He burned. He shook with chills, then drowned in his own perspiration. The skin of his left leg felt too tight for the flesh beneath. He knew he still lived, for his pain was too great for him to be in heaven. And though he was no angel, he didn't think he deserved hell.

The grating rattle of bones coaxed Zach from the swirling mists of shadow and darkness. He opened his eyes to the bizarre sight of a wizened old man bent over him, chanting in a strange monotone. The shaman was dressed in buffalo robes and wearing a headdress crowned with a stuffed sacred owl. When the shaman saw that his patient was awake, he ceased his chanting and placed a cup to Zach's lips, forcing a vile-tasting brew down his throat. Zach coughed, gagged, and tried to resist, but he was too weak to protest as the liquid slid down his throat.

Then he drifted off again. But when the hideous old man probed his flesh to remove the arrowhead, he screamed in pain. He had no idea how long he remained unconscious, or if he still had a left leg, but when he awakened later, the shaman was dancing around him, chanting and shaking those infernal buffalo bones.

"He is awake," Tears Like Rain said.

Her voice sounded like sweet music to Zach, and he turned his head to stare at her. He recognized her immediately.

The shaman dropped to his haunches, inspected Zach's leg, placed a claw-like hand on his forehead, and announced, "He will live." Abruptly he turned to leave, his strong medicine no longer needed.

"Wait!" Since her father and brother had been gone these three days past while her captive had remained unconscious, there was no one to explain that he was her slave. She knew Spirit Singer spoke little or no English, but she did know of someone still in camp who would convey the message. "Would you tell Painted Horse that I would like to see him?"

The shaman nodded and shuffled through the tent flap.

Zach watched Tears Like Rain warily. He understood none of what was happening. Why had she dragged him in out of the rain and engaged the tribal medicine man to treat his wounds? He asked her as much, but she stared at him blankly. He then tried a simple word, asking for water. Tears Like Rain's brow furrowed when she heard the word.

"Water," Zach repeated slowly. "I'm thirsty. Please."

Slowly Tears Like Rain's brow cleared, and she reached for the water jug. Delving deeply into the forgotten chambers of her brain, she had interpreted the word correctly and reacted.

Zach tried to rise to receive the water but was too weak. He was forced to rely upon the generosity of his captor to slake his thirst. Tears Like Rain didn't hesitate as she held up his head and put the jug to his lips so he could drink. With her hand resting at the back of his head, she had the sudden irresistible urge to run her fingers through his thick thatch of straw-colored hair. Fortunately, the arrival of Painted Horse saved her the embarrassment of doing something so unacceptable.

Painted Horse waited respectfully outside the tipi after he signaled his arrival. He would never think of barging inside without being invited. Nor would he compromise the virtue of a chaste maiden. A Cheyenne maiden's chastity was her greatest asset, and though Painted Horse had thrown his blanket over Tears Like Rain and exchanged a few private words with her beneath

41

its dark folds, it had always been in the company of her father. His courtship of the lovely maiden was progressing according to Cheyenne custom, and he was satisfied that she would be his one day.

Casting a furtive glance at the semiconscious Zach, Tears Like Rain stepped outside the tipi to speak with Painted Horse.

"Spirit Singer said you wished to speak with me," Painted Horse said, drinking in the sight of the woman he hoped to make his wife.

"Ai," Tears Like Rain said, thinking Painted Horse looked most handsome today, with his long, flowing hair adorned with feathers. Except for the bandages covering his healing wound, he appeared as strong and virile as her brother. "Since I have little knowledge of the white man's tongue, I wish for you to speak to the captive and inform him that he is my slave."

Painted Horse glanced inside the tipi, his face dark with disapproval. "It is not proper for you to be alone in the tipi with a male other than a husband or relative. I will ask my aunt to come and stay with you until he recovers enough for you to stake him outside at night like the dog he is."

Tears Like Rain bristled indignantly. Something inside her rebelled at the thought of being submissive to a man. She had always tried to be a dutiful daughter to White Feather, to be obedient and meek like the other Cheyenne women, but her stubborn nature refused to allow it. Some emotion within her made her as fiercely independent and proud as any of the braves. Sometimes women were allowed to join the war societies and fight beside their men. Secretly, Tears Like Rain hoped to be a soldier woman in the Dog Soldier Society one day.

"I am capable of managing on my own," she insisted. "Besides, the slave is no danger to me in his condition."

Painted Horse scowled. "I do not like it. Wind Rider asked me to protect you in his absence, and I promised to keep you from harm. It would have been best had you not interfered in tribal ritual and left the prisoner to his fate. Many of our people are questioning your motive for claiming the captive."

Stung by the reprimand, Tears Like Rain felt no inclination to explain her actions to Painted Horse, especially since she did not understand them herself. "No harm will come to me. White Feather had no qualms about leaving the slave in my charge. Will you speak to him as I asked?"

"If you wish it," Painted Horse said sourly.

Tears Like Rain squatted down outside the tent where she could listen to Painted Horse's words.

Though he understood nothing of what was being said, somehow Zach had guessed that the conversation concerned him. His curiosity was soon appeased when the tent flap was flung open and a muscular young brave entered. He watched warily as the brave stood over him, a fierce scowl darkening his bold features. Zach was startled when the brave spoke to him in English.

"You will live, White-eyes. But if I had my way, you would be feeding the vultures right now."

"Who are you?"

"I am called Painted Horse. I am here because Tears Like Rain asked me to speak with you in the white man's tongue."

"Tears Like Rain," Zach repeated slowly. The name rolled off his tongue like sweet honey. "Is she the woman who brought me here and treated my wounds? I am grateful to her."

A sneer twisted Painted Horse's lips. "Ai, Tears Like Rain claimed you, but not for the reason you think. Perhaps you will not be so grateful when you understand that you are to be her slave."

"Her what! You expect me to be slave to a woman?"

"Ai, that is the way of it, White-eyes. I would have preferred your death, but White Feather saw fit to grant his daughter's wish and gave you to her. You must obey Tears Like Rain in all things. If you fail to do so, you will be punished. Each night you will be chained to a stake outside her lodge, and if you complain you will be beaten. Do you understand?"

Zach was stunned. Slave to a woman? It was beyond comprehension. It was degrading and demeaning. Why would a woman who was half-white save his life for such a vile purpose? It made no sense.

When Zach made no reply, Painted Horse took great pleasure in prodding him none too gently with his toe. "Do you understand, White-eyes?"

Zach gritted his teeth against the sudden burst of pain when Painted Horse's foot connected with his wounded thigh. "I understand. But why would a woman who is half-white wish me for a slave?"

"Tears Like Rain is not white. She is Cheyenne in her heart," Painted Horse informed him with a snarl. "I do not know why she wanted you, but I will tell you that I do not like it. One day she will be my wife, but until that time she is free to do as she pleases, as long as her father agrees."

A skeptical look came over Zach's face. Who was the brave trying to fool? Tears Like Rain couldn't possibly be Cheyenne. Not one Indian trait marked her beautiful features. True, her skin and hair were dark, but her soft gray eyes betrayed her white heritage.

"You'd do well to heed my words, White-eyes," Painted Horse continued gravely. "I will be watching you. All the men have gone to Fort Weld for the Great Smoke except those who belong to the Shield Society. They were left behind to protect the camp. I was forced to remain behind because of my wounds. You will be treated like any other captive, and I will make certain you bring Tears Like Rain no grief."

Before Zach could form a reply, Painted Horse turned abruptly and swept out of the tipi.

Exhausted by the encounter, Zach contemplated everything that Painted Horse had told him. Evidently, the lovely half-breed maiden, Tears Like Rain, had spared his life because she wanted a slave. He was to be chained like a dog and made to do her bidding. If he refused to obey her every whim, he would be beaten. She must hate him very much to demand his complete subjugation, he reflected. But when he recalled the look of utter contempt in her eyes as she looked at him, he could indeed believe that she despised not just him but the entire white race.

Suddenly the wedge of light at the entrance of the tipi widened, and Tears Like Rain stepped inside. She stared dispassionately at Zach, her expression unreadable.

"So, White-eyes," she said in Cheyenne. "Now you know. When you have recovered, you will do as I ask, no matter how repulsive the task."

Zach's eyes fastened on Tears Like Rain in fascination. She was beautiful in her soft deerskin tunic and fringed moccasins. Tall and slim, she had a supple body and lush curves that proclaimed her a woman full grown. Her long black hair hung down her shapely back in a thick cascade of soft waves, and her skin glowed darkly. Zach noted that her lush lashes and arched brows were several shades lighter than the dark ebony of her hair.

"I don't care what Painted Horse says," he muttered to himself. "You are no Indian." Then more loudly, he asked, "Why did you spare my life? Why have you taken the trouble to save me from death and tend my wounds only to make a slave of me? How can you have no feelings for your own kind?"

Tears Like Rain frowned. In the past she had refused to speak the white man's tongue or even listen when she heard it spoken. She wanted nothing to do with white men who destroyed the People and ravaged their land. They lied and killed and stole while talking out of both sides of their mouths. They wanted to exterminate the People entirely.

Yet despite her contempt for the white man's language, the words coming from the soldier's mouth began to make sense. Some long-suppressed memory stirred deep in her breast. Vaguely, she remembered a sweet-faced woman who hugged and kissed her and called her Abby. And a strong, kindly man who let her ride on his shoulders. There was a brother she adored named Ryder and a little sister she loved fiercely. But those memories were from a different time, a different world. She was Cheyenne now, and she had claimed this white-eyes solely to humilate and punish him. Though his words unlocked secret places inside her, her mind refused to interpret them.

Zach watched Tears Like Rain's face closely, realizing that she understood more than she let on. He didn't know what to make of her. No matter how he looked at it, she had saved his life. As long as he had his life, he could endure slavery until he found a way to escape. And he would escape, he told himself fiercely. Being a captive and serving the whims of this slip of a girl rankled more than he cared to admit. He was a proud man. Never before had a woman held such total control over his life.

Tears Like Rain wondered why this man's complete subjugation gave her no joy. She was fascinated by his brilliant blue eyes and pale skin. With a start, she realized that her own skin would be as pale as his if she didn't stain it. The prickly hairs growing on his face and body were another source of curiosity. Indians did not have facial hair. She knew her brother scraped the hair off his face each day and supposed this man would have to do the same.

"My name is Zach."

Tears Like Rain nearly jumped out of her skin. She looked at him curiously.

"Zach." He repeated the name, hoping she understood what he was trying to convey.

"Zach?" Comprehension dawned as her lips formed the word. It was his name. Obviously he was trying to tell her his name. Why should she care? He was still a despised white-eyes.

"That's right." Zach nodded. "What is your name? You do have a white name, don't you?"

Tears Like Rain knew what he was asking but deliberately ignored his question. Instead, she repeated her name in Cheyenne. When her words were met with silence, she saw that Zach had drifted back into a world of darkness. She stared down at him dispassionately, then knelt beside him and threw aside the blanket covering him. Since he was unconscious, she decided it was a good time to change the bandage on his wound. She needed her slave healthy if he was to accomplish the tasks set for him.

Tears Like Rain's breath slammed against her ribs. She knew immediately that it had been a mistake to expose the captive. He was magnificent. He was also naked. Previously, Spirit Singer had tended the captive's wounds, and she had no idea that the shaman had stripped him naked. Every glorious inch of him was exposed to her startled gaze. His body wasn't sickly white as she had supposed. She was surprised to see that his flesh was tanned to a rich gold color. Broad of shoulder, slim of waist, with muscular legs and arms, he appeared every bit as strong and powerful as a Cheyenne warrior. Though his manflesh lay flaccid between his legs, it appeared impressive to her innocent eyes. Were all men so generously endowed?

A warm flush spread over Tears Like Rain's body, and she felt a tingling deep inside her woman's place. A shuddering sigh whispered past her lips. She did not welcome the effect Zach was having on her and quickly bent to her task. Working swiftly, she kept her eyes

49

averted as she cleansed the wound according to Spirit Singer's instructions and covered it with a fresh bandage. By the time she finished and left the tipi to start their meal, her hands were shaking.

Yet long after she had bared his body to her gaze, she could not forget the blatant virility and power of his muscular form. To her everlasting regret, the masculine perfection of his face and body was committed forever to her memory.

Chapter Three

Tears Like Rain stirred the pot of savory stew vigorously, wishing her thoughts could be dealt with as easily as the contents of the pot. Her slave's wounds were healing, and he was growing stronger. Instinctively she knew that he wasn't the type of man to accept the yoke of slavery meekly and that she must act to prevent his escape before he was fully recovered. Painted Horse had already accused her of coddling the white-eyes and demanded that she evict him from her tipi. He insisted that it was time her slave was taught his place among the People and treated with the contempt he deserved.

If Tears Like Rain held any doubt that Painted Horse was right, she had only to recall the unprovoked attacks on their tribe by soldiers and the massacre of innocent women and

51

children to renew her strong hatred for all white-eyes. She personally intended to make her slave pay for every indignity visited upon her people by soldiers from the surrounding forts.

Tears Like Rain glanced toward the tipi, her mind boiling as furiously as the pot she stirred as she examined her reasons for sparing the wounded soldier. She had acted with uncharacteristic recklessness, even for one as prone to rash behavior as she was. Her grandmother, Cow Woman, who had insisted on staying with her while the slave remained in her tipi, had been summoned to treat a sick child, leaving him unattended.

Forcing her mind to her task, Tears Like Rain tried to forget how the slave looked at her, how his bold glance made her feel, and the way her insides quivered when his captivating blue eyes slid over her. Deliberately, she forced herself to remember how those of his race wanted to exterminate the People and their allies living on the Great Plains. Not until she recalled the deceit and lies white men were capable of would she be able to enter the tipi and treat her slave with the contempt and hatred he deserved.

Zach cast a furtive glance around the tipi. Relief shuddered through him when he realized that he was finally alone, and he rose unsteadily to his feet. He had been secretly testing his strength whenever he was left unattended— which wasn't often enough to suit him. If

Tears Like Rain wasn't with him, a toothless old crone watched over him with an inscrutable expression. It was the old woman who saw to his needs when he was unable to see to them himself, not the beautiful half-breed.

His leg wound was healing well, thanks to the poultice the medicine man had provided, and Zach realized that his ordeal as a slave would soon begin. He stretched his left leg, wincing when pain lanced through him. Then he put his full weight on his wounded leg and was gratified when he found he could support himself. Completely nude—the tattered remnants of his clothes had been taken from him—he flexed his muscles, stifling a groan when they protested. He had been inactive far too long as he lay recuperating from his wounds. Unfortunately, it would be a while yet before he was mended enough to contemplate escape.

Zach took a few hesitant steps toward the door, willing himself to remain calm. If no one was guarding the door, he fully intended to wrap himself in a buffalo robe and walk boldly into the midst of his captors. He was anxious to test his position as slave and wondered what would happen to him if he walked boldly about the camp. He was two short steps from the entrance when Tears Like Rain burst through the opening. Zach froze, poised on the balls of his feet as he met the sharp, silver-eyed gaze of his beautiful captor.

Tears Like Rain skidded to a halt just inside the door, unprepared for the visual assault that met her eyes. Zach stood close enough for her to touch; the sight of his nude body rendered her speechless. She had seen him nude while he was lying unconscious and had chastely averted her eyes. But seeing him now, recognizing the latent power in his muscular legs and arms, the masculine beauty and strength in the set of his wide shoulders, narrow waist, and corded chest made her wonder at her daring in claiming such a virile man as her slave. A voice deep inside her conscience warned that this man would bring her more grief than she had ever known and perhaps change her life forever.

Zach stood his ground, fists clenched at his sides, his mouth taut with anger. He hated the way Tears Like Rain stared at him, as if inspecting her property and finding him lacking. Zach refused to be intimidated by the little savage, despite the disadvantage his nudity gave him.

"Where are my clothes?" Tears Like Rain gave no hint of understanding. Zach reached out and touched the fringe of her tunic. "My clothes. I want my clothes."

Abruptly, Tears Like Rain walked past him, rummaged in a parfleche hanging on a pole, and returned with a small bundle. She thrust it into his hands, then withdrew quickly, as if contact with him repelled her.

Puzzled, Zach shook out the brief swatch of material and was stunned to find that she had given him an Indian breechclout. Surely she didn't mean for him to go around in something as indecent as this, did she? Obviously she did, for she left the tipi and motioned for him to follow. Since Zach had no intention of going about totally naked, he donned the skimpy breechclout and limped out into the bright sunshine.

For a moment, he was so happy to be outside and to feel the sun on his face that he failed to notice the women and children gathered around him, pointing and snickering. Some of the younger boys picked up sticks and poked him cruelly. Tears Like Rain seemed not to notice as she ladled out two bowls of stew. She set his on the ground by his feet and motioned for him to sit down and eat. He looked around for a utensil, and when he saw Tears Like Rain pointedly ignore him while daintily eating with a buffalo horn spoon, he realized that he wasn't to be allowed that luxury. Laughter taunted him when he picked up a piece of meat and shoved it into his mouth. But Zach was too hungry to be bothered by their jeers.

He had scraped clean the first bowl and was about to ask for a second when Tears Like Rain took it from him and ordered him onto his feet. The group of women and children crowded around him when Tears Like Rain went into the tipi and returned almost immediately with a length of rawhide. Before he realized what she intended, she had looped it around his neck and pulled it tight. Zach's hands flew to his neck, intending to remove it.

Suddenly the crowd parted, and Painted Horse shoved through. He carried a Spencer rifle and his lips were twisted into a sneer. "Do not resist, White-eyes. It is your fate to be a slave. If you defy your mistress, you will be beaten."

"Beat me, then, for I will not submit willingly."

Tears Like Rain sneered at his defiance. Foolish white man, she thought derisively. He should be grateful for his life.

A sly grin split Painted Horse's dusky features. He picked up a stout stick and advanced slowly toward Zach. Several women and children followed his example. Painted Horse's blow fell first. In a matter of seconds, so many blows had fallen upon his back, legs, and shoulders that he was driven to his knees. Suddenly a voice rose above the din. Zach did not understand the words, but he recognized the melodic tones of Tears Like Rain.

"Stop! Cease now. I do not want my slave killed."

The blows stopped abruptly.

"Bah, you are too softhearted, Tears Like Rain. The white-eyes must be taught a lesson." Painted Horse's eyes glinted malevolently. His brother had been slain at Solomon Fork, and the urge for revenge was strong within him.

Tears Like Rain glared defiantly at Painted Horse. Since they were not yet married, he had no right to rebuke her. "He will obey." Turning abruptly, she went inside the tipi and returned with a water jug, which she thrust at Zach.

Fearing he would be beaten to death before escape was possible, Zach accepted the jug, struggling to wipe the defiant scowl from his face. His compliance pleased Tears Like Rain as she picked up the loose end of the leash she had placed around his neck and jerked him forward.

"Wait!" Painted Horse leaped in front of her. "Arm yourself. White-eyes are not to be trusted. Though the warriors of the Shield Society have remained behind to guard the camp, their numbers are few. You must not allow your slave to escape, for he will surely tell the soldiers where we are camped and lead them to us. Take my rifle."

It was a magnificent gesture on Painted Horse's part, and Tears Like Rain accepted his offer. Prodding her slave in the back, she pointed him in the direction she wished him to take. Clutching the water jug, Zach started forward, his gait slow and awkward due to his leg wound. Nearly all the women and children in the camp followed, eager to view the slave's humiliation.

Tears Like Rain could feel the white-eyes' silent rage as she jerked him forward by the neck leash. She knew what he was experiencing because she would have felt the same were it she who was his slave, and she felt vague stirrings of discomfort. Despite herself, she had to admire his courage. Bending to her will when he wanted to lash out was a sign of his mettle.

But Tears Like Rain was not fooled by his mock docility. His shrewd blue eyes gave him away. He was in full control of his senses, totally aware of his predicament, and was even now planning his escape.

"You cannot escape," she told him in Cheyenne. "The Shield Society will kill you before you reach the perimeter of the camp."

"I don't understand," Zach replied. "I know you speak my language—why won't you use it?"

"I—do—not—speak the white man's—tongue."

Stunned to hear the language she had tried to forget coming from her mouth, Tears Like Rain stopped abruptly. A tug on the neck leash brought Zach to a skidding halt. The stunned look on Tears Like Rain's face made him smile despite the cruel bite of the leather thong into the flesh of his neck. Goading her to speak English was his method of retaliation.

"I knew it! You do speak English."

"No!" Tears Like Rain's denial came too late as memory came flooding back to her, filling her brain with jumbled words and phrases. Her brow furrowed as she tried to cast them from her mind. She prodded him with the rifle. "Walk." She groaned aloud when she realized that she had used another word from the despised white man's tongue.

Zach started forward, his mind whirling with all kinds of possibilities now that he could communicate with Tears Like Rain. He turned to speak with her again and was silenced when she stooped, picked up a stout stick and began beating him about the back and shoulders. Hoots of laughter came from the women and children following behind. He flushed with anger. They had come along to be entertained, and he was providing the entertainment.

Soon they came to the bank of a stream, and Zach waded in to the extent of his leash and bent to fill the jug. He placed it carefully on the bank and returned to the water, intending to take the opportunity to wash himself as best he could in spite of his audience. When Tears Like Rain saw what he intended, she tugged on the leash.

"No."

It was all Zach could do to quell his rising temper. "What in the hell is wrong now? I merely wanted to wash myself. There is still blood on my skin, and I smell."

Tears Like Rain tugged on the leash. "No." Her slave must learn that he could do nothing without her approval. The Cheyenne were masters at rendering their enemies meek and biddable. Before she was through, she vowed, he would be completely submissive to her wishes. She would break his spirit and crush his pride until he was as compliant as a camp dog. She would prove to him that a white man was no match for a Cheyenne.

Their amusement having come to an end, the women and children began drifting back to camp. In the past, the chieftain's daughter had proven herself capable of handling potentially dangerous situations, and they had faith in her ability to do so now.

Zach looked longingly at the refreshing water and then at Tears Like Rain standing on the bank gesturing for him to return, and something inside him snapped. Grasping the leash with both hands, he gave a vicious yank. Caught by surprise, Tears Like Rain dropped the rifle and went flying head over heels into the stream. Zach reeled her in like a fish, hauling her up against him, sputtering in indignation.

"I'm not going to leave this stream until I've washed," he said, staring into the angry storm clouds of her gray eyes. There was a bitter challenge in his voice that dared her, defied her.

A startled gasp slipped past Tears Like Rain's lips. Standing this close, she felt overwhelmed by the solid, unyielding strength in him. Just a day or two ago, she could have sworn he was as weak as a kitten and no danger to her or anyone. But obviously she had misjudged him. He was extremely wily and dangerous, and she could see now that she would have to be on guard every minute. Silently she accepted the challenge he offered and issued one of her own. *I will master you, White-eyes. The Great Spirit will give me strength.*

Zach's eyes narrowed as he stared at Tears Like Rain. Her wet deerskin tunic clung to her nubile curves like a second skin. Her eyes were wide, her mouth slightly open, and her chest rose and fell as panting breaths escaped from her parted lips. Zach didn't know when he had seen anything more arousing.

Beneath his penetrating gaze, Tears Like Rain could feel her breasts swelling and her nipples puckering. Her whole body blushed beneath his heated gaze. A Cheyenne warrior would never look at a maiden like that. If a warrior was courting her, he might stop her on the way to the stream for a few minutes' conversation, but he would never say anything to cause her embarrassment or look at her with hot, probing eyes the way this man was regarding her.

Zach felt his body grow taut with desire. He had never encountered a more savage woman and felt himself responding with pure animal lust. Yet because he was her slave, she his mistress, the very thought of wanting the half-breed Indian filled him with revulsion. Obviously, she had lived too long with savages and was beyond redemption. She could never be taught to live with polite society. Yet, looking at her now, with her shiny black hair waving softly around her face and the curves of her lithe body clearly defined beneath her wet tunic, he had never wanted a woman more.

The urge to kiss Tears Like Rain was like a driving force inside him. Impulsively he reached for her, dragging her against the naked wall of his chest. Tears Like Rain's scream of protest ended in a gurgle of surprise when Zach's mouth clamped down on hers. This touching of lips was new and frightening. Cheyenne men and women touched cheeks to express intimacy, never lips. Sometimes a man licked his lover's skin, but being a maiden she had never experienced such things.

Zach's kiss grew urgent as his hands slid down her back to grasp the soft mounds of her buttocks. His breechclout provided small protection against the bold thrust of his manhood, and Tears Like Rain felt like a sparrow trapped within the talons of a mighty eagle. All-consuming rage lent her the strength to tear herself from Zach's arms. How could she have let this happen? The white-eyes was her slave, her enemy. Struggling fiercely, she reached for the knife strapped to her thigh and pressed it against his vulnerable neck.

"Touch me again, white man, and I'll rip your heart out," she snarled in Cheyenne.

Zach felt the prick of the blade and glanced downward to see a trickle of blood sliding down his chest. Though he couldn't understand the words spoken by the bloodthirsty little savage, he knew his life hung by a slim thread. She could slit his throat without a moment's hesitation and never blink an eye. Despite the threat to his life, pride demanded that he resist. "Go ahead and kill me. Death does not frighten me. It might be preferable to being a slave."

Slowly, Tears Like Rain lowered the knife, a brief flare of admiration turning her eyes dark. Then, whirling abruptly, she waded toward the shore where she had dropped her rifle. Picking the weapon up from the ground, she pointed it at him and ordered brusquely, "Come out!"

Though she had spoken in Cheyenne again, Zach knew exactly what she was asking. But defiance was a pulsating giant inside him. "Speak English. How can I obey when I know not what you are saying?"

"Come—out," she repeated in halting English.

"When I finish bathing," he answered boldly. Though Zach had no idea what the little savage would do, male obstinacy demanded that he challenge her authority. Kissing her had been a rash move on his part, but the pleasure was well worth it. Ironically, she had turned the tables on him. He had found himself so thoroughly enthralled by the kiss that it had left him shaken.

Calmly, he sat in the knee-deep water and proceeded to splash water over his body. Inwardly, he wasn't as calm as he pretended. He had no idea how Tears Like Rain would react. As he cleansed his body, he braced himself for the rip of bullets through his flesh. His pride demanded that he defy her authority and challenge her orders.

Tears Like Rain had never known a more obstinate man, nor one so foolish. She knew he had deliberately challenged her, but she couldn't bring herself to shoot him. "Get out now!" she ordered in Cheyenne.

"Speak English," Zach repeated slowly.

It amazed and angered Tears Like Rain that she was able to understand almost everything the white man was saying. Somehow he had dredged up those long-forgotten words from somewhere deep inside her. She had pretended ignorance of the language of her birth for so many years that she thought she had lost the ability to speak and understand it. She had even refused to listen to or speak with Wind Rider in the white man's tongue. Now she realized that she had never forgotten, just repressed the knowledge.

"Come out! You must obey me." Tears Like Rain's tongue twisted around the English words as she spat them out. It seemed strange to use the tongue of her enemy. Her expression was hard and uncompromising as she gestured with the barrel of the rifle.

Zach stood up, adjusted the breechclout that had become tangled beneath the water, and walked slowly toward the grassy bank upon which Tears Like Rain stood. Tears Like Rain watched him through shuttered lids. The strength and sheer masculine beauty of him flooded her with an anticipation so intense that she felt brittle, ready to shatter. The sun turned his hair into a golden halo and gilded his skin bronze. Because he hadn't shaved the hair from his chin, it sprouted like ripened wheat upon his square jaw. And except for the healing wounds scattered over his body, he was pure perfection.

The thought came to Tears Like Rain that she would have to provide her slave with a pair of her brother's deerskin leggings or be plagued by the sight of his blatantly male body day in and day out. She had thought that dressing him in a minimum of clothing would humiliate him, but he did not seem unduly embarrassed by his lack of proper clothing. When Cheyenne braves wore breechclouts, Tears Like Rain barely noticed, for it was the accepted manner of dress. But when this man dressed in the same fashion, she was aware of every nuance of his masculine frame.

When Zach reached the bank, Tears Like Rain grasped the tether attached to his neck, gave it a vicious jerk, and motioned for him to pick up the water jug and walk before her. He did as he was bidden, but not before sending her a mocking smile. As he walked back toward camp, he made careful note of his surroundings and filed the information away for future use. He was bound and determined to escape before the main body of warriors returned from their conference at Fort Weld.

Bone weary, Zach sagged against the pole to which he had been tied. His chores had been many and varied this day, but nothing had been more humiliating than when he had been ordered to squat beside an upright stake outside Tears Like Rain's tipi, where he was tied like an animal while the women and children watched. His hands had been bound together and attached to the stake with just enough slack to allow him to sit on the ground. No one had thought to provide him with a blanket. At least Tears Like Rain had fed him and allowed him to drink his fill, he allowed grudgingly. But she had not interfered when the children began dancing around him, throwing stones and poking him with sticks.

Perhaps it was because Painted Horse stood nearby, sneering at him with a particularly nasty smile, that Tears Like Rain did not interfere. Curiously, Zach wondered about the relationship between Tears Like Rain and the young warrior. Though he appeared respectful in all his dealings with Tears Like Rain, Zach could not help but notice Painted Horse's possessiveness toward her and the covetous way he stared at her when she wasn't looking. Painted Horse wanted the beautiful maiden, that much was certain, and Zach wondered if Tears Like Rain was attracted to Painted Horse in the same way. For some reason, the thought of the two of them together as lovers was disturbing. Had he known of the strict Cheyenne taboo against premarital sex, he would have been very much surprised.

Many Plains Indians, he knew, had no such moral codes. Premarital sex was permitted, even encouraged, with young maidens often offered to white men who visited the tribe. But the Cheyenne were not among those who permitted promiscuous behavior in their women.

Zach's thoughts scattered when a rumble of thunder brought an unwelcome onslaught of cold, stinging rain. It reminded him of the night Tears Like Rain had come to him and saved his life by bringing him into her tipi and treating his wounds. Would she come again? he wondered. He glanced expectantly toward the tipi, imagining her lying nude on her pallet, her lissome, golden-hued body curled warmly beneath her buffalo robes. His thoughts grew so erotic that he groaned aloud, his agony as much from repressed passion as from discomfort due to the elements. How could he want a heathenish little savage who took delight in his torment?

Tears Like Rain awoke to the splatter of rain on her face. Crawling from beneath the warmth of her buffalo robes, she closed the smoke hole at the apex of the tipi, then crawled back beneath the covers. She closed her eyes, willing herself back to sleep, but sleep would not come. She knew from experience how miserable one could be huddling in the rain. After a while, one's skin became cold and clammy and nothing could stop the body from shaking. She imagined the white man's discomfort and tried without success to forget it.

Why should she care if a lowly slave, a man no better than an animal, shook from cold?

It didn't matter.

Her eyes flew open when a loud groan penetrated the darkness of her tipi. She knew its source immediately and tried to ignore it. She had so many reasons to hate the pony soldier; she shouldn't care how miserable he was. When another groan followed close on the first, the truth dawned on Tears Like Rain.

She cared.

The reason for her caring frightened and angered her. Hate for the white race had been a part of her life for so many years that she felt shamed by her compassion for her slave. Yet it did not stop her from rising from her pallet, wrapping her body in a robe, and picking up another robe that lay neatly folded in a corner. Resolutely, she opened the tipi flap and stepped into the starless, ebony night. A brilliant streak of lightning and a clap of thunder hailed her exit from the tipi.

Zach shivered uncontrollably as he shook his head to dash the rain from his face. When Tears Like Rain made no effort to bring him in out of the inclement weather, he resigned himself to spending a miserable night crouching in the mud. He would have expected no less from the heartless little vixen.

Vivid lightning lit the moonless sky, and Zach looked up just as Tears Like Rain stepped from the tipi. His heart leapt in joy as she walked slowly toward him, clutching a bundle to her chest. Another streak of lightning revealed a flash of something white, and Zach's eyes widened when he realized that he had caught a brief glimpse of one of Tears Like Rain's legs through the opening of the robe. Incredulous, he waited breathlessly for another revealing glance, wondering if he had been imagining things. Shouldn't her legs be as golden brown as her face and arms?

Stopping inches from Zach, Tears Like Rain unfolded the buffalo robe she carried and placed it over his shoulders. "I do this because you are of no use to me when you are sick," she said in Cheyenne.

"I do not understand," Zach replied. He was as determined that she speak English as she was not to.

"I—" From somewhere deep inside her, Tears Like Rain dredged up the halting words to convey her meaning to Zach. "I—do not—want you to fall ill, for you will be of—no use to me." She turned to leave.

"Wait!" She hesitated but did not turn. "You are half white. You do not belong here with these savages."

Tears Like Rain whirled on her heel, her eyes blazing. "I am Cheyenne! Do not forget it, White-eyes. My people do not speak with forked tongues, nor do they kill unless provoked." Abruptly, her rash words skidded to a halt. She had spoken more words in the white man's tongue than she had at any time since she was six years old, and it shocked her.

"I am not your enemy. I have never killed an Indian," Zach said. "I have just recently arrived from the East and was wounded by your people while on my first patrol. I have never even drawn my weapon against your people."

"It—matters not," Tears Like Rain spat. "In time you would have killed, and done so willingly."

Zach had no answer, for he realized the truth of her simple statement. His orders were to attack and kill Indians, and he would have done so—but not women and children. That was something he could never do, no matter who had ordered it. But when he opened his mouth to tell Tears Like Rain his feelings, she was no longer standing beside him. She had quietly disappeared inside her tipi.

Chapter Four

Zach grimaced in revulsion at the buffalo skin stretched on the ground before him. The day before, one of the warriors from the Shield Society had spotted a small herd of buffalo. Led by Painted Horse, they had left immediately, returning late in the day dragging the meat, skin, and bones of several of the huge animals behind their horses on travois. As was their custom, the warriors killed only what they needed for their consumption. The meat and other parts were divided equally among the tribe members.

Zach's grimace of disgust brought a smile of amusement to Tears Like Rain's face. Without a word, she handed him a small fleshing tool made of buffalo bone and gestured toward the hide. Zach turned the tool over in his hands, a perplexed expression on his face. The thought occurred to him that it would make a reasonably effective razor to scrape off his beard.

"What is this for?"

Tears Like Rain made a sweeping motion with her hand, indicating that he was to scrape the tool against the buffalo hide. Zach realized then that he was to follow the example of the women who were kneeling beside a buffalo hide staked nearby on the ground, scraping it clean of tissue, fat, and hair. The stench made him gag, and he shook his head in vigorous denial.

"You—will do as—I say," Tears Like Rain insisted. More and more she was using the white man's tongue to issue orders, she thought guiltily. But it seemed the only effective way of communicating with her slave. "Your gut is as weak as an infant's."

The smug look on her face gave Zach the stomach to bend to his task. Her words stung. He could hear the other women laughing and jeering as he struggled to keep the contents of his stomach from spewing forth. Satisfied that Zach was following orders, Tears Like Rain turned to her own task of cutting up buffalo meat and stringing it on a frame to dry.

Some of the meat would be pounded into tiny bits and mixed with berries to make the nourishing pemmican they depended on during the winter months. Finding buffalo this late in the year was a lucky omen, Tears Like Rain thought, and she wondered if it meant that her people would be successful in persuading the soldiers to allow them to travel and live in peace wherever they chose.

Staring at his hands, slippery with slime and blood, Zach wiped them on the grass to remove as much of the filth as he could. At long last, the buffalo hide was scraped clean, and he sat back on his haunches to inspect his work, which had been harder than he would have thought. Suddenly, Tears Like Rain appeared at his side, holding out an iron pot filled with something disgusting. Zach recoiled in revulsion.

"What is it?"

Tears Like Rain grinned, relishing the startled look on her slave's face. She could hardly wait to describe what he was now required to do. "Buffalo brains."

Zach paled. "What am I supposed to do with them?"

"Rub them into the hide. It will make it soft and supple enough to make into clothes."

"Good God! If it is all as disgusting as this, it is no wonder your men avoid domestic chores." He couldn't help but notice that none of the warriors left in camp ever lifted a finger to help the women.

"Our men are warriors. Women's work is beneath them."

"I am a soldier. Why must I do women's work?"

"You are a slave." She indicated the long leash attached to his neck and tied to a nearby stake. "But for me, you would not be alive,

73

White-eyes. I could beat you, kill you, debase you in any manner I see fit and my people would not object. Here." She shoved the pot holding the brains at him. "Observe the women. They will show you how it is done."

Zach's stomach rebelled as he reluctantly accepted the disgusting mess, vowing to get even with the savage little half-breed for the humiliation she was causing him.

"Ho, I see you have found a fit duty for your slave, Tears Like Rain." Painted Horse's voice grated harshly in Zach's ears. The warrior's black eyes gleamed maliciously as he said, "It pleases me to find him wallowing in offal."

Zach stiffened. Male laughter filled the air as the warriors who weren't engaged in duties came to watch the white soldier perform degrading women's work. It was an insult no Cheyenne warrior would have stood for. Painted Horse's laughter was loudest of all. When Zach glared up at him, the haughty warrior placed his foot on Zach's backside and shoved, sending him sprawling facedown in the revolting mass of blood and brains.

Raising himself up on his haunches, rage surged through Zach as he glared into Painted Horse's cruel face. Loud hoots and howls from the amused warriors milling around added to Zach's humiliation, and something inside him snapped. Curling his hand around a clump of brains, he flung it into Painted Horse's face.

Tears Like Rain's loud gasp sounded like thunder in the ominous silence that followed Zach's rash act.

"White dog!" Painted Horse hissed as he dashed away the brains and gore with the back of one hand. "You will pay for this insult."

He barked out an order in Cheyenne, and immediately Zach was surrounded by warriors. One of them grabbed the leash still attached to his neck and jerked viciously, forcing him to his feet. When Painted Horse jabbed him in the ribs with the sharp end of his lance, Zach cast a surreptitious glance at Tears Like Rain, wondering if she would protest. He realized that he really had gone too far this time and that nothing short of a miracle would save him.

Tears Like Rain was shocked by Zach's reckless act of defiance. She could understand his defying her—she was a woman. But to challenge a man like Painted Horse was tantamount to a death sentence. Didn't he know that his rash resistance had doomed him? Her admiration for him grew despite her unwillingness to admit that this particular white man had qualities valued by the Cheyenne. She watched in trepidation as Zach was dragged to where Painted Horse's swift pony was tethered and the end of his leash was attached to the saddle.

"We will see how defiant you are when your flesh is torn from your bones by nettle and brush and your head is pounded into the dirt beneath my horse."

Painted Horse could hardly contain his glee as he leaped aboard his horse's back and dug his heels into its flanks. The horse jumped forward, jerking Zach's feet from beneath him. The leash tightened around his neck, and Zach grabbed onto it in order to keep from being strangled. Bouncing along the ground, he hung on with a desperation born of his innate instinct for survival. He had no idea how long he could hang on before he eventually tired and strangled to death, but he wasn't going to accept death easily.

Her face drained of all color, Tears Like Rain watched in mounting horror as Painted Horse took his terrible vengeance on her slave. She had been so stunned by the white soldier's reckless defiance and Painted Horse's swift rebuttal that she had been unable to interfere. But when she saw his flesh being literally torn from his bones as he was dragged behind Painted Horse's mount, a terrible rage seized her. The white man was her slave! If he needed punishment, she would mete it out in her own way, on her own terms.

Suddenly, Tears Like Rain became a whirlwind of motion as she leaped onto the back of the nearest horse and took off after Painted Horse. Since her horse wasn't hindered by a dragging weight like Painted Horse's mount, she easily caught up with him. When she drew abreast of Zach, she removed the knife strapped to her thigh, reached down, and slashed the tether attached to his neck.

He came to a tumbling halt. Painted Horse realized what she had done and howled in protest.

It had all happened so fast that Zach wasn't certain what had taken place. One moment he was gasping for breath, aware that he couldn't hold on to the tether much longer, and the next moment he was lying motionless on the ground.

Painted Horse slid from his mount, his eyes blazing. "Why did you do that?" His voice was like thunder as he rounded on Tears Like Rain. "Your slave insulted me. It is my right to punish him in any way I see fit."

"You have no right," Tears Like Rain flung back fiercely. "He is *my* slave. You have no right to interfere."

Realizing what had happened, Zach struggled to his feet. Once again the woman had come to his defense, and it stung to think that he had been unable to defend himself. The feeling of helplessness and frustration was more painful than the hair-raising ride he had just taken at the end of a rope. It seemed that his very life depended on the goodwill of a slim young maiden with the instincts of a savage.

"Once again I am in your debt," he gasped as his heart finally slowed to a steady pounding.

Tears Like Rain sent him a scathing glance. "You are my slave, not the slave of Painted Horse. Do not thank me yet, for my punishment is likely to be as severe as that of Painted Horse."

Painted Horse looked stunned. It was the first time he could ever recall hearing Tears Like Rain use the white man's language. "When did you learn to speak the tongue of the enemy?"

Tears Like Rain flushed but refused to be intimidated by Painted Horse. She was the daughter of White Feather, respected chieftain of their tribe, and her pride was as fierce as that of her father and brother. "The knowledge was always with me. I felt no need to speak the tongue until now. It is the only way I can convey my wishes to my slave."

She glanced at the white man, wincing inwardly at the bloody red welt ringing his neck. She wanted to treat it with soothing salve immediately but knew that showing compassion for the enemy would earn the contempt of her people.

"If you cannot control your slave, I will kill him," Painted Horse growled in rapid Cheyenne. "Your brother and father honored your request without considering the consequences. Were you my wife, I would have denied your foolish request."

Tears Like Rain bristled angrily. A few weeks ago, she would have been proud to consider taking a brave warrior like Painted Horse for a husband. She had happily agreed to the negotiations already in progress for their courtship and eventual marriage. She had not known he would be so demanding a husband. Now she was having second thoughts.

"I am not your wife, Painted Horse," she declared boldly. "Perhaps I never will be." Her eyes had turned a dark angry gray by the time she turned to confront her slave.

All the while Painted Horse and Tears Like Rain spoke, Zach tried to pick up a thread of meaning but failed. He had learned a few words of Cheyenne, but not enough to follow a conversation. But there was no mistaking the fact that Painted Horse and Tears Like Rain were arguing over him. When the beautiful little savage turned her compelling gray eyes on Zach, he could think of only one thing to say.

"Thank you."

Painted Horse heard Zach's words, and his hands clenched into fists at his sides. Then he turned abruptly, mounted his horse and rode away.

Tears Like Rain reached down and drew Zach up behind her on the horse. As she rode slowly back toward the village, he wondered how long Tears Like Rain would be able to keep Painted Horse from killing him. At least until he could escape, he hoped fervently. Then his thoughts scattered as his head grew heavy and his limbs threatened to give out. He would have fallen from the horse if Tears Like Rain hadn't hissed, "If you show them you are weak, they will ridicule and revile you."

Her stinging words sent renewed strength surging through his limbs. His spine stiffened, and he raised his head in grim determination. Though his head was spinning and his vision blurred, he managed to remain upright, determined not to display weakness before these savages.

"Come," Tears Like Rain ordered crisply as she dismounted and led the way toward her tipi.

Zach wasn't certain his legs would obey, but when she walked past him and did not glance back to see if he was following, he realized that she would offer no help with her people watching. He felt their eyes boring into him, surprised by their look of grudging admiration as he slid off the horse, then took one careful step, followed by another, and another. The tipi looked miles away, and each movement caused his body untold agony, but he dared not give in to his pain. He still had several feet to go when he felt his strength leaving him.

"Do not give up now!" The words whirled around his brain. Zach had no idea if they had been spoken by Tears Like Rain or if they were the silent dictates of his own will. Wherever they came from, they had the necessary effect. By sheer strength of will, Zach reached the tipi and followed Tears Like Rain inside.

Once inside, his legs crumpled beneath him and he fell flat on his face.

"Foolish white man," Tears Like Rain said as she stood over Zach. Her silver eyes betrayed her compassion.

A moment later, her grandmother entered the tipi, carrying an assortment of ointments and medicines with which to treat Zach's bruises.

Tears Like Rain gave her a grateful smile.

"Your slave does not appear to be badly hurt," Cow Woman said. Her sharp eyes did not miss the tender look her granddaughter was bestowing on the white man. "If you wish it, I will treat him."

"Thank you, Grandmother. He is no good to me as he is."

Cow Woman's wrinkled face bore the wisdom acquired with great age. She regarded Tears Like Rain through bright, intelligent eyes. "My heart tells me that this white man means more to you than you are willing to admit."

"Oh, no, Grandmother, you are wrong. You know how much I hate all white-eyes. If they have their way, our people will have no place to live. They chase us from our land, destroy our buffalo, make promises they do not intend to keep, and kill our women and children. How could I not hate them? I am Cheyenne."

"Your heart is Cheyenne," Cow Woman reminded her.

"I am Cheyenne in all but the color of my skin and hair," Tears Like Rain insisted. "The People's enemy is my enemy."

Cow Woman did not contradict Tears Like Rain, nor did she tell her granddaughter that she foresaw a day when the young woman would be faced with a choice. The old woman had seen it in a dream, and when she had spoken to Spirit Singer about it, he had agreed that Tears Like Rain would have to make a very difficult decision in the near future.

Setting out her pots of salve, Cow Woman turned her attention to Zach, lamenting the day he had been brought into camp. Because of him, she stood to lose her beloved granddaughter. But all this she kept to herself. Telling Tears Like Rain about her dream would serve no purpose at this time.

Zach awoke in a haze of pain. His throat was so raw, he could hardly swallow. It was dark and he could see little beyond the glowing embers of the dying fire in the middle of the tipi. As his eyes grew accustomed to the dim light, he noticed a sleeping figure reclining on a mat in one of the far corners. From the shape of the figure, Zach assumed it was the old woman who had treated his wounds. Tears Like Rain had indicated that the old woman was her grandmother.

Since Zach didn't see Tears Like Rain, he suspected that she had chosen to sleep elsewhere. That notion had no sooner formed in his mind than a figure appeared on the other side of the dying fire. Tall and slim, her supple body a tantalizing mixture of shadows and light, Tears Like Rain appeared to be readying herself for bed. Unaware that she was being observed, she undid the ties on her tunic and let it glide down her body to the ground.

The beating of Zach's heart was so loud, he feared Tears Like Rain could hear it, but nothing in her manner indicated that she knew that he was awake and observing her. As she shook out her long hair and combed her fingers through it, Zach felt a suffocating weight choking off his breath. The play of shadow and light upon her flesh teased and taunted him. Her breasts stood high and firm above an incredibly tiny waist. Her hips flared and tapered into long, firm thighs and strong athletic calves.

Shadow and light.

Torment and ecstasy.   .

What Zach saw tantalized him, but it wasn't nearly enough to satisfy him. When Tears Like Rain bent to unroll her mat, he caught a brief glimpse of a long elegant back and a hint of firm white buttocks. It took a few moments to control the powerful surge of desire before he realized the implication of what he had seen. Tears Like Rain's backside was as white as the purest alabaster! Zach stifled a groan of disappointment when she lay down on her mat and pulled a blanket up to her chin. Long after the even cadence of her breathing told him she was sleeping, Zach lay awake pondering the startling revelation. Tears Like Rain was no half-breed Cheyenne. She was white!

The implications boggled the mind.

If she was white, why was she claiming to be Cheyenne? And why was she defending the Cheyenne as if she was one of them? He didn't know the answer, but he certainly intended to find out.

The relentless stab of sunlight against his face awoke Zach the next morning. He opened his eyes to the stirring sight of Tears Like Rain combing her long black tresses. She sat beneath the open smoke flap at the apex of the tipi, and the same errant ray of golden sunshine that had awakened Zach filtered through the opening onto the shining glory of her hair. He watched for a moment, mesmerized, until he realized exactly what had captured his attention. Unbelievably, threads of rich sable brown provided glowing contrast to the pure black strands crowning her head. On closer inspection, Zach realized that the contrasting brightness was more prominent at the roots.

Given such overwhelming evidence, there was no disputing the fact that Tears Like Rain was white.

Tears Like Rain continued running the buffalo-bone comb through her hair until she felt Zach's eyes upon her. Her arms halted in midstroke as her gaze met the blue intensity of his gaze.

"You are white," Zach accused her as he pushed himself into a sitting position.

Tears Like Rain stiffened. "I am Cheyenne."

"Why do you hate your own race? Obviously you were stolen by Indians or you wouldn't be here."

"White Feather saved my life," Tears Like Rain insisted. "The Cheyenne did not steal me."

"Then they must have killed your parents. Obviously you were very young or you wouldn't have become so thoroughly Indian."

"The Cheyenne did not kill my parents."

"Are your parents still alive? Think how happy they would be to see you again."

Tears Like Rain's expression revealed little of her inner thoughts. "White Feather is my father. Gray Dove was my mother. I remember no other parents."

"But you had white parents," Zach stressed. "What about your brother? Is he white too?"

"Wind Rider is Cheyenne. He hates white-eyes as much as I do." Her harsh words sent Zach's heart plummeting. Obviously the Cheyenne had turned her into a bloodthirsty little savage. He had been so unaware of his surroundings when he was dragged into camp that he couldn't recall her brother and wondered if he was her true kin.

"Do you have a white name?" Zach asked, abruptly changing the subject. Perhaps probing into her past would jostle her memory.

"My name is Tears Like Rain," she replied stubbornly.

"How did you get your name? What does it mean?"

Tears Like Rain was silent so long that Zach feared she intended to ignore his question. When she finally spoke, her voice sounded hollow, as if the memory was a painful one. "When I was very small, I cried a lot."

"Why did you cry?"

Tears Like Rain grew angry. "Why must you torment me? I do not care to remember."

"Why?" Zach prodded relentlessly. "Why did you cry? It is my understanding that Indian children are taught not to cry. That when babies cry excessively, they are carried into the woods and left until they learn not to cry. The action is repeated until the children learn that to cry brings isolation."

Stunned, Tears Like Rain asked, "How do you know these things?"

"I haven't been in the West long, but I have a friend who has. He told me many things about the Cheyenne. He told me the Crow and Ute are natural enemies of the Cheyenne."

Tears Like Rain's shuttered expression told Zach that his words had disturbed her greatly.

"The Crow are as deadly as the lowliest snakes that slither on their bellies. When they raise their heads to strike, the Cheyenne chop them off. I have good reason to hate the Crow, and not merely because they are the natural enemy of my people."

Her animosity for the Crow was so potent that Zach could almost feel it. "Why do you hate the Crow, Tears Like Rain?"

Tears Like Rain's lovely features hardened. "You ask too many questions, White-eyes."

"My name is Zach. And I'm asking because I'm interested. You're white, for God's sake. Don't you ever long for your own kind? Don't you ever wonder what it would be like to live in a house and have the kind of comforts not possible with the Cheyenne? Indians are being hounded and driven from their lands. Soon there will be no freedom for them anywhere on the plains. Life as you once knew it will disappear, and you and your people will be forced to live on reservations."

"No!" Though everything Zach said made sense, Tears Like Rain could not accept it. Her people would survive; they *must* survive. Abruptly, she rose and stormed outside.

Zach didn't follow immediately. He spent several minutes testing his limbs before he was satisfied that his bruises were superficial and no bones were broken. Except for the throbbing pain from the welt across his throat, his injuries were bearable. As for the welt, he imagined he'd always carry the scar. The call of nature finally brought him to his feet and out of the tipi. Sending a sidelong glance at Tears Like Rain, who stood over a fire stirring a simmering pot, he headed toward the line of trees behind the village.

"Stop! Where are you going?"

Zach's steps slowed. "To relieve myself," he called over his shoulder. Since Indians did not consider discussion of body functions taboo, Tears Like Rain did not flinch at his words as her white sisters might have done.

"If you try to escape, you will be hunted like an animal," Tears Like Rain warned. "If you do not give your word that you will not try to escape, I will replace the leash around your neck and hold the end of it while you relieve yourself." She knew that a leash would cause him excruciating pain and hoped he was wise enough to realize it.

Perched on the horns of a dilemma, Zach balked against giving an outright promise not to escape. It surprised him that Tears Like Rain would trust him. Didn't she know that he could easily lie and do as he pleased once he was out of sight? "Why would you trust my word?" he asked when his curiosity got the better of him.

Tears Like Rain looked surprised. "A Cheyenne warrior would never give his word if he did not intend to keep it. But you are right. I was mistaken to trust a white man, for none has ever kept his word. We have been lied to before and trusted where we should not. I will get the leash."

"No, wait! I promise. The leash is not necessary." Nothing had humiliated him more than being led around by a rope. Besides, he was not honor-bound to keep a promise made to savages.

Tears Like Rain hesitated. But in the end she nodded tacit approval. Should Zach break his promise, he wouldn't get far with the warriors from the Shield Society guarding the perimeter of the village. They must be even more vigilant now, with most of the warriors gone to Fort Weld with White Feather for the Great Smoke. Their enemies were many and they must be vigilant.

Zach disappeared into the woods without a backward glance. He felt a fleeting regret for having lied to Tears Like Rain. But only a coward would meekly accept the yoke of slavery, and Lord knew he was no coward. He quickly did what he had come to do, then looked around to get his bearings. Since he had arrived at the Indian village, he had made careful note of his surroundings and knew that if he could reach the stream and follow it to where it joined the Arkansas River, he would eventually reach Fort Lyon. He thought of Tears Like Rain and suffered a pang of regret. Dismissing her from his mind with a toss of his head, he turned and headed in the direction of the stream.

Tears Like Rain grew disturbed when Zach failed to emerge from the woods in the amount of time she had allotted him. She had been a fool to trust him, she thought bitterly. All whites were alike. They did not know how to tell the truth and had no honor. Though she hated to admit that she had been wrong about Zach, she had to face the fact she had been too trusting.

"What is wrong, Tears Like Rain? You look distressed."

Tears Like Rain had been so distracted that she failed to note Painted Horse's approach. She dreaded telling the haughty warrior about Zach, for she knew he would accuse her of coddling her slave. But there was no help for it. She must admit her mistake to Painted Horse, and do it now. But before she could form the words, the peaceful morning erupted in violence as a war party of painted Crow warriors converged on the village.

They had come to raid, to steal what horses remained, and to capture slaves. Screams pierced the air as Crow raiders cut down men, women, and children viciously and indiscriminately. Painted Horse's courage was not lacking as he grabbed Tears Like Rain and shoved her behind him, drawing his weapon in her defense.

"Hide in the woods!" Painted Horse told her as he loosed an arrow at an advancing horseman.

Pandemonium reigned as the outnumbered Cheyenne fought valiantly to defend their women and children. Tears Like Rain did flee, but only as far as her tipi, where she grabbed her rifle and ran back outside. She could shoot as straight as any warrior and fight just as bravely.

Zach had nearly reached the stream when the unmistakable sounds of gunfire stopped him in his tracks. He listened intently, trying to make sense of the sounds coming from the village. From all indications, a battle was being waged in the Cheyenne camp. Obviously it was under attack. Surely not by soldiers, he reasoned, for they would do nothing to destroy the negotiations with the Indians now taking place. That meant one of the natural enemies of the Cheyenne had ridden into camp. Exultant, Zach realized that he had picked a most favorable time to escape. With the Cheyenne fighting for their lives, no one was likely to come after him.

Then he thought of Tears Like Rain, and her unspeakable fate were she to be captured by an enemy tribe. She could be tortured, raped, or worse yet, killed. Though it meant his return to captivity, Zach was stunned to realize that he couldn't abandon her. Whirling on his heel, he raced back to the village. He arrived in time to see a Crow warrior leap from his mount and drive Tears Like Rain to the ground. A bloodcurdling scream escaped her lips seconds before the Crow raised his arm and knocked her unconscious with the butt of his rifle. Then he straddled her, lifted her tunic and prepared to rape her.

Chapter Five

Zach's muscles screamed in protest as he lunged at the Crow, tumbling him from atop Tears Like Rain's body. Weaponless, he fought fiercely, aware that his life and that of Tears Like Rain were at stake. Stunned by the surprise attack, the Crow fell beneath Zach's relentless fury. But he recovered quickly, tossing Zach aside and leaping to his feet. The Crow had dropped his rifle when he raised Tears Like Rain's tunic, but when he whipped around to face Zach, he clutched a wicked-looking hunting knife in his fist.

Zach backed toward Tears Like Rain, fully prepared to protect her from the Crow at the expense of his own life. The Crow advanced on him, a menacing grin curving his lips as he slashed outward and upward with the blade.

Zach sucked in his gut and leaped nimbly aside. The Crow howled in rage, then quickly moved in for the kill. He would count coup on an enemy, and the woman would be his reward.

Zach measured the distance to the two weapons lying on the ground. Tears Like Rain's rifle had skidded out of reach when the Crow jumped her and was too far away to consider. The Crow's weapon lay where he had dropped it on the other side of the Indian maiden. To get it, Zach would have to reach across her body, thus giving the Crow an unfair advantage over him. Then a flash of light caught Zach's attention. Like the Crow, Zach had noticed the pale gleam of Tears Like Rain's exposed limbs and realized that the brilliant flash he had seen came from the sun glinting off the knife strapped to her thigh.

The Crow lunged forward and made a menacing gesture as Zach successfully dodged another vicious jab of the blade. Zach was standing so close to Tears Like Rain now that he could touch her with his foot. Confident that the enemy was at his mercy, the Crow moved moved in for the kill. Prepared for the Crow's attack, Zach dropped into a crouch, twisted slightly and whipped the knife from the scabbard at Tears Like Rain's thigh. He slashed upward at the exact moment the Crow lunged at him. The sharp blade caught the Crow in the belly and Zach gave it a vicious twist. His eyes wide with disbelief, the Crow made a slow spiral to the ground, dead before he hit the dirt.

Though many Crow were down, the battle was far from over. All around Zach, rampaging Crow warriors rode through the village, visiting death and destruction on the Cheyenne. Clutching the knife, Zach stood over Tears Like Rain's body, mentally fortifying himself as another warrior rode toward him swinging a tomahawk. Raw adrenaline surged as the need to protect and defend the helpless woman lying at his feet became his mission in life. He reacted swiftly, without thought for his own safety. Reaching over her with lightning speed to scoop up the rifle, he aimed and fired, grateful that the rifle was primed and ready.

An excellent marksman, Zach hit the Crow in a vital spot, felling him instantly. But no sooner had the warrior hit the ground than another took his place. Bracing himself, Zach continued shooting until he was out of ammunition. Then he found the Crow's rifle and emptied that too. When his ammunition was gone, he spat out a curse, scooped Tears Like Rain up in his arms, and raced for the tipi, dodging horsemen, flying bullets, and arrows.

Once inside the relative safety of the buffalo-hide lodging, Zach carefully placed Tears Like Rain on the bedroll and searched frantically for more ammunition for the rifles. He found it in a parfleche hanging from one of the upright poles. Kneeling in the doorway, he aimed at a Crow warrior who was tossing a flaming brand into a nearby tipi. Unfortunately, the Crow managed to set the tipi ablaze before Zach's bullet found its mark.

Then, as quickly as it had begun, the battle was over. The Crow retreated, taking half the Cheyennes' herd of horses with them and leaving dead and wounded in their wake.

The moment Zach realized the battle was over and Tears Like Rain was no longer in danger, he considered bolting while the camp was in an uproar, certain no one would miss him. But one look at Tears Like Rain's pale face and the shallow rise and fall of her chest changed his mind. He could always leave later, he maintained, once he was certain she was out of danger. She had taken a vicious blow to the head and needed to be treated immediately. He did not dare search his heart too deeply for the reasons behind his unwillingness to leave, for he feared what he would find.

Since Zach had little experience with sickness and methods of healing, he went in search of Tears Like Rain's old grandmother.

The entire camp was in chaos. Women were wailing over the bodies of children and fallen warriors, while others were dodging inside burning tipis to save whatever they could of their belongings. The surviving warriors, including Painted Horse, were already mounting their horses to ride after the Crow. Numerous cuts and bruises covered his body but obviously his wounds were not serious enough to prevent Painted Horse from joining the chase.

Zach found Cow Woman lying on the ground outside her tipi, an arrow protruding from her chest. She was dead. Since she was beyond mortal help, and Tears Like Rain still needed attention, he thought of the old shaman who had once brought him from the brink of death with his herbs and incantations. He found Spirit Singer inside his tipi, gathering the paraphernalia needed to treat the wounded. He seemed dazed but otherwise unharmed.

"You must come," Zach said urgently as he grasped the old man's arm. "Tears Like Rain is hurt and I don't know what to do for her."

Understanding nothing of what Zach was saying, the shaman shook himself free of Zach's grip and dismissed him with an impatient wave of his hand. But Zach was in no mood to be dismissed. "You are coming with me," he growled menacingly. "Tears Like Rain needs you." When the old man protested vocally, Zach grasped him by the shoulders and pushed him out the door. He continued pushing until they stood outside Tears Like Rain's tipi. Only then did Spirit Singer seem to understand and stop resisting.

Tears Like Rain lay exactly where Zach had left her. She hadn't moved a muscle. Her face was so pale that Zach feared he was too late. Only the slight rise and fall of her chest gave hint of the life that remained in her. Spirit Singer crouched beside her, searching for the source of her injury. He found a lump the size of an egg on her left temple. Zach noted that the delicate skin surrounding her eyes was already turning black and purple from the blow she had received.

Motioning toward the water jug, Spirit Singer indicated that he needed water. Zach brought it to him and watched closely as the old man poured some of the water into a bowl and emptied into it a packet of powder he had taken from inside the parfleche he carried around his neck. Then he found a square of soft deerskin, wet it in the solution, and placed it over the lump on Tears Like Rain's temple. Next he emptied another packet into the water remaining in the jug and held it to Tears Like Rain's lips so she could drink. More spilled down her chin than she swallowed, but Spirit Singer seemed satisfied. When finished, he rose with difficulty to his feet.

"Is that all?" Zach asked, alarmed. His primative treatment seemed so meager that Zach feared it wasn't enough to save Tears Like Rain's life. But Spirit Singer appeared unperturbed as he motioned toward the bowl and jug containing the herbs, indicating that Zach was to keep changing the cloths on Tears Like Rain's head and feeding her the infusion he had prepared. Then he turned abruptly and left.

During the following hours, Zach paid little heed to the utter turmoil of the camp. Three women, four children, and two warriors had been slain. The survivors began mourning their dead immediately. The bodies were taken to the sacred burial ground and placed on high platforms where animals of prey could not reach them. If Zach wondered about the wailing, he gave no indication as he tended Tears Like Rain as carefully as if she were his beloved. Which of course she wasn't. But since no one arrived to relieve him of his duties, he remained steadfastly at her side.

That night, Zach pulled his pallet close to Tears Like Rain and lay down beside her. Exhaustion claimed him almost immediately, and he fell into a fitful sleep. Sometime during the dark hours of night, Tears Like Rain began thrashing and muttering in her sleep.

"Mama! Where are you? I'm afraid."

Though Zach's body protested, he came instantly awake. Alarm shot through him. "What is it?" Tears Like Rain's eyes were open, but she appeared to be still sleeping.

"I want my mama. Why doesn't she come for me? Ryder is afraid too, but he tries not to show it. I can't help crying, Mama. Ryder says you and Papa are dead, and so is baby Sierra."

She began crying—deep, racking sobs that tore at Zach's tender heart. "Don't cry," he pleaded helplessly. "I won't let anything happen to you. By what name does your mother call you?"

A violent shudder rippled through her body. "My name is Abby." Her reply left him shaken.

"Abby," he repeated quietly, with great satisfaction. The name flowed like warm honey over his tongue.

Recalling Spirit Singer's advice, Zach fed Tears Like Rain—no, Abby, for he refused to think of her by her Indian name—more of the herbal mixture and changed the cloth on her forehead. When she quieted, he lay back down and contemplated everything Abby had said.

The next morning, Abby was staring at him when he opened his eyes and looked at her. He smiled. "Good morning, Abby."

Abby's eyes widened and she regarded Zach as if he had just lost his mind. "What did you say?"

"I said, 'Good morning, Abby.'"

"Why did you call me that?"

"That is your name, isn't it?"

"My name is Tears Like Rain." She raised up on one elbow, grasped her head in her hands and moaned. "My head. What happened?"

"Don't you remember? The camp was over-run by Crow. You were injured. Lie back down. The shaman left something to ease the pain." He placed a cup to Abby's lips, but she pushed it away, refusing the brew.

"I remember now. The Crow warrior . . ." She drew her breath in sharply and her words stuttered to a halt. She had no idea if she had been violated while she was unconscious. She needed to talk to her grandmother, and she must help wherever she was needed. "I must help care for the wounded and prepare the dead."

"The women have already seen to the dead," Zach told her, "and the shaman has taken care of the wounded. The Crow warrior who hurt you will never harm another woman again."

"How like the cowardly Crow to attack when our men are gone and the village is ill-prepared to defend itself. Were there many casualties?"

"A few," Zach admitted. He hated to be the one to tell her about her grandmother's death.

The rattle of buffalo bones at the entrance of the tipi announced a visitor, and Abby granted permission to enter. Summer Moon stepped inside.

"Oh, Tears Like Rain," she cried when she saw Tears Like Rain's pale face, "I wanted to come sooner but I was helping the women prepare the dead for burial. Spirit Singer said you were injured and that"—her eyes slid shyly to Zach—"you were being cared for. I saw the Crow attack you and feared he would kill you. Your white slave fought fearlessly to save you from harm. I am glad to see you were not seriously harmed."

Understanding nothing of what was being said, Zach remained silent as the two women spoke. When Abby turned to regard him curiously, he wondered what Summer Moon had said.

"Zach fought the Crow to save my life?" Abby was astounded. After the way she had treated him, she wouldn't have been surprised had he fled and left her to meet her ancestors.

Abby's heart soared. Though it defied reason, she was pleased that Zach had killed the Crow on her account. It was difficult to believe he had fought with the People to defeat their old enemy. Why would Zach help the Cheyenne when he could have escaped during the battle?

"He was truly courageous," Summer Moon rhapsodized. "He stood over your body and fought the Crow who tried to ravish you. Do you not remember?"

Tears Like Rain's breath came out in a whoosh of relief when she heard that the Crow hadn't succeeded in raping her. "I remember nothing after being struck." She closed her eyes, seeing an image of Zach, weaponless and weak from his ordeal the day before, protecting her from the Crow warrior.

Abby's ashen face alarmed Zach. Assuming that her visitor was tiring her, he said to Summer Moon, "You must go now and return when Abby is feeling stronger."

Summer Moon looked at Abby askance. "What did he say? I know you understand, for I have heard you speaking to him in the white man's tongue."

"He wants you to leave. He thinks you are tiring me."

Summer Moon regarded Zach thoughtfully. "He seems overly protective of you, Tears Like Rain. No wonder Painted Horse is jealous. Actually," she said, her eyes raking him assessingly, "he isn't nearly as ugly as I first thought."

Abby sighed heavily. "I think Zach is right. I am tired. We will visit again tomorrow. But first, you must tell me who of our tribe has gone to join their ancestors."

"Prairie Flower, Spring Grass, and Cow Woman were slain by the Crow. So were Crazy Horse and Eagle Hat. Four children are also dead. I'm sorry about your grandmother, Tears Like Rain."

The stricken expression on Abby's face worried Zach. Then he realized that Summer Moon must have told her about her grandmother. Letting out a curse, he quickly escorted the girl from the tipi, closing the tent flap securely to keep her from reentering. When he turned back to Abby, tears were falling like gentle rain from her gray eyes.

"I'm sorry, Abby, I know your friend told you about your grandmother. I would have told you myself, but I didn't want you to know until you were stronger. I know how much the old woman meant to you."

"Cow Woman was my father's mother, revered by all the tribe. She taught me many things when I was a child. She instilled pride in me. Because of her, I quickly learned to adjust to my surroundings. I will miss her."

Zach felt her grief as keenly as if it were his own. He dropped to his knees and pulled her into his arms. She stiffened, then relaxed, accepting his comfort.

Zach's arms tightened, amazed at how right and good it felt to hold Abby like this. He kissed her brow, enthralled by the sprinkling of rich, sable-hued hair that grew close to her scalp. He imagined how she would look if her hair were returned to its natural color. He recalled those brief, tantalizing glimpses of white skin normally not exposed, and a surge of desire made him shift uncomfortably.

"We all miss those we love," Zach said, recalling how bereft he had been when his parents had passed away. "But we learn to live without our loved ones. Don't you miss your parents? I know you were young when you came to live with the Cheyenne, but you must have thought about them often."

Abby's chin lifted fractionally. "White Feather is my father and Gray Dove was my mother. She was killed by white soldiers at Solomon Fork."

"I'm sorry," Zach said. "But I'm talking about your real parents. And what about your sister?"

Abby froze. "How do you know about my sister?"

"You spoke in your sleep last night. You told me your name was Abby and that you were frightened. You called out for your mother. You also mentioned Ryder."

"My brother," Abby whispered. "He is called Wind Rider. I do not know what happened to little Sierra. She was only three. White Feather told me later that he saw only bodies of adults at the site of the Crow attack. In my heart, I feel Sierra still lives. I know Wind Rider feels the same, but we do not speak of it."

"Did the Crow kill your parents, Abby?"

"That is what White Feather told me, and I had no reason to doubt him." Scathing contempt for the Crow colored her words. "I was only six, and it is difficult to remember." The horror of recall turned her eyes bleak. "I remember now that Ryder and I were away from the wagons when the Crow attacked. I recall nothing about the people traveling with us at the time. Ryder and I watched from afar as the Crow killed our parents and the others. Then the Crow came after us. White Feather and his warriors saved our lives. He adopted us and raised us as his own. The Cheyenne are my people. I owe them my life."

"No, Abby, you owe them nothing," Zach denied. "You are white. They should have taken you to the fort. No matter how strongly you deny it, you can't change the fact that you are not an Indian. Let me take you back to your people. Come with me, and I'll see you safely away from here. Surely you have relatives somewhere who will welcome you into their family?"

Abby shook her head in vehement denial. "I have no one. I can't even remember my last name." That wasn't entirely true. Wind Rider had told her never to forget her name, for one day she might have need of it. "I am Tears Like Rain," she repeated.

"You are white. Your name is Abby."

"I know nothing of the whites except that they are thieves and liars who steal from the Indians, break treaties, and want to annihilate my people. They kill our women and children. If I went to live with them now, they would hate me as much as I hate them."

"I wouldn't let them," Zach whispered against her brow.

"You couldn't stop them," Abby responded realistically.

Placing a finger beneath her chin, Zach lifted her face so that he could look into her eyes. "Look at me, Abby. Listen to what I say. Indians kill and raid with as much cruelty and impunity as white men. More, in some instances. Look what they did to your parents."

"The White-eyes are driving us from our lands. We must fight back if we are to survive. Our leaders have signed countless treaties in good faith, only to have them broken again and again. Our young men feel desperate and fight back in self-defense."

"Perhaps this new treaty between the Indian nations and the government will be successful," Zach maintained. "Black Kettle and the Southern Cheyenne want peace, but all the Cheyenne must agree to it before it can be successful."

"My people will never side with Black Kettle. He is willing to sacrifice his pride to appease the White-eyes, but we are not. White Feather has said he will never agree to follow Black Kettle to a reservation without a fight. Warriors like my brother and Painted Horse will fight to the death."

"It will be your death, too, Abby. I don't want to see you killed or hurt."

Abby's eyes narrowed suspiciously. "Why? Have I not wounded your dignity? Have I not enslaved you and given you humiliating duties to perform?"

"You have done all of those things, Abby, but you also saved my life. I cannot forget that."

"You have saved mine, so we are even. Now I offer you your freedom. When our warriors return, I will tell them that you escaped. When Father and Wind Rider return, I will explain to them what I have done. They will understand."

Zach gave her a startled look. "You give me my freedom?"

"It is for the best."

"I won't leave without you."

Abby shot him a contemptuous look. "Foolish white man. Do you not realize that you will not be given another chance when Painted Horse returns?"

"I will leave when you agree to come with me and not before."

"I will not go." Her expression was mutinous. She was every bit as stubborn as Zach. Her home was with the Cheyenne. It was the only home she could remember.

Exasperated but not defeated, Zach stared into the whirling storm of her gray eyes and felt the uncontrollable urge to kiss her.

Abby looked up at him, arrested. There was an unyielding glint in his eyes that both frightened and attracted her. His lips were so close that she could feel the soft flutter of his breath against her cheek. Instinctively, she knew he meant to press his lips to hers as he had done before, and the thought was so arousing that she offered little resistance when he lowered his head and covered her mouth with his. He kissed her hungrily, making her head spin as his tongue slid along her bottom lip, then thrust inside, tasting her sweetness.

Startled as much by his boldness as she was by her own acquiescence, Abby bit down hard.

Stunned, Zach howled in pain and thrust her away. "Little savage, why did you do that? Haven't you ever been kissed before?"

"I do not know about kissing. Indians do not press their mouths together in such a disgusting manner."

Zach stared at her in disbelief. "You find a kiss disgusting?" He couldn't imagine a culture where men and women did not kiss. "How does a young man court a woman he wishes to marry?"

"He brings gifts to her parents. If he is serious, and the girl agrees, he throws a blanket over her head for a few moments of private conversation. But always in the presence of her parents. It is all very chaste. Rarely do the boy and girl touch intimately. Cheyenne warriors learn to control their urges, and courtship is a long, drawn-out affair."

"Is Painted Horse courting you? Is that why he is so protective of you?"

Abby flushed. "Wind Rider has given Painted Horse permission to court me."

"Your brother? I would think it would be up to your father."

"In Cheyenne culture, it is the girl's brother who makes decisions for her and sees to her welfare. Wind Rider and I are very close. Closer than most Cheyenne brothers and sisters who only communicate upon occasion after a girl reaches womanhood and visits the—" She paused, searching her mind for the English word to describe the menstrual tent where women went during their monthly flow. But nowhere in her memory could she find the word she sought. Finally she shrugged and said, "I do not know the word, but once a girl's monthly bleeding begins, she rarely has contact with her brother. But it is different with Wind Rider and I."

Zach's eyes widened. He couldn't believe he had just heard Abby refer to a private bodily function as if there were no cause for embarrassment. The young women he knew would rather die than even hint at such a thing. "Do you always speak so frankly?"

Abby's brow furrowed. Had she said something wrong? Had she broken a taboo of the white world?

Recognizing her bewilderment, Zach explained, "Most young women of my acquaintance are too shy to speak of bodily functions."

"There is nothing shameful in the body or the way it works," Abby said, "but if I offended you, I am sorry." Zach's words had just given her another reason for remaining where she felt safe and comfortable. "As you can see, I would not fit into the white world. The Cheyenne are my people."

Exasperated, Zach shook his head. Was there no way he could talk Abby into abandoning the doomed Cheyenne nation and reentering the white world, where she belonged? It startled him to realize that he could not possibly leave until she agreed to go with him. Suddenly his eyes narrowed as he considered another alternative. If Abby refused to leave with him, he could always take her by force.

"Very well, Abby, if you won't leave, neither will I."

"That is your decision, White-eyes," Abby contended, "but I can make no sense out of it."

"Nor can I understand your aversion to returning to your own people. I'm certain a good family can be found to help you with your transition."

"Do not speak of it again," Abby said harshly. "I refuse to live with a people I do not understand and know nothing about."

Grasping her shoulders, Zach gave her a little shake. "Why are you so damn stubborn? I'm trying to save your life."

"Why do you care what happens to me?"

Her question caught Zach by surprise. Abby was right in assuming that he had no reason to care about her welfare, but that didn't stop him from wanting to see her safe with her own kind. She was the most courageous woman he had ever known, braver than some men of his acquaintance—though a bit more savage than he would like. She was beautiful beyond belief. Just looking at her made him ache. He wanted her. In his arms and in his bed. Yet he knew he was more than just sexually attracted to Abby. Somehow the contrary little savage had burrowed beneath his skin until he genuinely cared what happened to her.

"I am not stubborn, merely wiser than you. My friends are Cheyenne. My brother will see to my welfare. With your people I have nothing."

"You have me."

"Ha!" Abby scoffed. "You are my enemy."

"No, Abby, not your enemy. Never your enemy." He drew her close, staring deeply into the swirling gray depths of her eyes. It was like looking into the dark underbelly of a storm.

When his mouth slowly descended, a shudder shook her slender frame. Her eyes widened as she saw glittering specks stir to life in his eyes. His breathing quickened, and she saw his nostrils flare and his lips part in anticipation. She felt his arms tighten around her and the heat of his skin sear her flesh.

Then he was kissing her, and though the taste of him was familiar now, the passion he inspired in her innocent body was new and frightening. Cheyenne maidens were forbidden such sweet ecstasy until marriage. It wasn't right that she should respond to the touch of an enemy. She tried to tell herself that Zach was her enemy, that his kisses were shameful, that her response was wicked. But her body refused to listen to her mind. In all her twenty years, she had never felt more alive and vital, and a new kind of despair consumed her. By allowing her enemy to touch her in such a shameful manner, she was betraying her people.

Zach hadn't realized how carried away he was by the kiss until a groan slipped from his lips. Abby's mouth was incredibly sweet and naively responsive. He wanted to devour her, to lay her against the furs and teach her what it felt like to become a woman. He wanted to love her so well she'd wonder why she even considered lying with a savage like Painted Horse.

Zach's lips were boldly persuasive as they left her mouth and slid over her cheek, down the delicate length of her neck to the opening of her tunic where a slash of pale skin teased and beguiled him. Before she realized what he was doing, he pushed the tunic over her shoulders and down the length of her arms, baring the creamy paleness of her breasts. As smooth and pure as rich ivory, each perfect mound was crested with a perfect rosebud of delicate coral. A jolt of incredible pleasure seared through him when his lips closed over one nipple and drew it deeply into his mouth.

Abby's cry of shock and outrage went unheeded as Zach moved from one breast to the other, feasting upon the delicate morsels as if they were some exotic food and he was starving.

"Zach, no! You must not humiliate me like this. A Cheyenne warrior would never insult a

111

chaste maiden in such a vile manner."

Her words finally got through to him. "Insult? Humiliate? That is not my intention. I didn't intend for my emotions to get out of hand."

"A Cheyenne warrior would not allow himself to lose control. They train themselves to ignore the natural urges of their body. They are in control of themselves at all times."

Zach snorted in disgust. "I'm sorry if I don't measure up to Cheyenne men." Abruptly he released her, though to do so was almost painful. "Rest today. Your slave will find you something to eat."

Abby watched him leave. The tautness of his nearly nude buttocks, the proud bearing of his massive shoulders, and the stiffness of his back made her realize that he was every bit as impressive as a Cheyenne warrior. And though she'd never admit it, she had never felt the same kind of exhilaration or excitement with Painted Horse or any other man that she felt with this White-eyes.

Chapter Six

Abby saw little of Zach the remainder of the day as she rested inside her tipi. Her head still throbbed, and she slept off and on. She awoke once to see Zach searching through her brother's belongings. When he found Wind Rider's spare leggings and buckskin tunic and donned them, she did not protest. She had meant to give him something more substantial to wear as the days grew cooler and hadn't gotten around to it. When he glanced in her direction and saw her staring at him, he sent her a silent challenge. Abby chose not to accept it.

She realized that the only reason she was allowed to remain alone in the tipi with Zach was because the camp was in turmoil. So strict were the rules concerning unmarried women that Painted Horse would have offered vigorous protest and have likely sent one of his aunts to stay with her, had he known of her situation.

Zach donned the fringed leggings and shirt with great relish. If the Cheyenne had intended to humiliate him, they had succeeded when they forced him to walk around half-naked like a savage. The brief square of cloth he had been given to wear covered little more than his genital area. And though he was quickly learning that Cheyenne men felt no embarrassment over exposing their bodies in such a manner, he felt as if his dignity had been stripped from him.

Abby's eyes were hooded when Zach left the tipi. He was such a complex man that she didn't know what to make of him. She had given him ample opportunity to leave and he had refused. She had always hated the White-eyes. Yet, if Summer Moon could be believed, and she had no reason to lie, Zach had stood over her and fought side by side with the People against their Crow enemy. Conflicting emotions warred within her, increasing her headache, and she closed her eyes and willed herself to sleep.

Zach was appalled by the destruction wrought by the Crow raiding party. Besides the dead and wounded, tipis had been burnt, food destroyed, and personal belongings plundered. When he saw Summer Moon trying to salvage cooking implements from the ashes of a partially burned tipi, he lent a hand. When an old woman needed help with the awkward tipi poles she was trying to rescue from another ruined lodge, he quickly bent his back to the task. Before the day was over, the women were looking at him with renewed respect. They recalled how he had fought beside their men and saved the life of their chieftain's daughter. Now they offered him shy smiles where once he was given curses and beatings.

When Zach attempted to find the ingredients to cook supper for himself and Abby, Summer Moon came quickly to his rescue, offering a bowl of savory stew for him and Abby to share. When he brought it inside the tipi, Abby was sitting up, looking much improved.

"I've brought you something to eat." He sat down beside her and set the bowl between them.

"Did you make this?" Abby asked, taking up the buffalo-horn spoon Zach had found with the cooking pots. "It smells wonderful."

Zach grinned. "My cooking wouldn't taste nearly as good as this," he admitted. "Your friend brought it."

"Summer Moon?"

"I wasn't sure about her name, I've never heard you speak it in English." Zach chewed thoughtfully, paused, then asked, "Have you changed your mind about leaving with me?"

Abby regarded him crossly. "I will never change my mind. Do not ask again."

A short time later, Summer Moon came to visit. She gave Zach such a radiant smile that Abby was taken aback. When Zach left the two friends to chat, Summer Moon burst into excited chatter.

"Sky Eyes was most helpful today, Tears Like Rain. Did you order him to help the women?"

"Sky Eyes?"

"It is the name the women have given him. His eyes are as blue as the heavens on a cloudless day. There isn't a woman in the village he hasn't helped today. We are all grateful, for without his aid we wouldn't have accomplished so much."

Abby snorted in disgust. "He is the enemy. I have not forgotten how his kind killed Gray Dove."

"How can you consider Sky Eyes an enemy when he saved your life and cared for you so diligently? Even Spirit Singer is impressed. You should be grateful."

Abby felt a slow flush creep up her neck, recalling her shameless behavior when Zach caressed her bare breasts and claimed her mouth in that strangely arousing pressing together of lips that he called a kiss. Gratitude? No, she felt anger. Anger at the brazen way he made her feel and respond. Anger because he was badgering her to leave the People.

She felt despair.

The Cheyenne were an honorable people, who were taught to repress their sexuality. With one kiss, Zach had proven how much she differed from her adopted people in that respect. When Zach kissed and caressed her, she was aware of her receptive body and sexuality as never before. Her response to him was spontaneous and dramatic. Did Wind Rider share the same flaw? she wondered. Was it a trait she and her brother had inherited from their white parents?

"Of course I am grateful to Sky Eyes for saving my life," Abby said, using the name her friends had given him. "But that does not mean I must treat him as I would one of the People."

Zach chose that moment to reenter the tipi. "It's raining," he announced, sending Abby a meaningful glance. "I don't intend to sleep outside tonight." The challenge in his voice was unmistakable.

"What did Sky Eyes say?" Summer Moon asked.

"He said it is raining and that he intends to sleep inside the tipi tonight."

Summer Moon gasped in shock. "Then I will stay with you." She gave Abby a determined look. "Since Cow Woman is no longer here to act as chaperon, I will take her place."

"Sky Eyes is a slave," Abby scoffed. "If I say he will sleep outside, then he will do so."

"I do not think so," Summer Moon said, casting a sidelong glance in Zach's direction.

"What is she saying, Abby?" Zach asked. He was growing uncomfortable under their close scrutiny, aware that they were discussing him.

"It is not proper for you and me to share a tipi," Abby replied, "so Summer Moon has offered to stay with me."

Zach tried not to show his disappointment. "I would not harm you, Abby."

Abby grew thoughtful. Perhaps he wouldn't harm her, but he certainly would make life more difficult for her. Just the thought of being alone with him made her cheeks flush and her skin tingle.

"Summer Moon will stay," she said emphatically.

When Zach awoke from a troubled sleep filled with anguished dreams, he was startled to find Abby gone. He questioned Summer Moon, but she was unable to understand and merely shrugged her shoulders. It was the same with everyone he spoke to. No one seemed to understand what he was asking. As the day progressed, the mystery of her disappearance was not solved and Zach grew frantic. Most puzzling was the fact that no one seemed concerned about Abby's sudden disappearance. Not even Summer Moon, Abby's closest friend, appeared worried.

By evening, Zach was at his wit's end. Where could Abby have gone? he wondered desperately. Why did no one search for her? Was she not missed? When one of the women shyly offered him food, he took note of the fact that there was only enough for one person. It appeared that he was the only one concerned about Abby's absence. It occurred to Zach that Abby might be avoiding him so he couldn't badger her about leaving her people. Preparing for bed, his mind was in a turmoil. He was determined to turn the village upside down until he found her if she did not appear tomorrow.

By noon the following day, Zach had searched three tipis with little success. Now he paused before a tipi that stood apart from the others. From earlier observation, Zach had assumed that no family lived in that particular tipi, even though from time to time he had noticed various women enter and leave at different times. At first he thought it might be used for storage, but now he wasn't so certain. He took a step forward, intending to throw aside the flap and enter. Suddenly Summer Moon came careening toward him, flapping her arms and crying out a word he did not understand. He halted, thoroughly mystified as he tried to shrug Summer Moon aside. But she clung to him fiercely.

Zach's annoyance escalated when some of the other women joined Summer Moon as she tried to drag him away from the tipi. The thought occurred that Abby might have been taken seriously ill during the night and carried off someplace where he couldn't help her. That disturbing notion made him more determined than ever to enter the tipi and find out for himself.

Suddenly he was aware of horsemen riding into the village, and that the women and children were fleeing in panic. Zach spat out a curse, angry at himself for leaving the rifle behind in Abby's tipi. Had the Crows returned to finish their destruction? Casting a wistful glance at the tipi, he turned abruptly and

119

hurried off. He had reached the center of the camp when he was surrounded by several men on prancing horses. His relief was profound when he recognized White Feather and Wind Rider. At last, here was someone who could understand him and explain Abby's strange disappearance.

White Feather's intelligent eyes made a slow perusal of the village, missing none of the destruction left by the Crow raiders. His dark gaze settled disconcertingly on Zach. Since most of the women had gone into hiding at the first hint of trouble, Zach was the only one available to answer questions. The chieftain spoke to him in halting English. "What happened here? Where is my daughter? Where are the warriors left behind to protect the camp?"

"The village was attacked two days ago by Crow warriors," Zach said. "Your daughter was injured, and I do not know where she is. No one here can tell me what happened to her. Painted Horse and the other men went after the Crow raiders."

With an anguished cry, Wind Rider leaped from his mount, his eyes blazing. "How badly is my sister hurt?"

By now the women were creeping out of the woods where they had fled and crowded around the men, everyone talking at once. Summer Moon took it upon herself to tell Wind Rider what had happened. She spoke rapidly, gesturing wildly with her arms, catching the attention of White Feather, who drew closer so he could hear Summer Moon's words. His expression alternated from outright disbelief to amazement, and then to grudging admiration.

"You saved the life of my daughter," White Feather said as he turned to face Zach. "Tears Like Rain must have had a vision that you would one day prove your worth when she asked that your life be spared. Your courage shall not go unrewarded. You are free to go back to your people."

Wind Rider stepped forward, grasping Zach's forearm in a gesture of friendship. "Summer Moon said you fought beside our men, that you killed our Crow enemies and saved my sister's life. I have never known a white man willing to stand beside an Indian and fight the Indian's enemy. I am glad Tears Like Rain did not let us kill you. It pleases me that White Feather is freeing you to return to your people."

"That's all well and good," Zach said impatiently, "but I still don't know what happened to your sister."

Wind Rider turned to Summer Moon. They spoke for several minutes before he returned his attention to Zach. "There is no need for worry. Tears Like Rain has gone to the"—he could not recall the English word—"to the hut where all women go when during the time of their monthly bleeding."

Zach was stunned. "What! I never heard such nonsense. Do all Cheyenne isolate their women each month?"

"It is our custom," Wind Rider maintained. "During that time a woman's blood is defiling and dangerous to our virility and superior powers. Thus it is taboo to be around women when they are bleeding. Confining them to a special place where they will not pollute their fathers or brothers is the People's way of solving the problem. She can reenter social life after she had been purified in the sweat hut."

Wind Rider's explanation made Zach realize just how far removed their cultures were from one another. Everything the handsome white Indian told him seemed barbarous to him. But he was astute enough to hold his tongue.

"I wish to see Abby before I leave," he told Wind Rider.

Wind Rider gazed at Zach through narrowed lids. "Where did you hear that name?"

"From your sister. That is her name, isn't it?"

"Tears Like Rain does not speak the white man's tongue."

"She speaks it as well as you or I. We have been communicating for some time now. I know that the Crows attacked and killed your parents and you were raised by White Feather."

Wind Rider appeared dazed. "I—I cannot believe my sister revealed things of so personal a nature to you. I thought she had forgotten everything that happened those long years ago. When I would speak to her of them, she refused to listen or respond."

Wind Rider's gray eyes regarded Zach thoughtfully. Somehow this white captive had managed to penetrate deeply into his sister's mind and release memories that had remained concealed even from him. Though he had spoken to Tears Like Rain upon occasion in the white man's tongue, thinking she might one day have need of the tongue of their birth, she had denied all knowledge of the language and refused to speak it. Evidently she had listened carefully to the white traders who had visited the village and kept the language alive in her mind all these years.

"My son, I have just learned that Cow Woman is numbered among the dead slain by the cowardly Crow," White Feather said. The chieftain had been engaged in conversation with one of the women while Zach and Wind Rider spoke, and when he turned back to them his face was filled with grief. "We will spend this day and the next mourning our dead."

"I am truly sorry, White Feather," Zach said. "The attack was totally unexpected and cowardly. I will wait until your period of mourning is over before speaking to you about your daughter's welfare. If you love Tears Like Rain, you will listen carefully to what I say, search your heart, and act accordingly."

Wind Rider bristled indignantly. "White Feather is a good and wise man whose love has sustained us all these years. He will do what is best for my sister no matter what you tell him."

"I will listen to you, Sky Eyes, after I mourn my mother." He turned abruptly and walked away, his grief a heavy burden upon his shoulders.

"Sky Eyes?" Zach's brow furrowed as he looked to Wind Rider for an explanation.

"The women call you Sky Eyes," he explained. "White Feather does you honor by referring to you by that name. Besides mourning Cow Woman, he has much to think upon. The Great Smoke at Fort Weld did not go as we would have liked, but White Feather promised Black Kettle that he will take our people to Sand Creek as the soldiers asked and await further developments. Now I must join my father in mourning Cow Woman and the others."

At loose ends, Zach spent the next two days rehearsing his plea to White Feather. He hoped to persuade the chieftain to send Abby back to the white world. He had no idea why the militia urged the Cheyennes to settle at Sand Creek, but he'd be willing to bet it boded ill for the Indians. Abby might be as wild as the savages she lived with, but he couldn't bear the thought of her lying dead among her adopted people at some forsaken outpost on the prairie.

Abby emerged from the isolation hut shortly before Zach was summoned for his interview with White Feather. She looked somewhat pale but acted as if nothing was amiss. She greeted Zach cautiously when they met outside her tipi.

"Have you seen White Feather?" Zach asked.

"No. When Summer Moon brought food to me, she told me the men had returned from the Great Smoke. I am most anxious to see White Feather and Wind Rider. Do you know if the Great Smoke was successful?"

"I do not know." He paused, then said, "White Feather released me from captivity."

Abby's shuttered gaze gave Zach no hint of her thoughts. "So Summer Moon told me. I am surprised you are still here."

"Summer Moon kept you well-informed. Did she tell you White Feather has set aside two days to mourn the dead? I refused to leave because I wished to wait to speak privately with him."

She regarded him warily, curious as to what he intended to say to White Feather. "I know. That is why I have not yet greeted my father. I did not wish to intrude upon his grief. I also mourned my grandmother and our people during my time in the isolation hut."

"Tears Like Rain!"

Abby gave a glad cry when she saw Wind Rider running toward her. Since the Cheyenne were not demonstrative people, she did not throw herself into his arms as she longed to do. Instead, she smiled at him, her happiness at seeing him again clearly visible in the shining gray depths of her eyes.

"Welcome, brother," she greeted shyly. "Is our father well?"

"White Feather is weary, but he wishes to see you." He reverted to English as he turned to include Zach. "White Feather will speak to you now, Sky Eyes. He awaits you and my sister in the lodge of Spirit Singer."

Facing White Feather across a small circle formed by White Feather, Wind Rider, Abby, Spirit Singer, and himself, Zach thought the chieftain looked drawn and older. His noble face was deeply etched, and his fathomless black eyes held ancient knowledge of the dim future ahead for his people.

Abby felt certain she knew why Zach had requested a meeting with White Feather, and she was comforted by the thought that nothing he could say would make her father send her away if she didn't wish to go. The color of her skin might be white, but inside where it counted, she was Cheyenne.

White Feather's deep-set eyes seemed to sink deeper into his swarthy face as he stared at Zach. He took his time in speaking. He stared into space so long that Zach feared the old man had lost his voice. Finally, with great effort, White Feather spoke.

"On behalf of my people I thank you, Sky Eyes. I am grateful for my daughter's life. When offered freedom, you remained of your own free will. You asked to meet with me, and I have granted your request because I admire your courage. What is so important to keep you from returning to your people?"

Zach cleared his throat. "I wish to discuss your daughter. She is white and does not belong with the Cheyenne. I propose to take her to the fort and place her in a good home with a white family who will love her."

"Has Tears Like Rain expressed a desire to return to the white world?"

"Father, no, I do not wish to leave you or the People!" Abby's cry was a desperate appeal to her adoptive father. "Sky Eyes has no right to make such a demand of me. I wish to remain with you and Wind Rider."

White Feather nodded sagely. "I understand that you have spoken to Sky Eyes in the white man's tongue. Why have you kept knowledge of the language secret?"

Abby hung her head. "I was ashamed of being white, Father. Claiming knowledge of the tongue made me feel like a traitor. In truth, I had forgotten much until Sky Eyes began speaking to me and jogging my memory. I have no idea why Sky Eyes wishes me to return to people I hate."

Before White Feather could reply, Zach cut in. "If you care about your daughter you will realize that the days of freedom for the Indian are past. What did you learn at the conference held at Fort Weld? Were you given assurances that you and your people would be safe to live in peace and roam at will?"

"The Cheyenne and Arapaho met with the governor of Colorado Territory and the commandant at Fort Lyon to try to find a basis for peace. Black Kettle is old and weary of war and wants peace for his Southern Cheyenne. After many days of endless talks and deliberations, we received promises that Sand Creek, some thirty miles from Fort Lyon, was a safe place to camp, and that the village would be protected by soldiers from the fort as long as the village remained peaceful."

Abby snorted in disbelief. "And you believed them, Father?"

"Black Kettle chooses to believe them. We were urged to join Black Kettle's band at Sand Creek. In an act of good faith, Black Kettle and a small band of Arapaho relinquished their weapons to the soldiers. They will establish a camp on the banks of Sand Creek."

"And you, Father? Will you join them?"

"The council has decided to bend one more time to the will of the whites. If they do not keep their promises this time, we will go on the warpath with our Sioux brothers to the north."

Abby glanced at her brother, aware of his fierce scowl and the defiant set of his jaw.

"The War Dog Society will not go to Sand Creek," Wind Rider declared. "We will join the Sioux in their struggle for freedom."

"You're leaving?" A cold chill settled over Abby. What would she do without her brother? They had been together as long as she could remember, parting only briefly when Wind Rider went hunting or raiding.

Wind Rider's gray eyes, so like his sister's, softened with love. He had been her protector since he was a lad of ten, and he felt keenly his loss at having to leave her now. But his conscience would not allow him to join White Feather at Sand Creek to await an uncertain fate. The younger warriors of the War Dog Society agreed, and they had elected to ride north to join the Sioux, who were on the warpath against the White-eyes.

"I *must* leave," he told her sadly. "I do not trust the white man, nor can I meekly surrender like Black Kettle. White Feather understands my need to ride north."

"But what about me?" Abby cried. "Take me with you."

"Your sister's welfare is the reason I have asked to be heard by White Feather," Zach said, jumping into the conversation. "If you love Abby and wish her safe, it's imperative that she return to the white world. There is a family at Fort Lyon by the name of Porter. I know they would be delighted to take her in and teach her all she needs to know about white customs. They are good people and would treat her like one of their own."

"I have a family," Abby declared staunchly.

"Do you?" Zach questioned softly. "Your brother is leaving for the north, and he knows as well as I that it is dangerous for you to accompany him. I know nothing of what took place at the Great Smoke, but I am familiar enough with my own people to know that they are as numerous as the grass upon the plains. They will soon arrive in droves and require lands that once belonged solely to the Indian nations. Where will you go then? What will you do?"

He turned to White Feather, extending his hands in a gesture of pleading. "Abby is white. She need not share the Indian's fate. Surely you are wise enough to realize what is in store for your people. Do you wish the same fate for your adopted daughter? Think hard, White Feather, and understand that I speak because I wish what is best for Abby."

"Why should my daughter concern you, Sky Eyes?"

Zach flushed. Why indeed. "Because she once saved my life. And because I once saved hers. I cannot help but be concerned for her future. If you love her, you will order her to return with me to the white world she left as a child."

"No, Father, I will go with you and the People to Sand Creek," Abby protested violently. "I gladly accept the fate the Great Spirit has in store for you."

A fire kindled in White Feather's black eyes. He loved his daughter well, and the thought of bringing her harm caused him great pain. Yet his mind was filled with doubts. He was not certain that sending her back to white society was the answer. Intuition told him that everything Sky Eyes said was true—that Sand Creek might not be the safe haven the People hoped for. Ever since he had agreed with the council to join Black Kettle at Sand Creek, he had been plagued by signs and premonitions that disturbed him greatly.

When Wind Rider refused to abide by the white man's rules and settle at Sand Creek,

White Feather had felt grudging relief. He had no idea what was in store for the Cheyenne nation, but he feared there was no future for his people. He wanted a better life for his son and daughter.

Abby's gray eyes were softly pleading as they silently implored White Feather to ignore Zach. She was surprised to see that White Feather's dark eyes gleamed with suspicious moisture, and the need to ease his heavy heart was an ache inside her.

"My head and my heart go in opposite directions, Tears Like Rain," White Feather said at length. "My head agrees with Sky Eyes. You are white and should not be made to suffer the fate of the People. But at the same time my heart grieves, for I do not wish to part from the daughter of my soul. Perhaps our wise medicine man can provide me with an answer." White Feather turned to Spirit Singer and spoke at length.

Until now, Spirit Singer had remained in the background, listening intently but not speaking, for he understood little of the white man's tongue. Abby turned to Spirit Singer, her eyes fearful that he might agree with Zach and advise White Feather to send her away. When White Feather fell silent and the shaman spoke, it was in Cheyenne, and Zach cursed his inability to understand.

Zach had no idea what he would do if Spirit Singer decided that Abby must remain with the Cheyenne. Intuition warned him that they and all Indians were doomed, and he did not wish her to share their fate. Abby was too beautiful, too vital and alive to lose her life in a raid, or to starvation and disease. And she was white. He cared what happened to her. He didn't know why; he only knew that parting from her now would bring him unbearable pain. Zach had no idea if Sergeant Porter and his wife Milly would be able to tame the little savage, but he felt certain they would welcome her into their home.

Try as she might, Abby could not remain silent while Spirit Singer decided her fate. She didn't want to leave her people. She hated all whites. She did not understand them or their ways. And she despised Zach for wanting to take her away from all she loved and held dear.

"I wish to remain with White Feather and the People, Spirit Singer," she explained. "Can you not make Father understand that I prefer to share his fate?"

"What is your decision, Spirit Singer?" White Feather's eyes were bleak as he awaited the shaman's answer. "Should my daughter return to the white world with Sky Eyes?"

"I want what is best for my sister," Wind Rider contended, his eyes nearly as bereft as White Feather's. His decision to leave the Southern Cheyenne and join the Sioux had been made after much soul-searching.

"Only you can make that decision, White Feather," Spirit Singer droned in a singsong voice. "You must find the answer within your heart. You must seek a vision. Your vision will give you the answer you are looking for. I will join you in the purification hut to pray with you. After you have fasted for a day and a night, you must go forth and seek your vision. Only by prayer and fasting will you learn the path upon which your daughter must tread."

"So be it," White Feather acknowledged humbly.

Abby bowed her head in mute acceptance of the shaman's sage words. When White Feather rose to his feet and strode from the tipi, Zach turned to Abby. "What did the medicine man say?"

"Spirit Singer told Father he must seek his answer in a vision. He goes now to the sweat hut to fast and pray in preparation for his quest. After a day and a night of fasting and praying, he will go into the hills to seek his vision."

"You mean he must have a vision before he makes a decision?" Zach questioned in disbelief. He knew Indians were superstitious, but this was ridiculous.

"It is our custom," Abby said simply. "But I am not afraid. My heart tells me that the Great Spirit will give White Feather the only answer possible. Then you will leave and no longer badger me."

Chapter Seven

Painted Horse and the men of the Shield Society returned while White Feather was on his vision quest. They announced their victory over the Crow raiders with whoops and loud cries as they rode into the village driving the stolen horses before them and waving their coup sticks to display their trophies. Abby's stomach lurched sickeningly when she noted the fresh scalps adorning the men's coup sticks. She abhorred the practice of taking scalps, and she felt the same even now, when those scalps belonged to the despised Crow.

Spotting Abby immediately, Painted Horse cut two particularly fine horses from the string of ponies and led them toward her tipi, where he staked them near the entrance. Then he strutted over to where Abby stood beside Zach.

"I have brought your father a gift," Painted Horse said meaningfully. His dark eyes swept over her possessively. "I hope they please him."

"Father has gone on a vision quest," Abby informed him, shifting uncomfortably beneath his hot regard. It was obvious that his courtship was reaching a point when he already regarded her as his property. Once that would have pleased her, but now it produced only vague discomfort. When Painted Horse continued to stare at her as if he expected something more, Abby said, "You displayed great courage against the cowardly Crow. Your courage will be sung around the campfire." Basking in her praise, Painted Horse seemed to grow in stature as he puffed out his chest in a manly display of pride.

As if noticing him for the first time, Painted Horse sent Zach a withering look, his animosity palpable. "I am surprised to see you here, White-eyes. There was ample opportunity for escape during the battle."

"I will leave when I am ready," Zach said cryptically.

"Sky Eyes helped defend our village against the Crow," Abby was quick to add. "White Feather has given him his freedom."

"Sky Eyes," Painted Horse repeated with derision. "Why is he still here? I doubt it is because he is enamored of our people. More likely he is more enamored of you, Tears Like Rain, than the Cheyenne People."

A rosy flush crawled up Abby's neck as she searched her mind for an appropriate reply. She was angry at Painted Horse for inferring that she was responsible for Zach's presence.

"Come with me and I will explain." Wind Rider had approached them while they were talking. "Much has happened in your absence, Painted Horse. The village will move to Sand Creek soon to join Black Kettle. But I have decided not to accompany them. A few members of the War Dog Society have thrown their lot in with me. We ride north soon to unite with our Sioux brothers in their fight for freedom. We do not trust the word of the soldiers and are unwilling to sacrifice our freedom for a barren strip of land bereft of game and sustenance. You must decide for yourself if you will join us or go with White Feather to Sand Creek."

Painted Horse nodded, eager to learn what had taken place at Fort Weld during the Great Smoke. And why White Feather had gone on a vision quest. As to joining Wind Rider, Painted Horse wasn't so certain. If it meant losing Tears Like Rain, he would have to give it serious thought. Maybe he would go on a vision quest of his own. He needed a sign before he could make such a choice. After slanting Abby a long, searching look, Painted Horse turned to follow Wind Rider.

Zach eyed Painted Horse's departing back narrowly, strangely annoyed that the warrior already considered Abby his. The thought of Painted Horse possessing Abby gave Zach a hollow feeling of helplessness.

"How can you marry an Indian when you are white?" he asked impulsively. If he had given the words careful thought, he wouldn't have phrased them in quite that way.

"I am Cheyenne!" Abby maintained fiercely. "There is no finer warrior than Painted Horse. Any maiden would be proud to become his wife."

Zach noted with satisfaction that Abby did not say that *she* would be proud to be the wife of Painted Horse. "Why did Painted Horse bring the horses for your father?"

"They are gifts. Bride gifts, if you will. He is most serious about his courtship and wishes to conclude the negotiations."

"There can be no courtship if you are no longer with the Cheyenne. Those horses will serve us well when we leave here."

Abby's small chin rose at a stubborn angle. "That will not happen. Why do you insist upon taking me away from those I love? Is it because you hate me and scorn our customs?"

Zach looked stunned. "I don't hate you at all. I know far too little about the Cheyenne or their customs to judge them. You are white and do not belong here. I want what is best for you."

Abby gave him a derisive look. "Then go away and leave me in peace." Whirling on her heel, she stormed off.

*   *   *

Abby sat on the bank of the creek, idly trailing her hand in the water. She glanced down into the still water, staring intently at her reflection. Startled by what she saw, Abby felt as if she were looking at a stranger. She had not applied the walnut dye to her skin and hair in some time, and her complexion was paler than she had ever seen it. And the roots of her hair were a dramatic contrast against the inky strands that fell softly around her face. But what startled her most were the memories her image invoked. Dredged up from somewhere deep within her, the vision of her golden-haired mother hovered on the edge of her memory.

The image of that beautiful, tenderhearted lady of her memory seemed to stare back at her from the water. A strangled cry of denial came from her throat. It was as if everything Zach had said was true, that she really didn't belong with the Cheyenne. The image staring back at her was a visual denial of a life she had wholeheartedly embraced, the only life she wanted, or thought she wanted. With an angry flick of her fingers, she distorted the reflection until nothing but ripples remained on the water's blue surface.

Zach watched Abby from where he stood behind a tall cottonwood tree. He hadn't expected to find her here; he had assumed he was the only one who came to this secluded spot to bathe. When he saw her sitting on the bank, she appeared so deep in thought that he decided not to intrude. He started to turn away when he heard her cry out.

Thinking Abby had encountered some unknown danger, Zach burst from the trees. Startled, Abby jumped to her feet.

"You! How dare you follow me."

Zach gave her a sheepish grin. "I didn't follow you. When I arrived and saw you here, I intended to go away and leave you in peace, but then you cried out. Is something wrong?"

Abby glanced down at the water where her reflection had mocked her only moments before. She quickly looked away, determined to give no hint of her confused thoughts. "Nothing is wrong."

"Why did you cry out?"

She looked past him for a moment, as if stirred by visions no one else could see. The silence became so pronounced that Zach thought she hadn't heard him. He repeated his question.

Dragging her eyes back to Zach with marked reluctance, Abby slumped beneath the weight of his question. Her innermost thoughts and fears were none of his business. Wasn't it enough that he had already disrupted her life? If she hadn't spared his life, he wouldn't be here now dredging up painful memories or trying to take her away.

He would be dead.

That thought was even more painful.

Staring at her bent head, Zach suffered a moment of acute discomfort as her hair parted, exposing the vulnerable nape of her neck. His heart pounded furiously, and beads of sweat popped out on his forehead. With a shaking hand, he raised her chin so he could look into her eyes. A shimmer of sparkling tears turned her eyes into luminous gray pools, and Zach felt the almost desperate urge to pull her into his arms.

"Why did you cry out?" he asked again.

"You ask too much of me." Her words were a whisper of breathless air past her lips.

Zach sent her a melting smile. "I have not asked for anything—yet."

Abby shuddered, the hidden meaning in his words sending a thrill of apprehension down her spine. When he grasped her shoulders and pulled her hard against him, showing her by deed rather than word what he wanted from her if she were willing, Abby's face flamed and her eyes widened in sudden comprehension. The press of Zach's solid length against her body was like nothing she had ever felt before. Bodily contact between unmarried Cheyenne men and women was so rare that nothing had prepared her for the jolting pleasure of a fully aroused male.

Zach had kissed her before, and touched her, but never had she felt so threatened—or humiliated by the way her body reacted to his. She felt overwhelmed by fiery heat and burning shame and consumed by a dread colder than the deepest winter. It shamed her to know that her flawed body and weak mind could be bent to the will of a white man. When Zach's mouth lowered toward hers, her head snapped back.

"Let me go! Your vile behavior shames me."

"That is not my intention, Abby."

His arms tightened, and she could feel the tense power of his lean muscles against her pounding breast and trembling thighs, and every part of her felt the subtle throbbing of his desire. It enthralled her, beckoned her, frightened her, repelled her—and made her feel more alive than she had ever felt in her life. His mouth came closer, her protest dying in her throat as Zach's lips covered hers. Her strangled cry mingled with the hot rush of his breath and was returned in the form of a ragged groan.

Zach's kiss was more thorough than any he had previously bestowed upon her, and Abby felt a melting sensation deep within her most private places. She could feel the heat of him; it became a flame of overwhelming power and hunger radiating from his body to hers. In her innocent dreams, Abby had never imagined the kind of raw hunger she was experiencing. It both shamed and thrilled her—and made her angrier than she could ever remember being. How could a man, a white man, make her feel so intensely? Would it be the same with Painted Horse? Did her white blood make her susceptible to all men? To lust? Or was it only Zach who could move her so dramatically?

She gasped in outrage when Zach unlaced the ties on her tunic and shoved it roughly from her shoulders, baring the upper contours of her breasts. When his lips caressed those enticing curves, she renewed her struggles to escape his embrace. When his tongue left a moist trail on her burning flesh, her hands flailed ineffectually against the hard wall of his chest.

Zach knew he should release Abby, but his body worked independently of his mind. Some timeless emotion he would have been hard pressed to explain made his arms tighten as he pressed her against him from thigh to chest. She was soft and hard at the same time. Her lean, slightly muscular body was utterly feminine, innocently beguiling, immensely pleasing to his touch. And her mouth . . . It was sweetly intoxicating, full and lush and heady. Desire flooded his lower body, hot and swift and undeniable.

He wanted the little white savage more than he had ever wanted another woman.

He wanted her but could not have her. His body tensed and he deliberately concentrated on the slow inhaling and exhaling of his breath. By sheer force of will, he restrained the need that drove him relentlessly, forcing himself to relax before he lost complete control and took what he wanted. Zach was astute enough to realize that White Feather would never allow his daughter to return to the white world with a man who had taken advantage of her sexually. All Abby need do was cry rape and not only would his request be denied, but he could lose his life in the bargain.

With painful reluctance, Zach released his hold on Abby and set her aside. His action was so abrupt that Abby nearly toppled over backward. She caught herself and glared at him as if he were a loathsome insect too insignificant to crush beneath her moccasin. He supposed he had earned her contempt, but it was disconcerting to be regarded with such revulsion.

"Why did you do that?" Abby asked as she rubbed her kiss-swollen lips with the back of her hand. "I have told you repeatedly that I do not wish you to touch me."

"I'm not going to apologize, Abby, because I don't think you truly mean what you say. You're not too innocent to know how it is when a man wants a woman. Or that a woman can enjoy the act as much as a man. Nevertheless, it was contemptible of me to try to seduce you. I do not wish to earn White Feather's enmity. I can't deny I'd like to be the one to teach you how to be a woman, or how wonderful it can be between a man and a woman, but if I am to assume responsibility for you, it is best that I restrain my desire."

Abby frowned, not really understanding everything Zach said. "Why do you desire me? Surely there are white women more beautiful than I."

"I'm sure there are," Zach agreed, "but none that I know of. You're different, Abby. You're strong, courageous, loyal, and so disgustingly innocent, you make me want to protect you even as I yearn to make love to you."

143

"Make love? I do not understand."

Zach let out an exasperated sigh. "I want to bed with you, Abby. I want to put the man part of my body inside yours. I want to lie with you and bring you great joy. I want to love you."

Terror shivered through Abby. His erotically charged words slid over her like warm honey, doing things to her body that both thrilled and frightened her. She knew about intimacy. The bodies of men and women held no secrets for her, but never had she heard anything as sensual and arousing as what Zach had just said to her. She wanted to turn and flee, but something elemental held her rooted to the spot.

"You'd better go, Abby," Zach said harshly, "before I change my mind. I can only take so much. Unlike Cheyenne men, I have never learned the knack of repressing my sexuality." When Abby did not move, Zach growled, "Go on, get out of here!" She turned and ran as if the devil was after her. And indeed he was.

Zach watched her leave, his breath rasping from his chest in harsh, uneven gasps. His body was drawn as taut as a bow, and it took several minutes of intense concentration before he was relaxed and controlled enough to venture back to the village. He arrived at a moment of great excitement. White Feather had returned from his vision quest.

From a distance, Zach saw Abby standing beside her adoptive father. The chieftain appeared weak from his days and nights of fasting. His face was drawn; the furrows scoring his brow and cheeks were deeply etched, and his eyes were sunken into the hollows of his skull. He was leaning heavily upon Wind Rider as he spoke to Spirit Singer. Then Wind Rider, White Feather, and Spirit Singer disappeared into the shaman's tipi. Abby paused outside the tipi, turned, and looked directly into Zach's eyes. It was almost as if she had sensed his presence.

Their eyes met for a breathless moment, tense and expectant, before she beckoned him to her side. Without being told, Zach knew that White Feather had received his vision. He almost feared the chieftain's decision. On the one hand, he wanted to take Abby back to her own kind where she belonged; on the other, he feared she faced a far greater danger by being alone with him during their journey to Fort Lyon. Not until she was living with the Porters could he ease his vigilance and watch over her from a safe distance.

Milly Porter and her daughter Belinda could teach Abby how to act and behave like a lady. With Abby's looks, it wouldn't be long before she snared herself a husband. That thought brought Zach to a stumbling halt. That was what he wanted, wasn't it? The life he led was too dangerous and unsettled to keep Abby as his ward. Besides, gossip would destroy her if she were to live with an unmarried man. If and when he married, it would be to a woman who would fit into Boston society. One day he would return home to the life he was born to.

It bothered Zach that Abby's reputation would be severely damaged when word got around that she had been raised by the Cheyenne and had traveled alone with him to Fort Lyon. But he would do his utmost to squelch gossip and save her reputation. He forced himself to start walking again.

"White Feather has returned," Abby said when he reached her side. "Spirit Singer is interpreting his vision. We are to wait outside until we are summoned."

Abby could hear the low murmur of voices from within the tipi, and anxiety rose like bitter gall in her throat. She swallowed convulsively. What if White Feather's vision was not to her liking? Would he make her leave the People simply on Spirit Singer's interpretation of his dreams? She had always had a healthy respect for visions and their sacred meanings, but this time she wasn't certain she could abide by the dictates of a vision if it meant she must leave those she loved.

Abby's reverie was interrupted by the appearance of Wind Rider. "White Feather awaits you both inside the tipi."

Abby's heart was pounding as she searched her brother's face, seeking an answer to her unasked question in the stark planes of his face. She saw nothing in his inscrutable features but his abiding love for her.

Wind Rider held back the tipi flap and beckoned Abby and Zach inside. He entered behind them and indicated that they should sit.

Abby gave a cry of dismay when she saw White Feather. He looked older and more exhausted than he had before he'd entered the tipi.

Though Zach couldn't understand Abby's words, her obvious concern for White Feather was touching, and he knew how unhappy it would make her to leave her adoptive father.

"We will speak in the white man's tongue, daughter," White Feather said, allowing Zach the courtesy of understanding what was being said. "I spent three days fasting and praying for a vision. When none came, I feared I was not worthy enough to receive one, that I had not prepared myself properly. I began to despair. But on the night of the third day, weakened by thirst and hunger, the vision I sought appeared as I stood on a hill looking down upon the village."

Abby held her breath and waited anxiously for her father to continue. She had no idea that Zach was every bit as anxious as she.

"If my vision didn't concern both Tears Like Rain and Sky Eyes, I would not reveal it now. But once Spirit Singer interpreted it for me, I realized that it was meant to be revealed to both of you. And to Wind Rider," he added, including his adopted son in his narration, "for Wind Rider was also in my vision."

"Tell us, Father," Wind Rider urged. "What has your vision revealed?"

White Feather closed his eyes, and they appeared to sink even deeper into his skull.

His complexion was ashen beneath the rich copper of his skin, his lips bloodless. He related his vision in a harsh voice that was forced from his throat with great effort and personal pain.

"I stood on a hill looking down upon the village. The hour was sometime between dawn and daylight, and I had the feeling of bitter cold despite the mildness of the night. The village appeared deserted. In the distance, I saw Tears Like Rain walking in the direction of Fort Lyon. Sky Eyes was with her."

A hoarse cry escaped from Abby's bloodless lips. White Feather stared straight ahead. "In my vision, I saw Wind Rider walking north. I called out, but neither my son nor my daughter stopped or looked back. Before my vision ended, a small gray dove flew down from the heavens and alighted on my right shoulder."

Drained of all emotion, his strength ebbing, White Feather leaned back and waited. Wind Rider was the first to react. "What does it mean, Father?"

White Feather's harsh features softened somewhat as he regarded the adopted son he loved so well and who loved him in return. "I will tell you how Spirit Singer interpreted my vision," he said wearily. "The empty tipis represent our village once we go to join Black Kettle at Sand Creek." He directed his bleak gaze at Abby. "Spirit Singer has interpreted the next part of my vision to mean that Tears Like Rain will walk a different path from that of the Cheyenne."

148

"No, Father, I do not want to leave the People."

"The Great Spirit has spoken," White Feather intoned sadly. "There is no turning back from what is meant to be. You will return to the people of your birth and learn to live among them."

"What of me, Father?" Wind Rider asked fearfully. "Surely the Great Spirit does not intend for me to forsake those I love and care about. I will ride north—I knew that before your vision—but it is to fight whites, not to join them."

"I did not reveal all of my vision, my son. As I watched you walk away, I became aware that you were wearing white man's clothing. Spirit Singer could not tell me if that meant you would join the whites like your sister or if you were merely wearing the clothing as a disguise. With your sister it was more clear. Her destiny lies with the whites."

Abby's face drained of all color. She had been so certain White Feather would receive a vision favorable to her that she had never considered that she might actually have to leave her home. But a vision was sacred, made even more so by the fact that White Feather had shared it with them. Morally she was obliged to obey the dictates of the vision as interpreted by the shaman.

Wind Rider was riddled with confusion. He refused to believe his destiny lay with the white race he despised. If White Feather had seen him dressed as a white man, then there was a very good explanation. He was going north to Sioux country to fight for freedom for the People, and he would not allow himself to believe otherwise. Suddenly he recalled the small gray dove White Feather had mentioned.

"What of the gray dove, Father? What does Spirit Singer say about that?"

White Feather's expression became shuttered, and his lids lowered to hood his eyes. "Spirit Singer was uncertain as to the meaning of the gray dove." Actually, White Feather was keeping that part of his vision secret from his beloved adopted children. If they were aware of Spirit Singer's interpretation of that part of his vision, they would refuse to follow the path indicated by the Great Spirit through his vision.

Spirit Singer's wizened face had worn an expression of profound sadness when he told White Feather that the gray dove represented his dead wife, Gray Dove, and that it meant he would join her soon in the spirit world, where their souls would be reunited. In effect, White Feather had foreseen his own death in his vision. He accepted Spirit Singer's word with fatalistic calm and hoped he would have time to take his small band safely to Sand Creek before he met his death.

"Perhaps the dove meant that our mother is watching over you," Abby suggested hopefully.

"Perhaps," White Feather murmured, refusing to look at her.

Gathering his wits, Zach spoke for the first time since entering the tipi. "I believe your vision has clearly indicated what must be done regarding your daughter."

What Zach had just witnessed was something so extraordinary that it left him shaken. Indians were said to believe in mystical events and circumstances, and their visions were treated with awe and respect, much as in the white man's religion. As he listened to White Feather speak, he could almost believe the old man had seen the vision he had described so vividly. It was one of the most awe-inspiring experiences he had ever witnessed—not at all like the hocus-pocus described by skeptics. He felt privileged to be a part of it.

"I hear you, Sky Eyes," White Feather said wearily. "And it shall be as you say. But before I let my daughter leave the safety of my lodge, you must give your word that no harm will come to Tears Like Rain."

"And I would have your promise that you will protect my sister's virtue," Wind Rider said fiercely. His sister was too beautiful and naive to be set adrift in a society that would take advantage of her innocence. Parting with her would be the most difficult thing he had ever done.

"I can take care of myself!" Abby said defiantly. "If you insist that I leave the People, then let me follow my own destiny."

"You have my solemn promise," Zach vowed, ignoring Abby's outburst. "I will place Abby with a good family who will teach her the ways of her people. They have a daughter Abby's age, and she will have companionship. She will become my ward, and I will protect her reputation to the best of my ability.

"But you both must realize that gossip will plague her because she has been raised by Indians. I will do what I can to protect her reputation, but it will be up to Abby to conduct herself in an appropriate manner. I further promise to see that she marries a good man who loves her."

Abby bristled angrily. "I will marry no white man!" She glared at Zach through eyes as turbulent as a storm-tossed sea. "I will conduct myself as I always have. I do not need an arrogant White-eyes to tell me how to act. I take more pride in being Cheyenne than I do in that part of me that is white."

Zach rolled his eyes, aware that his work was cut out for him. Taming Abby was going to be a full-time job. If he was smart, he'd leave the little savage with the Cheyenne, where she obviously wanted to be, and forget all about her. But a niggling suspicion remained concerning Sand Creek. He strongly suspected a tragedy was in the making, one that involved White Feather and Black Kettle, and that if he let Abby go to Sand Creek, she would be trapped in the middle of it.

A sinking feeling in his gut warned Zach that he was taking on more responsibility than he could possibly handle. More than he wanted.

What if he was transferred from Fort Lyon? What if Pete and Milly Porter decided they wanted nothing to do with a white woman raised by Indians? What if Belinda Porter, a self-centered brat, didn't like Abby? What if white society shunned her? What if . . .

What if he couldn't keep his hands off her?

Zach was suddenly aware that he hadn't specifically promised to keep his hands off Abby, and he made himself a silent vow to keep a respectful distance from the enticing little beauty until he could place her safely with the Porters.

"You may leave us, Sky Eyes," White Feather said, interrupting Zach's mental observations. "I wish to bid my daughter farewell in private."

Chapter Eight

The numbness in Abby's limbs extended to her heart as she walked woodenly toward the horse Zach held waiting for her. She had already said good-bye to White Feather in an emotional outpouring of love and respect. Parting with friends and family who had been a vital part of her life for the past fourteen years had been heartbreaking, and when the time came to bid farewell to her brother, she had broken down and wept. Abby recalled his words and hoped they would sustain her during the weeks and months to come.

"Be brave, Tears Like Rain," he had admonished her. "Your heart is Cheyenne, and nothing will change that. In time you will learn to adjust to white customs and make a life among the people of our birth."

"I do not want to go, Wind Rider. Why must things change for us? Why can't the White-eyes let us live in peace as our people have done for generations? Why can't I go to Sand Creek with White Feather? I will miss you, brother."

"Only the Great Spirit knows the answers to your questions. White Feather's vision is a grim warning of things to come. Even I know the days of greatness for the Cheyenne are numbered. Sky Eyes is right—you should return to the white world where you will be safe."

"They will despise me," Abby said bitterly.

"I am confident of your ability to adjust to the change in your life," Wind Rider said with a sad smile. "I promise that before I leave for Sioux territory, I will visit you in the white man's lodge to make certain you are well. Intuition tells me that Sky Eyes will protect you, and so I must trust him."

"Your trust is misplaced, brother. Sky Eyes is white. He speaks with a forked tongue."

Wind Rider shook his head. "Have you forgotten that Sky Eyes fought beside the Cheyenne and saved your life?"

Abby flushed. She also recalled how he had kissed her and touched her and how her body still ached from a wanting that had been totally foreign to her until Zach had come into her life. "I have not forgotten." Her words faltered, unable to describe her desolation at having to part with her brother. "Take me with you, Wind Rider—I will make my home with our Sioux brothers."

Wind Rider's silver gaze slid away from Abby. Given the precarious existence he led, he feared his days on earth were numbered. When White Feather had described his vision of Wind Rider walking north wearing white man's clothing, Wind Rider interpreted it to mean that he was walking the path to the afterworld. He believed the white man's clothing he wore in the vision signified his white blood and the fact that he would meet his white ancestors in the afterworld. If he took his sister with him, she'd be left unprotected and alone once he departed this world. Besides, White Feather's vision indicated that he and Tears Like Rain would walk different paths.

"Though it pains me to part from you, Tears Like Rain, I cannot take you with me. Each in our own way, we must fulfill our father's vision."

Despair weighed heavily upon Abby's slender shoulders. "When will you go north? Do you leave immediately?"

"No," Wind Rider told her. "I will travel to Sand Creek with the People and see them settled before I take my leave."

They had parted then, and Abby knew a pain far greater than any she had ever experienced before. It was a pain that continued now as she walked to where Zach had waited patiently while she said farewell to Summer Moon and others gathered to bid her good-bye.

Zach's heart was heavy. He knew he was doing the right thing by taking Abby to Fort

Lyon, but he felt like a villain for separating her from those she loved. Yet if she remained, her life would be torn apart anyway. Her brother was leaving, and White Feather was taking his band to Sand Creek. White Feather was a wise man, who recognized the uncertain future of his people, and Zach respected him for giving permission for his adopted daughter to return to white society.

Abby's steps dragged as she approached Zach. She knew without being told that neither White Feather nor Wind Rider would be present to see her ride away from her home. They had already made their farewells; there was nothing more to say.

"Are you ready?" Zach asked solicitously. He didn't want to hurry her, but neither did he want to linger, for it would only make it harder for Abby to leave. The three-day journey to Fort Lyon was not without danger. There were still many miles of hostile territory to travel through, and the Crow and Ute might still be in the vicinity, raiding and plundering.

Abby sent Zach a look of utter loathing. She might have to travel with him, but she certainly needn't act as if she liked it. If she must live with whites, she'd do it on her own terms, without the help of the man who had torn her from the bosom of those she loved. Though Abby had told no one, she didn't plan on staying at Fort Lyon long. She intended to slip away and join White Feather at Sand Creek. Once she had returned to the People on her own, she believed her father would change his mind and allow her to remain. He would realize that she wasn't meant to live in the white world.

Disdaining Zach's offer to help her mount, Abby leaped agilely onto a black mare with a star on her forehead. Abby's back was rigid, her pained expression giving mute testimony to her misery. Zach mounted a sturdy painted stallion and grasped the leading reins of a packhorse carrying warm buffalo robes and food for their journey. He nudged his horse forward, aware that Painted Horse had approached Abby and was speaking to her in a hushed voice.

"I will kill Sky Eyes if you wish it," Painted Horse said earnestly. "We will be joined immediately, and I will take you with me to Sioux territory."

Abby's eyes widened. "I am honored, Painted Horse, but it will accomplish little to kill him. White Feather's sacred vision foretold my leaving. I must fulfill the prophesy of the Great Spirit."

Undaunted, Painted Horse stepped closer. "You were meant to be my woman. I will not let you go so easily. We will meet again, Tears Like Rain." Then he stepped back, his piercing black eyes effectively conveying his willingness to kill in her defense.

Abby suppressed a shudder. Not too many moons ago, she had been looking forward to becoming Painted Horse's mate. But that was no longer true. And it was all Zach's fault. He had come into her life and changed it, forcing her to accept a different future than she'd envisioned. Not long ago, Abby had thought her happiness depended on becoming Painted Horse's wife. How naive she had been.

Zach's patience was wearing thin. Painted Horse's intimate conversation with Abby annoyed him. He hoped the Cheyenne warrior wasn't plotting some mischief, for he wouldn't stand for it. Zach took small comfort in the fact that he had a weapon, and his fingers curled reflexively around the barrel of the Spencer rifle White Feather had given him. Abby had also been given a weapon, and they were both provided with ammunition. Knowing how angry Abby was at him, Zach hoped she didn't take it into her head to shoot him in the back. His mental musing slid to a halt when Abby nudged her horse and rode up beside him.

"I am ready, Sky Eyes."

As they left the village, Zach was aware that they were being followed, and he strongly suspected that Painted Horse planned some kind of devious mischief. He pretended not to notice.

When he called a halt around noon to eat and refresh themselves in a meandering creek, he casually mentioned that they were being trailed.

Abby sent him a look of utter disdain. "Of course we are being followed. It is Painted Horse. He is letting me know that he cares for me."

"How long does he intend to follow us? Surely not all the way to Fort Lyon. If he intends to ambush me and take you by force, he will have a fight on his hands."

"Painted Horse has already turned back," Abby said quietly. "He will not harm you unless I ask it of him."

"What! How do you know that?"

"I know," Abby replied cryptically. "Do not fear, Sky Eyes. White Feather will be most displeased if Painted Horse dishonors his pledge to allow you to leave in peace."

"You must call me Zach, for it is the name you will use at the fort. And for your information, I do not fear Painted Horse."

Abby sent him a scathing glance. "You should. Painted Horse is a formidable foe. Despite White Feather's wishes, he would have killed you had I allowed it."

Zach stiffened, his expression fierce. "Had *you* allowed it? No matter what you think of me, I am no coward."

Abby stared at him, unable to speak beyond the dryness of her throat. She had only to look at him to know he was no coward. He possessed the superb body and awesome strength of a Cheyenne warrior. She did not like to think that a white man rivaled a Cheyenne warrior in fitness and courage, but it was true. Try as she might, she could not deny the powerful attraction that existed between them, or prevent the enchantment he wove around her senses.

"I did not say you were a coward," Abby denied, flustered.

Zach reached out to touch her smooth cheek, shedding his stiffness the way a reptile sheds his skin. "Abby, must we always be at odds with each other? I know you are angry with me, but had White Feather wanted to keep you with him, he would have done so. Only a wise man would make the decision to send you back to the white world. I'll do everything in my power to see that you're happy with the transition. If you have relatives alive, I'll find them."

His fingers left a burning trail against her flesh, and Abby flinched. She feared the strange effect Zach had on her. He had but to touch her, and her body was no longer hers. It was his to do with as he willed. It took strict discipline and fierce will to resist the powerful allure of his innocent caress.

"I will do as you say, Sky—Zach. At Fort Lyon I will be friendless but for you. It would be foolish of me to destroy that small comfort no matter how much I despise you for taking me away from my people. We will have a truce."

"A truce," Zach repeated solemnly. He wanted more than a truce, much more, but it wasn't possible. He was astute enough to know that Abby would be unhappy in Boston, where he intended to live once the war was over and he had fulfilled his duty to his country. His brother and sister were anxiously awaiting his return. He had a new niece he'd never even seen.

Abby nodded and walked away, her hips swaying seductively beneath the supple doe-skin dress she wore. Zach thought she had never looked lovelier. Her tunic was bleached a soft buttercup yellow, embellished with colorful beads and fringed at the hem and yoke. Long sleeves protected her arms from the cold, and her beaded moccasins were laced to her knees. Except for her hands, face and neck, no skin was visible to taunt him, but Zach had never seen anything more tantalizing than her buckskin-clad form. Dimly he wondered how her skin and hair would look once they had returned to their natural color.

They traveled in silence most of the afternoon. The weather grew colder as the day progressed, and Zach removed a buffalo robe from the packhorse and placed it around Abby's shoulders. He was still dressed in Wind Rider's tunic and leggings, but from somewhere White Feather had resurrected his boots and presented them to him the day before he and Abby left the village. He was grateful for the small comfort of a familiar possession, and though the buckskins were warm, he'd feel more at ease once he donned his uniform.

Dusk came early and Zach called a halt. The wind was howling through the trees, and the early October chill gave promise of a hard winter. Beneath the shelter of a rocky ledge, Zach laid out the buffalo robes and built a fire. By the time they had eaten, Abby was yawning.

"Go to sleep, Abby," Zach urged. "Tomorrow will be a long day."

Abby cast a nervous glance at the scant distance between the two pallets before crawling beneath her buffalo robe. Zach disappeared into the darkness for a moment of privacy, and when he returned, Abby was asleep. He stared at her with the hunger of a starving man, wishing with all his heart that he could share her warmth. The soft womanly part of her beckoned to the hard manly part of him, and he gritted his teeth in deliberate denial of the gnawing need riding him. An anguished sigh slipped past his lips as he fought his demons and slid into his own bedroll.

Abby awoke screaming in terror. A dream she'd had countless times in the past had roused her from a deep sleep. She was six years old again, witnessing the brutal slaying of her parents and her own abduction. She saw it all—the mutilated bodies, the burning wagon, their ransacked possessions, and the terrible anguish she had suffered over the unknown fate of little Sierra.

Her cry awakened Zach, and he leaped to his feet, ready to do battle with an unknown enemy. He relaxed somewhat when he realized that Abby was having a bad dream.

"It's all right, Abby," he said in a soothing tone meant to allay her fears. "It's only a bad dream. What did you dream that was so terrifying?"

"I—I don't know," Abby said, unwilling to divulge the frightening details of her nightmare for fear they would continue. "I'm fine."

When Zach reluctantly returned to his pallet, Abby's tense words brought him back to her side. "Wait! I—I'm not ready yet for sleep. If we are to become friends, perhaps you could tell me about yourself." The fear of being left alone with her nightmare had reduced her to begging for favors. Like it or not, even Zach's company was better than being tormented by the painful memories plaguing her.

"Now?" Zach asked, astounded. "You want to talk now?"

"Now is as good a time as any. Tell me about your family. Where is your home? I know your parents are dead, but do you have brothers or sisters?" The sudden thought came to Abby that Zach might even have a wife. "Do you have a wife and children?"

Realizing that Abby was serious about wanting to talk and aware that her request was connected to the nightmare that had awakened her, Zach pulled his pallet next to hers and crawled inside, for the night air was sharp and cold.

"I have no wife. Nor do I have any children that I am aware of. I do have an older brother and younger sister. Both are happily married. I have two nephews and a niece I have yet to meet. My home is in Boston. Boston is on the coast of a great ocean called the Atlantic. What else would you like to know?"

Abby grew thoughtful. "Are there many people in the East?"

"More than you or I can count. And thousands of them are coming across the prairie to settle on Indian lands in the West. As land becomes more crowded in the East, migration West is more and more attractive. Soon locomotives will carry large numbers of people across the plains. Where open lands once stretched as far as the eye could see and beyond, there will be settlers populating cities and carving out farms."

A cold chill settled in the vicinity of Abby's heart. "If you speak the truth, it will mean the end of the People. Buffalo cannot survive under such conditions, and our livelihood will be taken from us."

"I think White Feather already suspects what the future holds for his people. That is why he decided to send you back to your own kind, where you will be safe."

"My own kind," Abby spat derisively. "My own kind will despise me because I am Cheyenne."

"I won't let them," Zach said harshly. "You are white." He knew there were those who would consider Abby a savage because she had been raised by Indians, and he wished he could protect her from such cruelty. Those same people would judge her harshly despite her white skin.

A tense silence stretched between them before Abby said, "Tell me more about yourself. Do you plan to return to Boston where you once lived?"

"It's my fondest hope," Zach admitted. "When the War Between the States started, I joined the army and my brother remained home to oversee the freighting business left to us by our father. Once my enlistment is up, he will expect me to return to help him run the business."

"I . . . see," Abby said slowly. "Is . . . is there a woman waiting for you in Boston?"

"Not really, though my parents had hoped I'd marry the daughter of their dearest friend. I suspect Deborah will grow tired of waiting and marry someone else in my absence."

"You do not seem overly concerned."

"It wasn't a love match. Deborah is a beautiful woman who knows her way around Boston society. We would have suited one another well enough, but love never entered into the picture. Isn't it the same in Cheyenne culture? Do you marry your men for love?"

"Courtship in our culture lasts four or five years," Abby explained. "Cheyenne women are noted for their chastity, and no Cheyenne male would do anything improper. The courtship and marriage involves the entire family, not just the girl chosen by the male. There is much discussion about the fitness and ability of the warrior, and his gifts to the parents help them make the proper choice. But if a girl does not favor the warrior, she does not have to accept him."

"Did you accept Painted Horse?"

"He is a brave warrior. And handsome. He would be the kind of husband a girl could be proud of. I found no objection to his suit."

"Did you love him?" Zach held his breath as he waited for her answer. For some reason it was important to know just how deep her feelings were for Painted Horse.

"I . . . admired him. He is very brave and cunning. I would have been a good wife to him."

Zach turned to face her, caressing her cheek with the back of his hand. "You will be a good wife no matter who you marry," he said earnestly. And he meant it. He hoped she would choose a man worthy of her.

His touch sent a trail of fire racing across her skin. She jerked away, stunned by her reaction to so innocent a gesture. In her entire twenty years, she'd never felt so attracted to a man. Cheyenne maidens were protected by such a stringent moral code that had she experienced the same kind of intense response with Painted Horse or any other Cheyenne warrior, she would have been shamed.

Yet with Zach she felt no shame, no embarrassment, even though it was wrong to enjoy the caress of a man who despised her way of life. She wished fervently that his touch did not make her feel alive in a way she had never felt before.

Mistaking her retreat for revulsion, Zach reluctantly pulled his hand from her cheek. He could feel the sweet warmth of her breath brush his face, and he had to clench his fists to keep from reaching out and taking her into his arms. From loving her.

"Go to sleep, Abby," he said gruffly. "That's enough talk for one night." The words were easier said than obeyed. Long after Zach heard the even cadence of Abby's breathing, he lay awake, his arms aching to hold her, his lips yearning to taste of her sweet nectar.

They were up and on their way early the next morning. The sun came out, and it was somewhat warmer than the day before but still cool for October. If all went well, Zach expected to reach Fort Lyon the next day. That meant he had to suffer only one more night of exquisite torture, knowing he couldn't touch Abby no matter how desperately he wanted her. He had given his promise to Wind Rider and White Feather to protect Abby, and he knew now that he was her greatest danger.

They stopped briefly at noon to partake of a cold meal consisting of dried pemmican, parched corn, and cold water. It was nearly sundown when they reached a branch of the Republican River, and Zach started looking for a likely place to spend the night. He spotted a grassy area partially protected by a dense stand of trees and motioned for Abby to follow him. They had just turned off the trail when the silence was broken by staccato bursts of gunfire and chilling war cries. They realized immediately that somewhere nearby a terrible battle was being waged.

The sounds grew intense as savage war whoops and guttural cries echoed through the stillness. Since Zach had no idea if the attacking Indians were Cheyenne or other hostiles, he grasped the reins of Abby's mare and led her deeper into the woods, where they couldn't be seen.

"Stay here," he whispered harshly, "while I try to find out what's happenning and offer whatever help I can."

"I will go with you," Abby returned. "If they are Cheyenne, we will be in no danger."

"What if they're Crow? Or Ute? Both are your enemies."

"I will go," Abby repeated stubbornly.

Zach cursed softly. There was no time to argue. "We'll leave the horses tethered here and slip through the woods. Stay behind me and don't say a word until we know what's going on."

Abby nodded, following close on Zach's heels. Shortly they came upon a scene straight from hell.

"Dear Lord!" Zach dropped to the ground, pulling Abby with him. An Indian raiding party had found a lone wagon which had stopped for the night beside the river and were attacking it with savage fury. "Which tribe?" Zach asked Abby, hoping she could identify the raiders.

Abby glanced over Zach's shoulder, her eyes wide with horror. She had witnessed attacks by soldiers upon Indian villages but had never seen the devastation wrought by raiding parties. The Southern Cheyenne usually attacked only when provoked. "They are Ute," Abby whispered harshly.

Zach rose to his knees, intending to go to the aid of the helpless victims, but Abby grasped his arm and yanked him down. "No, it is too late for you to help. If you go now, you will be slain. The Ute show captives no mercy."

Shaking off her clinging hands, Zach grudgingly admitted the utter futility of offering aid, yet he could not stand idly by while Indians attacked innocent people. He prepared to rush to their defense. Then abruptly the guns fell silent. He watched in growing horror as the last survivor was cut down and ruthlessly scalped.

"It is too late," Abby hissed. Succumbing to helpless rage, Zach sank to his knees on the cold damp ground. There was nothing he could do now but wait until the Indians left and see to the burial of the dead.

The Ute took their time, thoroughly ransacking the emigrants' possessions before leaving the scene of their attack. Dusk hovered on the edge of darkness when one of the warriors raised his coup stick in the air, gave a bloodcurdling cry, and rode off. One by one the other dozen or so warriors followed, carrying the looted possessions of their victims. Zach waited a full fifteen minutes before creeping out into the open, cautioning Abby to remain behind. Though she was probably accustomed to atrocities of this sort, mutilated bodies weren't a pretty sight, not even for a young woman raised by Indians.

Abby paid little heed to Zach's warning as she followed him into the clearing. She knew what she would find; it had been described to her often enough when their warriors returned from a successful raid and bragged about their exploits during the celebration of their victory. But she had not expected her own horrified reaction to the gruesome aftermath of death and destruction she found after the Ute's raid.

Six bodies lay on the ground. All were dead. Two were women, three were small children, and one was a man. All had been scalped, and their faces wore grimaces of horror. Both women had been raped and lay with their legs spread obscenely. But what affected Abby the most were the dead children. The Cheyenne would never harm a child; children were too precious. They would have been spared and raised with love, just as she and her brother had been. She stopped beside one of the children and saw that it was a girl. Bile rose in her throat, and she swallowed convulsively. It was a struggle to keep from spewing forth the meager contents of her stomach.

A kind of numbness slowly took control of her body as she crouched beside the little girl. The violent scene suddenly became her own nightmare. The face of the child lying in a pool of congealing blood became the face of little Sierra, looking exactly as she appeared the last time Abby had seen her fourteen years ago. The features of the man sprawled nearby resembled her father, and one of the women

171

had the beautiful, serene countenance of her mother.

A scream rose up in Abby's chest, lodged in her throat, and finally was forced past her lips in a keening wail. Her eyes were wide and fixed, her pupils dilated. She was no longer twenty years old. She was a child again, witnessing the murder of her parents and experiencing the despair of being forcibly ripped from the loving bosom of her family. If not for Ryder, she would have perished of a broken heart.

Zach clutched his rifle and whirled, the hair rising on the back of his neck when he heard Abby's eerie cry. He had expected to see the Ute converging on them and was bewildered when he saw Abby crouching beside the dead child, her eyes blank, her face contorted with terror.

"Abby, what is it? What do you see?" He held his rifle aloft, cocked and ready to fire, but saw nothing to justify the kind of panic she displayed.

He went to her then, realizing that she hadn't heard him. He should have insisted that she remain in the woods where she wouldn't have to view the carnage up close. Grasping her shoulders, he raised her to her feet and shook her roughly. "Abby, for God's sake, snap out of it!"

Nothing. Zach could have shaken her until her teeth rattled and she wouldn't have responded. With growing alarm, he tried to turn her around and lead her away, but she would not budge. Abruptly she dropped to her knees beside the dead child and began rocking back and forth and moaning as if her heart were breaking. Her lips moved in a wordless litany that produced no sound, and she was so distraught that Zach feared for her sanity. He realized that if he didn't remove her immediately from the scene of death and destruction, she was likely to lapse into a state of profound shock.

He bent and scooped her up in his arms, carrying her back to where they had left their horses, praying the Ute hadn't stumbled upon their hiding place. He uttered a heartfelt thanks when he found their mounts undisturbed where they had left them. He eased Abby onto her feet, supporting her with one hand while he removed their buffalo robes from the packhorse with the other.

When the robes were spread on the ground, he carefully guided her down and sat beside her, wrapping her in his arms. "Can you talk now, Abby? What happened back there? What frightened you?"

Abby stared at him through blank eyes. Her face wore a haunted look as terrifying visions from her past assaulted her memory. He touched her gently. "Abby, can you hear me?"

Her skin was as cold as ice.

He gazed into her unfocused eyes, and what he saw in their stormy gray depths made him shudder. They were filled with profound anguish. With all his heart, Zach wished he could absorb her pain and end her agony. She spoke in a hushed voice and he strained to hear her words.

"Sierra." She repeated the name over and over. Zach recognized it as the name of the sister Abby had mentioned before, and the cause of her distress became clear. Evidently the dead girl resembled her little sister, and all the horror she had repressed these past fourteen years had returned to haunt her, including the death of her parents and her own abduction.

Zach searched his brain for a way to release Abby from the chains of shock. With a need born of desperation, he pulled her hard against him and kissed her. Deeply, hungrily, with all the longing and urgency he had suppressed during the past days and weeks. At first she remained stiff and unresponsive, but Zach showed her no mercy as his lips moved over hers with reckless abandon.

Then, so slowly, Abby warmed to the heat of Zach's lips. Her body grew soft and supple as she burrowed into the welcome comfort of his embrace. When his tongue teased her lips apart, she opened to him, accepting without protest the hot, stabbing warmth. She wanted to forget what she had seen, escape the haunting memory that tugged at the fringes of her conscience, forget everything except the wonderful euphoria Zach's kisses brought her.

She wanted to feel again.

If Zach assumed he could control his ardor once Abby's senses returned and she began responding to him, he was badly mistaken.

The moment he felt the first spark of desire soften her body and tasted the hot spurt of passion on her lips, there was no turning back.

Chapter Nine

Abby felt her body warming to the powerful allure of Zach's lips. His kiss was at once gentle and hungry, his arms coaxing her from the frozen horror of her nightmare as they pulled her close, fitting softness to strength, molding her slender frame to one harder and more demanding. She offered not even token resistance, for the flame building within her dispelled the paralyzing horror of past memories. Zach's lips coaxed a response, banishing thoughts of right or wrong as a slow-building passion swirled between them.

The hard hand caressing her back in strong circular motions grew bolder, until reaching her hips he pulled her flush against him. Heat, searing, scorching, flowed over Abby like torrid currents of air, leaving her aching and wanting. Those terrifying visions dredged from her turbulent past slipped away, replaced by the breathless reality of Zach's lips teasing hers, of his tongue slipping into her mouth to taste her sweetness, of his hands boldly exploring the curves of her body.

Plunged into a swirling torrent of hot desire, Abby gasped for air as Zach searched the inside of her mouth. She never dreamed anything could feel so wonderful. Touching faces was not nearly so arousing as touching mouths. She writhed and moaned against him, her emotions condensed into a hot rush of exquisite tension that spread throughout her body in undulating waves.

Zach's kisses grew frenzied as he tried to withdraw from the explosion of passion between them. He failed utterly. His original intention had been to shock Abby back to reality with his kisses, not seduce her. Abby's response had surprised and thrilled him. But it could not continue. Zach knew that if he kept this up there would be no turning back. The need to make love to Abby was an ache inside him, and within a very short time the threads of his control would snap and he'd do something he'd promised himself wouldn't happen.

When Abby offered no resistance, Zach's kisses fell like gentle rain against her mouth, eyes, face, wherever her skin lured him. When his searching lips reached the pulsing hollow of her throat, she arched to give him better access, long past caring what her people thought of her disgraceful behavior. Her people had sent her away. She had been abandoned to the enemy, left to flounder helplessly in a world she knew nothing about, and Zach was the only tangible in her shattered life. That terrifying thought made her cling to him with the desperate tenacity of a drowning person.

Zach shifted, pressing Abby down on her back. His hands were shaking as he molded the firm roundness of her breasts. When he could no longer bear the obstacle of her clothing, he unlaced her tunic and slid it down past her shoulders, baring the soft white mounds to his gaze. His eyes dropped hot and certain to her breasts. Their pink crests were puckered into taut buds, inviting his intimate caress. He gave it freely, drawing one nipple into his mouth and laving it with the moist tip of his tongue. Abby gasped and cried out, lurching upward into the sudden heat of his caress.

Her passion mesmerized him, and suddenly it wasn't enough just to taste the sweetness of her flesh. He wanted more, needed more, had to have more or perish. His hands dropped to the hem of her tunic, gathering the material in his fingers as he slowly inched it upward above her knees. His right palm blazed a scorching path on the inside of her leg, sliding past the tender flesh of her inner thigh. A soft cry fluttered past her lips when she felt the heat of his hand caress her between her legs. It was the most intimate and arousing thing she had ever experienced.

Abby's cry seemed to bring Zach to his senses. A great shudder shook the length of his body as he raised his head and stared at her through passion-glazed eyes. His hand stilled, reluctant to leave that warm place where he longed to thrust his aching manhood. Fortunately, a small degree of sense returned before he lost complete control.

"Oh, God, Abby, stop me. I didn't mean to take my kisses so far."

Abby's thoughts scattered. Her skin was flushed and beaded with dewy drops of moisture. Her breasts tingled and burned where his lips had branded them, and the scorching heat between her thighs sent a message to her brain utterly foreign to her upbringing. She didn't want Zach to stop. She never wanted him to stop. The powerful emotions Zach had created inside her had swept away all thought of the violent deaths of her parents and the unknown fate of her little sister. If ever she needed the comfort Zach offered, it was now.

"I don't want you to stop," Abby said in a trembling whisper. "I—I need you."

Another shudder shook Zach as he reacted to her words. "You don't know what you're saying. I promised your brother I'd protect you."

"White Feather and Wind Rider no longer control my destiny," she said bitterly. "They relinquished that right when they sent me away. My life is my own to do with as I please." She reached up, dragging his lips back to hers. "I've never released you from slavery. You are still mine to command."

He watched her closely, watched the dewy moisture bead her skin, watched her silver eyes darken to stormy gray, watched her flesh grow rosy with the first flush of newly awakened sexuality.

His voice was rough with need as he rasped, "I want to love you so damn bad I ache. Your slave obeys, but don't say I didn't warn you. Tomorrow you will hate me."

Deep in her heart Abby knew Zach was right, but at the moment nothing mattered but his lips and arms and the way he made her feel. Enemy or lover, slave or freeman, white or Indian, it made no difference. Her white blood had betrayed her, making her susceptible to Zach's powerful magnetism. Tomorrow she might hate him, but she knew she'd blame herself even more. Despite that awareness, she rushed to embrace destiny with indecent haste.

Abby felt the cold bite of air against her fevered flesh as Zach slipped her tunic over her head and tossed it aside. His glance slid over her like warm honey, and her arms flew across her middle to hide herself, but he pulled her wrists away and shook his head.

"No, sweet Abby, do not hide yourself from me. You're beautiful. More perfect than any woman has a right to be."

Abby shivered. His erotic words affected her more profoundly than the cold. Zach pulled the buffalo robe over them and slid full-length atop her. Then slowly, with consummate skill and dedication, he teased her body to full, aching passion. The sweet valley between her breasts became a welcome haven for his tongue as he laved and teased the white mounds rising proudly on either side of it. When he sucked the rosy crests of her tightly curled nipples deeply into his mouth, the erratic beating of her heart pounded like thunder against his ear.

He dropped his head to her breast, his harsh breathing mute testimony to his shattered control. He struggled to suppress the urge to spread her legs and thrust into her like a wild animal, for his body demanded that he take her now. With a minimum of effort, he cast aside his clothes. Then he nudged her knees apart and settled into the cradle of her thighs. One plunge and he would attain paradise. Fortunately, his sense returned in time to prevent lust from turning him into a rapacious beast. He knew Abby was a virgin. Taking her without tenderness or restraint was unthinkable.

"The first time will hurt, sweetheart," he whispered into her ear. "I—I can still stop if you want me to." He prayed fervently that she wouldn't ask it of him, for he harbored grave doubts that he really could stop now.

Abby listened to the pounding in her blood and forgot the sexual restraint taught to her from childhood. She might curse the white blood that made her a creature of passion, but she would confront that later. "It will be

181

more painful if you stop now. I know there will be pain, and I am prepared."

"Oh, God, sweetheart, I've wanted you from the moment I set eyes on you."

His hand paused at the entrance of her body, testing her readiness to accept him. He encountered moisture, and heat, and smiled down into the glowing silver depths of her eyes. When his finger slid inside her, her eyes widened with disbelief and desire. His finger eased forward a scant inch. He felt her slick moistness tighten reflexively and encountered the barrier of her maidenhood. He eased back slightly, then pushed deeper. He heard her gasp, felt her arch against him and withdrew again. He rose above her, secure in the knowledge that she was ready to accept him.

Abby knew a moment of fear when he parted her thighs. There would be no turning back now, she thought, and experienced a pang of remorse. But the regret turned to urgency as the ache inside her pushed her over the edge of restraint.

Sensing her panic and fearing her withdrawal, Zach lowered his head and kissed her fervently, his lips tender, coaxing. And as she kissed him back, he pierced her cleanly. Abby jerked convulsively and cried out, the shock of penetration jolting her back to the harsh world of reality. Zach whispered soothing endearments into her ear, forcing his fiercely pounding heart to still as her virgin flesh stretched to accept him.

Abby had known there would be discomfort, but she hadn't expected the sharp stab of pain as Zach shattered her innocence. She felt herself stretching to accommodate his great size and blinked to dash away the tears from her eyes.

"I'm sorry, sweetheart," Zach said on a breathless whisper. "I don't want to hurt you. The pain will go away soon, and I promise you pleasure." When the tenseness began to drain from her body, Zach slid deeper inside her, sighing with sublime pleasure as her tight warmth closed around him.

"Damn," he groaned into her mouth, nearly out of his mind with the need to thrust and thrust and empty himself into her. Abby was the only woman who had ever come close to making him lose control. He couldn't recall when he had been so hot and eager, so near to bursting.

Abby felt her body soften; she could feel her moisture ease his entry, and the pain began to recede. Only a slight burning remained where they were joined—and something else. Tendrils of tingling sensation spread throughout her body, making it impossible for her to remain motionless beneath him. She moved her hips experimentally, and was rewarded by an agonized groan that slipped past Zach's lips. She writhed erotically, bringing him deeper inside her. Moaning, Zach grasped her hips, moving them to match his strokes, teaching her the rhythm that would give them the most pleasure.

If Abby had to describe the feeling of his man part sliding in and out of her woman's place she would not have found the words with which to do so. It was intensely arousing, profoundly pleasurable, deeply satisfying, but she knew there was more, much more, and waited for Zach to show her the way. There was no holding back now. She had already shamed herself in the eyes of the Cheyenne and decided to enjoy the fruits of her downfall.

"That's it, sweetheart," Zach encouraged her as Abby pressed her loins up to his, needing the strength and hardness of him in a way she had never thought possible.

Abby felt herself rushing toward a deep abyss. The buzzing in her head grew louder and she threw her arms around Zach's neck, fearing he would leave her before she found that place she searched for so desperately. He lowered his head, his mouth closing over her breast, capturing a hard, swollen nipple, and she cried out, begging for release from her anguish. Beads of perspiration clung to Zach's forehead as he fought to restrain his climax until Abby had reached hers, but his control hung by a fragile thread. "I want to wait, sweetheart, but I don't think I can." His voice was raw, harsh, ragged. His heart was beating so furiously that he feared it would burst from his chest.

Abby had no idea what Zach was referring to, but her body told her she would perish if he left her now. "Don't leave me, Zach!" she cried, unaware of what she was asking.

Zach felt the pressure building, felt his control slipping. Shifting his right hand from the soft mound of her buttock, he slid it deftly between their straining bodies. Raising himself slightly, he searched her tender slickness for the tiny bud of her passion. He found it nestled amidst a forest of sable curls and gently stroked it with the rough pad of his fingertip. The erotic friction sent her tumbling over the edge as she trembled violently and cried out.

"Zach, what is happening to me?"

"It's your first climax, sweetheart, don't fight it. Come to me, Abby, come to me now."

It started as a tingling where their bodies were joined, slowly building and spreading along nerve endings to every part of her body. A great shudder racked her as the first, blissfully erotic contraction began, and intense rapture sent sizzling heat pumping through her veins. Her mind went blank, and her thoughts ceased. The pleasure mounted until she was no longer flesh and blood. She was quivering sensation and tingling nerves as the agonizing thrill of her first climax sent her spinning to the stars.

He was losing control. Zach could not stop the hot tide that seemed to spill over inside him. He tossed back his head as his hips surged forward and he released himself in a torrent of raw, liquid flame. Sensual pleasure jolted through him. Velvet hard, his sex leaped inside her, emptying into her in hot spurts until he was replete. Still shuddering from the intensity of his release, he fell against her in a boneless heap.

Abby felt his weight pressing against her, and her arms tightened around him. She had allowed this mating between them, and she wasn't sorry. But it must never happen again. She had needed him and was honest in admitting it. But it was wrong. She and Zach walked different paths. She could not be happy anywhere but in the West. Living in a city like Boston would be like living inside a prison. Besides, she thought in self-derision, she wasn't foolish enough to think this meant anything to Zach besides a release for his body.

She had offered herself to Zach, given him her innocence, and enjoyed it. She had disgraced herself, shamed her people, and made it impossible to go back to them unless she remained unmarried for the remainder of her life. And after experiencing the pleasure Zach gave her, she doubted any other man could ever take his place. But he must never know that. He would go home to Boston, take charge of his business, and marry a woman suited to his way of life. She was Cheyenne, Abby told herself fiercely, and nothing would ever change that.

Zach raised his head, looking into the silver depths of her eyes. They were dilated so that the irises were narrow rings of smoky gray. He could feel the tension draining from her and rolled to his side, drawing her snugly into the curve of his body. She did not protest, but neither did she offer encouragement.

"You are angry," Zach said bluntly. Guilt at what he had done rode him mercilessly.

Abby regarded him squarely. "I am not angry. You did nothing I did not want you to do. What I did brought dishonor to my family. No man will ever want me now that I am no longer a maiden."

"That's not true!" Zach protested vigorously.

"Are your young women not chaste?" Abby asked. "Are they not virgins when they go to their husbands?"

Zach flushed, hesitant to tell her that the same rigid standards existed in the white world. Most young women were expected to remain pure until they married, but not all were. "Some are virgins, but not all," he hedged.

Abby grew thoughtful. "It does not matter, as I am unlikely to marry. The Cheyenne have abandoned me, and I refuse to marry a white man."

"Abby, I—"

"Go to sleep, Zach. I am tired." Deliberately she turned her back so he would not see the tears sliding down her cheeks.

"Very well, but we'll speak of this tomorrow. I knew that you would hate me; I should have listened to my conscience."

"I am not certain how I feel," Abby declared softly. "I do not wish to speak of it now."

A long sigh shuddered past Zach's lips as he turned and gathered Abby's slender body into his arms. "Sleep, sweetheart. This has been a trying day for you."

*   *   *

Her body was as cold as ice. Her overtaxed mind tried to thrust away the recurring dream, but it spun about her in a confused blur. A shudder racked her as past horrors came into frightening focus, sending her brain reeling from a vision straight from the darkest hell. A scream ripped from her throat, and she fought the arms pinning her to the ground. In her dream, some dark villain was dragging her away. She could smell the acrid scent of him, feel the terrifying strength of his bronze body. She didn't want to leave her parents, but she was so small and helpless.

Then her face was pressed against flesh—hard, warm, vibrant, sweetly scented with pine and smoke. The voice that spoke to her was not harsh, but softly comforting. The hands that stroked her were large and warm and soothing. She sensed no threat as they stroked and caressed, felt no peril as the tenseness left her and her body warmed to the persuasive heat of another.

"Hold me," Abby pleaded, distraught at the return of her nightmare. If they hadn't stumbled upon that Indian raid, she would not be having these painful recurrences of past horrors.

She clung to Zach with grim desperation, her cheek nestling against the curve of his neck. Soothed and comforted by the warmth of his body, she stirred and gazed up into his face. A haunting mixture of darkness and shadows played upon his handsome features.

"I'm sorry," she whispered, "you must think me a silly child to be frightened by a dream."

"What frightened you, Abby? Did you dream about your dead parents?"

Abby's answer surprised Zach. "I do not fear the dead. It is the living who frighten me. Despite your words to the contrary, the white people at the fort will not welcome me. They will shun and despise me because I was raised by the Cheyenne."

In the light of day, Abby would be shamed to admit to feeling fear. But in the darkest hours of night, when Zach's expression was hidden from her, her deepest fears spilled from her lips in a breathless rush. It mattered little if he laughed at her, for she was astute enough to realize that her fears were very real no matter how often Zach denied them.

"I won't let them hate you," Zach promised rashly.

"You won't always be around to protect me. I must take care of myself."

"Abby, I . . ."

"No, Zach, make no promises you cannot keep. No one knows what the future holds."

Zach wanted to promise her that she would be accepted without reservation by white society, but he knew how cruel people could be. He wanted to assure her that she would be happy with her own kind, but he could not see into the future. He wanted to tell her he'd always be around to protect her but feared it would be a lie. To compensate for his silence, he pulled her close, offering comfort with tender kisses and warm caresses. But given the new sensual awareness between them, within a very few minutes those kisses intended to offer comfort turned passionate, and the caresses offered to show compassion became bold and insistent.

"I can't believe I want you again," Zach whispered against her lips as he pulled her on top of him.

"Zach, no," Abby protested feebly. "I've shamed myself once with you tonight, I cannot do it again. I—I don't know what happened, or even how it happened, but repeating it will only complicate matters."

"I know," Zach said reasonably, "but that doesn't stop me from wanting you. I can't believe I made love to you after I promised myself it wouldn't happen." Reluctantly his arms fell away, offering her a choice of stopping or continuing.

With the length of her body pressed intimately against his, Abby felt the full potency of his masculinity and suffered a pang of remorse for being unable to leave the comfort of Zach's arms. But the warm rasp of his hair-roughened flesh against her sensitized skin made parting difficult. While he waited for her to make up her mind, Zach lifted his head and moved his mouth slowly over her half-parted lips, tasting her sweetness with gentle pressure. Then, even more gently, he pressed his tongue inside her mouth. The feather-light touch of his rough tongue against hers sent a hot flame shooting through her.

Thrilled by her unspoken willingness for him to continue, Zach's hands splayed across her back, and the heated flush of her skin sent a warm spurt of pleasure surging through him. He kissed her harder then, his tongue plundering her moist mouth in heated strokes that made her shudder with a resurgence of passion. The small moan he heard deep in Abby's throat gave him renewed hope, and his hand tangled in her hair, pulling her head back, tracing his lips over the delicate arch of her throat to the sweetly curved line of her breasts. After he lavished a few heated kisses in the valley between her breasts, he felt her sag against him.

Dragging in a deep breath, he found her mouth again, surprised when she began shaking. He drew his head back and stared at her. Her expression, reflected in pale moonlight, enchanted him. Her lips were slightly swollen from his kisses, and her breath came in soft pants. Long silky lashes shadowed her flushed cheeks, and he could feel her heart hammering against his chest.

"This is your last chance, sweetheart," Zach said as he pressed his groin into the soft hollow between her legs. "If you don't move this very minute, I'm going to make love to you again."

Abby's body refused to obey her mind. She couldn't move. All she could do was *feel*. Never in all her years had she imagined being with a man could make her feel so—so splendidly vital, so alive. Not even her previous disgraceful behavior with Zach provided the will to stop him. Just the thought of leaving the hard warmth of his body was painful. Unable to speak through the dryness of her mouth, she shook her head.

Zach groaned, pulling her closer, closer still, until not even a breath separated their bodies. He tried not to dwell on the promise given to Abby's brother, for making love to her had happened spontaneously, before either of them had time to consider the consequences. And having once tasted her sweetness, he was incapable of summoning the willpower not to do so again. Tomorrow, he vowed as he surrendered to the driving need of his body, tomorrow he would think about what had happened tonight and try to mend the damage.

"Spread your legs, sweetheart," he whispered into her ear as he guided her legs apart so that she was straddling his hips. Lifting her buttocks, he slid full and deep inside her. Zach gasped, feeling her stretch and tighten around him. "Am I hurting you?" he asked in a raspy voice so taut he felt as if he was strangling. "I can't believe how good you feel inside, like warm, slick satin."

Abby felt little discomfort this time when Zach entered her, only slight pressure—and pleasure. So much pleasure that she could hardly keep her hips still. But need for caution no longer existed as Zach grasped her buttocks and moved her up and down the solid length of him.

Exerting the most stringent control, Zach grew tense as he gritted his teeth in a valiant effort to contain the explosion of his seed into her tender depths. When he lifted his head and drew a nipple into his mouth, a shudder racked Abby's slender form and she cried out. The taste of her sweetness, and the scent of her womanliness were exciting him unbearably.

Besieged with sensation from every side, Abby surrendered to abandon. It was heaven; it was hell. She was hot; she was cold. Every muscle in her body was trembling; her breath was coming in hot, ragged gasps. Her entire body was being consumed by a raging inferno. He was driving her mad with intense, overwhelming need.

Zach lunged upward in a final thrust, and Abby felt the hot pulsating splash of his seed against her womb. Sparks flew up her spine and exploded in her brain as she climaxed. Hot spasms surged through her as she felt Zach's body jerk convulsively and heard his hoarse shout of release. Then everything went blank.

Abby regained her senses slowly, stunned by their passionate joining. She had known women received pleasure at such times if the man was skillful and patient, but she had never expected to experience anything as earth-shattering as this second mating with Zach. She was grateful that darkness prevented him from seeing her face, for her embarrassment was great. No virtuous Cheyenne maiden would give herself willingly or with so much abandon to a man before they were joined according to tribal laws.

"Abby." Zach's voice jolted her back to reality, but Abby was in no mood for conversation.

"I'm tired, Zach. Go to sleep. We'll talk tomorrow." She turned her back, refusing to be drawn into a conversation when her mind was reeling in confusion.

Zach sighed. "Very well. But we do need to discuss this—what happened tonight. Don't worry, I'll take care of you."

Indignation was bitter on Abby's tongue. "I told you before, I can take care of myself."

"Of course. Good night, Abby."

Despite his weariness, Zach lay awake until daybreak, trying to make sense out of what had just happened. By the time he fell asleep, mauve streaks colored the misty dawn. He was still sleeping when Abby rose at dawn and disappeared into the woods, returning a short time later with a handful of strange-looking herbs. Nor did he know that while he slept, she had built a fire and brewed a strong herbal tea. She had just drained a cupful of the brew when Zach awoke, watching her through slitted eyes.

"What are you drinking?"

Abby stared at him but did not answer.

"Abby? Answer me. What are you drinking?"

"Herbal tea."

"Where did you get the herbs?"

"In the woods."

"Are you ill? Why didn't you tell me?"

She regarded him narrowly. "I am not ill. The herbs are a remedy Cheyenne women use when they do not want to conceive a child."

Zach jerked upright, his face mottled with anger. The thought of Abby destroying their child was repugnant to him. "How do you know of such things?"

"All Cheyenne women are taught to prevent unwanted children. Cow Woman told me which herbs to use."

"I won't have you using vile, heathenish remedies," Zach ranted. He had no earthly idea why he was so upset except that he didn't want Abby endangering her life by taking primitive medicines.

With a calmness that belied her explosive nature, Abby rose to her feet and walked away. "I will not bear children neither of us wants."

Zach went still. That one sentence told him more about her feelings for him than anything she had ever said. "Where are you going?"

"There is a creek nearby. I wish to bathe."

Zach watched her walk away, enthralled by the seductive sway of her hips beneath the supple buckskin tunic. During the long night, he had made a decision concerning Abby. No matter how exasperating or stubborn she might be, he would make her understand that it was for her own good. He was an honorable man. His accursed pride demanded that he prove it.

Chapter Ten

Abby dawdled at the stream as long as she dared, her mind in a turmoil. How could she have allowed Zach to make love to her when it went against Cheyenne morals and principles? She might have excused the first time, but allowing him—no, inviting him—to do so a second time was inexcusable. She hugged herself and shivered, recalling how his fingers, so warm, so strong, so sure, had played upon her flesh, bringing her pleasure such as she'd never known existed. He had used her to slake his lust, and she had shamelessly encouraged him.

Zach had possessed her with the white heat of his mouth and burning thrust of his passion, and she had desired it with every fiber of her being.

Abby hung her head as a tear squeezed from

beneath a lowered lid and slid down her cheek. She had willingly surrendered to the clamoring of her flesh and welcomed Zach's loving. Feeling guilt now would change nothing, she thought bitterly as she dashed away the moisture gathering in her eyes. She was Cheyenne, she was strong, she would live through the humiliation and forget her shameless response to Zach. She must never forget that he was a white man. She had ample reason to mistrust the white race despite the fact that she was white by birth.

Once they reached Fort Lyon, she need never see Zach again, Abby thought with a hint of regret that she found disconcerting. She didn't intend to remain long at the fort in any case. It did not matter that White Feather had sent her to live in the white world; she simply could not obey him. Unable to linger a moment longer lest Zach come looking for her, Abby reluctantly walked the short distance to their camp.

Abby's pallor was so pronounced when she returned to camp that Zach grew alarmed. He knew she felt shame for what happened between them, but he was more to blame than she. He was the experienced one; he knew the consequences. What he hadn't counted on was the explosion of passion between them the moment their lips touched. What followed was inevitable. Nothing could have prevented their coming together, for Zach truly believed it had been preordained by fate.

"Are you all right?" Zach asked as he handed Abby a portion of the pemmican provided by

White Feather for their journey. "You look pale. Was it that nasty brew you drank this morning? I told you I don't hold with heathen remedies."

"I am fine," Abby replied evenly. "My people are not heathens. We believe in *Heammawihio*, The Wise One Above. We believe the spirits of the sun, the earth, the moon, and the water give us blessings and rule our lives."

"Sorry," Zach mumbled, "I didn't mean to offend you. Before we continue on to the fort, there's something we must discuss. About last night . . ."

Abby sent him a wary glance. She had grave doubts that anything Zach had to say would help their situation. "Forget last night," she cut in before he could finish his sentence. "It should not have happened, and I do not want to be reminded of it." She fastened her eyes on the ground, aware that her expression would betray her lie. She'd never forget how Zach's loving made her feel or the gamut of emotions she experienced in his arms.

"Look at me, Abby," Zach said, raising her chin so he could see her face. "We can't deny what happened between us. Lord knows, I feel badly about it. I truly didn't mean to take advantage of you, but the situation became explosive so quickly I couldn't stop. I want to make amends."

Abby's expression grew mutinous. "It would please me if you never mentioned my lapse again. What is done is done. I am as much to blame as you are. When we arrive at Fort Lyon, we will part and go our own ways."

"I warned that you would hate me in the morning," Zach reminded her, "but I'm not sorry we made love. That's why I'm prepared to do the honorable thing. We will marry when we reach Fort Lyon."

Abby's mouth fell open. "Marry? Marry a man who kills my people and drives them from their ancestral home?" Her eyes blazed with angry defiance. "I will not marry a White-eyes!"

"I promised your father and brother I'd protect you," Zach said reasonably, "and I failed. I will do what is necessary. It is my fault you lost your innocence. I couldn't control myself, and because of it you are no longer a maiden."

"You are foolish if you think I had no say in what happened last night. Do you think me a weakling with no will of my own? Bah," she spat disgustedly. "Cheyenne women are not victims who have no control over their lives. I will go to the fort, but I will not marry you. I will stay with your friends, but if I do not like them I will leave and join White Feather at Sand Creek."

"Be reasonable," Zach chided. "What we did last night could have made a child. I have little faith in your heathen's remedy."

Abby sent him a contemptuous sneer. "It has always worked for our women. The Cheyenne believe it is not good to have children close together in years."

"I have thought long and hard on this, Abby. It is in your best interest to marry me. Being alone with me now, like this, is damaging to your reputation."

"I care little what White-eyes think of me."

"It should matter, since you're going to live with them. You've much to learn, Abby, and I fear people won't be kind to you."

"I don't expect kindness from White-eyes. And I don't want a husband who feels pity for me. You told me you intend to return to Boston one day, and I would not be happy in a large city such as you described. Your family would not approve of me."

Zach sighed. Regrettably, everything Abby said was true. It would be heartless of him to marry her and take her to Boston, where she would wither and undoubtedly suffer in so restrictive an atmosphere. She was a free spirit who needed space to spread her wings and soar. In Boston she'd be like a captive bird, beating its wings against its cage trying to escape. But she was wrong when she accused him of feeling only pity for her. Zach wasn't certain how to describe his feelings for Abby, but pity had nothing to do with it.

"Leave my family out of this, Abby. I speak for myself. I can't force you to marry me, but I urge you to think about it."

"At least Painted Horse was honest in his desire to make me his wife," Abby said with scathing sarcasm.

A muscle in Zach's jaw jumped. "Are you calling me a liar?"

"Your misplaced honor is making you blind

to the difference in our upbringing. Marriage between us would be a disaster. My family name is Larson. They come from farm stock, not a socially prominent family like yours. Our worlds are too different. Please do not speak of it again."

Zach glared at her, undecided whether to shake her until her sense returned or kiss her until she was too weak to protest. He did neither as he shrugged his shoulders and turned away. If Abby refused his help, he wouldn't offer it again, even though he felt responsible for her. If not for his intervention, Abby would be on her way to Sand Creek with White Feather. Unfortunately, her prejudice against whites made helping her most difficult.

"There's the fort up ahead," Zach said as he pointed to the large structure visible in the distance.

Fort Lyon sat on a flat, arid plain in a wilderness populated mostly by Indians and wild animals. The few settlers who lived in the area were clustered around the fort, living in small cabins within sight of the stockade. Of late, the warring Cheyenne, Crow, and Ute had made living in the inhospitable area more dangerous than ever. With the war still raging in the East, the forts were severely undermanned, and the few army regulars depended on Colorado volunteers to help them protect settlers.

"It is not very impressive," Abby said disdainfully.

"Few forts are," Zach admitted, "but they were built for the protection of the settlers, not for beauty. Mostly Colorado volunteers man the fort now. When I first arrived at Fort Lyon, I heard that Colonel Chivington would arrive in November with six hundred members of the Colorado Cavalry, made up of men who had volunteered solely to fight Indians."

"White Feather told us that Major Wynkoop assured Black Kettle that the People would be protected by the soldiers as long as they remained at Sand Creek and were peaceful. But I have heard of Colonel Chivington. He has little regard for our people."

"I'm sure Major Wynkoop is a man of his word," Zach said with a confidence he didn't feel. Wynkoop had recently been replaced by Major Anthony, and no one knew if Anthony would honor the agreement with Black Kettle and the Southern Cheyenne. And from what he knew of Chivington, nothing good could come of the man's arrival with his six hundred Indian-haters.

They fell silent as they neared the fort. The gate was open and they rode through the entrance with little interference from the sentry, who blanched when he recognized the new arrival.

"Gawd damn, if it ain't Captain Mercer! We thought you'd been killed by them murderin' Cheyenne." He glanced slyly at Abby. "Where'd ya pick up the squaw, Captain?"

Zach bristled in sudden anger. "Show some

respect, Private. This lady is no squaw. She is Miss Abby Larson, a white woman who has been raised by the Cheyenne."

The private's gaze slid over Abby in an insulting manner. "Sorry," he gulped, nodding at Abby with a marked lack of respect. But Zach's quelling look was fierce enough to put the fear of God into him.

"He meant no offense, Abby," Zach said, wishing he could wipe the leering grin from the private's face.

"I am not offended," Abby insisted haughtily. "I am not ashamed of being Cheyenne."

Zach sighed, exasperated. "You are not Cheyenne. The sooner you realize that, the better off you'll be. I need to report to headquarters first; then I'll take you to meet the Porters. You'll like them, I promise."

Five minutes later, Zach and Abby were introduced to Major Scott Anthony, Major Wynkoop's replacement, who had arrived at the fort during Zach's absence. The commanding officer stared at Zach as if he were seeing a ghost.

"Captain Mercer, I was led to believe you were dead. Before he left, Major Wynkoop said your patrol had been attacked by a Cheyenne war party. All bodies except yours were accounted for. Everyone assumed you'd been captured and tortured to death."

"They were only half right," Zach replied. "I was captured, but I escaped torture and death with the help of the young woman standing before you."

Anthony tried to hide his contempt as he noted Abby's Indian garb and mistook her for an Indian. "Why would an Indian squaw save your life? Bringing her to the fort wasn't smart, Captain. These people have good reason to hate the Cheyenne. She won't be safe here."

Never had Zach come so close to striking a superior officer. Did the man have no eyes in his head? Anyone could see Abby was white. Or could they? Was she white only in his eyes?

"Before you judge harshly, Major, let me introduce Abby Larson to you. Abby is as white as you or I. She was raised by White Feather after her parents were killed. I talked her adoptive father into returning her to her own kind."

"Raised by White Feather, you say?" Anthony's voice held a note of disbelief. "If you have been in White Feather's camp as a captive and lived to tell about it, you are a lucky man indeed, Captain." He turned to stare at Abby. "Does she speak English?"

"I speak the white man's tongue well enough," Abby replied, looking down her nose at him. "I had just seen six summers when White Feather adopted me." She was careful to make no mention of her brother, for she didn't want his name associated with the renegades who were on the warpath.

"I'm sorry, Miss Larson, you don't look—that is, your skin and hair are—"

"—Darkened with walnut stain," Zach told

him. "I assured Miss Larson she'd receive a warm welcome from the white community. I hope I've not been premature in my assumption."

Anthony shifted uncomfortably beneath the intensity of Zach's blue eyes. "You were quite right, Captain Mercer. We are most happy to welcome Miss Larson into our midst. Will she be returning to relatives?"

"I have no relatives," Abby answered. "At least, none that I know of."

"I thought Sergeant Porter and his wife might take Abby in until she decides what she wants to do with her life, or relatives can be located. They have a daughter about Abby's age who can help her adjust to white society."

"I have no objection to that arrangement if it's agreeable to the Porters," Anthony contended. "Meanwhile, I'll look through the records for mention of relatives who might be willing to accept responsibility for Miss Larson."

"I have seen twenty summers, Major," Abby informed him, "and I am quite capable of looking after myself."

"Unless you marry quickly, you will have no means of support," Anthony said, not unkindly. "The Porters can't be expected to support you forever."

Abby sent Zach a telling look. She hadn't thought of that. The Cheyenne had no need for money; the land provided all they needed. But she was strong; she could work. "I will work to earn my keep."

"That won't be necessary," Zach interjected. "I don't expect the Porters to support Miss Larson. Since I was the one who convinced White Feather to let his daughter return to the white world, I will be responsible for her financially, at least until she no longer needs my support."

Abby felt herself teetering on the brink of seething anger. They were talking about her as if she were deaf and her opinions didn't matter. She wasn't a brainless idiot unable to think for herself. Major Anthony's contempt for her was potent enough to reach out and touch. Did he think her a savage who'd murder them all in their beds? Of course he did, she told herself. Her white skin made no difference, while being raised by Cheyenne made her capable of committing all kinds of foul deeds.

Zach would have done anything to protect Abby from this kind of prejudice. He knew hatred for Indians ran deep in this part of the country where suffering had been the greatest, but he never suspected it would be directed at one of their own kind. Would everyone at the fort consider Abby a savage? Lord, he hoped not. He didn't bring her here to be discriminated against and insulted.

"If you'll excuse us, Major, Miss Larson is tired after her long journey. I'll take her to the Porters, then report back here for a full explanation of what transpired during my absence." He saluted smartly and pushed Abby before him out the door.

"I told you they would hate me," Abby contended once they were outside.

"Not everyone feels as Major Anthony does about Indians. Besides, you aren't Indian—you're white."

"Tell that to your major. I want to go home, Zach. I want to join White Feather at Sand Creek."

"It's already been settled, Abby. White Feather decided that you don't belong at Sand Creek, and he's a wise man. Give it time. If you aren't happy, I'll personally escort you to Sand Creek. But you must allow yourself time to adjust to your new circumstances."

Abby frowned. "I don't like being a burden."

"Isn't it the same with the Cheyenne? You told me yourself that your brother was responsible for you. Didn't he provide for you and see to your welfare?"

"You aren't my brother."

Zach groaned and rolled his eyes. "Thank God for that small favor." The feelings he had for Abby were anything but brotherly. "Come along, I'll take you to the Porters."

Abby hung back. "What—what if they won't have me?"

Zach grinned. "Don't worry, everyone isn't like Major Anthony. Milly Porter will love you, and you'll like her. Trust me in this."

"Do I have a choice?" Her voice held a note of fear that was foreign to her nature, and Zach felt fleeting remorse for insisting that she leave those she loved.

"None at all. Just remember, I won't let anyone hurt you. If you had agreed to marry me, you'd be safe. It's still not too late to change your mind."

"What you ask is impossible. I told you before that I do not want your pity. If you must take me to the Porters, then let us go."

"Oh, you poor dear child," Milly Porter cried as she gathered Abby against her ample bosom. "What you must have suffered all those years. Thank God, Captain Mercer rescued you from those heathens. You must think of this as your home until relatives can be found to take you in."

Milly Porter seemed oblivious to the sudden stiffness of Abby's spine, or her fierce frown. From the moment tenderhearted Milly saw Abby, looking so lost and forlorn, her heart went out to her. After Zach's brief explanation, she had invited Abby to live with her and her family as long as she wanted. Pete Porter, as compassionate a man as his stout wife, extended his own invitation, just as Zach had hoped.

Pete Porter was an experienced Indian fighter, who had reached middle age through cunning and caution. He felt pity for the young girl separated from the white world and raised by Indians. He considered it his Christian duty to help civilize the girl, even though Zach had told him privately that Abby would be a reluctant student.

The one person in the family who viewed Abby's arrival with revulsion and distrust was lovely, willful Belinda, the only child of the Porters to survive infancy.

"I hope you don't think it presumptuous of me to bring Abby here," Zach said, once Abby managed to free herself from Milly's embrace. "I felt certain you'd welcome her."

"Land sakes, Captain Mercer, of course we'd welcome Abby," Milly said. "She'll be great company for Belinda. Isn't that so, dear?"

Belinda Porter gave her blond curls a careless toss, her irritation obvious. "You don't really expect me to keep company with a savage, do you, Mama?"

"Belinda! Mind your manners," Milly chided sternly. "I expect you to make poor Abby feel at home. She's been through a great deal. Where is your charity?"

"Charity aside, I'm not sure it's wise to open our home to the girl, Mama. Just look at her. She's a savage. How do you know she won't murder us all in our beds?"

"I hardly think that's likely, Belinda," Zach said with a hint of censure. "I'd hoped you and Abby might find common ground. There's much she could learn from you."

Belinda batted long golden lashes at Zach, her almond-shaped hazel eyes regarding him in a flirtatious manner that was not lost on Abby. "Do you really think so, Captain Mercer? I've always considered myself a lady, so perhaps I *can* be of some help. Are you sure she's not dangerous?"

"I will try to keep my knife sheathed," Abby said with scathing contempt. "I do not want to stay where I am not wanted."

"Now, now, none of that," Milly soothed in her motherly fashion. "I'm sure you two girls will do just fine together once you get to know each other. You can share Belinda's room, Abby. And we'll see about getting you something decent to wear."

Abby frowned. Something decent to wear? This was her finest tunic. She had donned it before arriving at the fort so she'd look her best. It was elaborately beaded and fringed and so soft that it molded her curves perfectly.

"Mama! You can't expect me to share my bed with a white savage!" Belinda turned to Zach, her eyes wide with mock horror. "Captain Mercer, surely you understand my fear. She isn't even tamed yet." She sidled up beside him, leaning against him in helpless appeal. She reached out and touched his arm, an innocent gesture, but one calculated to tantalize.

Assuming her fear was real, Zach grasped Belinda's small hands in his and gazed into her eyes. "I give you my word, Miss Porter. Abby is not dangerous to you or your parents. I ask only that you treat her kindly and teach her to adjust to the white world."

Belinda gave Zach a simpering smile. "Put like that, I can hardly refuse."

Zach returned Belinda's smile. "I knew I could

count on you. And now I must really leave, but first I'd like to have a private word with Abby if I might."

"Of course, Captain Mercer," Milly acquiesced graciously. "Come along, Belinda, you can help me pick out some of your clothes for Abby."

"I've duties to attend to," Pete Porter said as he ducked out the door.

Belinda shot Abby a venomous look before turning and following her mother into the bedroom.

Abby felt more bereft than she ever had in her life. She had told Zach that this wasn't going to work, and after meeting Belinda Porter she was sure of it. Not only did the beautiful young woman despise her for her Cheyenne upbringing, but Belinda was besotted with Zach, whether Zach realized it or not. It was as obvious as the nose on her face that Belinda was jealous of the time Abby spent with Zach and intended to make life miserable for her.

"It's turning out just as I hoped," Zach said on a sigh of relief. "You'll do fine here with the Porters. Belinda can teach you everything you need to know about being a lady."

"I'm sure she can," Abby intoned dryly. "Don't worry about me, Zach. I can take care of myself." *And I won't be here long*, she thought but did not say.

"If you need me, I won't be far away. My private quarters are just across the parade grounds. Number twenty-three." He stared at her hard, then said, "If you should find that your—Indian remedy did not work, come to me immediately. Meanwhile, I'll be around to check on you from time to time. We're so undermanned right now that I suppose I'll be kept quite busy, but I'll always find time for you."

After being with Abby on a daily basis for the past few weeks, Zach found it difficult to part from her. What he really wanted to do was take her in his arms and kiss her until her lips softened and she grew breathless.

"Have no fear; the herbs my people employ are quite reliable."

Zach stared at her lips, wanting to kiss her so badly it was like a physical blow to his gut. But he didn't dare, not with the Porters in the next room. "It's time I left. Be happy, Abby," he whispered softly before turning and walking out the door.

Abby stared at the door, her eyes bleak, her mind spinning dizzily. She remembered the night she and Zach had lain entwined in one another's arms, not as enemies but as lovers. He had taught her how to be a woman, and she had surrendered her innocence with the abandon of a fallen woman. She had gloried in all those wonderful, erotic things he had done to her and wanted it never to end. But as with all good things, it had ended, leaving guilt and remorse in its place. Unfortunately, not enough remorse remained to prevent her from wanting the sweet joy of his loving again—and again.

But she despised his pity and had rejected his proposal, knowing it was offered to salve his guilty conscience. He was white, and White-eyes couldn't be trusted. Her heart was too fragile to place into the keeping of a man who would break it.

"Is he gone?" Belinda walked into the room, her disappointment keen when she saw that Zach had already left.

"He is gone," Abby said flatly.

Belinda gave her a hard look. "Is there something between you and Captain Mercer that I don't know about?"

"I do not understand," Abby said, deciding to play dumb. "The white man's tongue is difficult for me."

"I think you understand perfectly," Belinda charged. "I know all about Indians. They're savage heathens without morals. How many Indian men have you lain with? Ten? Twenty? One hundred? Did you add Zach to your list of lovers?"

If Abby hadn't been so stunned by Belinda's vicious attack, she would have launched one of her own, wielding her blade with swiftness and dexterity. Parting the buffalo robe still hugging her shoulders, she fingered the hilt of the knife hanging in a sheath at her waist, tempted beyond endurance to plunge it into the blond witch's heart.

Belinda blanched when she saw Abby's hand close on the knife she hadn't been aware of until now. She backed away slowly, her fear palpable as she watched Abby's hand caress the hilt of the knife.

"You wouldn't dare," she hissed from between clenched teeth.

"Wouldn't I?" Abby countered. "You have insulted me with your mean words. The Cheyenne are honorable people. Their maidens are pure and chaste. I suggest you rethink your opinion of them or suffer the consequences."

"You're bluffing," Belinda challenged. "You wouldn't dare harm me. Captain Mercer placed you in our home. Think what it would do to his reputation. His responsibility toward you ended when he brought you to Fort Lyon." She laughed harshly. "He would never saddle himself with a savage like you."

"Perhaps he needs a woman like you," Abby said sweetly. "You may have him, Belinda. Perhaps he will even take you back to his Boston when he leaves here. But if I were you, I would not count too heavily on it. You do not look to be Zach's type."

"You call him Zach?" Belinda asked nastily. "No proper young woman would address a man by his Christian name."

"I am not Christian, so the rules do not apply to me. I earned the right when I saved Zach's life and made him my slave."

"Your slave!" Belinda's eyes nearly popped out of her head. "My God, it is worse than I thought. What exactly does a slave do?"

"Zach did whatever I asked of him," Abby said in a tone that mocked propriety.

Belinda's mouth was still hanging open when Milly entered the room. "Oh, is Captain Mercer gone? Such a kind man." She turned to Abby. "I hope you'll be happy here, dear. Why don't you go with Belinda. We chose clothes that should go well with your coloring. I hope you like them. After a nice hot bath and new clothes, you'll feel like a different woman. You must have gone through so much during those years with the Cheyenne. Did they mistreat you, dear?"

Abby knew Milly wasn't being deliberately unkind, but it angered her to think that people believed she had been mistreated by White Feather and his people when just the opposite was true. White Feather and Gray Dove had been the kind of parents a girl would wish for when her own were no longer available.

"I was not mistreated," Abby maintained, wanting to put the subject to rest once and for all. "I had a most happy childhood. My adoptive parents doted on me and Wind Rider."

"Wind Rider?" Milly asked curiously.

"Wind Rider is my brother."

"Your Indian brother?" Belinda asked contemptuously.

"My white brother. We were together when White Feather found us."

"Where is he now? Will he join you at Fort Lyon?"

"Wind Rider would never consent to leave the People."

"Your people are white, dear," Milly reminded her.

Abby's chin rose several notches, but she offered no reply. What could she say?

"Well, it doesn't matter. You're here with your own kind where you belong. It will work out, you'll see."

No, you will see, Abby thought as she followed Belinda to the room they would share. I will not stay long enough for it to work out.

Chapter Eleven

"I will not wear that instrument of torture!" Abby's set jaw and flashing silver eyes effectively conveyed her contempt of modern convention.

"But, dear, corsets are required wear for women," Milly said with a hint of annoyance. "You'll grow accustomed to it in time."

"Why is it necessary to wear one?" Abby questioned. "The dress fits just fine without one. Aren't two petticoats and a"—she searched her limited vocabulary for the word—"a chemise enough? My tunic is much more comfortable. I think it quite beautiful. I beaded it myself."

"Not wearing a corset is like going naked," Belinda said, eying Abby's slim figure enviously. She wished her waist were as slim and her breasts as full and womanly as Abby's. "And that tunic is positively indecent. I can see the outline of your nipples beneath it. Have you no shame?"

"The Cheyenne find nothing shameful about the body or its functions," Abby declared defensively.

"But you are no longer living with the Cheyenne, dear," Milly reminded her gently. "You must observe white customs if you are to get along in our society. Captain Mercer left you in our charge so that we may teach you proper conduct for a young lady."

"It's hopeless," Belinda sighed in exaggerated disgust. "It matters little that her skin is almost white again or that her hair is nearly free of walnut stain. Nothing will change her inside."

"I do not wish to hurt you, Milly," Abby said, "but I will not wear the corset. It is not good to confine the body so it cannot breathe. I will wear the dress and the petticoats to please you, but I refuse to torture my body with the corset."

Milly accepted defeat gracefully, but she definitely wasn't going to give up on Abby. Just getting her into the dress and petticoats had been a struggle. "Very well, Abby, we'll forego the corset for now. But I absolutely forbid you to wear the moccasins."

Abby looked down at her moccasin-clad feet, wiggling her toes in the roomy comfort of the soft buffalo hide. She had tried to squeeze her feet into the hard leather shoes Milly had purchased for her from the post sutler, but they pinched so badly that she considered them next to useless. As far as she could see, they were just another one of those senseless articles of clothing whites wore to torture their bodies.

"I see nothing wrong with my moccasins," she declared in the same tone of voice she had used when arguing over the corset. "Why must whites be so impractical when it comes to clothing their bodies? The Cheyenne—"

"And I repeat," Milly said sternly, "you are no longer living with those savages. You are white, you've always been white, you were born white. Now, about the shoes. You wouldn't want Captain Mercer to think I've been remiss in my duty, would you?"

Abby didn't care what Zach thought. It was foolish to think he cared about her. Nearly two weeks had passed since he had left her with the Porters, and she had neither seen nor heard from him since then. She had watched him as he rode out on patrol, but she had not spoken to him personally. It had hurt when she learned that Belinda had seen and spoken to Zach on more than one occasion—and had bragged about it afterward. Belinda made certain Abby knew that a handsome unattached male like Zach received more than his share of attention from the unmarried young ladies residing inside the walls of Fort Lyon.

Did he ever think about the night they had made love? Abby wondered wistfully. Was he making love to other women in the same way he had made love to her? She knew so little of the white world. But from what little she did know, it was obvious that white males had none of the sexual restraint practiced by Cheyenne men. She also had learned that women who slept with men for money came regularly to Fort Lyon from Denver. Belinda told her they were called whores. Did Zach think she was a whore for sharing his mat?

"What about the shoes, Abby?" Milly's high-pitched voice brought Abby abruptly from her reverie.

"I will consider wearing them," Abby promised. If White Feather hadn't sent her away, she wouldn't be forced to accept these stupid customs. She rued the day Zach Mercer had been dragged into their camp more dead than alive.

Wielding a fork and knife was not an easy accomplishment, Abby thought as she stabbed a piece of meat on her plate. It skittered across the plate and landed on the table beside her. Using her fingers, she picked it up and popped it into her mouth. Thinking no one was watching, she took a potato with her fingers and scooped it into her mouth.

"Really, Abby, must you be so crude?" Belinda rebuked her. "Use your fork."

"Fingers are more practical," Abby declared.

"But it's not the right way, dear," Milly explained patiently.

Being made to feel like an ignorant child shamed Abby, and she rose abruptly from her chair.

"Where are you going, dear?" Milly asked, peering at Abby over the top of her wire-rimmed spectacles. She hated to be constantly badgering Abby because she was genuinely fond of the girl, but Abby had much to learn if she was to survive in the white world.

"For a walk," Abby replied. Milly sighed, wondering from which parent Abby had inherited her stubborn streak.

"It's quite cold outside, and growing dark. Take a wrap and do be careful."

"For heaven's sake, Mama, she's not a child," Belinda said crossly. "Abby has been taking walks in the evenings since her arrival."

"Yes, I know, but nevertheless . . ."

"Belinda is right, Milly," Pete added in support of his daughter. "Abby is not a child, and I'm sure she can take care of herself." He smiled at Abby. "Don't stay out too late, Abby; the weather is turning bitter."

Abby returned Pete's smile. She genuinely liked the crusty sergeant. He was neither condescending nor disapproving; he merely accepted her. But he rarely interfered with what he considered "woman's business." "I am accustomed to living in the open. Do not worry about me."

She left the room, stopping only to exchange the tight shoes she had been forced to wear for a pair of comfortable moccasins. She'd feel safer carrying her knife, but it had disappeared shortly after she had arrived. She suspected that Belinda had taken it one night while she was sleeping.

"You really are too easy on Abby, Papa," Belinda said peevishly. "How do you expect her to learn if you give in to her so easily?"

"The girl is twenty years old, Belinda. It isn't my place to dictate to her. She's here to learn, and I hate to see her miserable while she's adjusting."

"How long will she be with us?" Belinda asked sullenly.

"Major Anthony is trying to trace her relatives. He looked up the records and found that her parents had hailed from a small town in Ohio. He sent a telegram to the authorities, and they are looking into the matter."

Abby had heard the conversation, having just returned from the bedroom before letting herself out the front door. When Pete mentioned Ohio, she recalled leaving that state and traveling to St. Louis, the gathering place for the wagon train. But try as she might, she could not recall any relatives who might still be living in Ohio. She had only Wind Rider, and she feared she might never see him again.

The November night was cold and crisp with a promise of snow. A few stars struggled to survive in the cloudy sky, and the sliver of moon was all but obscured by a frosty haze. Abby had made a nightly habit of strolling around the parade ground after supper because she enjoyed the solitude. She hated being confined by the four wooden walls of the white man's lodge and despised the lack of privacy.

Abby's mind wandered to happier times as she followed her normal course past post headquarters, the livery, enlisted men's barracks, and officers' housing. The circuit would be complete when she finally returned to the small group of houses set aside for the senior enlisted men and officers who had family with them. She paid little heed to the three men who lurked in the shadows of the barracks, smoking and talking in low voices.

"I told you that white squaw passed by the barracks about this time every night," one of the men whispered when he spotted Abby.

"Do you think she's willing?" the second man hissed.

"Hell, yes, she's willing," the third man shot back. "She's lived with savages long enough to think and act the way they do. You know Injuns have no morals. I reckon she'll be tickled pink to oblige all three of us. You can bet your boots Captain Mercer had his fill of her. Rumor has it he was her slave." He licked his lips, imagining the lascivious implications of that statement. "He probably serviced her the whole time he was held captive by the Cheyenne."

"Drag her behind the livery where no one will see us," suggested the first man. "I don't want to share her with the others. Maybe we can keep her as our private whore. Those prostitutes from Denver don't come out here often enough to suit me."

"Our private whore. Hot damn!" the second man said excitedly. "Look lively, men, here she comes."

Unsuspecting, Abby walked past the barracks, just as she had done on previous nights. She realized her danger a minute too late as the three men stepped out of the shadows into her path. Becoming the victim of assault was the last thing on Abby's mind as she tried to detour around them. When one of the men grasped her arm, she reached automatically for the knife at her waist, then remembered that she no longer had it.

"Let me go!" Her voice was calm despite her desperation. Unable to see the faces of the men clearly in the darkness, she knew instinctively they meant her harm.

"Not on your life, honey," one of the men growled as he started dragging her behind the livery. She struggled fiercely, managing to open up a gash beneath the eye of one of her attackers with her sharp nails.

"Little she-wolf! I'm gonna enjoy taming you. Why should Captain Mercer be the only one to sample what's between your legs? It ain't like you're a lady, living with Injuns and all. I'll bet you're real good at making a man happy."

"White dog!" Abby snarled viciously. "The only savages I know are men like you. Let me go!" She struggled to escape, but three pairs of hands forced her into the alley between the barracks and the livery. If she didn't do something fast, it would be too late for her. She

Thrill to the most sensual, adventure-filled Historical Romances on the market today...

FROM ▐█ *LEISURE BOOKS*

As a home subscriber to the Leisure Romance Book Club, you'll enjoy the best in today's BRAND-NEW Historical Romance fiction. For over twenty years, Leisure Books has brought you the award-winning, high-quality authors you know and love to read. Each Leisure Historical Romance will sweep you away to a world of high adventure...and intimate romance. Discover for yourself all the passion and excitement millions of readers thrill to each and every month.

Save $5.⁰⁰ Each Time You Buy!

Six times a year, the Leisure Romance Book Club brings you four brand-new titles from Leisure Books, America's foremost publisher of Historical Romances. EACH PACKAGE WILL SAVE YOU $5.00 FROM THE BOOKSTORE PRICE! And you'll never miss a new title with our convenient home delivery service.

Here's how we do it. Each package will carry a FREE 10-DAY EXAMINATION privilege. At the end of that time, if you decide to keep your books, simply pay the low invoice price of $14.96, no shipping or handling charges added. HOME DELIVERY IS ALWAYS FREE. With today's top Historical Romance novels selling for $4.99 and higher, our price SAVES YOU $5.00 with each shipment.

AND YOUR FIRST FOUR-BOOK SHIPMENT IS TOTALLY FREE!
IT'S A BARGAIN YOU CAN'T BEAT! A Super $19.96 Value!
▐█ *LEISURE BOOKS* A Division of Dorchester Publishing Co., Inc.

Get Four Books Totally FREE— A $19.96 Value!

▼ Tear Here and Mail Your FREE Book Card Today! ▼

PLEASE RUSH
MY FOUR FREE
BOOKS TO ME
RIGHT AWAY!

Leisure Romance Book Club
65 Commerce Road
Stamford CT 06902-4563

opened her mouth to scream.

"No you don't," someone growled into her ear seconds before a hard hand came down upon her mouth. "You know you want this, honey. Don't be shy—we ain't gonna hurt you. Just pretend we're Injuns. There's a pile of hay behind the livery, where we'll be nice and cozy."

It was as dark as pitch in the alley, and Abby mourned the loss of her knife. Did these men consider her without feelings because she had been raised by Indians? Inspired by desperation, she suddenly went limp. She prayed that her captors would relax their hold if she pretended to be agreeable. Her ploy worked. The hand was removed from her mouth.

"I knew you'd see it our way, honey. If you're nice to us, we'll make it real good for you— won't we, boys?"

"You're hurting me," Abby complained. "There's no need to be so rough."

Immediately two pairs of hands fell away, leaving the third man to hustle her through the alley. Summoning her strength, Abby turned her body toward the man holding her arm, raised her knee and kicked viciously at his groin, asking *Heammawihio* to guide her. The Wise One Above must have heard her plea, for her aim was true. Clutching his privates, the soldier howled and doubled over in pain. Swift as a fox, Abby turned and fled down the alley. She heard the men pounding after her and lifted her skirts to free her legs so she could run faster.

Abby had no idea in which direction she had fled until she glanced around to get her bearings and found herself on the opposite side of the parade ground, in the area housing bachelor officers. She had passed this way many times on her nightly walks and realized she was close to Zach's rooms. Since it was very cold out, and most of the fort's occupants were enjoying their supper, the parade grounds were virtually deserted. The sentry was stationed some distance away at the gate, and no one was nearby to come to her aid. She considered screaming, but if she did it would cause a stir, and perhaps she'd be blamed for what happened. Most people at the fort seemed anxious to think the worst of her, and she didn't want to embarrass the Porters.

"Hey, honey, what did you run for? I told you we wouldn't hurt you."

The men were pounding after her, and Abby had only a few precious seconds to make a decision. Her brief hesitation nearly proved disastrous. Hands tugged at her coat. Twisting her body, she managed to slide her arms out of the sleeves and slip away. Without a backward glance, she directed her feet toward number twenty-three, only a few steps away. She felt fingers grasping her arm just as her hands reached for the doorknob. There was no time to knock, or even wonder if the door was locked as she turned the knob and burst inside when the door opened to her touch.

Realizing that their prey had eluded them, her pursuers gave up the chase, cursing their bad luck at having been denied a night's pleasure.

Zach sat behind a desk piled high with papers. He had shoved most of them aside and was writing a letter to his brother, telling him that he was still alive and well and looking forward to returning to Boston. But the longer he stared at the sheet of paper, the more convinced he became that he would be lying if he told Paul that he wanted to return to Boston. Hard on the heels of that thought came the surprising revelation that he wanted to stay where he could keep an eye on Miss Abby Larson.

More than keep an eye on her, if the truth be known. He had deliberately kept his distance these past two weeks, allowing her time to settle in and adjust to the change in her circumstances. On more than one occasion, he had wanted to call on Abby, but Belinda had told him that the family requested that he not visit until she had adjusted to life in the white community. Reluctantly, he had acquiesced to their wishes, keeping tabs on Abby's progress through Pete and Belinda.

Zach was aware that the family was having a hard time dealing with Abby's rebellious nature. He himself had intimate knowledge of the little vixen's stubbornness. Though he had been busy nearly every minute of every day since his return to Fort Lyon, he hadn't been too preoccupied to remember how good it felt to have Abby in his arms, how incredible his pleasure when he thrust inside her and felt her tight warmth surround him. No woman of his acquaintance had ever responded to him with the same innocent passion Abby displayed. She was uniquely different. Few woman possessed the kind of courage and strength of character that had allowed her to adjust to the cultural shock of being captured by Indians at a young age.

An unexpected racket at the door of his modest quarters brought Zach surging to his feet. Suddenly the door burst open, and Abby rushed inside, panting raggedly, her eyes wild. She slammed the door behind her, leaning against it as she sought to bring her breathing under control. She wore no coat and was shivering uncontrollably.

Zach was beside her instantly, his arms supporting her as he led her inside. "My God, Abby, what is it? What are you doing here at this ungodly hour? Has something happened at the Porters?"

Swallowing convulsively, Abby shook her head. "N—no, everything is fine at the Porters. I always go for a walk this time of night. I didn't think—that is, I never had a problem before. Those men . . . They wanted to . . ."

When he finally realized what Abby was talking about, Zach's expression grew fierce. Gently pushing her aside, he opened the door and stepped outside, searching the darkness for the men who had threatened her. His fists were clenched, his body tense. Once he caught the men, he'd tear them limb from limb, then see them drummed out of the army.

What must the Porters be thinking to allow Abby to roam about the fort alone at night? The remote outpost was manned with a number of men who had joined the army to escape an unsavory past. Those men would think nothing of assaulting a woman like Abby, whose past association with the Cheyenne made her vulnerable to attack.

A vile curse slipped past Zach's lips when he spied Abby's coat lying on the ground nearby. It enraged him to think that the men had escaped so easily. Returning to his quarters, he shut the door and locked it. After hanging her coat over the back of a chair, he went directly to Abby, who stood in the center of the room looking confused and hurt. "Are you all right, Abby? Did they hurt you?" She shook her head. "How many were there? Did you know them?"

"It was dark," Abby replied. "I wasn't able to see their faces."

"What about their names?"

Abby searched her mind. "I don't think they mentioned names."

Zach spat out another curse. "Do you recall what they said?"

Abby stared at him, then nodded her head, her expressive face giving vent to her fear and anger. "Yes, they spoke. They accused me of— they said I had lain with men, many men. Even with you." Lightning flashed in the storm clouds gathered in her eyes. "How did they know I had lain with you? Did it give you pleasure to tell them about us?"

Zach paled. "My God, Abby, you don't think that I—that I would tell anyone what happened between us, do you? I have many faults, but bragging about women I've bedded isn't among them. Just calm down and tell me everything you can remember about those men. How many were there?"

She was still shaking, a natural reaction to the shock of being assaulted, and Zach led her toward the stove in the middle of the room. He sat down in the chair nearby, pulling her into his lap.

"Th—three men," Abby said through chattering teeth. "No names were mentioned, but I know I'd recognize their voices if I heard them again."

"Exactly what did they say?"

"They wanted to—to take me behind the livery and—and—"

"I get the picture," Zach said tightly. He hugged her fiercely, wanting to end her fears and protect her from vicious men and malicious gossip. "It won't happen again, I promise."

"Do not make promises you cannot keep," Abby said bitterly. She regarded him intently. "I want to go home, Zach. I don't belong here."

"You are home, Abby. Aren't you happy with the Porters? Have you been treated unkindly?"

"The Porters are not to blame," Abby contended. Except for Belinda, she thought. "I will never fit into white society."

"You must remain at the fort," Zach said urgently. "I've put off mentioning it to you, but something rotten is afoot. I don't know exactly what it is, but it involves Colonel Chivington and his Colorado volunteers. Until I know for certain what Chivington plans, I want you where you'll be safe. It's what White Feather would want for you."

"Do you think Chivington means harm to my people?" Abby asked sharply. "Black Kettle signed a treaty at the Great Smoke. I have heard of no raids by the People since they settled at Sand Creek."

"I don't know what Chivington's presence at Fort Lyon means, Abby. But I intend to find out soon."

"I must warn White Feather," Abby cried, pushing herself from Zach's lap.

His arms closed around her, preventing her escape. "What can you say? Neither of us knows what Chivington plans. You would only cause trouble and perhaps create problems where none exist if you go to White Feather now. Relax. As soon as you've composed yourself I'll take you home."

Home, Abby thought bitterly. She had no home. No one wanted her. Her people had abandoned her, and white society scorned her. "I do not want to go back to the Porters'." Her voice was taut with emotion.

A nerve jumped in Zach's jaw. "I'm afraid you have no choice. I'm only human, Abby. You're too much of a temptation to me. When you look at me like that, all I can think of is kissing those sweet lips until I create the same kind of wanting in you that you do in me."

She continued to stare at him, mesmerized by the fiery centers of his blue eyes. His lips were so close that she could feel the heat of his breath against her flesh. She shivered in response, and Zach answered with a groan as he surrendered to his need and lowered his lips to hers, taking that which he could deny himself no longer. Her mouth tasted like sweet wild honey, and Zach's arms tightened around her.

Abby felt utterly helpless, overpowered by his strength and masculinity as her soft body molded to his, her lips crushed beneath a mouth so demanding that it robbed her of her will. Her natural response was to close her eyes, open her lips to give him access, and slide her arms around his neck, but she resisted the impulse. It was so easy to be carried away by Zach. His hard kisses made her forget everything except how wonderful his loving made her feel. The memory of the incredible taste of his mouth and the feel of him inside her came back in minute detail, making her yearn to experience those feelings again.

Lifting his mouth from hers, Zach searched her face, alarmed at how easily he lost control where Abby was concerned. The power she wielded over him was frightening. These past two weeks he had fought his need to see and speak with her, but her erotic scent lingered in his nostrils, his skin remembered her touch, and his body ached to thrust into her velvet softness again. Now here she was in his arms, exactly where he had wished her all those long lonely nights he had tossed and turned in his cold bed.

"Dammit, Abby," he growled hoarsely. "Do you realize what you've done by coming here tonight? I'm not made of stone. Can you feel how badly I want you?" He grasped her hand, guiding it to his erection.

Abby's eyes widened as her fingers curled around him. Zach had said he wasn't made of stone, but the man part of him she held in her hand was hard enough to contradict his statement. Realizing the danger she had placed herself in by coming here, Abby's hand abruptly fell away, and she hugged herself tightly to still the aching need that made her breasts tighten and tingle unbearably.

"Zach . . ." His name tasted like sweet nectar on her tongue.

Zach's emotions had been stretched taut as he pulled Abby closer and kissed her again, stealing the words of protest he knew she would utter. He realized this was wrong, knew it better than Abby, but it made no difference. He wasn't deliberately seducing her; it had happened without premeditation or volition. It wasn't his fault that she had burst unexpectedly into his rooms seeking protection. The only thing for which he could blame himself was the certain knowledge of what was going to happen next.

Even as he kissed her, his hands were unfastening the front of her blouse. Then he was touching bare flesh, cupping her breasts, feeling them swell and harden beneath his caress. His mind vaguely registered the fact that she wore no confining undergarment beneath her dress.

Abby gasped at the raw pleasure surging through her and fervently prayed that Zach wouldn't—but he did. Her pupils dilated with pleasure as he lifted her breasts to his mouth and kissed them. Then he tongued and finally sucked them into his mouth until her nipples became diamond-hard. Her hands sought his hard body, intending to push him away, but the moment she touched him, the heat of his flesh radiating through his shirt scorched her and set her on fire for him. Her cry of surrender was all the encouragement Zach needed to strip away her skirt and blouse, scoop her into his arms and carry her to the narrow cot that served as his bed.

"Zach, we can't," Abby protested. Her words were in direct conflict with what her body demanded.

"I know," Zach whispered into her ear as he laid her down on the cot. He dropped a kiss on her mouth. "Do you really want me to stop?"

She was panting as if she had just run a great distance. "The Porters will be worried if I don't return soon."

"I know." He pulled off his shirt, ripping out buttons in his haste. His pants and long johns followed.

Abby's mouth went dry. Never had she seen anyone as magnificently male and wonderfully virile as Zach. Was it because she had never viewed men's bodies before in quite the same way as she was seeing Zach's? Her newly awakened sexuality made her aware of many things which she hadn't noticed previously. Did any man have shoulders as broad as Zach's? Or flesh as solid and muscles as powerful? Or thighs as strong? Buttocks as firm? Was any man as vibrant and vital as Zach?

She felt the solid weight of him press against her, and her arms opened in welcome. Moments before his mouth came down on hers, an unbidden thought came to her mind. She frowned, turning her head so that his mouth brushed her cheek. He drew back, looking at her strangely. "Is something wrong, Abby?"

"I'm not a whore, Zach. No matter what those men think. I was chaste until—until I met you."

Zach's face grew hard. "Forget those men. Forget what people think. They're all ignorant. I warned you what it was going to be like when people learned we had been alone on the prairie. I'm still willing to marry you. It's the only way to stop gossip."

Abby shook her head in vigorous denial. She couldn't marry Zach. She didn't intend to remain long at Fort Lyon. She'd be doing him an injustice by becoming his wife, then leaving him. The attack on her tonight had convinced her that she did not belong in the white world. Once White Feather learned how badly she had been treated, he'd have no choice but to allow her to remain at Sand Creek with the People.

Zach waited breathlessly for her answer. Truth to tell, he wasn't certain he wanted Abby to accept his offer. He doubted that staid Boston society would welcome her with open arms.

"I have already given my answer," Abby maintained. "Please do not badger me. All I ask is that you love me one last time before . . ."

"Before what?"

Abby flushed, aware of what she had been about to reveal. "Before I perish from wanting. Love me, Zach—make me forget those men who tried to violate me."

"I'll find them, sweetheart, and when I do they'll pay for laying their filthy hands on you."

His kiss was unbelievably gentle, his lips subtle and coaxing as his tongue pushed past the barrier of her teeth to explore the soft, sensitive interior of her mouth. His thighs pressed against her, letting the smooth head of his hard shaft rub against her belly and probe between her legs. Abby shifted beneath him and groaned as if in agony as he began to stroke and caress her, to arouse her to near madness with his hands and mouth.

"Open your legs, sweetheart," Zach moaned urgently as he nudged her knees apart. Abby obeyed instantly, the man scent of him making her wild to feel him inside her.

Lifting her hips, Zach thrust inside her, savoring his slide into ecstasy as her velvet warmth closed around him. He was rock hard; she was soft and yielding. They fit together perfectly. At that moment, Zach believed he was as close to heaven as he'd ever get. Stretched as taut as a bowstring, his control hung by a slim thread as her arms slid around him and her hands stroked the length of his back and the swell of his buttocks. He went still, forcing his breathing to slow to an even cadence.

"Oh, God, don't move, sweetheart!" His voice held a hint of panic as he fought the need to climax immediately. His eyes were closed, his brow furrowed as he forcibly restrained his rush toward fulfillment. Several long minutes of intense concentration passed before he felt himself capable of continuing.

At first his movements were slow and easy, allowing Abby to build gradually to that final moment of glory. Sensing his imminent loss of control, Abby's body responded to his urgency, rising to meet his strokes with hard thrusts that brought him inside her, full and deep. Driven beyond endurance, Zach's control snapped as his loins pumped vigorously, seeking the sweet reward of promised ecstasy.

"Come with me, Abby!" he cried as he flexed his hips and drove himself so deeply inside her that she felt him touch her soul.

His words shattered Abby's fragile defenses. Pulsating contractions shook her body in wave after wave of incredible rapture, sending her senses reeling. Her cries of ecstasy spurred Zach as he eagerly seized his own reward, spilling himself inside her.

Chapter Twelve

Dropping his head into the sweet hollow of her neck, Zach breathed deeply of her earthy scent, aware as he had never been aware before that Abby was someone special and precious. In that moment he realized that he must have had an unconscious reason for bringing her to Fort Lyon, and as soon as he was thinking clearly that reason would present itself. He greatly feared that once all the pieces fell into place, his life would never be the same. Yet if that life included Abby, he would welcome the change. Convincing Abby might be a problem, but he would face it when the time came.

Abby shifted beneath Zach, taking comfort in the solid weight of him resting atop her. Though she knew making love with Zach was considered wrong according to both the Cheyenne and white cultures, she felt no shame in the act. It might be the last memory she had of him if she left Fort Lyon as she planned. She looked up at him, searching his face for some hint of his thoughts. He smiled in response as he eased off her.

"I'd like to keep you here all night," he sighed regretfully, "but I fear I've already ruined your reputation by keeping you this long. Those men know where you've been and are vicious enough to spread gossip."

"The people at the fort already think the worst of me. They can do me no more harm. But you're right—it is time I left. The Porters will be worried."

"I didn't mean for things to get out of control, Abby, but I'm not sorry. Things always seem to happen when I'm around you. I'm taking a scouting expedition across the border into Kansas tomorrow. There have been reports of Indians raiding homesteaders. But when I return, there are things to be settled between us."

Abby averted her gaze, fearing her expression would alert Zach to her intention of leaving the fort. After what had happened in this room tonight, leaving was the only answer. Since there were no herbs in the woods for her to collect so late in the year, she could not afford to remain and become tied to Zach by a child. If Zach was going to be away from Fort Lyon for a few days, it would be the perfect opportunity for her to return to her people without being pursued. After literally falling into his bed tonight, Abby wasn't so naive as to think it wouldn't happen again. Something potent and compelling existed between her and Zach, and the longer she remained at the fort, the harder it would be to part from him.

"We will speak of those things when you return," Abby hedged as she rose from the cot and gathered her clothes from where Zach had flung them when he had undressed her. "I must return to the Porters before Pete comes searching for me."

Zach gave reluctant agreement, rising and helping her dress. "I'll see you home."

"There is no need."

"Don't argue, Abby. What happened to you tonight is a very real threat. What if those men had succeeded in raping you? Not only do I insist upon walking you home; I'm forbidding you to leave the house at night unescorted." There was an undeniable spark of challenge in his eyes.

Abby could see that arguing was useless, so she let his remark pass. Once she left the fort, it would no longer matter. Zach helped her into her coat, then asked, "Are you ready?" Abby nodded. He turned to open the door, then abruptly changed his mind. To her surprise, he pulled her into his arms and kissed her fiercely. "Just so you don't forget me while I'm gone." When he finally broke off the kiss, Abby's head was spinning and her legs trembling. Then he took her hand and led her out the door.

241

To Abby's horror, they found Pete Porter standing on the doorstep. He was staring at them in shock, his hand raised as if to knock. His face went stiff with disapproval when he saw Abby and Zach together.

"Sergeant Porter, what are you doing here?" Zach asked, all too aware of what Pete was thinking.

"I was just coming to ask your help in finding Abby. I've been looking all over for her. Milly and I were worried when she didn't return from her walk at her usual time." Pete's obvious disappointment at finding Abby in Zach's quarters sent guilt skittering through him. "Since I know she's in good hands, I'll return home, sir," Pete said formally. He saluted and turned to leave.

"Pete, wait, it's not, I mean—Abby was attacked by three men tonight outside my door. She appealed to me for help."

Pete's discerning gaze settled on Abby. He was too astute not to recognize her disheveled appearance and flushed features for what they were. Perhaps she really had been attacked; he'd never had reason to doubt Zach's word before. But intuition told him something had happened inside Zach's rooms tonight, something that made him question his captain's integrity. It grieved him to think that Zach was taking unfair advantage of Abby's innocence. Her ignorance of white morals made her prey to unscrupulous men, but he had never considered Zach a despoiler of innocent women.

"If you have the names of the men, Captain, I'll see that they are punished."

"Names weren't mentioned. And it was too dark for Abby to see her assailants. Keep your eyes and ears open, Sergeant. If they're attached to the fort I'll learn their identities if it's the last thing I do and see them punished. I was going to walk Abby home, but perhaps it would be best if you took over. And Sergeant Porter," Zach added with a hint of steel in his voice, "I see no need to tell anyone where you found Abby."

"I understand, Captain," Pete said, saluting smartly. He had lived a long time in this man's army, been in situations that required tact, and knew when to keep his mouth shut. Besides, he genuinely liked Zach Mercer. When the captain had arrived fresh from the war in the East, Pete had taken him under his wing and taught him things about the West and Indians that few men were privileged to know. He offered Abby his arm, and after a lingering look at Zach, she stepped out into the cold night.

Zach watched them walk away, annoyed that he had earned Pete's disapproval. When he had a chance to explain, he'd tell Pete how it was between him and Abby. That thought brought him up short. Exactly what would he say? That he couldn't keep his hands off Abby? That he'd taken her innocence during one reckless moment of explosive passion and hadn't been able to forget it? That his life was taking a different direction, whether he liked it or not? Yes, he decided, he could tell Pete all that and more. He could also say that he had never felt more confused or frustrated in his life. Whenever he thought about Abby, a strange, unsettling warmth radiated from some deep, mysterious place inside him.

"Is there anything you can tell me about the men who attacked you, Abby?" Pete asked as they walked across the parade grounds.

"I did not see them," Abby said in a small voice. "They tried to drag me through the alley. There were three of them. I'm positive I would recognize their voices if I heard them again."

"Don't worry, we'll find them," he said, patting her hand. "Captain Mercer won't let them get away with this. None of our daughters will be safe alone after tonight."

"I'm sorry, Pete," Abby murmured contritely. "I did not think I would be in danger. No Cheyenne warrior would think of assaulting a woman. If he did, he would be banished from the village."

"There are many unprincipled men in the Western army, Abby. They came west to escape the law. You must be ever on your guard, and you must never walk alone at night. Since I leave the fort tomorrow with Captain Mercer's pursuit expedition, you must promise to obey me in this."

"It will be as you say." It wasn't difficult to agree, for Abby knew she wasn't going to be at the fort much longer. But she didn't want to leave with Pete thinking ill of her. "Pete, about tonight . . ."

"No need to explain, Abby. You're old enough to know your own mind, but I suggest you think carefully before you let a man talk you into anything. You know so little of white men and their ways. I'd hate to see you ruin your life. Not that I don't think Captain Mercer is a good man. Just the opposite. But I know for a fact that he intends to return to Boston after the war in the East is over, and I don't think you'd be happy there."

Abby's heart gave a painful leap. Pete had just confirmed her own views of Zach's intentions concerning his future. She had refused his marriage proposal because she knew he didn't love her and she wouldn't fit into his world. The last thing she wanted was for him to be shamed by her ignorance of white customs.

"I know," Abby said resignedly. "Thank you for caring."

They had reached the house now, and Abby steeled herself for a confrontation with Milly and Belinda. Would they suspect she had been with Zach? Would Pete tell them despite Zach's request that he keep it to himself?

Milly rushed to meet her at the door. She sounded anxious. "My dear, where have you been?" Abby could see that Milly genuinely cared for her, and guilt gnawed at her.

Abby shed her coat, and Belinda's sharp eyes fixed on the front of Abby's blouse, noting that one of the buttons was undone. She made a slow perusal of Abby's person, not surprised to see that Abby's hair looked as if it had been hastily rearranged.

"Your walk must have been quite—strenuous," Belinda hinted. "Would you like to tell us about it?"

"There is nothing to tell," Pete interceded before Abby could think of an appropriate answer. "Abby lost track of time." He sent Abby a look that persuaded her to hold her tongue. "She's safe now, so I suggest we all go to bed."

Far from appeased, Belinda bade her parents good night and went to her room. Abby followed as meekly as her stubborn nature allowed, though she did not relish being alone with Belinda.

"Who did you meet on your walk?" Belinda asked the moment the door closed behind them.

"What makes you think I met someone?"

"Mama might be naive enough to believe you're an innocent virgin, but I know better. No woman who looks and acts like you is innocent. You've probably had vast numbers of men before you coaxed Zach into your bed. Is that where you were tonight? You have a look about you—like you've just lain with a man."

"How would you know how a woman who has just lain with a man looks?" Abby challenged.

Belinda flushed and looked away. A few months ago, she had thought herself in love with a young lieutenant and allowed him to make love to her. When she found out he was married, she felt no remorse over his death in an Indian attack, but she had never forgotten how wonderful it felt to take a man inside her. She'd welcome Zach Mercer in her bed, with or without benefit of marriage.

"I've got eyes," Belinda said snidely. "And I can tell when Papa is lying. Personally, I don't care how many men you meet on your walks, as long as you keep away from Zach Mercer. I want him for myself."

"I think Zach might have something to say about that," Abby returned cautiously. "Good night, Belinda, I'm suddenly very tired."

"I'll bet," Belinda smirked as she sought her bed.

Abby was watching out the window when Zach's patrol rode through the gates the next morning. Ice-laden wind seized the breath of both men and horses, forming a misty frost that hung around them like ghostly clouds. Once they were out of sight, Abby turned from the window and surveyed the small pile of belongings she had placed on the bed. Reverently she touched the medicine bag she wore around her neck. As long as she had her most prized possession, she could leave everything else behind without regret. But being practical, she knew she would need her warmest clothes. Her thick buffalo robe and fur-lined moccasins would be needed on the trip to Sand Creek.

Abby worked quickly, praying Belinda and Milly wouldn't return from the store before she finished. Placing everything she valued or might need in the center of the robe, she rolled it up and shoved it under the bed. When the time arrived to leave, she would be ready. Her tentative plan was to sneak out under the cover of darkness while the family was sleeping. Abby had been so careful that when Milly and Belinda returned a short time later, they had no inkling what she was up to.

Abby went to bed fully dressed that night. For a change, she had the room all to herself. Belinda had decided to share her mother's bed in her father's absence. Since she didn't intend to leave until the dead of night, she lay down and went to sleep immediately. When she awakened several hours later, it was with the certain knowledge that she wasn't alone. The window was open, and a cold breeze drifted across her face. She sensed no danger in the presence, so she waited.

"Wake up, little sister. It is Wind Rider."

Abby sat up, her face alight with incredible joy. "Wind Rider, you've come!" She was out of bed and in his arms instantly. Usual Cheyenne restraint was forgotten as brother and sister embraced warmly.

"I promised I would come to you before I traveled north to join our Sioux brothers."

"How is our father?"

"He is well, but our people are beginning to question the wisdom of Black Kettle. The land is barren and inhospitable. There is no game, and the promised supplies from the government have not arrived. Warm blankets and food are needed desperately. White Feather said he will remain only one moon longer, and if the soldiers do not keep their promises, he will lead the People north to join the Sioux and Northern Cheyenne."

"Take me with you," Abby begged. "I cannot stay here. I am despised and ridiculed for my Cheyenne ways. I do not like being laughed at and called savage."

Wind Rider regarded her sadly. "No matter how the whites feel about you, Tears Like Rain, you must remain with them. Things are very bad at Sand Creek. I fear the worst is yet to come. Not only the Cheyenne will experience bad times, but our Sioux brothers as well."

"I will share their misery," Abby persisted. "At least I will be with people who do not hate me."

"What about Sky Eyes? He promised to protect you. Is he just another White-eyes who speaks with a forked tongue?"

"I do not need Zach Mercer to protect me," Abby declared belligerently.

"Are you still at odds with the man?"

"At odds?" Abby frowned. At odds wasn't exactly the way she'd describe the potent attraction between her and Zach.

"You know what I am referring to. Are you

still angry at him for persuading White Feather to send you away?"

"I—no." She spoke the truth. How could she be angry with a man with whom she had made love with such wild abandon? The white man's word that came closest to what she felt for Zach would be love. But she wasn't ready to admit that, not yet anyway. Maybe never.

"Do the Porters treat you unkindly?" Wind Rider asked.

Abby tried to lie but could not. "No. Their daughter does not like me, but they do not treat me unkindly."

"Perhaps you will find a man you can love and respect and take him for a husband," Wind Rider suggested hopefully. "I think Painted Horse is resigned to the fact that he cannot have you. He has come with me so that he may speak with you."

"Painted Horse is here?" Abby asked, looking toward the open window through which Wind Rider had entered.

"He is waiting outside. We've watched for two nights to make sure this is the room you occupy."

"I usually share it with Belinda. It is fortunate that she is not with me tonight."

"Were she here, I would have found some other way to see you. Will you speak to Painted Horse?"

"I will see him. Does he ride north with you?"

"No, he must return to Sand Creek. His father

is ill, and he must stay to provide for his mother and two sisters. He came with me only to satisfy himself that you are well and happy."

A slow smile curved Abby's lips. If Painted Horse was returning to Sand Creek, what was to stop her from joining him?

"I must leave, Tears Like Rain. I do not know when I will see you again or even *if* I will see you again, but know that my love will remain with you always."

Tears welled up in Abby's eyes. Never seeing Wind Rider again was worse than—than never seeing Zach again! Losing either of them would be equally painful. But with Zach, she had no choice; they did not belong together.

"Don't cry, little sister. Keep me in your heart just as I will keep you in mine. If at all possible, I will see you again." Tenderly he kissed the top of her head, rubbed her cheek with his, and embraced her fiercely. Then he set her aside, searching her face as if to memorize it. After several poignant moments, he turned and left through the window.

Tears streamed freely down Abby's cheeks as she watched Wind Rider melt into the darkness and Painted Horse appear in his place.

"It is good to see you again, Tears Like Rain," Painted Horse greeted her formally. "When I learned Wind Rider was coming to see you, I convinced him to let me come along. Are you happy?"

Abby gave him a fond smile. If not for Zach, she would have been content to become the wife of Painted Horse. But she could not lie to him; she was not happy. Perhaps if he knew, he would take her to Sand Creek.

"It is good to see you also, Painted Horse. I wish I could tell you I am content, but it would be a lie. The truth is that I miss my father and the People. I do not belong in the white world. I wish to join White Feather at Sand Creek."

"Did Wind Rider give his permission?"

Abby snorted resentfully. "He wants me to remain here. He says our people are sick and starving and I should remain where I will be safe."

"Wind Rider is wise," Painted Horse said with marked reluctance. "As soon as my father is well, I will leave Sand Creek and join the Sioux to fight for justice. I agree with Wind Rider—all whites speak with forked tongues."

"I want to share the fate of our people," Abby said fiercely. "Take me with you to Sand Creek." Her voice was softly imploring, her words a desperate plea.

"White Feather would be most angry,"

"White Feather loves me. When he learns how unhappy I am, he will welcome me back."

Painted Horse gave her a doubtful look. "Perhaps it is so."

Abby's hopes soared. It would be much safer to travel with Painted Horse, but she would go by herself if there was no alternative. She told him so, emphasizing the fact that she would leave regardless of his decision.

"Wind Rider will be angry with both of us."

"Do not tell him, Painted Horse. Since you are traveling in different directions, when you leave the fort he need never know. Please, Painted Horse, help me."

Painted Horse's mind worked furiously. He had never lost his desire for Tears Like Rain, nor given up his dream of mating with her. "I will take you to Sand Creek on one condition. I still desire you. If you agree to our joining, I will not ride north after my father recovers. We will stay at Sand Creek and live in peace with our people."

"We will speak of it to White Feather," Abby hedged, unwilling to commit herself to Painted Horse when she knew he would think her shameless for giving herself to Zach. "If he is agreeable, the courtship can continue according to tribal custom." Since courtship often took as long as five years, she'd have sufficient time to come up with a reason for not marrying Painted Horse without revealing that she had violated Cheyenne moral code and was no longer fit to marry.

Her answer seemed to satisfy Painted Horse, except for a nagging suspicion he couldn't shake. "Perhaps you favor another. Has another warrior caught your eye?"

"You have my word, Painted Horse," Abby said solemnly. "No other warrior appeals to me." It was the truth. The only man who appealed to her was Zach. "When do we leave?"

"When Wind Rider and I part tonight, he

travels north into Sioux territory while I go only a short distance west to Sand Creek. I will double back and return for you tomorrow night. Where is your mare stabled?"

"She is stabled at the livery. Where will I meet you?"

"Meet me behind the livery after the fort has settled down for the night. I will take care of the sentry so we can ride safely out the side gate."

"Do not kill the sentry," Abby warned. "The soldiers will come after us if you do."

"Painted Horse, it is time to leave." Wind Rider's whisper came to them through the open window.

"Go," Abby said, "but do not tell Wind Rider what we have just discussed."

Painted Horse touched her cheek with a dark finger, then turned and ducked through the window. "Until tomorrow night," he hissed as he disappeared through the opening.

Abby leaned out the window, watching as Painted Horse disappeared into the darkness. She felt something touch her hand and realized that Wind Rider had remained behind.

"Good-bye, little sister," he whispered. "May *Heammawihio* keep you safe." His words warmed her heart long after he was gone.

Abby was a bundle of raw nerves the following day. Even Milly remarked upon her inability to concentrate and asked if something was troubling her. Abby merely shook her head, fearing Milly would suspect the reason for her nervousness. When Belinda decided to occupy her own bed that night because she didn't like the mattress in her mother's room, Abby's heart plummeted. How was she going to leave the house undetected with Belinda in the same room? But she was determined. Nothing would stop her, nothing. She would handle any obstacle in her way.

Night finally arrived, and not any too soon for Abby. She excused herself and prepared for bed. Belinda followed soon after. Fortunately Belinda fell asleep immediately, and by the time the hour arrived for Abby to leave, she encountered no interference as she eased from the bed and changed into her tunic and moccasins. But when she slid the buffalo robe from under the bed, Belinda awoke.

"What are you doing?"

"Nothing. Go back to sleep."

Belinda's eyes widened in fear as a beam of moonlight illuminated Abby's slim figure dressed in Indian garb and looking as fierce as any savage. "You're going to kill us in our beds!" Belinda cried irrationally.

Abby snorted in disgust. "Do not be foolish. I mean you no harm."

"Why are you dressed like that and sneaking around in the middle of the night?"

"You have nothing to fear from me."

"I don't believe you! You're going to kill us," Belinda repeated, growing hysterical.

Fearing she would scream and alert the entire

fort, Abby did the only thing possible under the circumstances. Doubling her fist, she swung at Belinda. Her aim was accurate. Her fist connected solidly with Belinda's chin, knocking her senseless.

"Sorry, Belinda," she muttered as she tore up strips of sheet to bind and gag the hapless girl. If an outcry was given too soon, she and Painted Horse might be followed and she didn't want to risk the possibility of that happening.

Hoisting the buffalo robe over her shoulders, Abby made her way cautiously through the dark house and out the door. Painted Horse was waiting for her behind the livery, the hackamore already on her horse in anticipation of her arrival. A tense silence swelled between them as Abby mounted and they rode off. Skirting the main area of the fort, they reached the gate in a matter of minutes.

They rode unchallenged through the side gate, which was to the right of the main gate and rarely locked at night. The guard was nowhere in sight, and Abby hoped Painted Horse had not harmed him, for it would be one more black mark against her. They traveled through the chill, misty predawn, continuing until the fort was well out of sight. It was bitter cold. Abby couldn't recall when she'd seen a colder November. Huddled in her buffalo robe, she concentrated on what she would tell White Feather when she arrived at Sand Creek.

* * *

Zach stared at the burning cabin in grim horror. They had found three bodies lying in the trampled yard—a man, a woman, and a small child. All were scalped and mutilated. The woman had been raped.

"Set the men to digging graves," Zach barked at Sergeant Porter. "There's nothing more we can do here. What do you make of it, Sergeant?"

Pete Porter picked up an arrow and studied it intently for several minutes. "Crow," he said with a knowledge born of experience. "Damn vicious savages. These poor people didn't have a chance."

Zach's patrol had crossed over the border into Kansas, but they'd found no sign of Indian activity. Then they circled back into Colorado territory and were only a day and a half out of Fort Lyon when they found the smoldering cabin and dead bodies.

"Do you think the wily bastards are headed to Sand Creek?"

"Not a chance," Porter said. "There's no love lost between the Crow and Cheyenne. Signs indicate a small raiding party, and they'd never ride into an enemy camp the size of Sand Creek. There's a small homestead a few miles to the north. Maybe they're headed in that direction. Should I take a few men and check it out?"

Zach weighed the options. Their supplies were short, and the cold weather made the men eager to return to the fort. They could be on a wild-goose chase. By now the Crow raiders could be holed up someplace in the hills. Lord knew it was cold enough to discourage the hardiest souls from venturing out. Still, as long as he was in the area, he should look in on the settlers and warn them of Indian activity.

"Take the men back to the fort, Sergeant Porter. I'll ride on myself and warn the settlers. I seriously doubt we'll find those Crow renegades in the vicinity. They've probably made camp in the hills and are dug in for the winter. Can't say as how I blame them. A warm fire would feel damn good right now."

"Are you sure, Captain?" Porter asked. "Corporal Osgood can take the men back and I can stay with you."

Zach shook his head. "You've a family waiting for you, Porter. No sense you traipsing around the countryside when there's no need. I'll just drop in on the settlers, see that everything is in order, then head back to fort."

"If that's your decision, then I'll abide by it," Porter said as he turned to join the men.

"Sergeant, wait." Porter halted, waiting for Zach to issue further orders. "This is personal, Pete," Zach said, addressing him in a confidential manner. "Take care of Abby. Have you learned anything further about the men who attacked her?"

"Nothing definite," Pete said. "I did learn that Privates Lentz, Flaherty, and Kramer were out of the barracks about the same time the attack occurred. You seem mighty fond of that girl. I should have known you wouldn't deliberately take advantage of her. I think you care for her."

Zach frowned. He knew the men named by Porter were crude types whose backgrounds were suspect. He intended to investigate when he returned to the fort. But it was Pete's words about the relationship between him and Abby that demanded a reply.

"About Abby, I—well, it's hard to explain how I feel about her. There definitely is something between us. I just don't know what. I did ask her to marry me, if that's what you're concerned about. But she refused."

"I understand, Captain," Pete replied, unwilling to delve too deeply into another man's private affairs. It did make him feel better, though, knowing that Zach's intentions were honorable despite the fact that marriage between them would definitely not be without problems. "I'll get the men digging those graves now."

An hour later, Zach watched the men ride off toward Fort Lyon. Then he swung his mount around and headed north into the wind-driven snow.

Chapter Thirteen

Abby clutched the buffalo robe tighter around her shoulders, grateful for the warmth provided by the heavy fur. It was growing colder by the minute and they had another hard day's ride before reaching Sand Creek. Given the natural Indian reticence to make small talk, she and Painted Horse did not converse much after leaving the fort. When hunger plagued them, they chewed on pemmican and buffalo jerky and ate snow to appease their thirst. They slept the first night in a wide crevice between two rocks, wrapped in their buffalo robes. It never occurred to Painted Horse to seek intimacy, for it wasn't the Cheyenne way.

They left the Arkansas River and were traveling north along a flat plain bordered by low hills. At the foot of the hills, a line of trees marked the beginning of the mountainous interior of Colorado. It was midday, and the icy wind was hurling snow and sleet at them, slowing their progress. The first inkling of trouble came when Abby chanced to glance toward the foothills and saw an Indian emerging from the trees. He wore full war paint and carried a rifle.

"Painted Horse, look!" Her warning came seconds after Painted Horse had seen the Indian for himself.

"Crow!" Painted Horse spat, recognizing the unique feather arrangement on the warrior's lance. Even as he spoke, three more warriors nudged their mounts through the trees. Then two more joined them, until six were poised like statues at the edge of the woods. "Ride, Tears Like Rain!"

Abby dug her heels cruelly into the mare's flanks, hanging on desperately as the valiant mount surged forward. The Crow warrior who had emerged from the woods first gave a bloodcurdling cry, signaling the beginning of the chase. The other warriors charged behind him, whooping and hollering at the top of their lungs. Though Abby's courageous little mare did her best to outrun the attackers, it soon became apparent that she couldn't keep up the grueling pace much longer.

"Leave me behind!" Abby urged Painted Horse, who was holding back his more powerful stallion in consideration of Abby.

"No! We will make a stand behind those rocks up ahead."

Abby glanced to the left, noting two huge boulders that had rolled down from a loftier perch at some time in the past and now rested at the foot of a hill. She needed no prodding as she urged her mare behind their meager protection.

"We have only one rifle between us," Abby gasped, wishing she had stolen a rifle from the Porters. "Give me your bow and arrows."

"Take the rifle, I will use the bow. There are only six of them. Two Cheyenne are better than six Crow any day. Aim carefully, Tears Like Rain, do not waste any bullets. And—" He hesitated, sending her a look that spoke volumes. "Save the last bullet."

Abby didn't need to be told what to do with the last bullet. Death would be slow and painful at the hands of the Crow. If they let her live after they raped her, she might be tortured or become the camp whore, used vilely by every man in the band. "I hear you, Painted Horse," she said solemnly.

"Here they come." His voice was taut, his sleek muscles jerking in response to the tension building inside him.

Abby watched in growing apprehension as the six Crow renegades rode within striking distance. Resting her rifle in a notch between the boulders, Abby waited until she had one of the Crow in her sights before squeezing off a shot. Painted Horse let loose a flurry of arrows at the same time. Unfortunately, because of the distance, the arrows were mostly ineffective. Abby's first shot hit its mark, wounding the Crow but not killing him. He was still able to ride and shoot, much to Abby's disgust.

Bullets flew back and forth furiously. One of Painted Horse's arrows felled a renegade who had come too close, and he lay sprawled on the ground nearby. But there were still five Crow riding in circles and shooting at them, making it difficult to aim and fire accurately. Abby grew frantic when she noticed their ammunition was low. She was concentrating so hard on keeping the enemy at bay that she failed to see one warrior break off from the main group and circle to the right, disappearing up the hill behind them.

Common sense told Abby that there was no escape, that she was destined to die a cruel death at the hands of her Crow enemies. Why hadn't she stayed at Fort Lyon? she wondered despondently, questioning her sanity. Did she so fear Zach's hold on her, or was it her own feelings she was trying to escape? Before she could consider the question, a bullet struck the rock behind which she was crouched, sending grit and dust into her eyes. She scrubbed furiously at her eyes while bullets whizzed around her. When her vision cleared, she sent a sidelong glance at Painted Horse. What she saw made her cry out in fear and horror.

Painted Horse lay in a pool of blood, felled by an arrow still protruding from his neck.

So many bullets and arrows had flown around them during the past few minutes—or was it hours?—that Abby had no idea when he had been struck down. She knew instinctively that Painted Horse was dead and she mourned his passing. He was a good and brave warrior. If he hadn't hung back to protect her, she felt certain he could have outridden the Crow.

Tears blurred her vision, but she forced herself to think coherently, not to give in to despair. She still had a few rounds of ammunition left, and she intended to use them wisely. Of one thing she was certain—they would not take her alive.

Zach regarded the small homestead nestled up against the hillside cautiously. From a distance the house looked deserted. It didn't appear as if the homestead had been under recent attack by Indians, for there were no outward signs of a raid. The house was standing intact and the yard seemed undisturbed. But no matter how tranquil the scene appeared, Zach sensed an unnatural emptiness, as if the place had been recently abandoned.

There were no animals in the corral, and the barn door hung askew, flapping noisily in the wind. No barnyard pets were visible; no chickens scratched in the yard. The eerie banging of the front door of the cabin caught Zach's attention. The owners seemed to have made a hasty departure. Cautiously, Zach started down the slight incline toward the house, his hand hovering near his holstered rifle.

"Hello! Anybody home?" The wind whipped away his words and flung them back at him. Zach expected no answer and was not disappointed when he received none. Dismounting, he pulled his rifle free and walked toward the house. "Hello! Is anyone home?" Silence.

Pushing open the door, Zach peered into the room. Dust balls rolled across the floor to greet him. He walked inside. If it wasn't for the dust and ominous silence, Zach would have sworn that the occupants had just stepped out for a few moments. Nothing appeared out of place. Dishes sat neatly on shelves, a pot of something congealed sat on the stove, and a child's doll lay beneath the kitchen table. He walked into the bedroom, noting that the beds had been stripped of linens and the closets emptied.

It didn't take Zach long to realize that the owners had left in haste, taking little except their linens and personal possessions. Had Indians scared them off? It certainly seemed reasonable to conclude that the homesteaders had left because of Indian activity in the area. Perhaps their livestock had been stolen and they feared the Indians would return. Realizing that there was nothing more he could do there, Zach remounted and turned his horse in the direction of Fort Lyon. If he rode hard, he could catch up with his men before they reached the fort.

Zach hadn't gone three miles in the driving snow and sleet when he heard gunfire. He reined his horse to a halt, listening carefully. Had his men run into a raiding party? Were settlers being attacked? Or were two enemy tribes waging war on one another? No matter what the cause, it demanded investigation. Urging his mount up the hill, Zach rode cautiously along a narrow ridge. His position gave him an unobstructed view of the valley while he remained virtually unseen from below.

He had covered about two miles when he spotted several Indians firing at helpless victims who had taken cover behind some rocks in the valley directly below him. He felt fairly certain that the raiders were Crow. And he noticed something else—one of those being fired upon was a woman. The woman turned slightly, giving him a full view of her profile. He froze. Were his eyes deceiving him?

Abby! He'd recognize her anywhere. My God, what was she doing here? When had she left the fort—and why? Was the warrior with her her brother? He counted four Crow warriors still mounted. One lay on the ground, and two of those on horseback appeared to be wounded but still capable of firing a weapon.

Zach's stared in horror when an arrow slammed into the warrior crouching beside Abby, felling him instantly. Spitting out a curse, Zach acted swiftly. Leaping from his mount, he scrambled down the hill, his legs churning vigorously. His heart pounded with fear when he saw a lone Indian directly below him, slowly sneaking toward Abby for a rear attack. Bringing his rifle up, Zach took careful aim, aware that Abby's life depended upon his accuracy.

Abby shoved the last three rounds in the rifle, recalling Painted Horse's words about saving the last bullet for herself. A sudden noise from behind her alerted her to danger seconds too late. She whirled at the same moment the Crow leaped at her from a ledge directly above her, a tomahawk raised in menace. In a reflexive act, she swung the rifle up and aimed. To her horror, the rifle jammed. Cursing the loss of her knife, she closed her eyes and prepared to meet *Heammawihio*. Dimly she wondered if Zach would mourn her.

A shot rang out. The Indian jerked in the air, then fell at her feet, his lips stretched in a grim parody of a smile. Stunned, Abby jerked her gaze upward. There, poised on a ridge immediately above her, stood a soldier in a blue uniform. It looked like—Zach! Relief shuddered through her. Mesmerized, she saw him fire several rounds in rapid succession, scattering the remaining Crow like leaves before the wind.

It never occurred to the Crow that a lone soldier would appear without support. Deciding they were outnumbered, they turned tail and ran. Shaking uncontrollably, Abby waited while Zach raced the rest of the way down the hillside. When he reached her, he grasped her shoulders, shaking her roughly. He was so damned angry at finding her in such a dangerous situation, and so horrified to think that she might have been killed, that he wanted to beat her and kiss her at the same time. He settled for a shaking.

"What in damnation are you doing here?" he ground out savagely. He glanced at her dead companion, relieved to see that it wasn't Wind Rider. "What were you doing with Painted Horse? Did you decide you couldn't live without him after all?"

Abby shook her head in vigorous denial, too distressed over Painted Horse's death to answer. It was her fault he was dead. If she hadn't begged him to take her to Sand Creek, he would have gotten safely away. She looked so stricken that Zach had difficulty maintaining his anger. His expression softened, and he drew her into his arms, hugging her fiercely. She was still shivering, and Zach realized she must be freezing. She had thrown off the buffalo robe in order to fire more accurately.

"Let's get out of here," Zach growled, casting a nervous glance at the departing Indians. He wouldn't be surprised if they strengthened their numbers and returned later. He picked up her buffalo robe and placed it over her shoulders. His motions were stiff, his voice tight with anger, and Abby knew his temper was on the verge of exploding. Not that she could blame him. It must have been a shock finding her here.

"Wait," Abby protested, "we can't leave Painted Horse like this. It's my fault he's dead."

Zach sighed in exasperation. "I doubt that. But if it will ease your mind, I'll pile stones on his body so wild animals can't get to him. The ground is too hard to dig a grave, and I don't have a shovel with me."

Abby nodded. "I will help."

"No, stay where you are. It's growing colder. Keep the buffalo robe around you. I had hoped to catch up with my men before nightfall, but it's already growing dark. After I finish here, I know of a place where we can spend the night. It's only a few miles away."

Abby slid Zach a mutinous look. She had no intention of obeying. "I will help." Zach stared at her, exasperated, then gave in.

It took nearly an hour to gather the stones they needed, wrap Painted Horse in his buffalo robe, and place the rocks atop his body. When they had done all that was possible, Zach went back for his horse. When he returned, Abby was already mounted on her mare and waiting. Grasping the leading reins of Painted Horse's mount, he attached them to his saddle. "Follow me," he advised Abby as he doubled back toward the deserted homestead.

Abby trembled with cold beneath the buffalo robe. Dimly she wondered where Zach was taking her and how severely he'd scold her for her reckless behavior. The anger seething within him was almost palpable.

Zach glanced over his shoulder at Abby, and when he saw that she was shivering beneath the buffalo robe, he spat out a curse, turned his mount around, and plucked her from the saddle. He seated her before him, holding her tightly and pulling the buffalo robe around them both so that their combined body heat could warm them. Within minutes, Abby had stopped shaking, drawing comfort from his lean hardness as she relaxed into his embrace. She must have dozed, for when she awoke Zach had already dismounted and was easing her from the saddle.

"Where are we?" she asked groggily. Darkness came early to the plains in November, and the vague outlines of buildings visible in the murky dusk piqued her curiosity.

"I found this deserted homestead earlier. It will provide us with adequate shelter during the storm. With any luck, the snow will stop before morning."

When Abby did not respond fast enough, Zach swept her from her feet and carried her inside. He set her down and lit a lamp. "I'll start a fire, then find shelter for the horses."

Light flooded the cabin, and Abby looked around curiously. She wondered why the tenants had left so abruptly, abandoning most of their belongings. Had they been frightened by Indian activity in the area? She glanced to where Zach knelt before the hearth, using kindling and wood shavings to start the fire. Nearly everything was just as the owners had left it. Firewood filled the firebox, kindling was stacked neatly beside the hearth, and the lamps were filled with oil.

"Where are the owners?" Abby asked when Zach stood up, dusting off his knees.

"Who knows? Maybe they got frightened because of all the Indian trouble and returned east. Maybe they didn't like the West. I'm just glad this cabin is still standing. It's going to be mighty cold tonight. This is better than sleeping in tents like my men are probably doing right now. Sit here before the fire while I take care of the horses. You might want to check the cupboard for something to eat. I still have jerky and dried biscuits, but anything you might find to supplement that meager diet would be welcome."

It didn't take long for the fire to warm the cabin. Abby threw off the buffalo robe and began a thorough inspection of the cupboards. There were no canned goods, but she did find a tin of flour, another of lard, and some salt. In the back of one cupboard she found a treasure trove of four wrinkled potatoes, three carrots, and an onion. While she waited for Zach to return, she started a fire in the cookstove, found a heavy iron pot, filled it with clean snow and set it on the burner.

"Look what I found!" Zach cried, holding up a fat rabbit, which he had skinned and cleaned. "The owner, whoever he was, set up traps out back. After I stabled the horses in the barn, I decided to take a look around."

Abby's gray eyes sparkled with pleasure. "It will taste wonderful with the potatoes, carrots, and onion I found in the cupboard. And I'll make fry bread with the flour and lard."

"A feast fit for a king," Zach remarked curtly, reminding her that he was still angry with her. "While it's cooking, we'll talk."

He stood before the fire warming himself while Abby set the rabbit and vegetables to cooking. Then she mixed up the flour and lard and placed the dough directly on the stovetop to fry. Her expression was solemn when she turned to face Zach. "What did you wish to talk about?"

"I think that's rather obvious, isn't it? How long have you been in contact with Painted Horse?" It rankled to think that she harbored tender feelings for Painted Horse. Was she thinking of the Indian warrior on those occasions when he, Zach, had made love to her? He was surprised at how angry that thought made him.

"Painted Horse came with Wind Rider when my brother rode to the fort to see me. I—I talked Painted Horse into taking me to Sand Creek with him."

"Why?" She could tell by his tone of voice that he was hurt as well as confused by her desire to leave Fort Lyon.

"I do not belong at the fort. I am not comfortable living with White-eyes."

"Dammit, Abby, you've got to stop thinking of white people as White-eyes! You're white. Your ancestors are white. You have as much right to be at Fort Lyon as any other white man or woman."

"My people are Cheyenne. I was adopted into the tribe. White Feather is my father." Her chin rose belligerently.

"Did you leave the fort because you missed Painted Horse and wanted to become his wife?"

Abby stared at him. She had left Fort Lyon because she couldn't afford to fall more deeply in love with Zach Mercer. He wanted to wrest her from those she loved and thrust her into a foreign society. They both knew he didn't really want to marry her, that he had proposed merely because he had taken her virginity and felt it was the right thing to do. She would lie to Zach before admitting that she held strong feelings for him. She didn't want his pity, nor did she want to ruin his life. People would despise her for her Indian upbringing and shun Zach for marrying a woman raised by the Cheyenne.

"I left for all the reasons you mentioned, and a few more you did not mention."

"You lie!" Zach roared, unwilling to believe that Abby wanted Painted Horse. That she'd rather marry Painted Horse than become his wife.

"I do not lie," she whispered through trembling lips.

Zach's eyes swept over her with smoldering anger. He saw through her lie so easily. His hot gaze lingered on her quivering lips, lush and red, just begging for his kisses. He lowered his head, dragging her hard against him as his mouth covered hers. For a brief instant of madness, Abby sought satisfaction in the hungry joy of his kiss, fearing that she had angered Zach beyond reason. A bittersweet sorrow flavored her fleeting taste of passion.

Suddenly he thrust her away, regarding her with wicked delight. "It pleases me that you enjoyed my kiss. Have you forgotten that the man you claim you love lies in a cold grave?"

Abby looked stricken. She *had* forgotten Painted Horse. If not for her, he would still be alive. She turned away, refusing to look at Zach and reveal how much she truly cared for him. She welcomed the pungent odor of burning dough that abruptly changed the direction of their thoughts and words.

"Oh," she cried, sniffing the air. "The fry bread is burning." Rushing to the stove, she ignored the searing pain as she used her bare hands to lift the crusty rounds from the burner. She was gratified to see that only the bottoms were burned; the insides still appeared edible.

"Dammit, Abby, look at your fingers," Zach admonished as he took her hands and held them up for his inspection. The pads of her fingertips were red and beginning to blister. Pulling her toward the door, he opened it and thrust her hands into the snow piled up on the doorstep.

Abby felt an immediate cooling but sensed that the burns weren't serious and would cause no lasting damage.

"What in the hell possessed you to do a thing like that?" Zach raved, still upset with Abby for insisting that she loved Painted Horse.

"I—I don't know," Abby said, shoving her hands behind her back. "There was no damage done." She turned away. "The stew is cooked. Let's eat, I'm hungry." Actually, her appetite had fled the moment Zach took her into his arms, but she wasn't going to admit that to him.

Abby watched him stomp to the table, aware that she was only fooling herself. Denying her love for Zach simply because of her distrust of the white race was crazy. She was swiftly learning that love knew no bounds. Love did not submit to reason or logic; it defied race, religion, and prejudice. Loving Zach Mercer had not been planned; it had been ordained long before she was born. If not, why had the Great Spirit introduced him into her life at a time when she thought her future was linked to that of Painted Horse?

Abby sat before the fire, listening to the wind rattle the windows. She shivered. The cabin wasn't nearly as cozy as a tipi in wintertime. But her thoughts weren't on the cold or ice; they were on Painted Horse and how his death was going to affect his family.

"Are you cold?" Zach asked, dropping down beside her. Abby shook her head. Her expression was so solemn that Zach felt obliged to add, "If it's any comfort, I am sorry about Painted Horse. I didn't know him well, but I'm sure he was a good man." Jealousy gnawed at him. Seeing Abby grieving for another man was like being kicked in the gut by a horse.

Abby said nothing as she continued to stare into the dancing flames. With Zach so close, she could barely think, let alone speak.

"Why don't you lie down and try to get some sleep? You've been through a harrowing experience and we still have a good day's ride ahead of us to the fort."

Sleep was the last thing on Zach's mind. What he truly wanted was to love Abby until there was no room left in her heart for any other man. But he couldn't be that insensitive, not when she was grieving for someone who meant a great deal to her. He spread her buffalo robe on the floor before the hearth, urging her to lie down. She obeyed woodenly, fearing that if Zach tried to make love to her, she'd not have the will to resist. He lay down next to her and slid his arms around her. When Abby stiffened, he said, "I just want to hold you while you sleep. No man wants to make love to a woman when she's thinking of another man."

The moment Zach touched her, the anger drained out of him. He could not blame Abby for leaving the fort and preferring Painted Horse over him. She had been taught to hate whites for their cruel injustice to the People. Unfortunately, she hadn't been treated kindly at the fort. But if he had it to do over, he would still insist that she leave the Cheyenne and return to the white world. Even White Feather had agreed that things looked bleak for his people, that

Abby did not deserve to share their uncertain future.

Abby's last thought before she slipped into a deep slumber was that she could grow accustomed to falling asleep in Zach's arms every night for the rest of her life.

Zach could tell by her slow, measured breathing that Abby was sleeping, and his arms tightened around her. For the time being he was content just to hold her, taking comfort in the knowledge that he was the man lying beside her, the man in whose arms she found solace. In time he would make her forget that she loved another.

As night sought its darkest hours and wind battered the small cabin, an enlightening peace settled over Zach. He finally knew what he had to do in regard to Abby. He was no longer offering her an option. His need was a driving force inside him; he would accept no refusal. He knew she would resist, that she would fight him, but this time he would win.

Chapter Fourteen

Abby stirred in her sleep, burrowing deeply into the curve of Zach's body, seeking his warmth. Zach felt the incredible heat of her and groaned as if in pain, his loins surging powerfully in response. The fiercest emotion he had ever experienced overwhelmed him, and for one heart-stopping moment he almost gave a name to that intense feeling he was experiencing for the first time. He ached to awaken her and make love to her as his body demanded, but instead he eased her from his arms, rose unsteadily to his feet, and turned his attention to the dying fire in the hearth. Bending low, he carefully piled on wood until flames shot up the chimney, spreading warmth throughout the room.

Even in her sleep, Abby felt the absence of Zach's arms, missed the warmth of his body, and she groaned in protest. Slowly she opened her eyes and saw Zach standing before the hearth, staring into the dancing flames. He had removed his jacket and shirt sometime during the night, and Abby thought him magnificent. The muscles in his broad shoulders and sinewy arms flexed and rippled as he bent to add wood to the fire. His back, muscled with corded strength, glistened in the golden light. His buttocks beneath his tight pants were high and hard and powerfully male. The tendons in his thighs and calves were long and athletic. Hot awareness thickened Abby's blood and pooled in her loins.

As if suddenly aware of her gaze, Zach straightened and turned, meeting her eyes. A slow smile alleviated his brooding features. "I'm glad you approve."

With a volition of its own, her gaze slid upward, lingering briefly at his loins, gasping at the sight of his heavy, hard manhood straining against his trousers. Tearing her gaze from that potent part of him, she jerked her eyes upward, over his broad chest, to his face. He was still grinning. Blood rushed to her cheeks when she realized that he knew what she was thinking. She searched his face for the space of a heartbeat before lowering her eyes.

"I—I don't know what you mean."

"Don't you? Your eyes tell me differently. If you keep looking at me like that, I'll lose what little control I have left."

He walked toward her with the swivel-hipped grace of a stalking panther. She tried to keep her eyes averted, but it was impossible. Their gazes met and locked. He lay down beside her, pulling her into his arms. "We've still a few hours until daylight."

Abby felt the tension in his body, the heat of his flesh, and the need for sleep fled like leaves before the wind. When he pushed aside the heavy cloak of her hair and placed a tender kiss on the nape of her neck, she nearly swooned with heady delight.

"Zach . . . I'm tired." Her words held a ring of desperation. If he tried to make love to her, she was lost. If he didn't, she would die. Either way she was doomed. A tense silence hovered between them.

"Foolish girl. Do you think the attraction between us will go away if I don't make love to you?" A vein pulsed in his temple, and flames leaped from the blue depths of his eyes, igniting the air between them.

"I'm hoping it will. It's wrong to lie with you. I fear I inherited a passionate nature from my white ancestors. As much as I admire the Cheyenne and try to emulate them, I cannot deny my white blood. If you care for me at all, you will not tempt me like this."

"Dammit, Abby, if you'd think about it, you'd realize the attraction between us has nothing to do with you being white or Cheyenne and everything to do with passion and emotions. The very air around us sizzles when we're together. When I touch you, something explodes inside me."

Abby clapped her hands over her ears and turned her back to him. "Stop! I don't want to hear those words. You have no right to say them."

He swung her around to face him. Abby went absolutely motionless. Her heart was beating in a frenzied, frantic motion. "I have every right in the world. You belong to me, sweetheart, whether you realize it or not."

"You are just saying that because—because you were the first to—to—" She flushed and lowered her gaze. "You feel pity for me, and I am too proud to accept pity. Don't you see how different our worlds are? Our destinies lie in opposite directions."

Zach shifted, bringing his chest into direct contact with hers so that she could feel his heart pounding. Her breasts were crushed fully against his bare chest, and he cursed the deerskin tunic that separated her flesh from his. His eyes caressed her lips, their lush fullness beckoning to him. Dismayed, Abby knew he was going to kiss her and tried to prevent it.

"D—don't." Her voice trembled. Zach seemed entranced by the tip of her tongue as it darted out to moisten the corner of her mouth.

His lips moved against hers in a raspy whisper. "Do you really want me to stop? I will—

just tell me you don't want me."

She wanted to stop him; she did want to. But when he unlaced the strings at the shoulder of her tunic, lowered it, and lifted a bare breast to his mouth, words failed her. When he took one erect nipple in his mouth, teasing it with his tongue, Abby grasped his head, crying out. Her intention might have been to push him away, but she held him to her fiercely, moaning as he sucked and licked her nipples.

"Tell me, Abby, tell me to stop while I still can. If not, I will make love to you as surely as daylight follows dawn." His eyes were blue flames, burning intensely. Abby's protest lodged in her throat. When she remained silent, hot blood surged to his loins in anticipation. Abruptly he slid her tunic down her hips and tossed it aside.

Rising slightly, Zach skinned off his pants. Abby's eyes widened as his manhood sprang free, engorged and fully erect. The sight of his male strength was so stirring that she closed her eyes and went still, her heart pounding erratically. But instead of entering her as she expected, she felt the glide of his hair-roughened body down hers and the heat of his mouth between her legs. Shock splintered through her, and her eyes flew open.

"Zach! No, you must not . . . Oh . . ." She tried to rise. He ignored her, pressing against her stomach to hold her down.

His tongue lashed her; his mouth ravished her. He gripped her buttocks and brought her up to meet his hungry lips, her exotic scent driving him wild. He had never lost control like this. No woman had ever captured his senses like Abby. He worshiped her with his mouth, kissing her as intimately as a man could kiss a woman, his tongue stroking over and into every crevice of luscious flesh he could find.

When he thrust a finger inside her, she climaxed violently, shuddering and gasping his name, spasm after spasm shaking her slender frame. With slow deliberation, he slid his body upward until he rested atop her, the muscles in his arms, neck, and shoulders straining, his need so urgent that he gasped in agony. Flexing his hips, he thrust into her hard. Abby arched to meet him. Her arms coiled around his shoulders; her legs gripped his hips. Their gazes collided. Then his mouth slammed down on hers.

When he felt her moist flesh surround him, his control snapped. He pushed his hips forward. Fast and deep, hard, hot, thrusting, withdrawing, groaning out his pleasure, telling her how wonderful she felt, how tight and hot. Abby pushed up her hips to meet him, wanting, needing, meeting the fury of his thrusting body with a fury of her own. Suddenly she gripped him fiercely as a gigantic wave seized her and tossed her upon a sea of intense, mind-shattering rapture. She shouted his name.

Zach's powerful buttocks tensed as he rode her faster, deeper, thrusting a final time, driving himself to a more dramatic climax than he had ever experienced in his lifetime.

They lay limp, drained, totally spent. He moved away from her slowly, reluctantly. Fearing she might be cold, he pulled her into the curve of his body. His own body steamed with heat, and his breath hissed from his lungs in harsh gasps.

Angry at herself for surrendering yet another time to Zach, a man with whom she shared no common ground, Abby tried to convince herself that the pleasure she shared with Zach was the result of defects in her nature. But she knew she was fooling no one but herself. Just imagining another man doing the same things Zach had just done to her made her sick to her stomach.

"Abby, don't go to sleep. Not yet. I want you to know the decision I've made regarding your future."

Abby's temper exploded. "You cannot make decisions for me! You are not my husband, my father, or my brother. I want to join White Feather at Sand Creek."

"That's a dead subject, Abby. White Feather doesn't want you there, and I will not allow you to go. Great danger exists at Sand Creek. I have no proof, but I've heard snippets of gossip concerning Chivington and his Colorado volunteers. I won't know for sure what's afoot until they arrive at Fort Lyon."

Abby frowned. "You are trying to frighten me. The governor assured Black Kettle that the Cheyenne would be safe at Sand Creek."

"Perhaps you are right, but it changes nothing where you are concerned. I intend to keep my promise to White Feather. There is only one sure way I know to protect you. We must marry."

Abby sent him a mutinous glare. "No."

An exasperated sigh hissed past Zach's lips. He knew this wasn't going to be easy. "Abby, be reasonable. Am I so disgusting that you can't stand me?"

Abby stared at him. Disagusting? She wanted to deny that the sight of him filled her heart with strong emotions, but she could not. He was white, and she was Cheyenne, despite the color of her skin and hair. Marriage to Zach would change her life too drastically. She couldn't cope in a society of strange customs and morals. Besides, he was only proposing because he felt sorry for her and enjoyed her body.

"You are not disgusting at all," she admitted cautiously.

"Am I ugly, or brutal, or cruel?"

"No! You are none of those things. You are white, Zach! I cannot live in your world."

Zach sighed wearily. "Go to sleep, Abby. We will speak of this tomorrow when you are more reasonable."

"We will not speak of it again," Abby insisted stubbornly.

285

"If you have not conceived my child before now, you may have tonight. No child of mine will be born a bastard. And I won't allow you to take those damn herbs," he said with fierce disapproval.

Since the herbs she needed had been destroyed by frost, and she had none of the dried variety, taking them was not an option. "I have no herbs. And I do not know what bastard means."

Zach's fierce expression softened. "A bastard is someone born to parents who are not married. In today's society, it is a bad thing to be born a bastard. A bastard is reviled and ridiculed all of his life."

Abby's chin rose fractionally. "A Cheyenne would never abuse or ridicule a child in such a manner. A child is not to blame if his mother committed a grave sin. But I shall not conceive your child. *Heammawihio* will not allow such a thing to happen."

Zach smiled in wry amusement. "*Heammawihio* is not the one filling you with his seed."

His words struck Abby like a dash of cold water. Her mouth snapped shut, and she turned her back on him, refusing to reply, for in truth she had no reply. When he touched her again, she stiffened. Zach gave a heavy sigh and allowed her her small defiance. Ultimately he would have his way. It was the only honorable thing to do.

It was what he wanted to do!

* * *

A weak sun shone through the dirty window of the snug shelter they had found during the storm. Abby stirred and stretched languorously, her body sated and content. She felt safe and warm beneath the buffalo robe. A tiny smile hovered on the corner of her lips.

"Dare I hope that smile is meant for me?"

Abby's eyes flew open. Zach stood before her, fully dressed. Her gaze flowed upward over his booted feet, past sturdy calves, bulging thighs, trim waist, and muscular chest, to his face. He was grinning, and her cloak of contentment slipped away.

"I wasn't smiling." Her voice had a defiant edge to it.

"You sure as hell could have fooled me," Zach said wryly. His grin widened. Abby could deny it until her face turned blue, but he knew she felt something for him. No one could make love as sweetly as she did and not mean it. His heart constricted painfully when he recalled how close he had come to losing her.

"As much as I hate to leave this cozy nest, we must return to Fort Lyon. If I don't return soon, I will be reported missing and a search party sent out."

Abby waited warily for Zach to make mention of his decision that they would marry when they reached the fort, and when he did not, relief shuddered through her. Perhaps, she hoped desperately, he had taken her words to heart and decided not to saddle himself with a wife who did not fit into white society.

Zach had fed the fire, and the room was warm. The smell of coffee wafted through the air, and Abby sniffed appreciatively. She started to rise and saw Zach staring at her. Heat rushed to her face when she realized she was naked. She saw his eyes kindle and recalled all the shameful, wonderful things she and Zach had done last night. She averted her gaze, ignoring his unspoken challenge.

"Would you please hand me my tunic?"

Aware of her discomfort, Zach chuckled, but he obligingly rescued her tunic and handed it to her. When she saw that he wasn't going to turn away while she dressed, she squirmed into the tunic beneath the buffalo robe. When she finally emerged, fully dressed, he gave her a look that melted her bones.

They left their private paradise after a quick breakfast of leftover fry bread and freshly brewed coffee. Abby knew better than to ask Zach to take her to Sand Creek. Experience had taught her that Zach could not be swayed by words.

The day was clear and cold; snow no longer fell, and the sun felt warm on Abby's back. The storm had dropped about two inches of wind-driven snow during the night, not enough to hinder their travel. Dusk hovered on the edge of darkness as Abby and Zach approached the fort.

Abby thought it strange that Zach had made no further mention of their marriage, and she supposed she should be grateful. Marriage to Zach Mercer was impossible—but oh, how she wished she had the luxury of giving her heart freely and unconditionally!

The sentry at the gate saw them and asked for identification.

"Captain Zach Mercer and Miss Abby Larson," Zach returned loudly.

The gate creaked open and they passed through. The sentry saluted. "Welcome back, sir. Sergeant Porter was getting worried. Your patrol was ambushed by Crow on the way back."

Zach frowned. Had they been ambushed by the same renegades who had attacked Abby and Painted Horse? If so, the Crow must have joined up with a larger band.

"How many casualties?" Concern colored his words.

"Three dead and two wounded," the sentry replied. "But word is that the count was much higher among the Crow. What was left of them escaped into the hills above Sand Creek."

"What about Sergeant Porter?" Zach asked tightly. He should have been with them instead of sending the patrol on ahead without him.

"The sergeant is just fine, Captain." He eyed Abby warily. "Where did you find *her*, sir?"

The sentry's voice was bitter with condemnation, and she wondered if he was the man Painted Horse had struck so that they could pass through the gate without being seen.

"It's a long story," Zach said, confused by the animosity in the sentry's voice. Was there something Abby had neglected to tell him?

"Where are you taking me?" Abby asked sullenly. She preferred not to return to the Porters after what she had done to Belinda.

"Oh, Captain," the sentry called after them. "Major Anthony left word that you were to report to him immediately when you returned."

Zach merely grunted as he reined his horse in the direction of the Porters' modest house.

"Zach, I don't think I should go to the Porters. You heard the sentry. I tried to explain that I'm no longer welcome at the fort, but you wouldn't listen. The Porters won't be glad to see me."

"You won't be staying there long, Abby." His words gave her a fluttery feeling in the pit of her stomach, but before she could ask what he meant they had arrived at the Porters' front door. Zach had already dismounted and was helping Abby from her horse when the front door opened and Belinda appeared in the doorway.

"Zach, Papa has been terribly worried about you. Come in. He'll be so glad to see you're alive and well. He feared the Crow raiders might have found you." Then she saw Abby and stiffened, her expression ferocious. "My God, what is *she* doing here?"

Grasping her hand, Zach led Abby past Belinda into the house. "I found Abby about a day's ride from here. She and—her companion were under siege by Crow renegades."

"You should have let them have her," Belinda said with bitter emphasis. "It would be no great loss."

"Zach, thank God you're safe!" Pete Porter walked into the room, followed closely by Milly. "I feared you'd encountered the same band of renegades we did." Abby wished she could disappear into the woodwork when Pete's censorious gaze settled on her. "Surely you don't expect us to welcome Abby back into our home after what she did."

A puzzled frown puckered Zach's brow. What in the hell had Abby done to earn such hostility? He knew Belinda didn't like her, but he'd assumed that was due to petty jealousy. When Milly gave Abby a cold glare and turned her back, Zach groaned in dismay, aware that she had offended the Porters in some unforgivable way.

"I had hoped you'd give her a place to stay for the night."

"Where did you find her?" Pete asked.

"She and her companion were pinned down by Crow raiders. I found them shortly after I left that settler's cabin you told me about, but I arrived too late to save Painted Horse."

"Who is Painted Horse and what was she doing with him?"

Zach sighed heavily. "It's a long story, Pete. Suffice it to say, Abby was on her way to Sand Creek."

291

"Too bad you didn't let the Crow have her," Belinda snorted. "Did the little savage tell you what she did to me?"

Zach whirled on Abby, his expression grim. "Did you deliberately forget to tell me something, Abby? What have you done to offend the Porters?"

Abby raised her chin to a defiant angle. "I had no choice. If I hadn't hit Belinda, she would have screamed her head off and awakened everyone in the fort."

"You hit Belinda?" Zach nearly choked on the words. "With what?"

"My fist. I had to. When Painted Horse offered to take me to Sand Creek, I did what was necessary."

"She bound and gagged me. I could have died," Belinda exaggerated. "She threatened to kill me, and I believed her."

Abby made a disgusted noise deep in her throat. "You lie. I would not have harmed you."

"I was pretty shook up when I returned and learned what Abby had done," Pete confessed.

"I really don't understand," Milly complained. "I tried to do my best for the girl."

Abby's expression softened. "I would never do anything to harm you or your family, Milly. I was desperate to leave the fort, and Belinda was growing hysterical. You and Pete have been very kind to me, and I won't forget it."

"Be that as it may," Milly sniffed, "we can no longer trust you."

"She can't stay here," Belinda insisted. "Find some other family to take her in. But I warn you, it won't be easy."

Zach struggled to hold on to his temper. He was so angry with Abby that he wanted to turn her over his knee and paddle her. "Does Belinda speak for the entire family, Pete?"

Pete sent Zach an apologetic look. "I love my daughter, Captain. Belinda is my only child. I won't do anything to endanger her life. I don't believe Abby is dangerous, but I must do what I think is best for my family."

"It would only be for one night."

"One night?" Belinda asked curiously. "Have you already found another family to take her in?"

"I refuse to stay where I am not wanted," Abby insisted belligerently.

"Be quiet, Abby." Zach's curt reprimand warned her that he was at the end of his tether. She had given him enough trouble for one night.

Belinda sent Abby a smug grin. It was about time the little savage was put in her place. Maybe now that Zach knew how brutal Abby was, he'd return her to her beloved Indians.

Zach's next words jolted Belinda's complacency. "Abby and I are going to be married as soon as I can make the arrangements. Probably tomorrow." His announcement brought a cry of denial from Abby and total silence from the Porters.

Belinda was the first to find her voice. "You can't mean it! The woman is a savage. I know you probably feel responsible for her since you were the one who brought her to the fort, and you were unchaperoned during the time you were together, but I prefer to believe you behaved like a gentleman. Besides, no one would expect you to marry a white savage, no matter what went on between you."

"Oh, dear," Milly said, looking as if she might faint. "I do hope you know what you're doing, Captain Mercer."

"Believe me, I am perfectly sane," Zach assured them.

Pete seemed the least perturbed by Zach's announcement. He knew Zach was an honorable man and felt that marriage to Abby was probably for the best, especially since he was reasonably certain Zach and Abby shared an intimate relationship. Abby needed a strong man to tame her, he reasoned, not envying Zach the chore.

"I think we're being a little hard on Abby," Pete said, earning a poisonous glare from his daughter. "We must consider her miserable background. She's had to adjust to a whole new way of life."

"She hit me, Papa!" Belinda reminded him. "You can't be thinking of letting her back into the house. Besides, once Zach realizes he's making a mistake, he'll change his mind about marrying Abby."

By now Abby's anger hovered on the edge of madness. How dare Zach decide her fate without considering her feelings! "I will marry no one against my will."

"Be quiet, Abby," Zach repeated. "The way I see it, you have no choice. Have you forgotten our little talk back at that abandoned cabin?"

Belinda's eyes narrowed. "Abandoned cabin? You were together in an abandoned cabin?"

"All the more reason for them to marry," Pete contended. "Under the circumstances, I think we should offer Abby the hospitality of our home for one more night."

Milly added reluctant agreement, but Belinda was clearly hostile to the idea. "I will not share a room with her."

"I didn't intend for you to, daughter," Pete said. "Since I have duty tonight, you may share your mother's room."

"Thank you, Pete," Zach said, vastly relieved. "I'd like a word in private with Abby before I report to Major Anthony."

Abby waited until she and Zach were alone before turning on him in fury. "Why did you tell them we were going to be married?"

"Because we are," Zach replied, unruffled. "And I expect you to behave tonight. No more running away. And leave Belinda alone. One doesn't repay kindness by hitting the daughter of one's host. You should have told me, Abby. Is there anything else I should know?"

Abby swallowed convulsively. "I'm sorry about Belinda. I never intended to hurt her."

"I know." His expression softened. "But that still doesn't excuse your behavior. I must go now. I'll let you know as soon as all the arrangements are made."

"Zach, wait! There *is* something else."

Zach's rolled his eyes, his patience all but shot. "Why doesn't that surprise me?"

"Painted Horse took care of the sentry so we wouldn't be challenged when we left the fort."

"Exactly how did he 'take care' of the guard?"

Abby shrugged. "I suppose he—rendered him senseless."

"You'd better hope that's all he did," Zach warned ominously. "Major Anthony will be furious if the sentry was seriously hurt. Good night, Abby. I'll see you tomorrow."

Abby was startled when Zach reached for her and pulled her hard against him.

She gasped as his arms clamped around her and his mouth came down hard on hers with a primal growl of pure need. His tongue prodded her lips apart and thrust inside, boldly weaving his special magic in her body, her senses, her soul.

Her heart.

The kiss continued for an eternity, and when he abruptly broke it off, Abby was panting to catch her breath. He smiled at her with slow relish. "Tomorrow." His voice was rich and deep with promise. When he walked out the door, her heart was beating like a trip-hammer.

Chapter Fifteen

Major Anthony's mouth gaped open, his eyes wide with disbelief. "You what! I don't believe I heard you right, Captain Mercer. Did you say you intend to marry Miss Larson? After what she did to Miss Porter and Private Henley? You must be out of your mind."

"Perhaps," Zach allowed, beginning to doubt his own sanity. "But nevertheless, Abby Larson and I will marry as soon as it can be arranged with the chaplain. Tomorrow, I hope."

Major Anthony's eyes narrowed speculatively. "What's the rush? Frankly, I'd say you're thinking with your loins. Granted she's a fine-looking piece, but hardly deserving of your name. She was raised by savages, for God's sake. Think, Captain! Think of how your family will react when they learn you've married a white squaw."

Zach's jaw tightened, and he said very calmly, "I'd be proud to introduce Abby to my family, Major. You don't know her like I do, so how can you judge her? And I'd appreciate it if you wouldn't call her a squaw. Her blood is as pure as yours or mine. She had no control over the way she was raised."

"Perhaps not, but you can't deny that she acted like a savage when she attacked Miss Porter. The poor girl could have been killed."

"Miss Larson exaggerates, Major. No real harm was done to her. And you said yourself, Private Henley was merely knocked unconscious and not seriously hurt."

"But the fact remains that both were attacked."

"Are you forbidding the marriage?"

Anthony assumed a thoughtful expression. He had no authority to forbid a marriage between two consenting adults. He could advise but not forbid. "You are free to marry whomever you please," he said dismissively. "I hope you don't live to regret it. Just don't expect the residents of the fort to extend your wife a warm welcome."

Zach had no delusions about Abby's reception. He supposed that by now everyone had heard what had happened to Belinda and the sentry. "Thank you, Major. Am I dismissed?"

"I know you're tired from your long ride today, but I want your opinion about the Crow renegades who attacked your patrol. Do you think they're still in the area? Sergeant Porter said they rode toward Sand Creek after the attack. Should we assume they have joined the Cheyenne camped there?"

"I seriously doubt they have joined the Cheyenne at Sand Creek. The two tribes are natural enemies and have nothing to do with one another except for occasional raids into each other's territory for horses and captives. It's my personal opinion that we'll have no more trouble from them until spring."

Anthony hesitated, then said. "I suppose you've heard that Colonel Chivington and his Colorado volunteers are expected at the fort."

"I've heard the rumor," Zach said, his interest sharpening. "They say he has six hundred cavalrymen under his command, most of them men who volunteered solely to fight Indians. What could he possibly want at Fort Lyon? Except for a few Crow raiders, there are no hostiles about. Especially at this time of year."

Though Anthony was aware of Chivington's mission, he did not so much as flick an eyelash as he said, "We will learn soon enough, won't we? If you have nothing further to add, you are dismissed, Captain."

"There is one thing more, Major. I request permission to move with my bride into one of the vacant houses on Officers' Row. My bachelor quarters are inadequate for two people."

"It's against my better judgment, but permission granted. I will hold you personally responsible for your wife's behavior. Until she proves herself trustworthy, I suggest that you keep a tight rein on her activities."

Zach kept a tight rein on his temper. Anthony's opinion of Abby was so unfair, he knew if he didn't get out of there immediately he would explode. Saluting smartly, he whirled on his heel and left the room. He went immediately to the chaplain's office, hoping to arrange for a brief wedding ceremony in the chapel the next day. The chaplain, more tolerant than Major Anthony, agreed to perform the ceremony at two o'clock the following afternoon. On his way home, Zach stopped in at the orderly room to see Pete Porter, who was on duty that night.

"I need a witness to my marriage, Sergeant," Zach said without preamble. "I'd be damn grateful if you'd do the honors."

"Belinda will have my skin, but I'd be happy to act as witness, Captain. And I'm sure I can talk Milly into it, too. She was mighty fond of Abby until . . ." His words faltered and he looked away. Then he cleared his throat and said, "We'll be there."

Zach's face lost some of its tenseness. "I knew I could count on you, Pete. I'll trust you to get Abby to the chapel at two o'clock tomorrow afternoon." He turned to leave.

"Captain, when we spoke earlier I failed to mention the names of the men who were killed by the Crow. Privates Lentz, Flaherty, and Zelmer were killed outright. They had been scouting ahead with Privates Kramer and Talbot. Kramer and Talbot were wounded but are expected to make full recoveries."

"Lentz and Flaherty? Weren't they the men we suspected of attacking Abby that night on the parade ground?"

"Those were the ones. We might never know the truth now, unless Kramer decides to talk."

"Let me know when the man is well enough to stand up to questioning. I'm not ready to drop the issue yet. Good night, Pete. It's been a long day."

Belinda listened to her mother's loud snores and knew from experience that nothing short of an earthquake would awaken her. Quiet as a wraith, she slid from bed, dressed quickly, and left the room. She paused briefly at Abby's door, heard nothing to indicate that Abby wasn't sleeping, and moved down the hall toward the front door. Her cloak was hanging on a hook and she slipped it on, pulling up the hood to hide her face before letting herself out the door. Frost crunched beneath her feet as she made her way along the perimeter of the parade ground. She reached Zach's quarters without incident and paused outside Zach's door to gather her courage. Though it was very late, a light appeared around the edges of the drawn window shades, indicating that Zach hadn't yet retired. Taking a deep breath, she rapped sharply on the door.

Zach had just put his signature on a letter telling his brother about his marriage and was reaching to douse the light so he could retire when he was startled by a knock at the door.

His first thought was that Abby had left the Porter house without permission again. Did she hope to change his mind at this late hour? He flung open the door, spitting out a curse when he saw a woman whose face and figure were concealed by a cloak and hood. Grasping her arm, he pulled her inside.

"Dammit, Abby, what in the hell are you doing here at this time of night? There is nothing you can do or say to change my mind."

Belinda threw back her hood. "If Abby can't change your mind, perhaps I can."

Astounded, Zach gaped at Belinda. "Belinda! What in God's name are you doing here?" Finding Belinda on his doorstep was so unexpected that he could only stare at her.

"I'm here to change your mind about marrying Abby, Zach," Belinda said, stepping closer. Her eyes settled disconcertingly on the patch of bare chest visible in the vee of his open shirt. The sight was so arousing that her breath caught in her throat and her tongue flicked out to lick her dry lips. She wondered if the same fine hairs furred his entire body.

"This is too much," Zach flung out disgustedly. "Don't you realize your reputation will be ruined if someone saw you enter my rooms? What in the world were you thinking?"

"It's worth it if I can change your mind. How can you want to marry a woman who's lain with Lord knows how many Indians? I'm not naive enough to think you haven't been intimate with her during all those times you've been alone, but no one will condemn you for that. You're a man—you were tempted by a conniving little whore."

Zach stiffened. "Abby is not a whore." His voice held an edge to it Belinda had not heard before. "Why should you care who I marry?"

Belinda smiled archly, narrowing the space between them until her breasts brushed his chest. "Because I care about you. I care a great deal. When you first arrived at Fort Lyon, I realized that you were the kind of man I've been waiting for all my life."

Zach was astounded. Granted, Belinda was an attractive female, but she had never appealed to him sexually. He thought of her as Pete's daughter, nothing more, nothing less. He had no inkling that she was attracted to him. "I'm sorry, Belinda, it just never occurred to me that you would read more into our friendship than was there. I didn't intend to give you the impression that we might become—close. No matter, it's too late now. I'm going to marry Abby."

Belinda paled. "Surely you don't love that little savage, do you? Look at me, Zach—I'm much prettier, and a darn sight more civilized. I'll never be an embarrassment to you like Abby is bound to be. And," she added, her eyes dark with promise, "I'll be a good lover."

"Dammit, Belinda, don't talk like that!"

"I mean it, Zach. If you don't believe me, let me prove it to you. Make love to me." She dropped her cloak, her fingers working to unfasten the buttons on her bodice. Before Zach realized what she intended, the edges of her dress gaped open and she was fumbling with the ties of her chemise.

Desperation released Zach's frozen limbs as he reached for her cloak and threw it around her shoulders. "Don't compromise your virtue, Belinda. Leave now and we'll both forget this ever happened. Believe me when I say I'm not interested in making love to you."

A look of utter disbelief came over Belinda's features. "Why—why you *do* love her! You actually love the little savage."

Zach's brow furrowed. Love? That notion would bear some thinking about. "Perhaps," he answered slowly.

"Well," Belinda sniffed haughtily. "I can see I'm wasting my time. Goodbye, Zach, and good luck. You'll need it."

Relieved, Zach opened the door. "Would you like me to escort you home?"

Sending him a scathing look, she flounced off into the dark. "I want nothing to do with a man who fancies himself in love with a savage," she threw over her shoulder.

Would he ever understand women? Zach wondered as he closed the door behind Belinda. Of all the women in the world, why was Abby the woman he wanted? Why couldn't he want someone suitable, like Belinda, someone who would love him in return? Someone who wouldn't act as if he were dirt beneath her feet. It wasn't simply that Abby was unique, or that the attraction between them was so intense and alive that it sizzled. His feelings were so damned confusing, it made his head ache. Without his realizing it, Abby had invaded his mind and body and crept into his heart.

Since he had never experienced love before, he wondered if what he felt for Abby would qualify.

The day was cold and blustery. Fluffy flakes of snow sifted down from a gray sky, dusting Zach's face and hair with white as he waited in the doorway of the chapel. He glanced at his watch and saw that it was five minutes past two, with no sign of Abby or the Porters. He gave the chaplain a nervous smile and glanced out the door again. He trusted Pete to get Abby to the church, but he still couldn't help being nervous, aware of Abby's marked reluctance to marry him. If they didn't show up soon, he'd be forced to take matters into his own hands.

"Perhaps we should take care of the paperwork while we're waiting," the chaplain suggested helpfully.

"Good idea," Zach replied, his voice taut with worry. What if Abby had run away again? What if . . . He turned away from the door and followed the chaplain inside the chapel.

Zach signed his name to the marriage document and looked up just as Milly came rushing through the door. "Captain Mercer, Pete and Abby will be here directly, but I wanted to warn you before they arrived. I didn't think Abby would be so stubborn. There was nothing I could do to change her mind."

Zach listened to Milly with growing alarm. What in the hell had Abby done now? But before he could form his thoughts into a question, he heard a commotion outside the chapel.

"Oh, lordy," Milly groaned, "it's too late. Don't say I didn't warn you."

Abby suppressed a smug grin when she saw the small crowd trailing behind them. She knew they were making fun of her, but she didn't care. It was her fondest hope that once Zach saw the spectacle she had made of herself, he'd realize that marriage wasn't right for them and cry off. Being stared at would be worth it if it changed Zach's mind. She had argued with Milly and Pete until she had finally worn them down.

Standing before the chapel now, Abby took a deep steadying breath, raised her chin, and stepped inside. The group of curious onlookers stopped just short of the door. Abby's heart fluttered wildly in her chest as Zach turned and looked at her, his expression inscrutable. He narrowed the gap between them, and she steeled herself for his harsh words of disapproval. What she received were words of praise—so unexpected that they left her speechless.

"You look beautiful." Nothing could have shocked her more than his honest admiration.

Abby had been absolutely positive that Zach would be so embarrassed if she showed up wearing her beaded tunic and moccasins that he'd withdraw his marriage proposal.

Zach's warm regard slid over her like warm, thick honey. He had never seen any woman as lovely as Abby in her Indian finery. Reaching just below her knees, the hemline of her tunic touched the tops of her knee-high moccasins. Her hair, grown out to its natural sable, was fashioned into a single braid that caressed her narrow waist. It was held in place by the beaded headband crowned by an eagle feather.

"I tried to dress her properly," Milly complained, wringing her hands, "but she refused. You know how obstinate she can be. I know she's a sight, Captain. Perhaps you can persuade her to return home and change into something decent."

Unable to tear his eyes from her, Zach grasped Abby's hand and drew her toward the altar where the chaplain stood waiting. "Abby is perfect just the way she is."

Abby suppressed a groan. She wanted to annoy Zach but had earned his approval instead.

"This is the wedding dress I wish to wear," she announced, trying her best to anger Zach.

"I approve," Zach said quietly. "It's quite appropriate."

"You approve?" Milly asked, aghast.

Unable to take his eyes from Abby, Zach nodded. "Shall we proceed with the wedding?"

Abby's face drained of all color. She had been so certain Zach would reject her. She was beyond understanding a man like Zach Mercer. He was looking at her as if he held some small degree of affection for her. Don't be foolish, she scolded herself. Zach lusted for her—she already knew that—and felt pity for her.

Abby felt her knees shake as the chaplain began reciting the words that would join them. She had often dreamed of becoming a wife, but in her dreams her husband would have copper skin and hair as black as midnight. She glanced at Zach from beneath lowered lids, noting how the light reflected off his sun-streaked hair and how magnificent he looked in his uniform. Just gazing at him made her forget everything but the way he brought her to the brink of madness with his body, mouth, and hands. If Zach truly loved her, she would do all in her power to make this marriage work.

Zach repeated his vows in a loud voice. When it came Abby's turn, she looked at Zach askance, unclear what she was supposed to do or say.

"Repeat after the chaplain," Zach whispered into her ear. Abby did as she was told, looking absolutely terrified when Zach placed a ring on her finger and the chaplain pronounced them man and wife. Dimly she wondered when Zach had had time to buy a ring and arrange all this.

Congratulations were brief and subdued. Milly went home immediately, and Pete returned to duty, leaving Zach and Abby staring at each other in awkward silence. Abby looked confused when it came time to sign the marriage paper, realizing that she couldn't write and afraid Zach would laugh at her. But Zach solved the problem by having her place an X on the document, which was witnessed by the chaplain. Once the legalities were attended to, she noted that Zach was grinning from ear to ear.

"You don't have to look so happy," Abby said tartly.

"I can't help it. Don't worry, sweetheart, it will work out. You'll see. I can protect you properly now. One day you'll realize this is for the best."

Abby stared at him. "I think . . ." She hesitated, dropping her gaze. Zach placed a finger beneath her chin and tilted her head so he could look into her upturned face.

"What, Abby? Tell me what you think."

"I—think you're brave to marry a 'white savage' like me. Why *did* you marry me when there are other women more suitable?"

Zach's expression grew thoughtful. It was a question he'd asked himself many times. Would she believe him if he told her he cared about her? Or would she laugh at him? He decided he'd rather not know. "It's cold, Abby, and standing here is doing neither of us any good. Let's go home. It isn't much, but it's the best I can do for now." He grasped her arm, leading her toward a row of neat little houses across the parade ground.

"Where are you taking me?"

"To our new home. I moved from my bachelor quarters into married officer housing. Most of the wives left the fort at the first sign of Indian trouble, leaving several vacant units. Ah, here we are."

Zach held the door open as she walked inside, following close on her heels. "I hope you'll be comfortable here."

The small house resembled the one occupied by the Porters, down to the plain, functional furniture. Someone had built a fire in the stove in the parlor, spreading warmth throughout the small house. "It's not a tipi," Abby said wistfully, "but I suppose it will do." She peeked into each of the rooms, surprised to see that her clothing had been brought from the Porters and hung neatly on hooks in the bedroom.

"I had one of my men carry your belongings over while we were at the chapel."

When she walked into the kitchen, nodding approvingly at the neat rows of canned goods lining the shelves, Zach said, "I arranged for them to be delivered this morning."

"You've thought of everything."

"Everything except how to make you accept this marriage."

Abby felt the heavy weight of his blue eyes warming her and turned to stare at him. His gaze was steady, hot, intense. She felt the breath slam out of her as he took a step forward. Then another, and another, until she felt his hot breath fan her cheek.

"Whether I accept it or not makes little difference," she said shakily. It was difficult to think, let alone speak, with Zach standing so close to her. It was the nearest she had come to admitting that she was finally resigned to their marriage. "I just wish . . ."

"What, Abby? What do you wish?"

"I never pictured myself living in a wooden house or wearing white women's clothing. I never imagined a husband with white skin and blue eyes. Had I married Painted Horse, it wouldn't be because he pitied me."

"Is that what you think?" His voice was harsh with an emotion Abby did not recognize.

"I can think of no other reason." A flare of stubborn resistance kept her from admitting that she cared for him more than he cared for her. If she weren't Cheyenne, and he weren't white . . .

He wrapped his arms around her, drawing her into his embrace, spreading kisses across her jaw to her full red lips. "Are these the kisses of a man who feels pity for his wife?" His mouth grew hard, demanding, his tongue sweetly tormenting as it slipped past her teeth to explore inside her mouth.

Abby groaned and swayed against him. She felt the inflamed ridge of his manhood through her clothing and undulated against it. A hoarse growl rumbled from Zach's chest as he caught her beneath the knees and lifted her from the floor. She gave a small cry of protest as she felt herself powerless in his arms, but his ravenous kisses drove all the differences that separated them from her mind. She wanted to believe Zach cared for her, and for a brief moment of madness she *did* believe it.

Abby felt her feet touch the floor, her body slowly sliding down the hard length of his. She felt as if her bones were melting. Her eyes rested on the bed. She licked her lips, attempting to speak three times before forcing the words from her throat.

"It's—the middle of the day."

Zach grinned. "So it is." His fingers moved to unlace the ties at the shoulders of her tunic. "I want to undress you, Abby. I want to see every part of you in the daylight. I want to take my time and love you properly. You're my wife now, and we've got the rest of the day and night before I have to return to duty."

Wife! Zach wanted to shout out the word. Sing it from the highest tower. He had never thought much about marriage before, though he knew he would probably marry one day. Since meeting Abby, he decided that spending his life with any other woman did not appeal to him. Abby was dead wrong if she thought he pitied her. His emotions went deeper—much deeper.

Abby stood motionless as Zach slowly peeled the tunic down her arms, baring her breasts. He paused briefly, staring at them, then shoved the tunic down past her hips. Lifting her by the waist, he stripped the tunic from her and tossed it aside. She closed her eyes as he knelt before her and removed her moccasins. She felt the heat of his mouth caress her as he feverishly feasted on the silky softness of her skin, kissing and sucking her breasts greedily, encouraged by her soft moans of pleasure. She gasped and quaked like a leaf when he ran his tongue up and down the insides of her silken thighs.

Grasping his head, she tried to shove him away, shocked by the terrible need growing inside her, a need only Zach could assuage. Then her thoughts scattered as he buried his face in the soft curls at the base of her belly and his tongue delved into the moist crevice between her thighs. Her legs buckled, and she cried out his name. His control shattered, he scooped her up in his arms and carried her to the bed. Dazed and aching, she watched him undress. His manhood was huge and swollen, and a reckless compulsion seized her. She sat up and reached for him. His sharp intake of breath turned into a shout as she wrapped her hand around him.

She was amazed to feel him grow even larger. Growing bold, she stroked him, enthralled at how soft and velvety the skin felt over the rock-hard flesh. She moved her hand down, then up, then down again. Shudders wracked his body, and his moans of delight filled the air. Suddenly he stiffened and his hand stilled hers. She glanced up at him, surprised to see an intense, almost painful expression on his face. He pushed her down on her back, kneeling over her.

"Two can play at that game," he gasped as he spread her legs apart and slid down the length of her body. Then she felt his mouth between her legs, felt his tongue delving hot and hard into her slick moistness. As nimble and skillful as his fingers were, they were nothing compared to what his tongue was doing to her. It was an instrument of sweet torture, a devil's tool devised solely to torment her.

She felt the flames of hell devouring her, stroking her, lashing her, dipping inside of her. Incredible waves of intense pleasure flowed over her, in her, around her, and she feared she would die if he didn't stop.

"Zach! Please stop! I can't stand it." Her heart was pounding so hard, she feared it would explode.

But Zach had no intention of stopping. The sweet essence of her and the scent of her womanliness were exciting him unbearably.

Powerful sensations battered Abby. Her breath squeezed from her chest in hot, ragged gasps. Her entire body was an inferno as Zach took her to the brink, holding her suspended until she was trembling uncontrollably, every nerve in her body screaming, begging for release. Never had she felt so driven with intense, overwhelming need. A scream rose in her throat, and then for a blessed moment the pressure abated.

She was dimly aware of Zach's body rising above her. Her fingers dug painfully into his shoulders as he plunged into her, his hot, pulsating shaft thrusting inside her. Bolts of lightning flew up her spine, exploding in her brain as she climaxed. Zach clenched his teeth as he felt her tightness squeezing him, exerting superhuman willpower to keep from following her too soon. His body was slick with sweat, his muscles knotted as Abby's shuddering spasms released the mechanism that held his own powerful climax in check. He flexed his hips, drove deep, and roared in joyous fulfillment.

Reluctant to part their bodies, Zach rested atop Abby, breathing raggedly, his heart pounding. He gazed down at her and saw her staring up at him, her eyes glazed, a dazed expression on her face.

"After that, do you still believe pity is what I feel for you? I'm not sure what I feel right now, but it sure as hell isn't pity."

Abby went still, her eyes wary. What kind of game was Zach playing? "What do you feel, Zach? There's no need to lie to me."

"I'm not lying, sweetheart. Would I force you into marriage if I didn't have strong feelings for you? I'm an honorable man, but I'm not a stupid one. Nothing or no one could force me into marriage if I truly didn't want it. You're just going to have to live with the fact that there's more between us than you're willing to admit."

She felt him swelling inside her again, and her mind went blank. She wanted to believe that Zach cared for her, but the thought was as frightening as it was pleasing. She and Zach didn't belong together, even though her heart was filled with all these confusing feelings, feelings that might be described as love were she to give them a name. Her mind utterly rejected the idea that she loved Zach. Undeniably, they had an overwhelming affinity for one another, but she assumed it was purely sexual.

"Did you hear me, Abby?" Zach repeated when Abby remained silent. "You can't deny the emotions that bind us, even if they are just physical."

"I'm not denying our attraction," Abby gasped as Zach moved inside her, thrusting and withdrawing, arousing her anew and scattering her thoughts. Then words failed her as Zach reversed their positions, rolling her atop him, her long legs straddling his loins. Passion sizzled and leaped from his body to hers and back again as indescribable sensations shuddered through her. She moaned as he drove himself deeper inside her, seeking the ultimate depths of intimacy. Like a storm releasing its full fury, wind-tossed pleasure buffeted them, sending them whirling and churning into gale-swept rapture.

Chapter Sixteen

Abby stretched languorously and snuggled down beneath the quilt, too exhausted to stir from her warm nest. Her body tingled pleasantly and a dreamy smile curved her lips as she recalled her wedding night and all the wonderful ways Zach had brought her body to pleasure.

"I hope that smile is for me."

Abby's eyes flew open, heat rushing to her cheeks. Zach was standing beside the bed, fully dressed, looking at her with a warmth that made her body flush and squirm beneath the covers.

"I—was thinking," she said, too embarrassed to admit that she had indeed been thinking of him.

"Of what?" Zach prodded relentlessly.

"I find it difficult to believe that we are truly wed, especially after I fought so long against it."

"Are you sorry?" His expression hardened, all hint of amusement banished.

Abby's lids fluttered down to shutter her eyes. "I think you are the one who will feel regret over our marriage."

"Why don't you let me be the judge of that." His smile sent the blood pounding through her veins.

"Where are you going?" she asked, frantic to change the subject. If he continued questioning her so closely, she feared she'd admit things she'd buried deep in her heart.

"The honeymoon is over, sweetheart. I have to report for duty this morning. Stay in bed as long as you wish. If there is anything you need, make a list and I'll give you money to purchase whatever is necessary."

Abby sat up in bed, pulling the quilt tightly against her bare breasts. Her gray eyes were suddenly dull with misery, causing Zach to sit down on the bed and pull her into his arms.

"What is it, Abby? Have I done or said something to disturb you?"

Abby shook her head. "No, it's just that— well, I cannot read or write the white man's tongue."

"Damn!" Zach blurted out, cursing his stupidity. Of course Abby couldn't read or write. And she probably had little knowledge of money and how it was used, since Indians bartered or traded for whatever they needed. "I'll teach you whatever you need to know," he promised. "It will take time, but we have plenty of time."

"Your friends will think me ignorant." It was just as Abby had predicted. She knew she would be ridiculed in the white world and feared Zach would come to hate her for her ignorance. Her woeful lack of knowledge was one of the reasons she had refused to acknowledge that her feelings for Zach were much stronger than she wished for them to be.

"Don't belittle yourself, Abby," Zach admonished sternly. "You'll learn to read and write, you'll see." He emphasized his words by tilting her head and planting a lingering kiss on her sweet lips.

Abby melted against him, savoring the warmth of his lips, opening her mouth to his probing tongue, her body reacting violently to his kiss. Would it always be this way between them? she wondered dimly. His kiss deepened, and her arms crept around his neck. Suddenly she felt cool air brush her breasts as Zach lowered the quilt to her waist. She cried out when his lips left hers and journeyed downward to her breast. When he found a ripe nipple and suckled vigorously, she arched against him and gasped out his name.

Suddenly Zach sighed and thrust her away. He was breathing hard, his eyes glazed with passion, his expression pained. "Dammit, sweetheart, I don't have time for this. I can't believe what you do to me. I feel like a callow youth whenever I'm with you. If I had my way, I'd never let you out of bed. But reality has a way of interfering." He kissed her hard. "That's going to have to do me until I return tonight."

Reluctantly he rose to his feet. Abby watched him leave the room, her expression thoughtful. She never imagined it possible to feel the things Zach made her feel. Guilt rode her when she thought of Painted Horse. She had never experienced with him the same giddy rush of sensation she did with Zach. But then, she had never really been alone long enough with Painted Horse to explore those feelings. If only she could rid herself of her mistrust of whites, she thought dismally. She truly wanted to be happy with Zach; she just didn't know how to accomplish such a feat.

The day passed slowly for Abby. She spent time familiarizing herself with the kitchen and its unfamiliar implements. She was quite adept at cooking over an open fire, but the huge iron stove made her nervous. She did her best with the food Zach had purchased and managed to have a meal of sorts on the table by the time he arrived home that evening.

"Did you go out today?" Zach asked as he ate the tasty stew Abby had prepared.

Abby shook her head. She had no desire to leave her safe nest.

"Tomorrow I want you to go to the store and buy some clothes. Something warm for the winter. Don't worry about money. The storekeeper won't cheat you—I've found him quite honest. One day soon I'll teach you how to read and write and you'll feel more at ease."

"Do you have enough money for my purchases?" Abby asked curiously. She had never questioned Zach about his wealth or lack of it. In Indian society, wealth was measured by the size of a man's herd of horses, and she wondered if it was the same in the white world.

A chuckle rambled though Zach's chest. "I'm quite rich by anyone's standards. My brother and I inherited a prosperous freighting company, and since our parents' deaths we've branched out into the mercantile business. We even ship goods west."

"Your herd of horses must be very large."

Zach found Abby's naïveté refreshing. "We keep horses only for our personal use."

Abby merely nodded, embarrassed at her ignorance. There was so much to learn.

That night Zach made love to her as ravenously as he had the night before. After he fell asleep, Abby tried to convince herself that they could indeed be happy together, that in time their differences would become less glaring and she could reconcile herself to the fact that she was no longer Tears Like Rain, adopted daughter of White Feather, but Abby Larson, wife of Captain Zach Mercer.

The next day was bitterly cold. Before he left for the day, Zach urged Abby to venture out to the store and buy herself a warm coat and boots, and anything else she needed, such as staples and fresh meat. In order to save her embarrassment, he told her to charge her purchases.

With marked reluctance, she started out for the store that crisp November morning. To her chagrin, she felt hostile eyes follow her as she trudged across the parade ground. She supposed there was ample gossip floating around about her marriage and speculation about Zach's reasons for marrying a "white squaw." Holding her head high, she hastened her steps, sighing in relief when she entered the store and saw it was empty.

She took her time examining the coats, keeping in mind Zach's words that money was no problem and she should buy whatever pleased her. She had finally chosen a woolen cloak lined in warm fur and was about to take it to the counter when the door opened and Belinda Porter entered on a chilly gust of wind. She was accompanied by another woman whom Abby recognized as the wife of a young lieutenant. Abby tried to make herself as inconspicuous as possible, but Belinda's sharp eyes spied her immediately.

"Well, if it isn't the new bride," Belinda said in a mocking tone. She saw the expensive cloak Abby was holding and her eyes widened. She couldn't begin to afford anything so luxurious. "Are you spending your husband's hard-earned money already? You have expensive tastes for a savage."

Abby's fists clenched at her sides. She wanted

to fly at Belinda and tear her eyes out, but at the last minute common sense prevailed. Drawing on her pride, she lifted her chin defiantly and said, "My husband is a generous man. He told me to buy whatever I wished regardless of price. Were you interested in this particular cloak, Belinda?"

Belinda flushed, aware that her father could not afford to purchase so fine garment for her. Disdaining a reply, she turned to the young woman with her and said, "Have you met Mrs. Mercer, Cathy?"

Cathy Pringle stared at Abby with avid curiosity. "So you're the woman raised by Indians." She smiled slyly, looked to see if anyone was listening, then asked, "Are Indian squaws the wanton creatures we're led to believe?"

Appalled, Abby was never made more aware that Indians were more civilized than most whites. A Cheyenne would never ask so personal a question. Suddenly she thought of a perfect rebuttal. "Are white women really the wanton creatures Indians are led to believe?"

The repeat of her question flustered Cathy. "Of—of course not," she denied vehemently.

"It is the same with Indian women," Abby allowed as she deliberately turned her back on the women and made her way toward the front of the store. She placed her purchase on the counter and said in a loud voice, "Please charge this to Captain Mercer. And do you have any boots in my size?"

When the storekeeper appeared not to hear her, Abby saw that his attention had been diverted by a commotion taking place outside.

"Oh, look," Belinda cried, peering out the window. "It looks as if Colonel Chivington and his Colorado Cavalry have finally arrived. Papa said they've come to fight Indians." Her eyes slid spitefully to Abby. "You don't suppose they're going to Sand Creek, do you? They're the only Indians I know of hereabouts."

Abby rushed to the window, stunned by the impressive sight of hundreds of blue-coated soldiers riding through the gate and assembling on the parade ground. Rumor had it that Chivington was bringing six hundred cavalrymen with him, and it appeared as if the rumors were true. Could Belinda be right? she wondered fearfully. Did Chivington intend to attack the peaceful Indians at Sand Creek? The only Indians she knew of who were on the warpath were the northern Sioux and some Crow. Was White Feather in danger?

Dismayed, Abby watched as a big, rough man riding at the head of the column dismounted and strode into post headquarters. She knew without being told that he was Colonel Chivington, a man despised by the Cheyenne for his cruelty and intolerance toward Indians. She had heard that Chivington was a former minister, a man of God, but if that was so, then somewhere along the way he had lost his holiness. When she spied Zach speaking to one of the cavalry officers, a chilling premonition settled over her.

Was Zach's patrol going to join Chivington?

Abby flung the door open, hoping to divert Zach. She spared the shopkeeper a brief glance as he called out, "Mrs. Mercer, your package! What about the boots?"

"I'll be back," Abby replied as she hurried out into the cold. Disappointment churned inside her when she saw Zach end his conversation and hurry into headquarters after Colonel Chivington. She had no intention of waiting until he came home to tell her what was happening, for there could only be one reason for Chivington's arrival. Turning abruptly, she retraced her steps back to the house. White Feather must be warned about Chivington and his intention to attack Sand Creek, and she had no time to waste.

Zach rapped on the door and entered Major Anthony's office without waiting for an invitation.

"I'm glad you're here," Anthony said as he motioned Zach inside. "I don't think you know Colonel Chivington. Colonel, Captain Mercer is my right-hand man."

Zach saluted smartly, his eyes wary. He wasn't impressed by the big, bluff man, nor did he like his arrogant manner. He had heard nothing good about the former minister who considered it his mission in life to kill all Indians.

"Captain Mercer," Chivington said curtly. "Major Anthony tells me your patrol is to ride with my regiment."

"Ride where, sir?" Zach asked cautiously.

"Haven't you told Mercer, Major?" Chivington asked, rounding on Anthony.

"Not yet," Anthony hedged. "I was waiting for you to arrive."

"Yes, well," Chivington said, turning to Zach, "no harm done. My regiment is going to wipe out those heathen savages camped at Sand Creek. We leave immediately."

Stunned, Zach merely stared at Chivington, realizing that the religious zealot was utterly without mercy. Crude and belligerent, he obviously believed he was an instrument of God, delegated to rid the world of an abomination. Zach had heard that his volunteer regiment consisted of barroom toughs and Denver riffraff spoiling for a fight. When Major General Curtis, Chivington's superior, declared, "I want no peace till the Indians suffer more," Chivington was more than happy to fulfill his wishes.

"Arm your troops, Captain, and requisition ammunition for the attack," Major Anthony ordered brusquely.

"Surely you jest," Zach said. "There are no hostiles at Sand Creek. The Indians camped there are peaceful. The Cheyenne handed over their weapons in return for amnesty. Governor Evans promised they would be left in peace as long as they caused no trouble."

"Believe me, Captain, this is no jest," Chivington boasted. "Our mission is sanctioned by God and General Curtis. Cheyenne raiders plundered several small Colorado settlements and murdered and mutilated the bodies of a family on an isolated ranch. Continual Indian raids have closed down the main road to the East, leaving Denver virtually isolated. Now we demand vengeance. We must kill and scalp all heathen Indians and rid the world of a threat to all mankind. With God's help, we will find the camp of Black Kettle and annihilate it every man, woman, and child."

Tears spiked Abby's lashes as she hurried home. She recoiled in horror when she thought about Chivington's reason for being at Fort Lyon. Her mind worked furiously. Intuition told her that Chivington and his six hundred armed cavalrymen were going to attack peaceful Cheyenne at Sand Creek, and more than likely Zach would take part in the unprovoked attack. Her hatred and distrust of whites, including Zach, was never more potent as she recalled the countless reasons she had opposed marrying Zach. She felt certain he was going to join Chivington's attack on her people, and her heart ached with the knowledge.

Her first thought was that she had to warn White Feather before it was too late. Without waiting to learn whether or not her assumption about Chivington's attack and Zach's participation was correct, she ran the rest of the way home.

327

*   *   *

Unaware that Abby had any inkling of Chivington's intention to attack Black Kettle at Sand Creek, Zach tried to remain diplomatic while voicing his objection. "Far be it from me to criticize, sir, but your proposed attack will bring you no glory. I fear you will be judged severely for organizing an unprovoked attack upon unarmed Indians."

"I didn't ask for your opinion, Captain Mercer," Chivington roared. "You heard Major Anthony. Arm and provision your men. You have one hour to prepare. You're dismissed, Captain."

Zach cast a sidelong glance at Major Anthony, saw that he was in complete agreement with Chivington, and realized that he had no recourse but to obey a direct order. After a brisk salute, he turned abruptly and stalked from the room. How could he obey an order that compromised his honor? How could he take part in what was likely to be a massacre? How could he ever face Abby if he went to Sand Creek and killed men, women, and children she had grown up with and considered her family? How could he expect Abby to love him if he performed despicable acts of cowardliness?

Zach went still. Love? Had he actually thought of love?

How could he not have realized it before? The strong emotions he felt had to be love. Furthermore, he wanted Abby to love him in return.

After careful consideration, Zach did what his honor demanded of him. He drafted a document resigning his commission and gave it to an astounded clerk to be filed through proper channels.

Abby was out of breath when she rushed into the house but ignored the need for rest as she searched frantically for her tunic, moccasins, and buffalo robe. She found them at the bottom of a trunk and quickly shed the trappings of white civilization, once again donning her comfortable Indian garb. This time, she vowed, she'd not return to the white world. No matter how much she loved Zach, for her feelings must certainly be love, she could never live with a man with neither conscience nor honor. Anyone who would attack unarmed people was undeserving of her love.

There was so much commotion on the parade ground and so many men crowding the fort that no one noticed the lone Indian woman. As Abby rode through the throng of people, she heard bits and pieces of conversation. It came as no surprise to learn that Zach's patrol was to join Chivington's regiment.

Zach's mind was in a turmoil. He was torn between duty and his honor. In a daze, he went through the motions of issuing orders and seeing that his men were properly armed and provisioned, aware that there was absolutely no way he could follow orders and still live with himself.

By the time the allotted hour was up, Zach's troop was mustered on the parade ground with Chivington's men, but Zach was not among them. He had placed Lieutenant Pringle in charge of the troop and took himself off to headquarters, his face grim with determination, his mind finally at peace with the decision he had made—the only one he could live with.

"What are you doing here, Captain?" Anthony asked. "I was just about to join you. I don't intend to miss out on this operation."

"I'm not going," Zach said tightly. "I've thought it over thoroughly and realize that I simply cannot take part in an act that will likely go down in history as a cowardly and cold-blooded slaughter."

"You're deliberately disobeying an order?" Anthony asked, dismayed by Zach's act of open defiance.

"I can't disobey an order if I resign my commission. I've already written a request to be relieved of duty and given it to the clerk to be put through proper channels. According to latest reports, war in the East is nearly over. I've never shirked my duty and would still be fighting in the war if I hadn't been assigned to the Western Army."

"It's because of that damn squaw you took as a bride," Anthony said with a hint of disgust. "I knew she'd bring you to grief. You'd have a brilliant career ahead of you in the army if you hadn't allowed yourself to become emotional over some white squaw. I'm sure there are other women more worthy of your name."

"I'm sure there are many worthy women in this world, Major, but none suits me as well as Abby. Of course my wife figures in my decision to resign, but it goes beyond that. I'm sure if you stopped and thought about it, you would agree with me that no glory will be gained by this unprovoked attack upon peaceful Indians."

"My sentiments are not yours, Captain. I could court-martial you for insubordination, but in view of your exemplary war record, I won't. Meanwhile, since you obviously will be of no use to us on this campaign, feeling as you do, you're relieved of duty, effective immediately. I'll see that your request is given immediate attention. Now if you will excuse me, I have duties to perform."

Zach felt as if a great burden had been lifted from him as he stood at attention while Anthony strode from the room and out the door. He followed close behind and waited at the edge of the parade ground as the huge body of men rode through the gates in the direction of Sand Creek. As he watched them disappear over the horizon, he had an uncontrollable urge to go home to Abby, to hold her in his arms, to love her. He had no idea how to tell her that Chivington was on his way to annihilate the Cheyenne nation, or how to convince her that he could do nothing to change the course of history.

Zach's heart constricted with fear when he entered the house and found it empty. The potbellied stove was cold, having been deprived of firewood for some hours, and Zach felt a chilling emptiness that had nothing to do with the weather seeping into his bones. When he went into the bedroom and saw Abby's clothes scattered around the room, he knew immediately that she had already heard about Colonel Chivington's mission and assumed she went to warn White Feather. A harsh curse left his lips when he thought about the danger that awaited her at Sand Creek.

Only one thought entered Zach's mind as he discarded the uniform he had worn with pride and donned the buckskin pants and shirt he wore during off-duty hours. Whatever he attempted now was strictly on his own, since he was no longer a member of the Federal Army. His resignation had severed the ties that gave him authority to command men. If he was to save Abby, he must rely on his own resources and instincts.

Zach made one detour before leaving the fort. He stopped at the quartermaster's to turn in his uniform, sword, and service revolver. The weapons he kept were his personal possessions, as was the horse that had carried him through some dangerous situations before he had been assigned to the Western Army. He rode through the gates of Fort Lyon a full hour after the departure of Chivington's Colorado regiment. But since he could travel much faster than the larger body of men, he felt confident he'd reach Black Kettle's camp on Sand Creek long before the Indian fighters did.

Bone weary, Abby reached Sand Creek just as dusk was settling over the barren land. She had ridden without respite or food since leaving Fort Lyon, spurred by the knowledge that even now Colonel Chivington and his regiment were within striking distance of the Indian camp. She had encountered the slow-moving regiment hours ago and had been astute enough to give them a wide berth as she skirted around them.

Since Abby had never been to Black Kettle's camp before, she followed the creek for some miles before she spied the settlement of more than two hundred tipis stretched out along the banks of the creek. Her ride through camp was followed by curious stares. Most of these people belonged to Black Kettle's tribe, and she recognized few of them. When she asked directions to White Feather's camp, her fluent Cheyenne brought an immediate reply from one of the women. She was told to follow the creek around a bend, that White Feather had settled his tribe a short distance from Black Kettle's on the bank of the creek.

Abby recognized White Feather's tipi immediately by the vivid paintings on the outside that portrayed brave feats from his life. She recalled painting some of the symbols herself, under Gray Dove's direction, of course. She was spotted and recognized immediately by those she had lived with for many years and had come to love. At the first cry of recognition, men, women, and children came running out of their tipis to greet her. But Abby had eyes only for White Feather, who strode toward her, his expression a mixture of joy and concern.

"Father!" Abby cried as she slid from her mount and rushed into White Feather's outstretched arms. "How good it is to see you again."

"Why are you here, daughter?" White Feather asked, trying to maintain his dignity while his heart was overflowing with love.

"I've come to warn you," Abby blurted out. She had no idea how much time remained before Chivington's army reached Sand Creek, but she did know that haste was of the essence.

"Warn us? What do we have to fear?"

"Please, Father," Abby begged, "hear me out. A regiment of six hundred men are on their way to Sand Creek. We must warn Black Kettle so he can lead his people to safety."

White Feather looked puzzled. How could this be when the army had promised them a peaceful existence if they settled on Sand Creek? "Come inside where it is warm, daughter. We will talk and decide what must be done." He held open the flap of the tipi, and Abby slipped inside. She was surprised to see Summer Moon bent over the fire, stirring something in a pot.

"Summer Moon, what are you doing in my father's lodge?"

Shifting her gaze from Abby, Summer Moon looked at White Feather for direction.

"I was lonely after you and Wind Rider left," White Feather explained, sending Summer Moon a tender look. "I am still a vigorous man and decided I needed a wife. Summer Moon's parents were agreeable to a match, so I took her as my mate. It was a good decision," he added, drawing himself up proudly. "Summer Moon may already be carrying my child."

"Do not be angry with me, Tears Like Rain," Summer Moon said shyly. "White Feather is everything I could desire in a man. I am very happy. And perhaps I will give him a child of his own loins soon."

Stunned, Abby stared at White Feather, seeing him through Summer Moon's eyes. He was not old in years, perhaps forty, for he had still been a young man when he and Gray Dove had adopted her and Wind Rider. He was tall and virile and still handsome, his flesh smooth and supple over thick, ropy muscles. She could not blame Summer Moon for loving such a man.

"I am not angry," Abby said gently. "It is time Father took another wife. I am happy for both of you. But enough of that. You must leave Sand Creek immediately, while it is still dark. If you do not, many of our people will die."

A small cry escaped Summer Moon's lips and she hugged her stomach, thinking of White Feather's child.

"How do you know this, Tears Like Rain?" White Feather asked sharply. "Where is Sky

Eyes? Why have you come all this way alone? Is Sky Eyes just another white man who speaks with a forked tongue?"

Dragging in a steadying breath, Abby answered White Feather's first question. "I know this because I saw Colonel Chivington ride into the fort with over six hundred men, all reported to be Indian haters."

White Feather frowned. "That proves nothing. What makes you think they are coming to Sand Creek?"

"I don't think, Father, I know," Abby said earnestly. "I passed them scant hours ago. We must warn Black Kettle; then you must lead our people away from here. Think of Summer Moon."

White Feather was slow to comprehend what Abby had told him. He didn't want to believe that the white man's word meant nothing, that betrayal and death stalked them even as Tears Like Rain spoke. "Why would they attack peaceful people? Perhaps they were on another mission," he suggested hopefully.

Abby shook her head in vigorous denial. "They are coming to Sand Creek, and my husband is riding with them."

"Your husband?" This from Summer Moon, whose dark eyes widened at Abby's mention of a husband.

"I—I married Sky Eyes," Abby admitted with a shaky smile. "I had no choice, really."

White Feather searched Abby's face; then he grunted, as if satisfied with what he saw in the silver depths of her eyes. "It is what I hoped for when I sent you away. I believed, even then, that you had strong feelings for the White-eyes. I see that I was not mistaken."

Abby flushed. "I should have never allowed myself to fall in love with a White-eyes. Whatever I felt for him died when he joined Chivington's ranks to attack unarmed men and innocent women and children."

"Are you so sure Sky Eyes has done what you said?" Summer Moon asked. "Did he tell you himself that he is joining Chivington?"

Abby shook her head. "I did not wait around long enough, but when I left I saw Zach's men join Chivington's on the parade ground and heard them talking. But enough of this. You must go to Black Kettle, Father, and convince him to leave Sand Creek immediately."

White Feather nodded thoughtfully. "I will do as you say, daughter, because I believe you. But it will not be so easy to convince Black Kettle. After I speak with him, I will decide what is best for my people."

"Hurry, Father," Abby urged. "There is so little time left."

Two hours later, White Feather returned. Deep lines were etched into his brow and his eyes were dulled with sadness.

"What is it, Father?" Abby asked, alarmed by the bleak look in his eyes. "What did Black Kettle say?"

"Black Kettle does not believe the army will break its word. He will remain at Sand Creek with his people and greet Colonel Chivington when he arrives."

"What of you, Father? What will you do?"

White Feather directed his gaze at Summer Moon. So young, so innocent, perhaps already quickening with his child. "At dawn I will lead our tribe from Sand Creek. I do not have the same kind of trust for White-eyes that Black Kettle does. That is why I did not insist that our people surrender their weapons like animals led to slaughter."

"Dawn may be too late!" Abby protested. "Chivington could arrive while we sleep."

"I do not believe so large an army will travel through the night. No, daughter, dawn will be time enough to leave. Our people will need a good night's sleep to prepare them for what lies ahead. Sit down and eat with us," he said. "Afterward I will go to warn our people so they will know what to expect. You will spend the night in my tipi, and you can help Summer Moon prepare for our departure."

Relief shuddered through Abby, grateful that White Feather wasn't going to send her away. She would never agree to return to Zach knowing he rode with Chivington.

Chapter Seventeen

Zach heaped a thousand curses upon the black, moonless night that made him lose his bearings. Unlike Chivington, he did not have the advantage of an Indian scout, and though he had trailed Chivington for several miles, he passed the main body of the regiment sometime during the night. Zach wasn't surprised that the religious zealot intended to ride through the night without respite in order to surprise the Indian village while it still slept.

Then he lost his way in the dark and became disoriented shortly after he had passed Chivington's slow-moving regiment. His relief was abundant when he finally stumbled upon Sand Creek—but it was short-lived when he realized that dawn was scant minutes away and Chivington was so close that he would probably arrive simultaneously with the light of day.

Zach was right on target in estimating Chivington's arrival. His regiment had traveled throughout the night, at times leading their horses through the darkness in order to arrive with the dawn on animals fresh for the attack. Even as Zach viewed the sleeping village from a ridge overlooking the site, Chivington's men had paused on the outskirts of the village to mount their horses and inspect arms. At Chivington's side was another Indian hater—Major Dowling, who cruelly boasted that it was easy to get *any* information out of an Indian just "by toasting his shins over a small fire. . . ."

Abby awoke as the gray dawn turned the eastern sky murky. The very air was charged with sinister vibrations. Her heart was pumping so fiercely that she feared it would jump out of her chest. Glancing over at White Feather's pallet, she was relieved to see that he also sensed impending danger and was already on his feet, donning his warmest garments, for the day was bitter cold.

Abby rose at the same time, noting that Summer Moon was now on her feet and moving silently around the tipi, gathering supplies to prepare their morning meal.

"There is no time to eat," Abby said anxiously. "Something is dreadfully amiss; I can sense it."

White Feather looked pensively into the distance, his body tense. "It is so, daughter. I will alert the People." He hurried from the tipi, and within minutes Abby heard people moving about, dismantling tents and gathering possessions.

"I will help," Abby told Summer Moon. "Where are the horses kept? We must pack quickly and load our belongings on travois."

"The horses are corralled at the edge of the village, near the woods." Summer Moon's voice trembled.

When Abby reached the corral, she found several braves already there, culling their horses from the herd. White Feather had judiciously forewarned his people the night before of a possible attack, and an air of urgency prevailed. She gathered White Feather's horses quickly and started back toward the tipi. She had no idea that her movements were being observed from a ridge a short distance away.

Zach paused briefly on the crest of the ridge and observed the sleeping village. Approximately two hundred tents stretched out along the banks of Sand Creek, reaching nearly to a dry creek bed and wooded area beyond the encampment. He knew those tents held five hundred souls, including more than three hundred women and children. As Zach's eyes swept over the cluster of tipis, his heart constricted with fear. He had hoped to find the campsite abandoned, confirming that Abby had convinced White Feather and Black Kettle of their danger from attack. He was disappointed to see that the Cheyenne slept peacefully, unaware of their danger.

Zach spit out a curse. How in the hell was he going to find Abby and White Feather among so many? His glance traveled a short distance beyond the main village to a bend in the creek, where a dozen or so isolated lodges were clustered.

Looking closely, he perceived a flurry of movement in the cluster of isolated tents. The murky daylight revealed men and women dismantling tipis and leading horses from a makeshift corral. He tried to convince himself that it was White Feather's band taking steps to leave Sand Creek while the main village still slept. Fear sizzled through Zach, realizing there was too little time for White Feather's people to gather all their belongings if they hoped to escape Chivington's fury. Making a hasty departure could mean the difference between life and death.

Then Zach saw Abby, illuminated by a narrow band of daylight that appeared on the eastern horizon. He'd recognize Abby's slim, athletic form anywhere. She was leading a string of horses toward one of the tipis. Spurring his mount, he rode down into White Feather's village, shouting Abby's name.

The Indians moved with such quiet purpose that Abby recognized Zach's voice immediately. She whirled, her eyes blazing with unsuppressed anger. Zach sawed on the reins, bringing his horse to an abrupt halt. Leaping to the ground, he grasped her arms and pulled her forcefully against him.

"Dammit, Abby, what in God's name are you doing here? Chivington's men are just minutes away."

Abby's eyes widened. "Minutes away? Didn't they stop for the night? I warned White Feather, but he wouldn't listen." She glared at Zach, reason giving way to incredible anger. "What are you doing here? Are you the vanguard of his army? Did he send you ahead to scout out the village? How could you, Zach? How could you join an army sent to kill unarmed men and innocent women and children?"

Ignoring her rage, Zach shook her, trying to bring some sort of order to her thinking. "Dammit, Abby, we've no time for this! Chivington will be here momentarily. Where is White Feather? He must move his people out immediately."

"They are still dismantling their tipis and packing their belongings," Abby said. "Why have you come? What will your superiors say when they learn you have left the main body of troops and ridden here alone?"

"You're just going to have to trust me, Abby. I'm no longer with the army. Now, where's White Feather?"

"I am here, Sky Eyes." White Feather had seen Zach riding hell for leather into camp and was eager to speak with him. "What is it you wish to tell me?"

"You must leave now, with all haste! Chivington's regiment is poised just beyond the village. Leave your tipis behind. Take your horses, warm clothing, and whatever food you can carry. I ask that you trust me, White Feather. I love your daughter too much to lie to you."

Even as they spoke, the muffled sound of riders echoed through the frosty dawn. White Feather stared hard at Zach for the space of a heartbeat, nodded his head, and called out to his people. His voice was tense and urgent, his words harsh and grating. His orders were obeyed instantly as men gathered their wives and children and waited for White Feather's direction.

"Lead them along the dry creek bed stretching beyond the village to the woods," Zach said. "For God's sake, hurry!"

"I will do as you say, Sky Eyes." He turned to Abby. "We must say farewell once more, daughter. If the Great Spirit wills, I will take the People across the border into Kansas." Tears gathered in Abby's eyes as she watched White Feather hurry to where Summer Moon waited.

"Go, Father," Abby urged. "Take Summer Moon to safety. I will warn Black Kettle and catch up with you." But White Feather did not hear her. The exodus of his people had begun—and not a moment too soon, as gunfire resounded through the stillness of dawn, heralding the arrival of Chivington's volunteer regiment of Indian haters. Left Hand, an Arapaho chief, was cut down with one of the first bullets as he came from his tipi to see what the commotion was all about.

Grasping Abby's waist, Zach flung her atop her horse. Then he took her reins and rode away in the same direction White Feather had taken.

"We can't leave like this!" Abby cried. "We must warn Black Kettle."

"It's too late," Zach bit out from between clenched teeth. "He should have listened to you before."

When they reached the creek bed behind the main village, Abby glanced back over her shoulder, crying out in terror when she saw the carnage taking place in Black Kettle's camp. The horror would be etched into her brain for all time, never to be forgotten. Chivington's volunteers had burst through the murky dawn with no warning, raking the settlement with lethal gunfire. She saw Indians, buck-naked, appear at the openings of their lodges, and troopers tearing down the ridge to cut them down with guns and swords. She saw Black Kettle stagger out of his tent, unable to comprehend what was happening, his face a mask of confusion as he ducked into his tipi, emerging moments later waving the Stars and Stripes. When that seemed to do little good, he tried hoisting a white rag on a stick to prove that he was friendly. Unbelievably, the Indians made no move to defend themselves. They milled around in clusters, wondering why this was happening and what would happen next. What followed was deadly, heavy shooting into their midst.

Chivington's orders were "Kill and scalp all, big and little; nits make lice." The troopers rode through the camp, killing every Indian who moved and then mutilating their bodies, saving some parts as grisly souvenirs of the day's action. One group of women and children were cut down in the act of appealing for their lives, while half-crazed troopers used a lost toddler for target practice. All women were cold-bloodedly raped and killed. Flight was the only escape from the unprovoked massacre and a few did get away to spread the word of the white man's atrocity through the grasslands and mountains. Those who escaped sought shelter in the creek bed or hid in the woods, digging holes and pits in which to hide. Fugitives found hiding in the woods were murdered. Black Kettle was the last to leave, still unable to comprehend the carnage dealt his people by Chivington's regiment.

"Don't look back," Zach urged when he heard a shrill wail escape Abby's lips. He knew without looking what was taking place on Sand Creek and thanked God for his timely arrival. They were traveling along the dry creek bed now and had nearly reached the woods when a cavalryman came bursting from the trees, heading directly for them.

"Zach!" Abby's warning was unnecessary, for Zach had already seen the trooper. He tried to swerve in another direction, but it was too late—the rider was already upon them. Zach braced himself to meet an attack, and when none came he took a closer look at the man giving chase. He was stunned when the trooper called out his name. Abruptly he reined in.

"Captain Mercer! Abby!"

"Sergeant Porter!" Zach was as surprised to see Porter as Porter was to see him.

"What in God's name are you two doing here, Captain? Lieutenant Pringle told me you resigned your commission and left the army. After I heard what Chivington intended, I had a good idea why, but I never thought I'd find you here."

"It's a long story, Pete," Zach said, glancing nervously over the sergeant's shoulder. Had he brought others with him? If so, where were they? "Suffice it to say that Abby heard about Chivington's mission and left the fort without my knowledge to warn White Feather. I couldn't let her be slaughtered with the others and came after her. I barely arrived in time to save her and warn White Feather. What are you doing away from the main body of soldiers?"

Porter flashed Zach a disgruntled look. "If I had your courage, I would have refused to take part in this wholesale slaughter. Chivington's men are half-crazed by hatred for Indians, even unarmed ones such as these. When the order came to kill women and children, it was more than I could stomach. While the others were busy raping women and spilling the blood of innocent babes, I rode for the woods. I'm sure there are others who feel just like me. Mark my words, Captain, one day the nation will know the truth about Sand Creek. I wouldn't be surprised if there's an investigation when the truth comes out."

"If I have anything to say about it, the nation will know sooner than Chivington would like," Abby said vehemently.

Zach spun around when shouts and sporadic gunfire echoed through the woods, followed by troopers chasing survivors who were trying to escape into the nearby woods.

"Go on," Porter urged, "get the hell out of here. Go back to Fort Lyon. Chivington's regiment will be here for several hours doing their dirty work. You'll have plenty of time to reach the fort before they do. No one need know you've been here."

"Thanks, Pete. Everyone should have a friend like you. If you ever need a favor, just ask."

Abby held on for dear life as Zach grasped her reins, pulling her horse forward with a jerk that nearly unseated her. They raced along at a furious pace until the sounds of battle could no longer be heard and they felt certain they had avoided pursuit. Zach wondered if Pete was responsible for their narrow escape and blessed the friendship that existed between them despite the difference in their military rank. When Zach finally stopped in the shadow of a hill, their horses were foaming at the mouth, their bodies slick with sweat.

Abby slipped from her mount, falling to her knees and burying her face in her hands. If she lived to be a hundred, she'd never forget the sight of people being slaughtered at Sand Creek. She had thought the attack that killed Gray Dove had been bad, but it was nothing compared to the magnitude of the massacre at Sand Creek.

Zach fell to his knees beside her, hugging her fiercely. "Try not to think about it, sweetheart. It will only bring you distress."

"Distress! If distress was all I felt, I'd be happy. If you hadn't arrived when you did, White Feather and his people would be dead. I tried to persuade Father to leave last night, but he thought there was still time, that Chivington would camp for the night and arrive later in the day."

"What about Black Kettle? Didn't White Feather tell Black Kettle about Chivington?"

"Oh, yes," Abby said bitterly. "We warned Black Kettle, but he chose not to believe his settlement was going to be attacked. Not after Major Wynkoop and Governor Evans of Colorado assured him that his people were safe there. Black Kettle had no reason to believe those men would break a sacred trust."

"It's not your fault," Zach consoled her. "I get chills every time I think of what could have happened to you if I hadn't arrived in time. My God, Abby, I could have lost you!" His arms tightened around her, as if trying to absorb her into his skin. "We must leave if we want to reach the fort before Chivington," he said, raising Abby to her feet.

Abby stiffened, her eyes seeking his in disbelief. "What! You expect me to go back to the fort after what has happened? If I saw Chivington or any of those men who took part in the slaughter today, I'd take a knife to them. I'm going after White Feather. I've been to Kansas territory before—I know where to find him. When I catch up with White Feather, we will find Wind Rider and be a family again."

"What about me?" Zach asked harshly. "Does it mean nothing that I love you, that I quit the army for you, that I risked my life to warn you and White Feather today?"

Abby's silver eyes widened. "You love me? Really love me?"

Zach nodded, unable to find the words in his heart to tell her just how much he loved her. It took a tragedy like Sand Creek for him to realize that she was his life and he couldn't live without her.

"Don't you understand? I cannot live in your world." The anguish of her words was reflected in the gray dullness of her eyes. "Not after today, certainly not after what I witnessed. Your love comes too late."

"I'm not going to let you go, Abby. Don't you realize what today's attack means? The survivors will spread the word. All-out war will be waged by every Plains tribe who hears of the incident. War and bloody skirmishes could go on for years, but it will end in defeat for the Indians. Do you think I'd allow you to die of starvation? Or be slain by men like Chivington?

No, Abby, you're staying with me, like it or not.
I love you too much to let you go."

Abby stared at Zach, wondering when she had
come to love him so dearly. But she feared their
love might not be enough to save their marriage. She had hated him when she assumed he
rode with Chivington's volunteers, and felt
overwhelmed by love when she learned he had
quit the army rather than obey an order that
compromised his honor. But now her heart was
empty, having been drained of everything but
hatred for white men and their cruelty toward
a helpless, downtrodden people. It would take
a miracle for love and respect to survive in such
a hostile atmosphere.

"It's time we left," Zach said as he placed his
hands around Abby's waist and hoisted her onto
her mare. "If we ride hard, we can reach the fort
before dark. And I swear to you, sweetheart,
we won't stay long. I'm taking you to Denver
until arrangements can be made to take you
home."

"Your home," Abby reminded him. Her biting sarcasm was not lost on Zach. "The West
is my home."

"You'll adjust."

"Have I no choice?"

"None whatsoever. I'm making the choice for
both of us. You'll love my family, and they'll
love you. Almost as much as I do," he added
meaningfully.

Before she could reply, Zach slapped her
horse's rump and they were off, riding hard for

the fort. Abby's stomach rumbled from hunger, but since neither of them had any food with them, they did not stop to eat. Zach preferred not to shoot any game, as there was a remote possibility that some of Chivington's men had followed them. They rode in silence throughout the cold, dreary November day and reached the fort as the last dregs of daylight gave way to the first onslaught of darkness.

The fort appeared deserted. Only a skeleton force had been left behind to defend the women and children residing inside the walls. Zach and Abby's entry through the gates was barely noted by anyone except a sleepy sentry. Zach took her directly to the little house they had shared as husband and wife. Since his resignation, he was no longer entitled to government quarters but he didn't intend to remain long at the fort. Only long enough to gather their belongings and allow Abby a night's rest before riding the short distance to Denver.

Abby appeared deep in thought as Zach lit a fire in the stove. Since entering the house, she could not stop shivering and she stared through Zach as if in a daze, wrapping herself tightly in her buffalo robe.

"Abby." She looked at him blankly. "I'll fix us something to eat; then I want you to go to bed." She appeared not to hear. "Did you hear me? Sit close to the stove. You must be frozen."

She did not move. Shrugging, Zach went into the kitchen, deciding there was nothing more he could say to ease her suffering. He felt like hell himself. Watching the slaughter of helpless, unresisting Indians was enough to turn the strongest stomach. He was still shaking over Abby's close call as he lit the cookstove and put water on to boil. As he scoured the cupboards for food, he recalled with vivid horror every detail of Chivington's attack upon the Cheyenne, and how close Abby had come to death. When the water had boiled, he carried a cup of tea to her, disturbed to find her standing exactly where he had left her, staring dully into space.

"I've brought you something hot to drink," he said, offering her a cup of tea. "Dinner will be ready soon. Nothing fancy, just beans and bacon, but it will stick to your ribs. You must be as hungry as I am." He placed the cup in her hands. "Dammit, Abby, you've got to pull yourself together. White Feather and his people are safe. Your brother is in no immediate danger, and you're here with me where no one can hurt you."

Abby turned to him, the dullness of her eyes turning smoky with rage. "I don't want to be safe. I want to be with White Feather. The People will be devastated. I want to help them."

"There's nothing you can do, sweetheart. I'd give my right arm if you hadn't witnessed Chivington's attack. I promise to take you where you'll never be in that kind of danger again."

"These senseless attacks won't stop just because I'm not here to witness them," Abby charged. "War in the West will go on and on until there are no Indians left."

Zach flushed, realizing the truth of her words and unable to offer a solution. "I'm sorry, Abby. I wish I could offer more than comfort. Come into the kitchen. Dinner will be ready in a few minutes."

Despite Zach's best efforts, their meager meal was a dismal failure. Though both had been plagued by hunger throughout the day, eating was difficult while memories of what had taken place at Sand Creek were so clear in their minds. After a few bites, Abby excused herself and went to bed. Zach followed shortly afterward.

The moment Zach slid into bed beside her, she stiffened, unable to bear his touch— not tonight when her hatred for the white race gnawed at her like a hungry beast. It would be a long time before she would forget that Zach had once belonged to the same army that killed and raped without mercy. She had been against marrying a white man from the beginning, and intuition told her she should have listened to her conscience and resisted more vigorously. She had lived too long with the People during her formative years. She had accepted their ways and had become one of them. Her heart was pure Cheyenne—until Zach Mercer had ridden into her life and changed it forever.

When Zach's arm slid around her waist, she panicked and cried out. "No! Don't touch me!

I can't stand it, not tonight. Tonight I hate all white men."

"You don't hate me, sweetheart," Zach whispered against her temple. "I'd never hurt you."

Abby stiffened in revulsion, unable to bear him touching her, wanting only to be left alone in her misery. "Please, leave me alone."

Feeling rejection keenly, Zach turned away, more hurt than he cared to admit. He only wanted to offer comfort, to try in some small way to alleviate her suffering. It devastated him to think that Abby's hatred for white men included him, regardless of how passionately she responded to his loving. It wounded him deeply to consider how effortlessly she scorned his love. Perhaps she was right after all. Maybe their marriage couldn't survive. If she remained rigid and unbending in her attitude toward him, there would be nothing left for them to build on.

Abby felt the stiffness in Zach's spine, recognized his anger, but couldn't find it in her heart to seek or offer comfort. Her love for him suddenly seemed insufficient to compensate for the terrible things that had been done to the Cheyenne by men under his command. It was true that Zach had quit the army rather than lead his men against those poor souls at Sand Creek, but the carnage was too fresh in her mind to forgive and forget so easily. Everything she knew about white men made her more determined than ever to return to the People. After a long time she fell into an uneasy sleep.

*　　*　　*

Abby came slowly awake. She felt sluggish and lethargic, as if her mind and body worked independently. A glance told her that Zach had already left, and she was glad for the privacy. She couldn't abide his sympathy or his pity. She arose quickly and looked for her tunic and moccasins. They were not where she had left them the night before, and she had a sneaking suspicion that Zach had taken them away so she would be forced to wear the clothing he had purchased for her. He probably thought she would be too conspicuous dressed in Indian garb, especially now, when feelings were so high against Indians.

Didn't he know she was proud of her Indian upbringing? Didn't he know she hated to be reminded that she was white? The knowledge that she belonged to a race who committed atrocities without remorse filled her with rage.

Dressing quickly in the hated dress and petticoats white women seemed to set such store by, Abby saw that it was much later than she'd thought. She wandered aimlessly into the kitchen, helping herself to leftover bacon from the night before. But the greasy mess must have upset her stomach, for she had no sooner swallowed her first bite than her insides rebelled. It took tremendous concentration to keep from emptying her stomach of the offensive food. Her innards had just settled down when she heard a commotion outside on the parade ground. Grabbing her coat from a hook, she hurried out the door.

Abby watched in growing horror as Chivington's regiment rode through the gate and mustered on the parade ground, triumphant and anxious to tell the world of their victory. With them were seven terrified women and children who had been taken prisoner. But the prisoners went virtually unnoticed, as everyone's horrified gaze fastened on over one hundred fresh scalps decorating the troopers' saddles and rifles.

Revulsion, disgust, and disbelief rose up like bile in Abby's throat, gagging her. She fought desperately to keep the meager contents of her stomach from spewing forth as people from the fort gathered around the troopers, celebrating the great and noble victory of American arms and superiority.

Then she saw Chivington, basking in the admiration of the crowd, and she did something she had never before done in her life. The world around her turned black, a void opened up under her feet, and she slid to the ground in a faint.

Zach emerged from the infirmary just as Chivington's regiment and the regulars from his own company rode through the gates of the fort, displaying bloody scalps taken from dead Indians at Sand Creek like badges of courage. He spat out a curse and turned abruptly toward home. He wanted to protect Abby, fearing her reaction when she viewed the grisly trophies of the slaughter. His fear escalated when he saw her standing on the perimeter of the parade ground. Her face was as white as the dusting of snow beneath her feet. Her eyes were glazed as she stared blankly at the bloody scalps the troopers had taken as proof of their victory.

Pushing through the milling crowd, Zach feared he wouldn't reach Abby in time as she seemed to totter drunkenly and began a slow spiral to the ground. He called her name, but by then it was too late. Her hands fluttering helplessly, she crumpled to the frozen earth in a boneless heap.

Chapter Eighteen

Abby hated Denver. The sheer size and complexity of it overwhelmed her. After she had fainted on the parade ground, Zach had taken her almost immediately to Denver. He had installed her in the best hotel in town, bought her new clothes, and tried to protect her from the talk racing like wildfire through the city. Locally, Chivington was hailed as a hero who had rid the world of a threat to mankind. His defeat of murdering Indians in a fierce battle was joyously acclaimed by one and all. According to Zach, the newspapers were full of stories about Chivington's daring efforts to force the remaining Plains tribes onto reservations.

Though Abby had been in Denver only a few days, she longed for the wide open spaces of the prairie. She found it difficult to breath in the mile-high city and felt as if she was hemmed in by the surrounding mountains, beautiful though they might be. Some tribes felt at home in such surroundings, but the Cheyenne were Plains people, content to roam the vast prairie grasslands in search of buffalo.

Abby paced the huge room she had grown to hate these past few days, waiting for Zach to return. Since the night she had asked him not to touch her, he had been cool and remote, taking care not to intrude upon her privacy. It was almost as if her careless words had killed something inside him, for he had not initiated the slightest intimacy since that night she had rebuffed him. But instead of being pleased by his consideration for her feelings, she was hurt by his lack of warmth. With the passage of time, she had come to realize how unfair she had been to Zach. He had quit the army for her sake and tried to tell her he loved her, but she wouldn't listen.

Truth to tell, she hadn't realized how much she had come to rely upon his caring and his understanding. And now she didn't know how to go about reestablishing the intimacy they once shared. She missed dreadfully that crooked smile of his, the way his blue eyes sparkled when he made love to her, and the incredible feelings he aroused in her.

Abby was so heartsick over the way things were deteriorating between them that she decided to open her heart fully and admit her feelings. She loved him, but she greatly feared the differences in their upbringing would tear them apart one day. A woman raised by Cheyenne Indians was no fit mate for a man of Zach's station in life. He needed a wife who understood the ways of society and who could move freely within its structure—something she could never do.

She walked aimlessly to the richly draped window, staring morosely at the falling snow. She was so engrossed in her dismal thoughts that she didn't hear the door opening or see Zach step inside the room.

Zach paused just inside the door, enthralled by the sight of Abby standing in the diffused light of the window. She was as lovely as a picture, with her rich sable hair framing her beautiful face. She looked so vulnerable that his heart nearly broke with the need to take her in his arms and comfort her. But Abby did not want comfort from him. What she longed for was freedom, something he could not—would not—give her. He loved her too much. He would be the happiest man alive if she could love him half as much he loved her.

When he'd finally reached her after she fainted on the parade ground, he had been more frightened than he had ever been in his life. Fortunately, she had regained her senses quickly. In order to save her from further grief, he had taken her to Denver posthaste. Regrettably the change of scenery hadn't lifted her mood.

He felt as he were continually walking on eggs around her, and he didn't like it one damn bit. He ached to make love to Abby, but her remoteness made it all but impossible. Forcing himself on a woman wasn't his style, even if the woman was his own wife.

To make matters worse, she regarded his white skin as if it were something loathsome. Incredibly, Abby still considered herself Cheyenne. No matter that her skin was far whiter than his; her sympathies, customs, and morals were pure Cheyenne.

Abby felt his presence before she saw him. Funny how she always seemed to know the moment Zach was nearby. She felt the warm slide of his gaze across her rigid back and slowly turned to face him. Her breath caught in her throat. Every time she saw him, she discovered something new about him. This time it was the incredible length of his lashes and the way his eyes crinkled at the corners when he smiled at her. There was so much she admired about him.

He was a man without pretense. A man who had demonstrated raw courage and determination time and again. She liked the fact that he wouldn't compromise his honor. Yet she came close to hating him for taking her away from her people and a life she had been happily content to follow until he had come along. He infuriated her; at times he made her weak-kneed and trembly. He never failed to touch an emotion deep inside her.

She wanted him to make love to her again but didn't know how to ask.

They stared at one another for so long that Abby felt compelled to say, "You left early this morning. Long before I awakened."

Zach shrugged, narrowing the space between them. He peeled off his sheepskin jacket and tossed it carelessly into a chair. "I had an appointment with the governor and I didn't want to be put off, so I arrived at his office early. Have you had lunch?"

"You spoke with the governor?" Abby asked, ignoring his inquiry about lunch. Her interest was definitely piqued. In fact, she showed more interest in Zach's meeting than in anything since their arrival in Denver. "What about?"

"I couldn't live with myself if I didn't try to right the wrong that took place at Sand Creek. I tried to tell the governor the truth about what really happened."

Abby grew excited. "What did he say? Is Colonel Chivington going to be punished?"

Zach released a heavy sigh. "I had the distinct impression that Governor Evans knew exactly what was going to happen the moment Chivington left Denver with his regiment. He seemed unimpressed that the Cheyenne were mostly unarmed or that their camp was full of women and children. During the conversation, I learned that Chivington's men had massacred three hundred Indians, mostly women and children. Only seventy-five of the victims were male, among them the great chiefs War Bonnet and Stands In Water."

The moment the words left his mouth, Zach wished he could call them back. Abby's face turned whiter than the falling snow outside the window and she swayed dizzily. He put out a hand to steady her. "Are you all right?" Anxiety made his voice gruff.

"I—yes. I won't faint again, I promise."

She was so pale that Zach wasn't so sure, but he gave her the benefit of the doubt. "Sit down, sweetheart. Have you eaten today?"

Actually, Abby hadn't felt at all like eating and didn't bother going down to the dining room for either breakfast or lunch. Since fainting that day at Fort Lyon, she'd experienced mysterious bouts of queasiness, and her stomach sometimes rebelled at the food she and Zach were served in restaurants. Indian food was far more digestible and certainly tastier than some of the fancy concoctions white people ate, she decided. She attributed her strange malady to the change in diet and promptly forgot about it.

"I'm not hungry," Abby said, deftly fielding Zach's concern. "Tell me more about your visit with the governor. Does he refuse to reprimand Chivington for his terrible deed?"

"It looks that way," Zach said with bitter emphasis. "I even went to Major Curtis, Chivington's superior, and tried to explain what I saw at Sand Creek."

"Did he listen to you?"

Zach snorted derisively. "The man said he wanted no peace with the Indians till they suffered more. He seemed only too happy that Chivington had fulfilled his wishes. I'm sorry, Abby, but it's going to take more than one man to get the truth out. But mark my words, others will be as disgusted as I was, men like Sergeant Porter who took part in the massacre, and word will get out sooner or later. Meanwhile, I'll continue to do my best to see justice done."

Abby gave him a shaky smile. If she could be the kind of woman Zach needed, she'd be content to be his wife. She doubted there was another man like him in the entire world. "Thank you."

Abby's sincere gratitude was the first honest emotion he'd had from her in many days, giving him renewed hope for their future. If only he could touch her heart in the same way he had earned her gratitude.

"I have a surprise, sweetheart. I thought you might enjoy going to the local theater. I saw the playbills advertising a Shakespeare play and bought tickets for tonight's performance. I'm sure you'll enjoy it. It will help take your mind off the terrible events of the past few days."

Abby looked puzzled. "A play?"

Zach smiled indulgently. "I'm sure even Indians playact at times. It's where people assume characters and act out their parts."

Abby's brow lifted. "Oh, yes, our braves often playact during ceremonies. Sometimes they are animals, but more often they demonstrate their bravery with tales of their cunning. It is very enjoyable."

"And so will be tonight's performance."

Abby sat entranced as the actors on stage brought the final scene of the first act of *The Taming Of The Shrew* to a finale. Never had she imagined anything more stimulating, more mesmerizing, than the people on stage pretending to be characters in the play. The costumes alone were a feast for the eyes. When the curtain came down to thunderous applause, Abby sat back in her chair, her eyes glowing.

"Are you enjoying it so far?" Zach asked, aware that his question was unnecessary. Her expression more than compensated for her lack of words.

"Oh, yes, I . . ."

Her words came to a halt when a man walked onto the stage, motioning for quiet. When he had everyone's attention, he said, "Ladies and gentleman, tonight I have the great pleasure of bringing to you as an added attraction some of our brave Colorado volunteers, who rode with Colonel Chivington on a mission important to all of us in this theater. Our courageous volunteers, men who risked life and limb to rid the world of murderous Indians who have been slaughtering helpless settlers, offer for your viewing pleasure their awesome array of war trophies. Ladies and gentleman, I give you our illustrious Colorado volunteers!"

The theater went wild as a half-dozen men in uniform marched onto the stage from the wings and ranged themselves prominently before the cheering audience. Abby's view was momentarily blocked by a woman in the seat ahead of her, who surged to her feet in order to participate in a standing ovation. When she returned to her seat, allowing an unobstructed view of the stage, Abby's breath slammed from her chest. She was struck nearly dumb by the gory exhibition unfolding before her eyes. The cavalrymen were grinning widely as they proudly exhibited some of the scalps taken at Sand Creek. Several women screamed, and a few men had the decency to look away, but most people stared in open fascination at the grim reminder of what had taken place at Sand Creek.

Before Zach realized what Abby intended, she surged to her feet, her voice trembling with rage as she alone challenged the Colorado volunteers. "No, it's not true! There is nothing brave or courageous about men who murder peaceful, unarmed Indians, or rape helpless women, or use little children for target practice."

"Sit down, lady," one of the cavalrymen shouted from the stage. "You don't know what you're talking about."

Zach, fearing that the audience would turn ugly, tried to pull Abby back into her seat. "Sit down, sweetheart—there are too many here for us to do battle with."

But Abby was too incensed to listen to reason and wrested her arm from Zach's grasp. Beyond fear, she continued her tirade. "I saw with my own eyes what happened at Sand Creek! I saw children skewered and women raped. I saw soldiers slit their throats when they cried out. I witnessed unarmed men killed while trying to protect their families. Soon others will step forward and tell the truth about this cowardly attack. There have to be a few men under Chivington's command who were as sickened as I by what they saw."

A hush fell over the theater. Heads turned in Abby's direction, each person weighing her words in his mind and heart. Suddenly a man in the audience shot to his feet. Zach recognized him instantly.

Private Kramer. The man Zach suspected had taken part in the attack on Abby at Fort Lyon.

When Zach had returned to Fort Lyon from Sand Creek, he had attempted to speak with Private Kramer before taking Abby to Denver. He had gone to the infirmary expecting to find the man recovering from his wounds. He was stunned to learn that Kramer had deserted.

Men like Kramer never stuck around long in one place. They joined the army to escape the law and left when it seemed expedient to do so. Obviously, Kramer had had enough of Indians and didn't fancy getting killed like his friends.

"Don't believe a word that white squaw says," Kramer shouted at the stunned audience. "Hell, she's a savage herself. She was raised by Cheyenne, ate with them, lay with their men, and probably helped take scalps from white people like you and me."

People around her recoiled in horror, and Abby realized that these ignorant men and women preferred to believe the popular version of what had happened at Sand Creek. Though she didn't know the man who had spoken up against her, there was something familiar about him. That voice—where had she heard it before?

Suddenly the woman in front of her turned, shaking her fist in Abby's face. "White savage! Filthy squaw! You're a disgrace to the white race."

Zach surged to his feet. He would have single-handedly fought every man and woman in the theater before he'd see a single hair on Abby's head harmed. He sent Kramer a menacing glare. Kramer was astute enough to realize his mistake. Aware that he was a deserter and fearing he would be returned to Fort Lyon to face court-martial and imprisonment if he were apprehended, he made a hasty exit, pulling along the woman he had brought to the theater with him.

Zach suppressed the urge to give chase, deciding it would be safer for Abby if they left themselves. Abby offered only token resistance when he dragged her from the theater, but by then her good sense had returned. By the time they reached their hotel, they were out of breath and panting.

"That wasn't very smart, Abby," Zach said, trying to keep his temper. "I want your promise that you won't do anything so damn foolish again. That crowd could have torn you apart. Indians aren't a popular subject in Denver."

"They had to be told the truth," Abby said, unrepentant. "I couldn't let them go on thinking those men were heroes. Who was that man, Zach? He seemed to know all about me. I didn't recognize him, but his voice—it sounded vaguely familiar."

Zach assumed a thoughtful look. Abby's recognition of Kramer's voice was all the proof he needed to believe the man had attacked Abby at Fort Lyon. He'd do all in his power to see the man imprisoned for desertion.

"I've been aware for some time that Private Kramer was one of the men who tried to rape you at Fort Lyon. He had been confined to the infirmary while recovering from severe wounds acquired in a raid that killed his two accomplices. When I tried to question him, I learned he had deserted. I won't rest until Kramer has been put in prison for his crimes."

"I don't want to think of him," Abby said, shuddering. "Or those men at the theater displaying their gruesome trophies. I want to forget. Oh, Zach, help me forget—please help me forget." The plea was torn from her throat. Zach glimpsed the overwhelming sadness in her eyes, heard the panic in her voice, and would have walked on fire to ease her suffering. He folded his arms around her, hugging her so fiercely that she could feel his heart thumping erratically against her breast.

He felt her move against him, so alive, so vital—so damn hurt and utterly lost in a world she did not understand. He lifted her face, looking deeply into the silver pools of her eyes, wanting to understand exactly what she wanted of him. But she closed her eyes, denying him her inner thoughts. Left to his own devices, he lowered his head and kissed her—kissed her deeply, ravenous for a taste of her sweetness, a sweetness that had been denied him since Sand Creek. Her lips trembled beneath his and parted, allowing him the intimacy he sought so desperately.

He loved her, he knew that now. He had loved her forever. No, not forever—beyond forever. Heat shimmered between them, raw and intense, bursting and spreading rampantly. He touched her breasts and she gasped. They felt heavy, heavier than he remembered. He caressed her nipples through the material of her bodice, encouraged when they hardened beneath his fingers.

Her body seemed to melt into his, welcoming his touch. She invited more of the same with inarticulate little gasps and subtle movements of her body. He kept on kissing her. Her lips, her cheeks, her chin. The sensitive cord running down the side of her neck, the erratic pulse beating at the base of her throat.

"Love me, Zach, I need you so." Her words were uttered in a voice so low Zach thought he had mistaken her meaning. But when she repeated them, his heart leapt with unsurpassed joy. A ragged cry escaped him, and she felt herself being swept up and laid back on the bed. Her eyes were glazed as she watched him shed his clothes, marveling at the speed with which he stripped. Then, with shaking hands, he undressed her.

He sensed her urgency as he undressed her, felt her tremble as he kissed each part of her body that he bared, his lips searing and wet. Then he was touching her, his hands circling her breasts, curving around her bottom, skimming over her hips, caressing between her thighs, touching her there, where she had already grown damp from wanting him. She felt the hard arousal of his manhood pressing against the softness of her flesh. When he bent his head and touched her, parted her, caressed her with his tongue, her body jerked convulsively.

She felt the warm moistness of his mouth bathe the sensitive folds of her inner flesh, and her fingers tightened around the firm muscles of his shoulders. Tendrils of hot desire swirled up inside her as his relentless tongue delivered its liquid heat. Supple and pliant beneath him, her skin was damp, her hair tangled as he feasted at the portals of her femininity. She moaned softly. Her head began to thrash from side to side, her body to writhe.

He found the tiny bud of her sensuality and mercilessly played upon it, laving, teasing, bringing her to shuddering ecstasy with the caress of his lips and tongue. Her body glistened with the golden sheen of her sweat, her hips undulated, and she clutched desperately at his shoulders, his sweet torment driving her to distraction.

"Please," she whispered raggedly.

"I want more than anything to please you," he murmured against her swollen flesh.

Suddenly the fire within her grew too painful to endure, too hot to contain, too wonderful to resist. It burst forth, sending her into a sweet spiral of sensation so powerful that she felt herself slipping from reality. She was aware of nothing but the splendor of his hands upon her flesh, of his mouth and tongue driving her to erotic heights of ecstasy, of the comfortable weight of him between her legs. The feeling grew until she was arching wildly against him. She cried out as something inside her burst, sweet, wild, achingly beautiful.

Then he was over her, atop her, thrusting into her hard, and the heat and hunger began inside her again. How could it be? She had given so much, how could she possibly give more of herself? Not only was it possible, but Abby found herself straining toward that celestial plateau again, eager to experience once more the bursting stars, the delicious heat, the heightened awareness of her flesh. He felt so good inside her; the fullness of him stretching her, the weight of his hair-roughened limbs pressing against hers, the hardness of his muscles, the rocking of his hips, the rigid thrust. . . .

"My God, you're so incredibly tight! I've never known anything so sweet."

She opened her eyes. His were blazing into hers, so blue that she might have been looking into a cloudless sky on a summer day. His arms, so strong, so sleekly muscled, held his body above hers as he thrust into her, again and again, his face strained with tension. Grasping his shoulders, she pulled him down so her lips could reach him, showering frenzied kisses on his damp flesh, wherever she could reach—his neck, his shoulders, his chest. Then their lips met in mutual passion as Zach thrust his tongue into her mouth, groaning when he tasted the hot, honeyed sweetness.

Suddenly he cried out her name and Abby felt him thrust even harder into her. His body tensed, his hips flexed, thrusting, faster, harder, until he shuddered and exploded within her. His climax released the fire and hunger inside her as she split into a million pieces of shimmering ecstasy. She felt the heat of his seed pouring into her, felt his fullness stretching her, felt his tension draining, felt her own body relaxing, and she went limp. After a while she smiled up at him.

He smiled back at her and fell to her side, breathing hard, his body slick with sweat. He pulled her against him, brushed the tangle of damp hair away from her face, and whispered into her ear, "I love you, Abby. I swear to you that one day you'll love me as much as I love you."

He said it with so much feeling that tears came to Abby's eyes. She truly regretted being the wrong kind of woman for an incredible man like Zach, and hated not being able to tell him she already loved him. Didn't he know the kind of abuse he'd suffer for loving a woman who didn't fit into society?

"What are you thinking, sweetheart?"

"I'm sorry I embarrassed you tonight, but I couldn't help it. When I saw those scalps, I went a little crazy. I warned you that marrying me would bring you grief."

"Don't be foolish, Abby. I'm proud of you. You've more courage than any woman I know. I'd rather have you than a hundred insipid women who have never experienced the hardships you've had to endure." Tenderly, Zach wiped away the tears shimmering on her cheeks. "I don't want you to be sad. Taking you east will be good for you, you'll see."

"Have—have you already made arrangements to leave?" she choked out.

"I wish it was that simple. The weather is against us. We'll have to wait till spring. I've wired my brother, though, and he's expecting us."

"What will we do in the meantime? I don't know much about money, but this hotel suite must be terribly expensive."

Zach grinned. "Money is no problem. I told you that before. You've married into a wealthy family, Abby. I'm wealthy enough to give you whatever you want."

"I want to stay in the West." Her impassioned words nearly broke Zach's heart. He wanted what was best for Abby, but he truly felt that removing her from the source of painful memories was the best thing he could do for her.

"Trust me to do what's best for you, sweetheart." He hugged her fiercely. "Let's get dressed and go downstairs for a late supper. Neither of us have eaten much today, and I'm famished."

Abby didn't feel much like eating, but she reluctantly agreed. In fact, her stomach felt as if butterflies were dancing inside it. All the while she dressed, her distress became more acute. She tried to hide it from Zach, but when they were finally ready to go downstairs, Abby was sweating profusely from the effort of keeping the contents of her stomach where they belonged. Zach seemed unaware of her distress until he ushered her out the door and noticed the fine sheen of sweat gathered on her brow.

"Are you all right, sweetheart? You look peaked."

She swallowed hard and gave him a bright smile. "I'm fine. I probably just need something substantial in my stomach."

He took her arm and they proceeded down the stairs. When they reached the lobby, people gathered there in groups stopped talking and turned to stare at them. Had gossip about the fiasco at the theater tonight preceded them? Abby wondered dimly. Her suspicions were proven correct when people began whispering behind their hands, sending them curious glances and making snide remarks that were a little too loud. She clutched Zach's arm tightly, realizing that her outburst had cost Zach the respect of his peers.

"Pay them no heed," Zach whispered into her ear.

They had almost traversed the length of the lobby when the manager of the hotel appeared out of nowhere. "Mr. Mercer, may I have a word with you and your—wife in private?" He turned abruptly, expecting them to follow him into his office.

"What is it, Mr. Mayhew?" Zach asked once the door was closed behind them. His face was taut, his expression unreadable, giving no hint of his inner rage.

"Ahem—well, you know how business is affected by adverse gossip, Mr. Mercer." He let his eyes stray to Abby, then slid them away with a shudder. "And since the hotel business is precarious in times like these, it's in the hotel's best interest to avoid controversy."

"Exactly what are you trying to say, Mayhew? What controversy are you speaking about?" Zach's eyes bored into the hapless Mayhew with relentless fury. The man cleared his throat and judiciously retreated.

"Yes, well, the management would appreciate it if you took your patronage elsewhere. A hotel of this caliber does not cater to undesirables. I'm sure you'll find one of the hotels across town adequate for your needs." His nose rose several inches in the air, and his gaze settled on Abby with something akin to loathing. "Of course, if you'd like to stay here without your squaw, you'll be more than welcome."

Red dots of rage exploded behind Zach's eyes. In two long strides, he was standing toe to toe with the slender manager. With incredible ease, he hoisted the man in the air by his collar, shaking him until his teeth rattled. "If you ever again refer to my wife in such a disparaging manner, I will personally see that you are in no condition to insult any other lady. As for leaving your establishment, we'll be more than happy to vacate our room, since I have no intention of exposing my wife to gossipmongers and bigots like you."

Abruptly he released his hold on Mayhew's collar, and the man dropped like a sack of potatoes at Zach's feet. "Now if you'll excuse me, my wife and I were just going to dinner."

He turned to offer Abby his arm, alarm shooting through him when he noted her sudden pallor and pinched features. "Abby, it's all right— don't let him distress you." Taking her arm, he turned her toward the door.

But Abby knew it wasn't all right. Nothing would ever be all right again. Her outburst at the theater had cost her dearly. She had ruined Zach's life. Why couldn't she have kept her mouth shut? And to make matters worse, her head spun dizzily and she was going to embarrass herself by being sick. The thought had no sooner left her head than the room started rotating around her. A void opened beneath her feet and she slumped against Zach. This time he was there to catch her.

Chapter Nineteen

Abby savored the moist coolness against her brow, comforted by the dark, misty world in which she had taken shelter. She knew that once her eyes opened, life would go on as before—unfair, cruel, and relentless.

"Abby."

Her name came to her as if from a great distance.

"Open your eyes, sweetheart."

Unable to resist the lure of his husky voice, Abby forced her eyes open. She saw Zach bending over her, his eyes anxious as he bathed her brow with a cloth dipped in cool water.

"I don't care what you say. I'm taking you to the doctor first thing tomorrow. Women don't usually faint for no reason."

Abby frowned in consternation. Zach was correct, of course. She had always been healthy and free of disease—and had never fainted before. There had to be a reason. . . . She considered her symptoms, which included nausea, malaise, and two episodes of fainting, and suddenly recalled that other women of the tribe had often complained of those very same symptoms. Of course, they had been . . .

With child.

My God, was she carrying Zach's child? From what she knew of the condition, it seemed altogether probable. Now that she thought about it, the last time she had visited the isolation tent was over two months ago, when she was still living with White Feather and Wind Rider.

"Are you feeling better?" Zach's voice was fraught with anxiety. "Perhaps I should find a doctor right away."

"No!" Abby sat up gingerly, encouraged when the room did not spin around her. "I'm fine, Zach, truly."

"You're not fine, sweetheart, and we need to find out what's wrong with you."

Abby bit her lip, considering her dilemma. Should she tell Zach what she suspected or wait until she was certain she was with child? She decided to wait, although she had no intention of going to a white man's doctor. She had heard too many horror stories about doctors who bled their patients, weakening them unto death, while the Cheyenne relied mostly on herbs and prayers to heal the sick. Besides, childbirth was a natural and private process. When the time arrived for a Cheyenne woman to give birth, she simply went off by herself and didn't emerge until after her child was born.

Sliding her legs over the edge of the bed, Abby pushed herself to her feet. "We'll talk about doctors tomorrow. How did I get to our hotel suite? The last thing I remember is fainting in the manager's office."

"I carried you here when you fainted. Do you think you could eat something?"

Feeling much better, Abby suddenly realized that she was hungry. "I'm famished. Shall we go to the dining room?"

"You're not leaving this room. I asked the chambermaid to bring us a tray; it should be arriving any minute." He pulled a chair close to the table.

Abby sat down, waiting for Zach to tell her what they were going to do now that they were being forced to vacate their rooms. When he made no mention of the angry words spoken in the manager's office, she broached the subject herself.

"What are we going to do? If the management of this hotel wants us to leave, others will be just as reluctant to rent us a room."

A soft curse slipped past Zach's lips. "I didn't want to distress you by talking about it right now. Don't worry, I'll think of something. I could buy a house in Denver. That will solve our immediate problems. But it might take a few days."

"No! Please, I don't want to live in Denver." Her voice trembled with fear, giving vent to the turmoil roiling inside her. "Big cities frighten me. I feel confined by the mountains." If Zach bought a house in Denver, he might want to remain. Living in Denver would be just as bad as living in Boston.

"Abby, be reasonable. You don't want to go to Boston; you don't want to live in Denver—what do you want?"

Her eyes were softly pleading as they searched Zach's face. "I want to live on the prairie. If I go to Boston, I will never see White Feather or Wind Rider again. And I can't remain in a city whose residents think of Indians as wild savages."

There were few Western cities that did not consider Indians wild savages, Zach thought. Reminding Abby of Indian attacks upon settlers would only add to her distress. "I'll find temporary lodging while we make up our minds about what we want to do until travel becomes possible. The most important thing right now is finding out what's wrong with you."

Abby opened her mouth to reply, but a knock on the door forestalled her answer. "That's the chambermaid with our tray," Zach said, opening the door. He instructed the girl to place the tray on the table.

The chambermaid entered with marked reluctance, her frightened gaze darting to Abby before approaching the table. Obviously she had heard gossip about the "white squaw" and expected Abby to pull out a knife and murder her. She placed the tray on the table with unwarranted haste and ran from the room.

"That's exactly what I was talking about," Abby said disgustedly. "I'm sure the girl thought I was going to attack her."

Zach felt his color rise. It was true—ignorant people did fear her—but he'd never admit it to Abby. He silently vowed to spend the rest of his life protecting her from biased and ignorant people.

"Eat your supper, sweetheart. We'll be gone from this hotel tomorrow, and you won't have to worry about these bigots."

"Will it be any better at another hotel?"

Zach did not respond, but Abby already knew the answer.

Abby stared out the window of the shabby hotel she and Zach had moved into several days ago. It was a far cry from the luxurious suite at the Denver Arms they had previously occupied, but the manager here offered no objection to their occupancy, as long as they paid their rent. Abby's glance wandered aimlessly to the noisy saloon directly across the street. It was the kind of inn one usually found on seedy streets far removed from residential districts.

Zach had left her at the hotel while he went to inquire about rental houses. They had eaten lunch first at one of the restaurants in the vicinity, and she could feel the greasy mass roiling in her stomach. Zach hadn't been happy with their choice of temporary lodging. In fact, he was so distraught over the accommodations at the rundown inn that he vowed he would have them out of there within days. Gossipmongers had been swift to spread stories about Abby, and when Zach attempted to register at the higher-class hotels, he was politely informed that there were no vacancies.

As Zach predicted, serious repercussions followed the Sand Creek Massacre. Gory details of the unprovoked attack spread far and wide across the plains, and reports reached Denver that two thousand Indians—Cheyennes, Arapahos, and Western Sioux—were gathered along the banks of Cherry Creek to plan retaliation. When Zach informed Abby of this newest development, she wondered if either White Feather or Wind Rider were among those Indians camped nearby.

Abby stared down at the snowy streets from her second-floor window, watching people hunched against an icy December wind make their way with difficulty along the narrow thoroughfare. Suddenly a flash of movement from the saloon across the street caught her attention. She watched with growing alarm as a young girl, younger even than she was, burst through the door of the saloon, her ragged clothes flapping in the wind. Dirty brown hair, lank and lusterless from infrequent washings, whipped around her pinched face, and her thin frame seemed lost in the baggy dress that was much too short for her spindly limbs. Though she wore no wrap, she seemed impervious to the bone-chilling cold.

A burly man, shaking his fist in a threatening manner, was hard on her heels. His eyes were narrowed vindictively in his angry, bloated face. A warning cry burst from Abby's lips as the man reached out and grasped the girl's flapping dress, bringing her to an abrupt halt. When she fought his efforts to subdue her, he clouted her hard alongside the head and flung her to the frozen ground. He continued to pummel her while she lay on the ground. Abby reacted instinctively. Grabbing her cloak from a chair, she flung it over her shoulders and rushed recklessly to the girl's defense.

By the time Abby reached the street below, a curious crowd had gathered to watch the man's cruel abuse of the defenseless girl. While most seemed reluctant to interfere, Abby had no such qualms. Pushing her way through the crowd, she saw the brutish man grab the girl's arms and haul her roughly to her feet.

"You little bitch! Did you think you could escape me? I own you, Hannah McLin. I own every inch of your worthless Irish hide." He shook her viciously to emphasize his words. "You're bonded to me for seven years, and I ain't about to lose your services. It's long past time you started paying for your keep. Get yourself inside, girl." He gave her a violent shove.

"No! You can't make me!" Her voice held a strange lilt Abby had never heard before. "It's not right. I'll work my fingers to the bone in your saloon, but I won't whore for you."

"You'll do as I say. All women are whores at heart. Now get your worthless bones upstairs. There's a line of customers waiting for your attention."

Abby had heard enough. If no one else would come to the aid of the hapless girl, she would. She'd already disgraced herself in Denver. One more indiscretion would certainly do her no harm. She took one step forward—and stopped in her tracks when she came face-to-face with a man she knew as well as she knew herself.

Dressed in white man's clothing, his dark hair clubbed at the back of his neck, a wide-brimmed hat pulled low over his silver eyes, Wind Rider stepped into Abby's path. When she would have cried out his name, he put a finger to his lips, cautioning her not to give away his identity. Abby cast a regretful glance at the girl, who was now being shoved inside the door of the saloon, and meekly followed Wind Rider as he led her away from the crowd. She wished she could have helped the girl, but the shock of seeing Wind Rider in Denver and the need to speak with him sent her good intentions flying away.

"I wanted to help that poor girl," Abby said, sickened by what she had seen. "Why would no one help? Why must people be so cruel to one of their own kind?"

"I don't know the why of it," Wind Rider said, recalling the helplessness of the girl and the look of utter defeat in her startling green eyes. He'd almost interfered himself, in spite of the fact that he couldn't afford to involve himself in white man's business.

"What are you doing in Denver? Where is Sky Eyes?"

"I am here." Zach had been returning to the hotel when he saw the crowd gathered and went to investigate. The sight of Abby speaking with a strange man had made him wild with jealousy. He didn't recognize Wind Rider until he was close enough to identify his handsome brother-in-law's deep voice. "The question is, what are you doing here, Wind Rider? And what is Abby doing on the street when I told her to remain inside unless I was available to accompany her?"

"I wanted to help the girl," Abby said, glancing toward the saloon. The crowd was beginning to break up, and she could no longer see the girl or her abuser.

"What girl?"

"She came running out of the saloon. A man gave chase and began beating her. He said he owned her. That she belonged to him for seven years. No one tried to interfere, so I—"

"So you thought you could help," Zach said with a hint of exasperation. "The girl is a bound servant. She sold her services for seven years to pay for her passage to America. Evidently the man was her master, and she was trying to run away. He had every right to stop her."

"Did her master have a right to force her to do—vile things?"

"Abby, forget the girl. There's nothing you can do. I'd rather hear what Wind Rider is doing in Denver."

Wind Rider tore his gaze from the saloon, trying to forget the disturbing vision of the helpless girl being cruelly mistreated by her master. If white society allowed such injustices, he wanted nothing to do with the white world. Indians could be cruel, but never to one of their own. He recalled vividly the terror in the girl's green eyes, the utter despair, and he shook his head to clear it of thoughts that should not concern him.

But as he turned his attention back to Zach and Abby, he had a momentary flashback of the mute appeal in girl's green eyes, and was strangely disturbed. He had been startled when she had found him in the crowd, and when their gazes met and clung, he couldn't shake the feeling that they were destined to meet again. He shook his head to rid it of unsettling thoughts.

"You've heard about the tribes camped on Cherry Creek, haven't you?" Wind Rider replied in answer to Zach's question. "The tribes have gathered there to discuss retaliation for the massacre at Sand Creek. Since I pass so easily for a white man, I've come to Denver to help spread the truth about what happened there."

"You *are* a white man," Zach reminded him.

"Perhaps my skin is white," Wind Rider admitted tersely, "but my heart is Cheyenne. Nevertheless, I've been going from saloon

389

to saloon, telling all who will listen that Chivington's version of Sand Creek is all lies. And it seems that I'm not the only man interested in the truth. I heard that a Captain Silas, a regular from Anthony's army, refused to follow the order to kill indiscriminately and has been spreading the word that the attack on Black Kettle's camp was nothing but wholesale slaughter. Did you know he was found murdered in an alley last night?"

"I heard," Zach said grimly. He thought of Pete Porter, who had also refused to obey the order. "One way or another the truth will come out."

"Have you seen or heard from White Feather?" Abby asked anxiously. "He fled with our people from Sand Creek scant minutes before the attack. They had to leave all their belongings behind, and I feared they would not reach safety."

"I have not seen our father, Tears Like Rain. But I heard he reached Kansas territory safely. I fear he has no stomach left to fight. It is up to the younger braves to defend our lands."

"*Will* there be fighting, Wind Rider? Is retaliation being planned?" This from Zach, who feared that the prairie would explode soon in bloody warfare.

"Tribal leaders have decided that peace with the United States is simply not possible. What do we have to live for? The white man has taken our country and killed our game. But not satisfied with that, he now kills our wives and children. There will be no peace. We have raised the battle-ax. We will fight to the death."

A small cry escaped Abby's bloodless lips, and her face grew so pale that Zach feared she would faint again. His arm came around her protectively. "Are you all right, sweetheart?"

Unable to speak after envisioning the bloody uprising and senseless deaths of both Indian and whites, Abby nodded.

"Is my sister unwell?" Wind Rider's handsome face wore an expression of deep concern. "I must return to camp very soon. If something is wrong with Tears Like Rain, I wish to know."

"It's nothing," Abby quickly assured him.

"We will let the doctor determine that," Zach told her.

But Abby, fearing she might never see Wind Rider again, couldn't let him leave thinking she was seriously ill. He also had no idea that she and Zach were married. She hadn't meant to tell Zach he was to become a father in this manner, but the situation demanded that she make her condition known to her brother before he left Denver, perhaps to ride to his death.

"I am not sick, Zach, not in the way you think," Abby began hesitantly. "I am with child. Wind Rider, Zach and I were married several weeks ago."

"Ho!" Wind Rider shouted, slapping Zach's back. "I am to be an uncle. Welcome to the family, brother-in-law."

"Good God!" Abby's announcement rendered Zach speechless. Why hadn't he suspected it? He had been so consumed with Abby's safety and arranging their trip to Boston that he hadn't used the sense God gave him to realize she was pregnant. "Are you sure?" he asked sharply. It would be impossible to take a heavily pregnant woman halfway across the country, which meant they couldn't travel to Boston in the spring as he'd planned. Though he hadn't meant to convey a negative attitude, his expression hardened and his brow furrowed into a frown.

"As sure as I can be," Abby replied, hurt by Zach's response to what should have been cause for rejoicing. Did he not want children? They had never discussed the possibility. But if he didn't want children, why had he forbidden her to take the herbal concoction that prevented pregnancy?

"I am glad you told me," Wind Rider said. "When I came to Denver, I did not expect to see you, sister, but now that I have, I leave knowing that you have married well and made a place for yourself in the white world. No matter what happens on the plains, you will be safe with Zach. My future is uncertain. If I should die, my one regret is that I failed to learn what happened to our little sister, Sierra. My heart tells me she is alive somewhere and wondering about us."

Bright tears gathered in Abby's silver eyes. "May the Great Spirit protect you, brother, and may we meet again." He gave her a brief but fierce hug, aware that they were standing on a public street.

Wind Rider turned to Zach. They clasped hands. "I envy you, Zach. You have a wife who loves you and a child on the way. I have no hopes of finding that kind of happiness. I am not likely to survive this war and regret that I will leave nothing of myself behind for posterity. Cherish what you have and thank your God for a chance at happiness."

"You don't have to return," Zach said earnestly. "You're white, Wind Rider. Stay in Denver. I will help you adjust to a new way of life."

Wind Rider shook his head. "I cannot. I must fight for Indian justice. Sand Creek cannot be forgotten, nor can it be forgiven." His burning gaze seared into Abby, as if memorizing her features. Then he turned abruptly and strode away.

"Wind Rider!" Abby reached out, willing him to turn back, but he did not. His back was straight, his jaw clenched as he fought the urge to remain behind with his sister and Zach, to accept the way of life he had given up when he became Cheyenne. But he could not. Cheyenne culture was too deeply ingrained in him.

If Abby could have seen his face as he walked resolutely away, she wouldn't have recognized him. The moment he turned his back, he changed. The chiseled planes of his handsome features turned hard and remote, his silver eyes glittered savagely, and he looked every bit the proud Indian warrior. But as he passed the saloon his step faltered. Once again he recalled the bedraggled, brown-haired girl whose haunted green eyes still taunted him. Appalled that he would even give the white whore a second thought, he turned the corner and was lost from sight.

Zach led Abby toward the hotel. "Let's go inside. You'll catch your death out here in the cold."

Abby sent him an uneasy glance. She thought his voice sounded distant, and she shivered as if from chill. Was he angry with her for being pregnant? she wondered dismally. Or merely annoyed for not being told before now? The moment they were inside their shabby room, she turned to face him. "About the baby, Zach, I—"

"It's my fault." His voice was ripe with self-condemnation. "I should have taken better care of you. You have enough problems right now without my adding to them. I should have allowed you time to adjust to your new way of life before putting a babe inside you. My damn lust for you was my undoing. Merely touching you makes me forget everything but the need to love you."

Her heart plummeted down to her toes. She was right! Zach was anything but pleased about her pregnancy. "I didn't know you felt so strongly about it."

Zach plunged his hands through his hair. "Do you know what this means? It means we can't possibly travel to Boston in the spring. We'll have to wait until the baby is born. And by the time the child is old enough to travel, it will be winter again." He sounded distraught, not at all like a man who had just been told he was to become a father.

"My child will never know the wonders of the prairie," she said wistfully, "or experience the miracle of open spaces and tranquil skies."

Abby had no idea how dramatically her words affected Zach, or the results her words would bring. Suddenly he stopped pacing and whirled, staring at her hard, his expression thoughtful. In the space of a heartbeat, a subtle change came over him. "Dammit! This hotel is no place for a pregnant woman. I'm going out, Abby. Don't leave this room until I return. Have the chambermaid carry up lunch and dinner if I'm not back." Whirling on his heel, he strode toward the door.

"Zach, wait—what's this all about? If it's about the baby, tell me."

"Of course it's about the baby, Abby. There's so much I want to say, but it will have to wait until I return. There's something important I must do first." Then he was gone, his whirlwind departure leaving Abby stunned.

Where had Zach gone? Obviously he wasn't excited at becoming a father. He had acted as if he had something more important to do than discuss their child. Did he think she had deliberately set out to spoil his plans to return to Boston? It wasn't as if she had planned this pregnancy, she told herself, or done it all on her own. She didn't know what kind of reaction she had expected from him, but it certainly wasn't indifference.

Well, she thought defiantly, if Zach didn't want their child, she would take herself off and join Wind Rider. Cherry creek was so close to Denver that she could reach the Indian campsite within hours. But would the Sioux welcome her, a white woman raised by Cheyenne? They had accepted Wind Rider, but he was a trained warrior, willing to wage war against the whites. With White Feather so far away in Kansas, joining him was out of the question. Especially with the plains about to erupt in bloodshed.

Abby's head was spinning and her mind in a turmoil as she lay down on the bed to sort out her thoughts. Her condition and the events of the afternoon conspired against her, and she fell into a deep sleep. When she awoke hours later, it was dark, she had solved none of her problems, and Zach still hadn't returned. Rising, she washed her hands and face and realized suddenly that she was famished. She opened the door to her room to summon the chambermaid and saw Zach striding down the hallway. His step was jaunty and he appeared excited. She stepped back into the room and watched warily as he followed her inside, closing the door firmly behind him.

Anger seethed through Abby. How dare he look so pleased with himself after the abrupt way he had left her? Didn't he realize how much he had hurt her by refusing to talk about the baby? By acting as if it were all her fault that he wouldn't be able to travel to Boston in the spring as he had planned? Deliberately she turned her back, refusing to give him the satisfaction of knowing she had been devastated by his cool reception to her pregnancy.

Zach was so excited by what he had accomplished in so few hours that he was completely oblivious to Abby's anger. He so wanted to please her that he could hardly contain his exuberance as he came up behind her and pulled her hard against him. His hands roamed freely over her breasts, and he was amazed that he hadn't noticed the added fullness before. Suddenly he wanted her. Wanted to feel her moist warmth welcoming him into her body, wanted her naked beneath him, crying out and writhing as he brought her to pleasure. He turned her in his arms, kissing her fiercely.

Sensation flowed through Abby's veins like sweet, thick syrup, and briefly she surrendered to the torrid heat of his kiss. But when she recalled his abrupt manner earlier, she pulled from his arms. Zach looked puzzled. "What's wrong, sweetheart?"

How could he be so dense? Abby wondered dully. "If you don't want our child, then you don't want me."

Her words set him back on his heels. "Not want our child? What in the hell are you talking about? Of course I want our child. Why do you think I've run myself ragged this afternoon making arrangements for our future? My God, Abby, I love you! Haven't you heard anything I've said? Nothing pleases me more than having a child with you."

Abby eyed him skeptically. "You didn't sound pleased. You acted as if a baby would prevent you from carrying out all those plans you've made."

Zach flushed guiltily. "I'll admit I was shocked at first, but only because I'd finally realized how selfish it was of me to impose my will on you. If you were going to risk your life bearing my child, it occurred to me that I could offer you something in return. I love you too much to see you unhappy." The corners of his mouth turned up in a crooked smile.

Abby searched Zach's face, more confused than ever. "Will you please tell me what this is all about?"

Zach's grin grew wider, transforming his expression into one of dazzling promise. "It's a surprise, sweetheart."

Chapter Twenty

Abby's beautiful features wore a sour look. "Surprise? I don't like surprises. Especially not surprises that have to do with my future."

He cupped her chin, raising her face for his tender perusal. Then he lowered his head and kissed her, telling her with his body that he'd never do anything to hurt her. And no matter how angry or upset Abby might be with Zach, she responded to his touch as she always did, with sizzling passion.

A low growl escaped Zach's throat as he pulled her close, drawing her deeper and deeper into the web of his love. But was it love on Abby's part? He wanted desperately to believe that Abby loved him, though she'd never admitted it to him. Thank God he was a patient man. He could wait for Abby to love him, and one day she would, he silently vowed.

Abby burrowed deeper into the heady warmth of Zach's arms, thinking how lucky she was to have him. Her thoughts returned to that poor, terrified girl from the saloon, and she felt safe and protected in his embrace. She sensed it in the hard strength of his chest beneath her cheek. She perceived it in the dependable comfort of his arms surrounding her. She knew it in the sincerity of his words. At that moment she came closer to telling him she loved him than at any time since their marriage. There was not even a remote possibility of her leaving him, no matter how much she might damage his reputation when they settled in Boston.

With a muted groan, she answered his hunger, conveying her feelings by deed while the words remained imprisoned in her throat. She opened her mouth to him and he tasted her sweetness with a soul-searching sweep of his tongue. She groaned again, clutching his shoulders lest she plunge from the face of the earth. When Zach's lips slid down the length of her neck, licking the sensitive hollow where her pulse beat furiously, the flame within her became a wildfire, blazing out of control.

"Oh, Zach, will it always be like this between us?"

"I don't know about you, but I'll never stop wanting you. Only one thing would make me happier than I am while making love to you, and that would be hearing you admit that you love me as much as I love you."

Abby's mouth went dry. Why couldn't she let old prejudices die? Why couldn't she let go of the Cheyenne way of life and accept that she was white? No man, Indian or white, would ever mean as much to her as Zach. She was going to have his baby! But the opportunity to speak passed as she felt the incredible warmth of Zach's hands on her bare flesh and realized that he had unfastened the bodice of her dress and was pushing it down her shoulders.

"Love me or not, I know you want me."

"Oh, yes, Zach, yes," Abby moaned as his lips burned a path to her breasts. Bending her over his arm, he drew a rosy nipple into his mouth, sucking first one then the other, while he continued to undress her. Abby was awash in sensation.

"God, I love your breasts," he muttered against her fragrant flesh. "Everything about you is perfect. I wouldn't change a thing."

"I'm going to be growing larger very soon."

"You'll be even more beautiful then."

As her last garment fell from her, Zach swooped her into his arms, intending to carry her to the bed, but Abby couldn't wait. She went wild in his arms, kissing his nose, his cheeks, his mouth, tearing his shirt open and running her fingers over his hard nipples, touching them with her tongue, nipping, biting, teasing his flesh unmercifully.

Abby was needy, but Zach was needier, tempted beyond reason by the erotic touch of her hot mouth and greedy fingers. Turning her in his arms, he wrapped her legs around his waist and braced her against the wall. Then he was kissing her, tongues entwined, breath mingled, while his large hands teased her breasts, stroking the erect nubs until she writhed against him and cried out in frustration.

"Ah!" Zach cried, tearing at the opening of his trousers to release his sex. It rose strong and proud from a thick forest at the juncture of his thighs, and Abby writhed against him as she felt the velvet-sheathed rod probe between her thighs. "See what your teasing has done to me?"

When he grasped her buttocks and shoved her down hard on his huge erection, Abby cried out his name. He couldn't remember when he'd been so all-fired eager or so rock-hard.

When Abby started to move, he held her still with the force of his hands. "No, for the love of God, don't move! I couldn't bear for it to end so soon."

Braced against the wall, her legs gripping his waist, Abby hung suspended, waiting for Zach to control the compelling need to thrust himself to completion. She felt him swell inside her, felt his slickness mingling with hers, and didn't dare breathe as she struggled to bring her own passion within bounds. His harsh breath tickled her ear, and perspiration from his brow dripped on her breasts.

The waiting became sweet agony.

She thrust against him experimentally, and a damn burst inside Zach. Desperation drove him, mingled with the throbbing, almost painful need for release. He slid forward, his hips jutting back and forth, sliding deeper and deeper into her slickness, withdrawing, thrusting deeper, harder, faster. . . . She arched against his powerful strokes, her legs gripping him almost desperately, her arms kneading the corded muscles of his arms and shoulders, her mouth leaving moist circles on his chest, her teeth nipping, teasing, driving him wild.

With a shuddering cry, Abby tensed, and shock wave after shock wave set off contractions in her body that Zach felt clear down to his toes, sending him headlong toward his own reward.

Abby collapsed against him, too drained to respond to the passionate kiss he gave her afterward. With her legs still clasping his middle, he carried her to the bed and laid her gently down. She watched through glazed eyes as he shed his rumpled clothing. His sex hung limply between his strong thighs and she smiled to herself, recalling how he had filled and stretched her only moments before. Even at rest, she thought him magnificent.

There was no denying he was a strong man. Her fingers still tingled with the memory of the hard-muscled strength of chest and shoulders. And he was handsome. Whipcord-lean, with thick wheat-colored hair that she loved to run her fingers through. His strong jaw hinted at the firmness of his character, and his blue eyes had the ability to see right through her. Just looking at him made her knees go weak and her stomach churn. She was a fool to think she could live without him.

Zach joined her on the bed. "I didn't hurt you, did I? I don't recall when I've ever been so out of control. You're the only woman who can do that to me, Abby. I feel weak as a kitten."

"Weak enough to tell me what the surprise is?"

Zach gave her a mischievous smile. "No, not that weak, but I'm most eager to have you keep trying to weaken me enough to reveal my secret."

Abby did her level best to bring Zach to his knees, but nothing, not even her scintillating seduction, loosened his tongue. She allowed him no respite as she loved him with her hands and mouth, driving him to the brink of madness and beyond. She learned his body as she never had before, caressing, fondling, refusing to bow to his superiority, until her own growing need compelled her to straddle him and take him into her body. She rode him mercilessly, and when they both exploded in climax, she still hadn't convinced him to reveal his surprise.

To Abby's chagrin, Zach continued his secretive manner after that night of unparalleled loving. He bought a wagon and made Abby promise to stay safely ensconced in the hotel while he made mysterious trips that lasted until nightfall. She had no idea what he was up to and feared he was preparing for a journey to the nearest railhead. She knew he was anxious to return East as soon as possible, and she dreaded the thought of leaving the west. She also knew that Zach had sent several telegrams to his brother, hoping one or more of them would get through. Since Sand Creek, telegraph lines had been cut and Indian activity had increased despite the cold weather. She feared that with the advent of summer, death and destruction would explode into full-blown warfare.

Zach smiled to himself as he loaded the wagon with supplies and staples, making a mental list of merchandise already purchased and those still needed. He wanted everything perfect for Abby. He had just hoisted himself onto the unsprung seat of the wagon he had parked in front of the mercantile when he heard his name being called. He whirled in the direction of the voice and saw Pete Porter sprinting across the road toward him.

"Pete!" Zach cried exuberantly. "What are you doing in Denver? God, it's good to see a friendly face."

Pete returned Zach's greeting with a jaunty wave. "I was just on my way to your hotel, but you've saved me the trouble. Join me for a drink and I'll tell you all about it." A grin spread from ear to ear as he pumped Zach's hand.

Together they went into the nearest saloon, selected a table in a quiet corner, and ordered drinks from the barmaid who came to take their order.

"What's going on, Pete?" Zach had been a part of the army so long that he felt keenly the loss of camaraderie and command. But he had no regrets for what he had given up; he had gained much more in return. His honor and Abby's regard meant more to him than his command. Nothing in the world could have persuaded him to ride with Chivington and Anthony.

"Thanks to your dispatch, we took Private Kramer into custody last night. We found him hiding in a local whorehouse. One of the whores had taken a shine to him and was protecting him. He's cooling his heels in jail, waiting for us to take him back."

"I assume you're part of that detail."

"Damn right," Pete growled. "I jumped at the chance. I haven't forgotten what he did to Abby. By the way, Major Anthony asked me to deliver your discharge papers." He reached into his inside pocket, removed a folded document, and handed it to Zach.

Zach saw the barmaid approach with their drinks and waited until she had left before unfolding the paper and scanning the contents. He was surprised to feel so little emotion. He was beginning a whole new life with Abby and had no regrets. He refolded the document and slipped it into his pocket.

Porter cleared his throat. "How is Abby?"

"She hates Denver, but she's fine otherwise. Right now she's angry at me for not revealing my plans for our future, but I want it to be a surprise."

"I thought you were heading east as soon as the weather breaks."

"I was, until—" He paused, grinned foolishly, then asked, "Did I tell you I'm going to be a father in the summer?"

"Well, I'll be," Pete muttered, returning Zach's grin. "Congratulations. I reckon that changes your plans some."

"You'll never know how much. In fact, let me tell you about them." Zach spoke in glowing terms about his plans, including how and where he and Abby would live and raise their children. When he had finished, Pete sat back and whistled.

"My God, you really do love her, don't you? And to think I blamed you for seducing her. I even let Belinda talk me into believing you had an understanding with my daughter. You might be interested in knowing that I sent Belinda back east to live with my sister. She needs a husband to keep a tight rein on her, and I feared she'd settle for one of the worthless drifters who joined the Western Army to escape the law."

"I never had designs of any kind on Belinda," Zach said earnestly. "It was always Abby, from the moment I first set eyes on her."

"I know that now, and I wish you all the happiness in the world. I'll admit I had my doubts. Abby was a wild one. I didn't think she'd ever adjust to white ways. She's the fiercest little

Cheyenne I've ever seen."

Zach threw back his head and gave a shout of laughter. "You've described my wife perfectly. Why don't you come back to the hotel with me and judge for yourself whether she's been tamed? Just don't expect too much."

"I just might do that," Pete replied. "We won't be starting back to Fort Lyon until morning."

The words had no sooner left his mouth than a soldier came bursting through the door, spotted Pete, and wove his way through the room toward him. "Sergeant Porter, some of Private Kramer's friends busted him out of jail and they hightailed it out of town. I've already rounded up the detail and they're waiting outside. Do we ride after them?"

"Damn right!" Porter said, jumping to his feet. "Sorry, Zach, some other time. Tell Abby that Milly and I will be right proud to call on her in her new home. In fact, I'm sure Milly will want to help with the birth."

"She'd like that, Pete." His expression was envious as he watched Pete stride across the room and out the door. He almost wished—no, that part of his life was over, he told himself. Nothing meant more to him than Abby and their unborn child—and the children to come after that. The only thing that would make him happier was to have Abby tell him she loved him as much as he loved her.

Abby's sweat-slicked body reflected the soft glow of lamplight, turning it to burnished gold.

She lay panting in the aftermath of release, her passion-glazed eyes regarding Zach with silver wonder. How could each time they made love possibly be better than the last? Yet it was. His hand rested lightly on the slight rise of her stomach, his gaze bathing her with tender admiration. The rapid rise and fall of her full breasts captured his attention, and he bent his head to lick a drop of moisture from the succulent buds.

"You please me so well, sweetheart." He loved watching her face when she reached her climax. Loved it even more afterward while her body still glowed from his loving, and her lips were lush and swollen from his kisses.

Abby smiled lazily. "Next you'll be saying you've tamed me. But don't make the mistake of thinking I don't remember my Cheyenne ways. If you don't tell me what you're planning for us soon," she warned in mock anger, "you'll find out just how savage I can be."

His eyes gleamed wickedly. "Oh, I already know. You show me every time I hold you in my arms and make love to you."

"I'm serious, Zach. Trying to guess the surprise you've planned makes me weary. What if I can't bear the shock?" Her body trembled from an emotion Zach recognized as fear. He sought immediately to put her worst fears to rest.

Bringing her cooling body into his embrace, he pushed the tangled hair away from her forehead and whispered into her ear, "It was cruel of me to make you wait, but I wanted everything to be perfect. You won't have to wait any longer. Tomorrow we're going home."

Abby swallowed convulsively. "Home?" Try as she might she could not keep the tremor from her voice. Would tomorrow be the last day she would see her beloved prairie? Would she never see Wind Rider or White Feather again?

"I'll try to make the trip as comfortable as possible for you. You can ride in the wagon bed if you'd like, and there are plenty of blankets to keep you warm."

"Isn't travel dangerous now? Considering the Indian problem, I mean. And what about the weather? What if we're snowbound and—"

Laughing at her long list of excuses, Zach placed a finger against her lips. "Would I place your life and that of our unborn child in danger? We won't be going far in the wagon, Abby. Nowhere near Cherry Creek where the tribal chiefs have gathered with their tribes. Go to sleep now. I want you refreshed for our trip tomorrow."

"I don't want to go to Boston."

"I know."

"I told you long ago that we should never have married."

"You did."

"We're from different worlds. We're as different as night from day."

Zach rolled his eyes. "Thank God for the difference."

"I don't know how to be a proper wife to a man prominent in society."

"I couldn't agree more. Are you finished?"

Abby sent him an oblique look. "Can't you be serious?"

"Not when you talk nonsense. Will you just wait until tomorrow before making these earth-shaking statements that are totally without foundation?"

"I can't help it."

"Do you trust me, Abby?"

That was a foolish question. She trusted Zach as much as she loved him. She just didn't happen to be the right wife for him. She hated the thought of having him regret introducing her into Boston society. Her ignorance would reflect badly upon his family. Why didn't he realize that?

A bubble of resentment burst inside Abby. Damn him. She knew what he was hinting at. He wanted to hear her tell him she loved him. Didn't he understand that her emotions were in a turmoil? He was tearing her away from the only way of life she had ever known. He once was her captive, but now she was his by virtue of marriage. And the child she carried bound them to one another forever.

And yet . . . All that paled in comparison to the tangled web he had wound around her heart. Because Zach was a white man, she had been afraid to feel, to give, to love. But his love and patience had slowly but surely eroded those fears, allowing her own love to burst forth. And like it or not, trust was a part of that love.

"I trust you, Sky Eyes." The name slipped out unconsciously.

"Then allow me to make this decision concerning our future, Tears Like Rain. I've done a lot of thinking and planning these past few days, and I think you'll be pleasantly surprised with the results."

The weather was cooperating beautifully, Abby thought as Zach lifted her onto the seat of the wagon and covered her legs with a thick robe. The sun was warm enough to melt the light dusting of snow that had fallen the day before, and the lull in the weather couldn't have been more welcome. The wagon was loaded with supplies too numerous to list, so Abby didn't even try. She couldn't imagine what Zach intended to do with such an enormous amount of food and sundry items. Surely he didn't intend for them to travel to Boston by wagon, did he? Tied to the back of the wagon, their mounts snorted and pawed the ground.

"Are you comfortable, sweetheart?" Zach asked as he climbed up beside her and took up the reins.

"I wish you wouldn't be so mysterious about this, Zach." Her mouth curved downward into a pout.

"Are you sorry to leave Denver?"

"You know I'm not."

"Then sit back and enjoy the ride. I promise we will be at our destination before nightfall."

Abby gave a skeptical snort. "Before nightfall? You mean we'll arrive at the place where we'll stop for the night, don't you?"

Zach sent her a brilliant smile. "No, sweetheart, we'll be at our final destination, and that's all I'm going to say. You'll just have to wait and see."

For the first time in weeks, hope flared in Abby's breast. Against her better judgment she had married Zach, knowing he intended to return to Boston one day, and she had fought it tooth and nail. Had he finally adjusted his thinking? And if so, what had provoked his abrupt change of heart?

The sun continued to smile on them as they plodded eastward. At noon Zach stopped and produced a picnic lunch he had purchased at the hotel. He appeared to have forgotten nothing. They stretched their legs for a spell, and a short time later continued their journey. The sun had barely settled on the western horizon when Zach drove the team of horses to the top of a knoll and stopped.

"We're home, sweetheart."

Abby had been dozing, her head resting comfortably against Zach's shoulder when the low rumble of his voice jerked her awake. "What? What did you say?"

"There's our new home, nestled below in the lee of the hill."

"But—but that's the abandoned homestead where we took shelter!" She recalled vividly lying before the hearth on her buffalo robe, making love with Zach.

"It's no longer abandoned. I found the young couple who owned it in town, and they were more than happy to sell it to me. Since the Indian trouble, they feared living out here and wanted to return east. They were thrilled with my offer."

"That's your surprise? You're not taking me to Boston? Oh, Zach!"

The look of wonder and joy in Abby's eyes was all the thanks Zach needed. "During the past week, I've made several trips out here, furnishing the house with everything we need to make it livable. The last of the supplies are in the wagon. Most of the buildings are intact, and in the spring we can do whatever work is necessary to make it even more comfortable. I plan on building another room for the baby. I'll fix up the barn, and then—"

He went on and on, amazing Abby with his enthusiasm. Zach a farmer? He was the last person alive she'd expect to enjoy farming. She stared at him as if in a daze. He gave her a quick hug, slapped the reins against the horses' rumps, and drove them to their new home.

"Do you intend to farm?" Abby couldn't help but pose the question. She just couldn't picture Zach behind a plow.

Zach grinned foolishly. "Hell, I don't know beans about farming. I've got a better plan.

I've been in contact with my brother. He's taking charge in Boston, and we're going to expand our business to the western frontier. Our wagons will transport the goods, and I'll arrange for their disposal at this end. Come spring, I intend to build a trading post where Indians can come to trade without fear of being cheated."

Abby was so choked up she couldn't speak. Moisture gathered at the corners of her eyes, and she dashed them away with the back of her hand. Zach had done all this for her! He had given up his dream of returning to Boston for her sake. At that moment she loved him so much, her heart was bursting from it. She wanted to tell him immediately, to shout it to the world. She turned to him, her eyes shining.

"We're here," Zach said, reining in and jumping to the ground. He hurried around the wagon, lifted Abby from the seat, and set her down outside the door of the snug little cabin. "Go inside and take a look around while I drive the wagon into the barn and unhitch the horses."

He was so eager for Abby to see her new home that he rushed her inside before she could tell him what was in her heart. He knew exactly where the kerosene lamp was and lit it, then hurried back outside to finish his chores. Abby was disappointed that she hadn't found the opportunity to tell him how she felt, but there would be plenty of time later, she thought, happily anticipating his return. All her doubts concerning her love for him and their ability to live in harmony had all been dispelled when she saw what he had done for her. Tears blurred her vision when she looked around the room, now softly illuminated in the golden glow of lamplight. It was just as she remembered it.

She walked into the cozy parlor, her gaze resting fondly on the hearth as pleasant memories tickled her conscience. She wandered into the kitchen, frowning when she saw dirty dishes and the remnants of food littering the table. Zach had never been negligent about cleaning up after himself before, and she wondered why he had left the mess on the table. Suddenly she heard a noise and her keen intuition told her she wasn't alone. Had Zach entered through a back door?

"Zach, is that you?"

No answer.

"Zach?"

An ominous silence made the hackles rise on the back of her neck. Every instinct screamed of danger. She spun around, intending to escape through the door as quickly as possible and warn Zach.

"Get away from the door, or I'll blow you away."

The harsh voice came from the dark recesses of the bedroom, stopping Abby in her tracks.

"Who are you? What do you want?"

He walked into the light, pointing a regulation army Colt revolver at her. His face was hard, his lips curled in a derisive sneer. Abby recognized him immediately. He was the man who had stood up in the theater and shouted accusations at her. Zach had said his name was Private Kramer and that he was one of the men who had attacked her at Fort Lyon. But Zach had told her he had been apprehended and taken into custody.

"I see you recognize me. I didn't know who owned this homestead, but I made myself at home anyway. The house looked deserted, and with the army hot on my trail I figured it was as good a place as any to hide out. Now I'm glad I found this place. I can finish what I started with you back at Fort Lyon. I always heard squaws were wild in the sack."

Abby sucked her breath in sharply. "My husband is out in the barn. Leave now while you still can."

A hoot of laughter rumbled past his lips. "I ain't afraid of Captain Mercer. Heard tell he's not in the army anymore. Rumor has it he resigned and was relieved of duty when he refused to join Chivington's regiment. Some accused him of being a coward, but you and me know that's not the reason, don't we, Mrs. Mercer? He didn't want to kill his wife's people. If I was able, I would have ridden with Chivington willingly. Those damn savages killed my best friends."

Abby froze as she heard Zach's footsteps crunch across the frozen ground toward the door. Kramer moved swiftly. In two long strides he reached Abby's side, yanked her hard against him to shield his body, placed a grimy hand over her mouth, and pointed the gun at her head. Then he waited for Zach to walk into the house.

Zach was bursting with excitement and happily anticipating Abby's reaction to his surprise when he entered the house. He couldn't wait to find out what she thought of her new home. He had worked tirelessly to buy and furnish the homestead in preparation for her arrival. He wanted a place worthy of her and hoped she was pleased with his efforts. It had taken a while, but he had finally realized that Abby would wither and die in a city the size of Boston. If he tried to settle anywhere but in the West, he would have a most unhappy wife on his hands. Besides, he liked the West. Except for the family business, which his brother could handle quite adequately, there was nothing to keep him from living wherever he pleased. Society never did hold much interest for him.

Abby and their children were all he needed, all he wanted. They would manage quite nicely on their homestead.

He lifted the latch and swung open the door, his smile stretching from ear to ear. In his mind he pictured Abby's shining face, expressing her joy, her gratitude, her love. Never in his wildest dreams did he imagine she wouldn't be alone, or that someone would be pressing a gun to her head.

"Come in, Captain. Me and the missus been waiting for you. We're gonna have us a party, and you're invited to watch."

Chapter Twenty-One

Zach stepped into the room, his eyes searching for and finding Abby immediately. His face hardened with barely suppressed fury when he saw her pale face turned to him in mute appeal. He had been stunned to see Kramer holding a gun to Abby's temple. He had assumed Kramer was far from Denver by now.

"Close the door, Captain, and keep your hands where I can see them."

Zach did as he was told, careful not to antagonize Kramer.

"I didn't know this was your place, but I can't say I'm sorry to see you. I never did like you, or your squaw."

"My wife is no squaw," Zach said with quiet menace as he took a step forward. He wasn't wearing his handguns, and he cursed his stupidity for leaving his Spencer rifle leaning against a stall in the barn. He had been so anxious to learn what Abby thought of her new home that he had been careless. If he lived through this, he'd never grow negligent again.

Kramer's arm tightened around Abby's waist. "Stay where you are, Mercer, if you want to keep your woman healthy."

"Harm one hair on Abby's head and you're a dead man," Zach ground out from between clenched teeth.

"It's not her hair I want to touch—leastways not the hair on her head," Kramer hinted crudely.

Kramer's words sorely tried Zach's control. "If you hadn't deserted when you did, you would have been charged with attempted rape. You and your friends terrorized Abby."

"You can't prove a thing," Kramer charged sullenly. "And my friends are dead, thanks to those savages your wife is so damn fond of."

"Let Abby go, Kramer. You've nothing to gain by harming her. Do whatever you want with me, but let her leave."

"So she can bring the law here? No way, Mercer. Besides, me and your squaw have some unfinished business." His eyes darted across the room, coming to rest on a box sitting on a bench. It was filled with linens Zach had brought to the house on a previous trip. "Tear one of them sheets into strips," he ordered brusquely. "When you're finished, bring them here and drop them at my feet."

Zach knew what Kramer intended and stalled for time. "Why?"

Kramer spat out a vile oath. "You ain't dumb, Captain. I can't get on with my"—he leered at Abby—"business with your squaw until you're taken care of. Do as I say if you care about your woman."

His arm dug cruelly into Abby's middle, and she whimpered in pain. She tried to bite the hand clamped over her mouth, but it tightened like a vise against her lips. Helpless rage seethed through Zach. For the moment Kramer was in control, but not for long, he silently vowed. Some way, somehow, he'd get himself and Abby out of this situation safely. There was too much at stake to allow the deserter to get away with this. He and Abby were about to embark on a new life together. She and their expected child were too dear to him to allow harm to come to them.

"Stop dawdling, Captain." Cautiously, Kramer removed his hand from Abby's mouth. "Tell your husband he'd better do as I say," he growled. Even though Zach was unarmed, Kramer feared him. He had seen Zach in action too many times not to respect his prowess.

"Pay no attention to him," Abby rasped through dry lips.

Kramer's arm was like a steel band around her middle as he warned harshly, "Don't be a fool, Captain. I hold the upper hand. If you value your wife's life, do as I say."

His mind working furiously, Zach moved with alacrity, ripping one of the new sheets he had purchased into long strips. When he finished, he carried them to Kramer, dropping them at his feet. "What now?"

"Now your wife is going to tie you to the chair over there, nice and tight. Don't try anything foolish 'cause I'll have my gun on her the whole time."

Zach's protest never left his throat. The sound of approaching riders sent his head whipping around to stare at the closed door.

"Sonuvabitch!" Kramer spat viciously. He knew there was more than one horsemen by the commotion they made as they rode into the yard. "Who in the hell is that!"

Zach grinned. "Why don't you just give up, Kramer, and make it easier on yourself?"

"I ain't giving up," Kramer growled. "I won't spend the best years of my life in prison. Why in the hell do you think I joined the army in the first place? The law was after me, and I needed a place to hide. I left when it suited me to leave."

Desperation rode Kramer as someone pounded on the door. He began dragging Abby toward the bedroom. "Go ahead and answer the door, Captain, but if you say anything to give me away, I swear I'll kill your wife. Just act nice and calm and get rid of them as soon as possible."

He was at the bedroom door, shoving Abby inside, when their unexpected visitor called out, "Zach, it's Pete Porter. Open the door."

"Christ! Don't let him in," Kramer hissed.

"If I don't, he'll suspect something," Zach warned. "Porter and I are friends, remember?"

"Shit! All right, but don't say or do anything suspicious. Just remember, I have your wife and I'm desperate. I've killed before." Then he disappeared into the bedroom, leaving the door ajar so he could hear what was being said.

Zach opened the front door, forcing a smile as he greeted Pete. "Come in, Pete. What brings you out here this time of day?"

Pete stepped inside and closed the door behind him. "We've been tracking Kramer and lost his trail a few miles back. We saw your lights from a distance and thought we'd stop in and see how you and Abby were doing. And since you've got an empty barn, my men would appreciate having a place to bed down for the night, if it's all right with you."

Fear raced through Zach. He had no idea what Kramer would do when he learned that Pete and his detail were bedding down in the barn. Yet to refuse Pete's request would raise all kinds of suspicions in Pete's mind. "I have no objection, Pete. You're welcome to the barn."

While Zach was talking, Pete's sharp eyes made a quick perusal of the room. His keen

423

senses told him something was amiss. Then he saw the strips of torn sheet lying on the floor and he knew.

"Did you and Abby just arrive, Zach? It's damn cold outside, and there's no fire in the hearth. Where's Abby? I'd like to give her my regards."

Zach slid his gaze toward the bedroom door. "We just arrived, and I haven't had time to lay a fire. Abby went directly to bed. The trip was exhausting. You know how frail Abby is."

Pete sent Zach a curious look. Abby frail? Funny, Zach had never mentioned that Abby's health was frail. According to Zach, Abby's pregnancy was progressing normally. He'd even hinted that Abby was as feisty as ever.

"Abby really hated to leave Denver," Zach continued, hoping Kramer wouldn't think he was rambling. Somehow, without alerting Kramer, he had to convey to Pete that all was not as it seemed. "She really loves big cities and wearing fancy dresses. I'm afraid living so far out is a big disappointment to her."

"Let me give you a hand with the fire," Pete offered, convinced now that Zach was trying to send him a message. He knew that Abby hated big cities and much preferred wearing a doeskin tunic and moccasins to donning underwear and layers of petticoats.

Pete knelt beside the hearth, laying kindling and firewood on the grate. Then he removed a match from an oiled pouch and set them ablaze. "There, that ought to warm things up."

He rose cautiously, his eyes wary, his senses alert. "Well, that should do it. Anything else I can do for you before I join my men in the barn?"

"Nothing, Pete, thanks. Oh, there is one thing. Be sure and tell Belinda that Abby sends her love. They became close friends during the weeks Abby was living in your home."

Pete's eyes widened. That cinched it! He knew for a fact that Belinda and Abby hated one another's guts. "I understand, Zach," he said as he gave Zach an imperceptible nod and turned to leave.

Zach sent Pete a wobbly smile, his relief so profound his knees felt weak. He felt reasonably certain Pete understood his silent message.

The moment the door closed behind Pete, Kramer hissed from the bedroom, "Bolt the door and bring those strips of cloth in here. And the lamp—don't forget the lamp."

Zach did as he was told, sliding the bolt home first, then picking up the lamp and strips of cloth. He set the lamp on the nightstand, then looked for Abby, desperate to know she was unharmed. Kramer was still holding her before him like a shield, his gun pressed against her temple.

"You're wise to do as I say, Captain," Kramer growled ominously.

"Too bad I can't say the same for you," Zach taunted. "Why don't you leave while you have a chance? There's nothing to gain by hanging around here. With troopers billeted in the barn, you can't possibly get away. A gunshot at this time of night would bring them rushing into the house."

"Oh, I'll leave," Kramer said, leering at Abby, "but not before I take care of unfinished business with your squaw. I've been waiting a long time for this. There will be plenty of time to leave after I finish. And don't think I won't hesitate to kill either of you. I'm a desperate man. Prison doesn't appeal to me."

"We won't give you any trouble," Abby promised, making plans of her own. She wasn't as helpless as Kramer thought. Had he forgotten she was raised by Cheyenne and learned their ways at an early age?

"Damn right you won't give me any trouble. One false move and I'll kill your husband. Now tie him up. Good and tight or you'll answer to me."

When Abby moved too slowly for his liking, he gave her a vicious shove, sending her to her knees. She glared at him, her eyes spitting silver flames. When Zach would have rushed to her defense, she placed a restraining hand on his arm and shook her head.

"That was wise," Kramer said, having observed her effort to restrain Zach. "Now tie him up. First his hands behind his back and then his ankles. And make the knots tight." He watched closely as Abby bound Zach's arms and legs as directed.

Zach's burning gaze bore into Kramer with the intensity of an inferno flaming out of control, causing Kramer to take an involuntary step backward. "You won't get away with this, Kramer." Sweat broke out on Zach's forehead. He wondered what was keeping Pete, and harbored the terrible fear that Pete had misunderstood the message he was trying to convey.

"Shut up, Mercer." Spying an unused strip of cloth lying at Zach's feet, Kramer picked it up and stuffed it into Zach's mouth. "There, that should take care of you. If you want to watch while me and your squaw have us a good time on the bed, be my guest."

He pulled Abby toward the bed. When her knees touched the edge, he gripped her waist and flung her across the soft surface, sending her skirts flying above her knees. He grinned lewdly and inched them higher with the barrel of his gun.

Zach's heart leaped into his mouth when he saw Abby grasp Kramer's hand, stopping the upward slide of her skirts. "Wait! Why don't you let me take off my clothes? Why hurry? This way both of us can enjoy it."

Kramer's mouth fell open, hoping he hadn't misunderstood. "You want to take off your clothes?"

Abby shrugged. "Why not?"

Kramer slanted a exultant grin in Zach's direction. "Did you hear that, Captain? Your squaw fancies me. I'm gonna enjoy this. Yes, sir, I'm gonna really enjoy it. Okay, honey, strip." He leaned back on his heels, leering at her with avid anticipation. "I didn't expect you to be so agreeable. I certainly have no objection to seeing you buck naked."

Refusing to look at Zach, Abby slowly unbuttoned her bodice, baring her shoulders and the upper swells of her full breasts. "Why not put your gun on the nightstand?" Abby suggested slyly. "Don't you want to use both your hands?"

Kramer's eyes gleamed brightly as he considered her suggestion. Then he shook his head. "I ain't stupid, honey. Go ahead—I can hardly wait to see more."

Abby sat up, bracing herself against the headboard. She shrugged her shoulders, thereby releasing one strap of her chemise, practically exposing a plump breast. A low groan came from Kramer's throat, inflamed by Abby's slow seduction. But she was too slow for what he had in mind. The gun slipped unheeded from his fingers as he reached out with both hands to rip away the bit of cloth concealing Abby's breasts from his lewd perusal.

Zach watched in disbelief as Abby wove a web of seduction around Kramer. He knew Abby well enough to know she wasn't going to submit to Kramer meekly, and he feared that she was playing with fire. He expected Porter and his men to burst in upon them at any moment and prayed Abby's dangerous game wouldn't backfire before they arrived. Kramer wasn't a man to be put off. Another fear was that she'd be hit by flying bullets. He'd be devastated if she or their child were harmed.

As Kramer reached for Abby, her hands slid beneath her skirt, searching for the knife she had strapped to her thigh just this morning. She had found it in her belongings after she left the Porter's house to marry Zach and had kept it with her since that time. She wore it from long habit and instinct, recalling the many times it had saved her from great harm. And since she had expected to journey across the prairie, she wanted to be prepared for any of the many dangers she knew existed in the untamed West. Abby shuddered in revulsion as Kramer leaned over her, his hands brushing her flesh, his foul breath gagging her. Her fingers closed on the hilt of the knife just as she felt the tug of Kramer's rough fingers on her chemise.

In a flash she yanked the blade from its sheath and up between their bodies, pressing it against Kramer's jugular. She was expert with a knife, having been taught by Wind Rider, and was fully prepared to use it to defend herself and the man she loved.

Kramer's hand stilled, his fear palpable as he looked down into the savage silver depths of Abby's eyes. He felt the warm trickle of blood down his throat and the pressure of the blade pricking his flesh and knew he looked death in the face. With just a little more pressure, the blade could easily sever his jugular.

Slowly Abby rose from the bed, pressing the blade deeper, forcing Kramer to back away. Then she kicked his gun beneath the bed with her toe in the event Kramer took it into his head to make a reckless dash for it. She could tell by the wild expression in his eyes that he was planning something, and she wished she could untie Zach before he put his plan into action. But she knew that was impossible. She didn't dare take her attention or her eyes from a man as desperate as Kramer. There was only one thing she could do, but even that was risky.

"Walk," Abby ordered, motioning with her head toward the door. If she could get Kramer outside and scream her head off, Pete Porter would be bound to hear and come running. The blade dug a little deeper, and Kramer took a step backward. Then another, and another, grinning all the time. He intended to disarm Abby once they were in the darkened parlor. If he had to kill her to do it, so be it.

Zach watched in trepidation as Abby backed Kramer out the door and into the darkened parlor. The fire had burned low, pitching the room into darkness and shadows. He knew what she planned and wished he wasn't lying on his back trussed tighter than a Christmas turkey.

He nearly died inside when he heard a commotion in the parlor and enough racket to rouse the dead. Then he heard a woman scream and a man grunt, and fear such as he'd never known before sent adrenaline rushing through him. While Abby had been busy with Kramer, he had been secretly struggling with his bonds. Abby's scream provided him with the extra burst of strength needed to wrest his hands free of their bonds, untie his ankles, and rush into the parlor, pulling the gag out of his mouth as he went.

Inside the cramped confines of the tiny parlor, all hell was breaking loose. The front door crashed open beneath a tremendous force, and Pete Porter rushed inside, gun drawn, followed closely by his men. In the dim light of the parlor, all Pete could see was Abby standing before the hearth and Zach rushing through the bedroom door to reach her.

"Where is Kramer!" Pete asked, searching the room for the deserter. "I know he's here."

"My God, Abby, are you all right?" Zach demanded, trembling uncontrollably. He had been so certain something terrible had happened to Abby that seeing her standing by the hearth, looking pale but otherwise unhurt, left him shaken. "Where is Kramer, Abby? Did he hurt you?"

Suddenly Abby became the center of attention. No one seemed to notice the body stretched out at her feet. Zach was the first to see the knife in Abby's hand and the blood dripping from it.

"My God, what happened?"

Abby held the knife up and looked at it curiously. "I didn't kill him." Her voice was calm, almost too calm. "I could have done so easily enough." She looked down, a sneer on her lips as she nudged Kramer with her toe.

"Keep that little savage away from me," Kramer pleaded hoarsely. Blood was gushing from a neck wound that had missed his jugular by a scant inch. "Get me out of here—I'm bleeding like a stuck pig."

"Take care of him," Pete ordered. Two men jerked Kramer to his feet and hustled him out the door. All but Pete followed. He turned to Abby, searching her face to make sure she was unharmed. "He won't escape this time. If he doesn't bleed to death before we reach Fort Lyon, he'll be court-martialed and sent to Dodge City to face a murder rap. We just learned he's wanted there for the murder of a lawman. Are you both all right?"

Zach's temper exploded. "You took your damn sweet time breaking in! What in the hell kept you? We could have both been killed."

"Now hold on," Pete hastened to explain. "We tried to devise a plan. What if we charged in here and either you or Abby or both of you were injured? Or worse yet, killed? Kramer was desperate. He could have killed both of you before we overpowered him. We saw the light in the bedroom and were watching to make sure he didn't escape through the window. Unfortunately," he apologized lamely, "we failed to come up with a plan and time was against us. We decided to burst through the door and trust that the element of surprise would work in our favor."

"While you worked out your lame strategy, Kramer tried to rape Abby," Zach growled, placing his arm protectively around Abby's shoulders.

Pete jerked his gaze to Abby, noting that her bodice had been hastily pulled up and clumsily buttoned. "My God, he didn't!"

Abby sent him a smile that set his mind at ease. "He tried, Pete, but he didn't succeed."

"You should have seen her, Pete," Zach said with obvious pride. "She was magnificent. I'm glad I failed in my attempt to tame my savage little wife. The knife she keeps strapped to her thigh came in handy."

Pete sent Abby a look of utter amazement. "I'll never underestimate you again, girl. I'm glad you're not my enemy."

Abby smiled serenely. "I may be white, but I'll never forget my Cheyenne ways."

"Thank God," Zach offered gratefully.

When Pete saw the exchange of heated glances between Zach and Abby, he cleared his throat and said, "Best I leave you two and see to my prisoner. We'll probably be gone before daylight, so I'll bid you both good-bye now. I'll bring Milly around to see you first chance I get. She's lonesome now that Belinda has gone east."

"I'd like that, Pete. You and your wife were good to me and I appreciate that."

"Well, then, good night." He let himself out the door, pulling it shut behind him.

"No sense locking the door," Zach said, noting the sprung lock, "since the wood has been splintered almost beyond repair. Don't worry, though. Pete and his detail will be extra vigilant tonight. Thank God he decided to stop in and check on us." He turned Abby to face him. Her eyes shone like pure silver in the soft glow of the dying fire. "But I doubt you needed Pete or anyone else," he added wryly. "You were doing pretty well on your own. I'm so proud of you, sweetheart." He pulled her into his embrace, pressing her against his pounding heart.

"I couldn't let that animal touch me." She shivered, recalling with revulsion how she'd felt when his hands brushed her bare flesh. No man had that right but Zach. Zach was her husband, and she loved him. And he deserved to know exactly how she felt.

"Come on, Abby, let's go to bed. You're shivering, and I'm afraid you've had more than your share of excitement tonight. I get cold chills when I recall how helpless I felt while Kramer was slobbering over you. I promise I'll never be caught unaware again." His arm tightened around her shoulders as he led her into the bedroom.

He brushed her shaking fingers aside when she tried to undo the buttons on her bodice. "Here, let me do that." He undressed her tenderly, with great patience and care, finding her nightgown and pulling it over her head. Then he tucked her into bed. Abby looked at him expectantly, disappointed when he started to leave the room.

"Aren't you coming to bed?"

"I'm going to find us something to eat. I won't be long."

A good half hour passed before he returned with a tray. He set it on the bed, urging her to eat. It wasn't much, but he had made hot tea, sliced bread and cheese, and added a crisp apple. After she had eaten her fill, he pulled off his outer clothing and slid into bed in his long johns. "I just want to hold you, sweetheart." His arms brought her against his heart. "I didn't get a chance to ask how you liked your new home. Do you feel like talking?"

"I'd very much like to talk," Abby agreed with alacrity, still too overwrought by the night's unexpected events to sleep. "What about Boston? I know how much you wanted to return to your home."

"I couldn't do it, sweetheart. If remaining in the West means so much to you, it would be selfish of me to tear you away."

Abby's eyes grew misty with unshed tears. "What about your life? Why would you give up your dreams of returning to your family business for me?"

"I love you," he said simply. "And it's not as if I'm giving up so much. I genuinely like the West. And it's about time Mercer Freighting Company broadened its horizons. Our business will thrive in the West. Besides, I'm gaining much more by remaining." His fiery eyes stroked over her like lapping tongues of flame. "After the baby is born, we can take a trip east and you can meet my family. So, what *do* you think about the homestead? It's not much right now, but it will be a real home after I build on in the spring."

435

"I love it, but not as much as I love you."

Zach's mouth dropped open. He had waited so long to hear those words that he thought he had imagined them. He lifted her chin and studied her with blunt appraisal. The truth of her words was clearly visible in the silver depths of her expressive eyes, and a slow smile spread across his handsome features. He lowered his head and kissed her, long and thoroughly. When he raised his head, Abby was smiling back at him.

"I've loved you for a very long time, you know."

His eyes twinkled mischievously. "You could have told me before instead of letting me think it was my body you cared about."

"I love that too. But there was so much fear in me."

"I'd never hurt you, Abby."

"Perhaps not, but I could hurt you. I feared your peers would despise and scorn you when you brought home a bride raised by Indians. I didn't want to do that to you. That's why I couldn't tell you how I felt."

"Don't you realize by now that idle talk doesn't bother me? You should have trusted me, Abby."

"I didn't fit in," she argued. "You saw how folks talked about me at Fort Lyon. I'm totally ignorant of white ways. I can't read or write. You were forced from the army on my account."

"No one forced me to do anything I didn't want to do. Besides, you're the most intelligent, courageous woman I know."

"And you'll be happy here, truly?" How she wanted to believe him!

"Truly. What will it take to convince you?"

Her eyes sparkled mischievously. "Love me, Zach. Love me now, on our very first night in our new home."

"Say it again, Abby."

She placed her lips against his and whispered, "I love you, Zach Mercer. Forever and always."

"Forever and always," Zach repeated as he bore her back onto the bed with a throaty, impatient growl.

Historical Note

The Pike's Peak Gold Rush in 1858 brought settlers and miners to Colorado to stay. In the following years, Colorado officials sought to open up Cheyenne and Arapaho hunting grounds to white development. But both the Cheyenne and the Arapaho refused to sell their lands and move to reservations. Governor John Evans decided to force the issue through war. He ordered volunteer state militiamen into the field under the Indian-hating military commander, Colonel John Chivington.

In the spring of 1864, Chivington launched a campaign of violence against the Cheyenne and Arapaho, his troops attacking any and all Indians, plundering their possessions and burning their villages. The often unprovoked attacks triggered swift and brutal retaliation.

Indians went on the warpath, raiding outlying settlements. This period of conflict is referred to as the Cheyenne-Arapaho War (or Colorado War) of 1864-1865.

During those years, Indian raiders blazed a burning path of destruction across the prairie, fueled by atrocities meted out by officers of the United States Army whose orders were to wipe out the proud Indian race.

The massacre at Sand Creek was one of those battles in which the Cheyenne, after having turned in their weapons as a gesture of peace, were attacked without provocation by Colonel Chivington's Third Calvary. Black Kettle's small band of Southern Cheyenne were cut down as they raised a white flag of truce and an American flag. Black Kettle escaped but was killed later in another unprovoked attack by General George Custer. Afterward, pockets of Cheyenne resistance remained, and as the army continued their pressure, the Cheyenne joined with the Comanche and Kiowa to fight in the Red River War. Later they allied themselves with the Sioux and Northern Cheyenne in the fighting at Little Bighorn in 1876.

Author's Note

The events leading up to and including the Sand Creek Massacre are as accurate as I could make them within the framework of my story. White Feather and his band of Cheyenne are figments of my imagination and to my knowledge no such tribe escaped the massacre before Chivington's regiment attacked. Nor was any warning given of the attack beforehand. I'd like to think some honorable man refused to take part in the attack, and that he did so for the love of a woman.

As you might have guessed, *Tears Like Rain* is the first book in my Trails West trilogy. If you've wondered about Wind Rider and what the future holds for him, you will find out in the second book of the trilogy. *Wind Rider* tells the story of the handsome white Cheyenne, brother to Tears Like Rain, and his struggle to find a place for himself on a Western frontier torn apart by war. The last book of the trilogy, *Sierra*, will bring you Sierra, sister to Wind Rider and Tears Like Rain, separated at a young age from her siblings. Her absolute certainty that her brother and sister still live sends her on a reckless quest to find them. I hope you enjoy the hopes, dreams, and loves of my Western heroes and heroines.

I enjoy hearing from my readers and answer all mail I receive. If you'd like a newsletter and bookmark, please write to me in care of Leisure Books at the address inside this book. A self-addressed stamped business envelope is appreciated.

All My Romantic Best,

Connie Mason

Connie Mason
Bestselling Author of *A Promise Of Thunder*

"Connie Mason tempts her readers with thrilling action and sizzling sensuality!"

—Romantic Times

When he sees Cassie Fenmore sneaking down the stairs of a fancy house, Cody Carter thinks her a tasty confection he can have for the asking—and ask he shall.

When she meets Carter on the Dodge City train, Cassie believes him a despicable blackguard capable of anything—like denying the two adorable urchins who claim to be his children.

When Cody and Cassie learn they are to share the inheritance of the Rocking C Ranch, they have no doubt trouble is brewing. But neither can guess that, when the dust has settled, all their assumptions will be gone with the wind—replaced by a love more precious than gold.

_3539-1 $4.99 US/$5.99 CAN

PROMISED SPLENDOR
CONNIE MASON

Winner of the *Romantic Times* Storyteller of the Year Award!

"I won't cheat you, Glenna," Kane Morgan swears in the heat of passion. "I promise you'll find only pleasure in my arms." And pleasure—searing, breathtaking, exquisite pleasure—is what she does find as Kane takes her innocence amidst the whispering pines of the Colorado wilderness. Flame-haired Glenna longs to give him her soul as well as her body, but she cannot promise her heart until she brings her father's murderer to justice.

__3438-7 $4.99 US/$5.99 CAN

Winner of the *Romantic Times* Storyteller of the Year Award!

Cool as a cucumber, and totally dedicated to her career as a newspaper woman, Maggie Afton is just the kind of challenge brash Chase McGarrett enjoys. But he is exactly the kind of man she despises. Cold and hot, reserved and brazen, Maggie and Chase are a study in opposites. But when they join forces during the Klondike gold rush, the fiery sparks of their searing desire burn brighter than the northern lights.

___3376-3 $4.99 US/$5.99 CAN

CONNIE MASON — A PROMISE OF THUNDER

Winner of the *Romantic Times* Storyteller of the Year Award!

Storm Kennedy can't believe her bad luck! With six million acres of fertile territory open to settlers in the Oklahoma Territory, she loses her land claim to Grady Stryker, the virile Cheyenne half-breed she holds responsible for her young husband's death. And the only way to get it back is by agreeing to marry the arrogant Stryker and raise his motherless son. But while she accepts his proposal, Storm is determined to deny him access to her last asset—the lush body Grady thinks is his for the taking.

_3444-1 $4.99 US/$5.99 CAN